FAMILY RESEMBLANCES

Also by Anne Cameron

FAMILY
RESEMBLANCES

Anne Cameron

HARBOUR PUBLISHING

Published by
Harbour Publishing Co. Ltd.
P.O. Box 219, Madeira Park, BC V0N 2H0
www.harbourpublishing.com

Cover photo by Image Source. Cover design by Silas White.
Author photo by Peter A. Robson.
Printed and bound in Canada

Harbour Publishing acknowledges financial support from the Government of Canada through the Book Publishing Industry Development Program and the Canada Council for the Arts; and from the Province of British Columbia through the British Columbia Arts Council and the Book Publisher's Tax Credit through the Ministry of Provincial Revenue.

The Canada Council | Le Conseil des Arts
for the Arts | du Canada
since 1957 | depuis 1957

BRITISH
COLUMBIA
ARTS COUNCIL
Supported by the Province of British Columbia

National Library of Canada Cataloguing in Publication Data

Cameron, Anne, 1938–
    Family resemblances / Anne Cameron.

    ISBN 1-55017-301-4

    I. Title.
PS8555.A5187P35 2003   C813'.54   C2003-911159-8

For my children
Alex
Erin
Marianne
Pierre

my grandchilden
Sarah
David
Daniel
Terry
Sheldon
Jen
Andy
Joan
Emily
and for Judy, Fran, Roberta, Bruce, Reta, Dymph, Deane, Nelle,
Hannah, Barbara Jean and Yimmy, the best support system anyone ever
had. Thora Howell asked for this story, actually nagged me about it.
Thank you!

and
especially
for Eleanor
"Whatever your little heart desires, kiddo"
"Well, at least it's never boring"

ONE

In the earliest image Cedar Campbell could dredge out of the splintered mess that passed for her memory, she was sitting on a swing, riding higher with each shove, the breeze warm on her face, the taste of dust in the air. Up and up and up until at the top of each pendulum swing, front and back, she could see over the fence and across the dirt road, to where the railway tracks glistened in the summer sun.

She had no idea who was pushing the swing, and less of an idea what had gone before or what was to come. All she had was that image: a pair of legs in blue jeans, bare feet in leather sandals, a Band-Aid—or something—holding her second and third toes together, and the up-and-down, up-and-down, back-and-forth motion, and an ever-expanding and shrinking vista. Up and up, larger, farther, down and down, smaller, closer, up up back and up, larger, then down, forward and down, the world shrinking again.

Her mother Kate had named her Cedar as the punchline to a bitter, unspoken, unfunny private joke. Cedar was born in May, nine months after Kate had turned nineteen. She had celebrated at a family picnic, to which Gus Campbell had not been invited because every member of Kate's family detested him. When night fell and everyone else was sound asleep, Kate slipped out of her bedroom window and ran down to the creek, where Gus sat on his jacket, smoking hand-rolled cigarettes and sipping from a jug of the best local hooch, a pale yellowish liquid with a slightly oily shine on it. General opinion was you could run freight trains on the stuff. One time when Gordon Bridges' lighter ran dry on him, he had dribbled some hooch into his Zippo, and it burned so hot that it was ruined.

Gus offered Kate a sip, and she took it. They sat talking softly, kissing occasionally, and Kate had a couple more sips, the first alcohol she'd ever tasted. The kissing increased, the passion intensified, and Kate conceived her child on a bed of cedar boughs, the rich woodsy scent making her almost as dizzy as the few sips of hooch.

She was so full of the idea of being in love, so excited by her secret thoughts of herself and Gus as a couple, that she hardly noticed it when she missed her period a couple of weeks later. When she missed the second one, though, she did notice, and she realized that she was, as local custom put it, in trouble. Up a stump. With a bun in the oven. Caught.

Naturally she turned to her older sister Marg for advice and help. Marg was married to Hank Keller, six feet two inches of incredible muscle topped by a headful of raven-black hair.

"It's not fair! You and Hank have been married four years and you still haven't got caught. I make one mistake . . ." And on she mourned, conveniently forgetting that it wasn't one mistake had been made but several dozen repeat episodes—nearly every night, in fact.

"Stop feeling sorry for yourself." Marg was more than willing to help, but no way would she indulge Kate by listening to a litany of all-my-luck-is-bad. "I don't know how many times you have to be told. When you start diddling around, the question isn't *if* you'll get pregnant, but *when*."

"What am I going to *dooooo?*" Kate wailed.

"Not a lot you can do. Unless you want to take the chance that Jennet took, and go see old Dr. Forbes."

Kate jumped at the mention of Gus's sister. "She *died!*"

Marg rolled a cigarette and handed it to Kate, then rolled another for herself, and waited.

"Momma will kill me," Kate whispered.

"No, she won't. But by the time she's through I-told-you-so'ing, you might wish she had killed you."

"And Poppa . . ."

"Well, he's had his heart broken before and survived. Anyway, the first thing you have to do is talk to Gus."

Gus's reaction to the news knocked a little more of the romantic glow off Kate's bubble. By the time she told him, she had spent a couple of nights lying awake, fantasizing, and had settled on the scenario where she told Gus and he stared at her, stunned, then grinned from ear to ear, cuddled her close, and said things that made her feel safe.

Instead, he damn near went into orbit. "Jesus Christ!" he yelled, his face pink with anger. "Thunder, lightning and dynamite, don't you know *anything?*" And he proceeded to tell her just what he thought of dumb-ass girls who don't know how to avoid the inevitable.

"But, Gus—"

"Oh, to hell with it!" he raged. "Just leave me alone, will you? I have to *think* here, I have to figure out a way to get us out of this goddamn miserable mess!"

Gus stomped off, leaving Kate at the bus stop wondering what it was she had done that had got him so angry. Why was *she* the stupid one? She hadn't done it to herself. She almost began to get angry with him, but the thought of life on her own with a bastard child was so terrifying she didn't dare tell Gus Campbell to take a long walk on a short pier.

She told her mother. Karen Larson sat at Marg's table with a cup of tea cooling in front of her and stared at the oilcloth, white with bunches of red cherries on it. Karen did not rant, she did not wail, she just stared at the oilcloth cherries for long, silent minutes and then said, "Gus Campbell. Dear God in heaven, please." God did not answer Karen's prayer.

Rather than tell Kate's father, Karen went to her sons Hugh, Wade and Forrest. They calmed her down, then went to see old Colin Campbell, a short, bald-headed, powerful man who bragged that he had the biggest chest in the district and fists hard enough to smash a coal seam with one punch. When Kate's brothers showed up with a dozen home-brewed beer, they found the stubby jut-jawed coal miner sitting in a wicker chair on his front porch, smoking the pipe his wife Mary wouldn't allow in the house.

"Evening, sir," Hugh said politely.

"Good evening, young man," Colin answered, jaw tightening, eyes narrowing. "And who might you be, may I ask?"

"Hugh Larson, sir. These are my brothers, Wade and Forrest."

"Would you care to sit?" The old man sounded as welcoming as a dog chained up too long in the hot sun.

"Thank you." Hugh brought out a bottle of cold beer and held it out. The old man took it and pried off the cap with his teeth, showing off just a little.

Karen Larson's boys sat on the steps. They opened their beers with a church key, so as not to challenge the old man.

"Larsons, eh? You any relation to Olaf?"

"He is our father, sir."

"Good man," Colin nodded. He sipped his beer. "Who brewed this?"

"We did." Hugh grinned. "Had to do it all in the shed behind the hen house because our mother is four-square against."

"Your mother was a Swenson before she married up with Olaf, I believe."

"Yes, sir. Humboldt Swenson's daughter with his first wife Freda, the one who died."

"Sad thing, that."

"Yes, sir."

"And so why are you here, young Hugh Larson?"

"Well, sir, there's a bit of a problem needs addressed."

"A problem concerning me?"

"One of your sons, sir."

"And which might that be?" The old man drank again, his Adam's apple bobbing. When he lowered the bottle, it was almost empty.

"Angus, sir. The problem concerns our sister Kate."

Old Colin emptied his beer, handed the bottle to Hugh, accepted a full one and popped it with the church key. No need to show off now. Damn Angus! You'd think his middle name was Trouble.

"Has he been disrespectful? I won't tolerate disrespect toward a woman."

"Our sister is with child," Hugh said.

"And is she pregnant with my grandchild, then?"

"Yes, Mr. Campbell, she is."

"Dinna fash yersel', laddie," Colin said, lapsing into broad Scots for a moment. "There'll be no Campbells I'm aware of who go by any name other than ours. Will you trust me to handle it?"

"Yes, sir."

"Fine, then. You make a good beer, no taste of yeast at all. Have the fish been active down your way?"

"Creek's a bit full because of autumn rain." Wade spoke for the first time. "But the fish are hungry. If you're interested, I could show you a good pool."

"Or you could bring me the odd trout now and again, and save my old legs the hike." Colin tipped his head, not quite smiling.

"I can only hope that when I'm the father of six sons and two daughters, my own legs are as strong as yours."

Colin laughed and drained his beer. He was proud of his strength, and proud of his reputation as a man who could whip any fool who got in his way.

The Larson boys headed home, leaving the rest of the beer with Colin. If the old man said he'd take care of it, then he'd take care of it.

Gus came home after midnight, smelling of whiskey, his smile lopsided and his clothes rumpled. He was surprised to see his father and two of his brothers sitting on the porch drinking tea and obviously waiting for him.

"Been out, have you?" Colin asked mildly.

"Yes, sir." Gus sat on the steps, rolled a cigarette, then handed the makings to his father.

"Sparking a young lady, I suppose."

Gus grinned.

"Kate Larson?"

"No." Gus stiffened slightly.

"When was the last time you saw Miss Larson?"

"Two weeks ago. I'm through with her."

"Oh, I don't think so, my son."

"It's not mine!" Gus flared.

"Of course it is."

"I won't!"

"Of course you will."

"I tell you, I won't! The girl's a fool."

"She wasn't alone in her foolishness. You wanted the tune, now you pay the fiddler, my boy."

"I made no promises."

"I've taught all my boys the same, Angus. There's things a man can wear."

"And who wants to take a bath with his gumboots on?"

"Don't be crude, there's no call for it. You'll do the right thing by this girl."

"Father, I—"

"You think we don't know about the others you've left behind you, as if babbies were puppies to be given away? There's at least two I know of down on the reserve. I've done nothing about them because the girls' families don't want us involved. But Karen Larson's sons came tonight and I told them not to worry."

"You had no right to tell them that, without talking to me about it!"

"I'm talking to you now."

"Well, and I won't!"

"Oh, you will, my son."

When Angus Campbell stood in front of Olaf Larson to tell him he wanted to marry Kate, Olaf read the whole story in the bruises on Gus's face and in the stiff way he walked. Olaf's heart did not break, but it did crack.

Wade Larson made it a point of honour to take fresh-caught trout to Mary Campbell at least twice a month, always enough for the entire clan to have a good fill. It wasn't an onerous honour-binding—Wade Larson loved to fish, especially for river trout, although if they weren't biting he wasn't too proud to go out on the chuck in a rowboat to jig for cod. Sometimes he took cod or red snapper over to the Campbells' place, and Mary always treated him as if he was a special guest, until she began to treat him as a friend. Wade knew how particular Mary Campbell was about her friends, and honoured her by taking crab to her at least once a month. Mary Campbell wasn't sure what to do with the crabs, especially as they were still alive when they arrived in her kitchen, but her sons knew very well what to do with them, and if Mary never really learned to enjoy the taste, her boys did. Colin refused to allow a bite of crab to pass his lips. What he didn't say, but Mary knew full well, was that it bothered him that the crabs were boiled alive. He would go outside, regardless of weather, to avoid hearing the clitter and scritch of their claws against the side of the big pot. Mary alone knew how soft-hearted Colin really was.

Cedar was born the following May, and Sheila Callahan's daughter

Beverly arrived less than a month later. Ewen Campbell had offered to marry her in Gus's stead, but Sheila refused. Kate Larson Campbell couldn't even begin to imagine how terrible it must be to have to face what Sheila was facing. Kate was so grateful to Colin and his sons that she vowed to bend over backward to be friendly. She was even more grateful to Gus. She read the message implicit in his battered appearance and surly attitude, and decided to set it aside.

The wedding was small but the reception wasn't. It was held in the hall where the schoolchildren played in rainy weather, and their parents held union meetings, quilting bees, Christmas concerts, bridal and baby showers and funeral receptions. Kate and Gus would just as soon have passed on it, but Karen Larson held firm. "Tongues will wag sooner and nastier if you don't have a party. Give yourselves a few months' peace and quiet, there will be enough said when the child comes."

"They can all go to hell for all of me," Gus snapped.

"Many of them will, I'm sure," Karen said, feeling her concern turn to cold hard anger. To her amazement, Gus grinned and his resistance vanished. She knew then that what they said about him was true: he was like a weather vane, turning in a variable wind, riding the peaks and valleys of emotion. She wondered if he'd been born like that. She was glad she didn't have to live her life with him, and sorrier than ever that her daughter would.

By law there was no alcohol allowed in the hall, but John Riley, who owned the Domino Club, lived across the road from the reception and he was neighbourly. He had a large roofed porch, and those who took a nip could go over there, indulge themselves, and wander back again—unless, of course, they stayed for a second and possibly third nip, prices reduced in honour of the occasion. A few of the rowdier men bought pint bottles and hid them under the steps at the side of the hall. Some of the teen-aged boys found the bottles, but even though they all drank too much too fast and got the heaves and hurls, none of them was dim enough to go inside and ralph all over the dance floor, so most people preferred to ignore their silliness.

All the women brought something for the buffet—cold sliced chicken, turkey, ham, pork or beef, spiced meat loaf, potato salad, three-bean salad, five-bean salad, seven-bean salad, and more kinds of cakes, pies and dessert loaves than could possibly be eaten. Besides being neighbourly and having a great porch, John Riley played violin and guitar. He and his sister Bridget, who also played the guitar and was a marvel on the piano, coaxed several other musicians into joining them, and the first people out on the dance floor were, of course, Kate and Gus. "Oh," everyone said, "don't they look happy." They all noticed the way Gus was flirting with Bridget Riley, who, as everyone knew, was no better than she should be, music and all notwithstanding. But what else could you expect from Gus Campbell?

There was no honeymoon trip to Niagara Falls or anywhere else. They drove away from the reception in the car Gus had borrowed from Tamas, and went straight to the little house they had rented.

Kate didn't talk about her wedding night with anyone. Three days after her wedding she was back at her job in the hospital, pushing a heavy mop down the hallways, stripping and scrubbing beds after patients had been discharged, remaking the beds for those being admitted, disinfecting bathrooms, serving meal trays and helping get people in and out of bed. She and her friends at work joked that the only thing they didn't do was brain surgery—for that, people had to go to the cleaning staff at the city hospital.

She worked until the end of April and her co-workers had a tea for her after her last shift. Nothing fancy—some sandwiches, some matrimonial cake, some lemon squares, and gifts for the baby.

Her first week without work she slept almost the whole time, slept as if she'd been hit on the head with a brick. By the end of the week she felt more like herself, the constant dull ache of fatigue was gone, her ankles were normal size again and she could cook and eat meals without feeling like throwing up.

Gus went out every night after supper. He had his volunteer fire practice and he had his trout fishing, and he had what he called his "spare-time job" at John and Bridget Riley's Domino Club. Some people actually did play dominoes at the club, but mostly they played one of the many kinds of poker. There was a pool table but it was mostly for recreation; nobody was interested in putting down good money for that silly game. You went to the Domino Club for real games of chance, not for something as boring as bowling.

Kate didn't go to the Domino. The only women tolerated there were Bridget, who owned half of it, and Jacqueline Conrad, who might not even be a woman, for all anyone knew. They called her Jake or Big

Jake, and once in a blue moon, when they had nothing else to talk about, they wondered aloud about her sex life. Big Jake always had money, was a good poker player and owned her own fish boat. She dressed in jeans, shirts with collars, and cowboy boots. In the wintertime she added a V-neck sweater. She was damn near six feet tall and built like a brick shithouse. Nobody had ever seen her with anyone who seemed to be a lover or a shack-job, but everyone had assumed for years that she preferred women, so now they thought they knew for sure. Why else would she go over to the city so often? And, they whispered and winked, what man would want a big, independent-minded woman who could break his back if she squeezed with those powerful legs? Mind you, they admitted, if she was more normal sized and less muscular she'd be one helluva lookin' woman with those big blue eyes and that sun-streaked blondy-brown hair and a smile that could just about light up the town.

Gus said he was going to the Domino Club, and because Kate had never been in the place she had no way of knowing whether he did or not, so she assumed that's where he was. And sometimes she was right. But the spare-time job was exactly that—he covered on the houseman's days off, and sometimes took over so the regular man could go grab a good meal, and even have a hot bath and fresh clothes if the game had been going on for a long time.

The rest of the time Kate thought Gus was at the Domino, he was actually having hell's own good time with another woman. He called it "squiring," but others had less vague names for it. Pussy bandit, pole vaulter, tomcat, running around, screwing around, effing around, messing around, bed hopping—whatever they called it, Gus got away with it because he was good looking, charming when he tried, and oodles of fun, and the town had more than its share of widows, grass widows and plain old lonely women. Fishermen's wives were on their own for months at a time, loggers went into camp and stayed anywhere from six weeks to three months, and some of the guys who worked the tugs were a week at sea or longer. Sometimes, when he was half-cut and joking with some of his envious friends, Gus said he should be given a government allowance or a union pension so he could devote all his time to keeping the wives from committing suicide out of discontent and frustration.

He could easily have gone into camp and made good money, but he preferred to work for a company that logged the slopes close enough to town that the men rode to work every morning in jitneys or crummies. Most mornings he left home by six and walked to the corner, where he was picked up by the company vehicle and bounced over half-built dirt roads to the logging site. By eight he was setting chokers, his lean, long-legged body moving quickly and easily as he raced to attach the cables, then raced to get out of the way so the machine operator could tighten the line and haul the log to the load site.

Gus didn't go into the mines like his father and some of his brothers. He'd tried that, when he was younger and first quit school. He hated the mine, hated the darkness, the musty smell, the grinding repetition and the stomach-churning danger. He'd tried fishing with his oldest brother Ewen, but that didn't suit him either. Logging did. He liked the smells of fresh-cut wood, of fuel and machine oil, of crushed moss and trampled bracken, he loved being outside, even when it was pouring rain, and he knew he was good at his job. Every year at Loggers' Sports Day his company entered him in the chokerman competitions, and most years he won. That was something else Gus Campbell liked—whatever he did, he had to win.

He came home from work one night, tired and looking forward to a good hot bath and a nice supper, only to find a plate of sandwiches covered with a damp cloth, and a note that said simply, "Took Kate to hospital at quarter to five. Marg." He took the sandwiches into the bathroom with him and ate them while running water into the tub. He'd been looking forward to this bath all day and by God he was going to enjoy it.

When Gus showed up at the hospital at 7:30, Kate's face was flushed and damp, her eyes bright with excitement and nervousness. Marg was sitting beside the bed knitting something out of soft pale yellow wool. Gus supposed it was something for the baby, but he didn't ask. At midnight Kate was moved to what they called the Labour Room. Gus sat holding her hand and wondering how in hell things had got themselves so balled up that he had wound up stuck like this.

He hadn't felt the slightest hint of passion or even sexual interest since Kate's body had begun to change and she had started to look, from the chin down at least, more like his mother than any woman a man like himself would want. He told her he was afraid of hurting the baby and she believed him and thought him kind and loving, but in reality, the bigger her pregnancy, the more disgusted and repelled he was. At least, thank God and the devil, she didn't get varicose veins like some did.

By 1:30 he was nodding off in his chair and when Kate told him to go home again, he did. He slept until it was time to get up and hurry off to work, packing his own lunch and muttering to himself about it. He was halfway up a slope setting beads and pouring sweat when the baby was born, and he knew nothing about it until he got back home again and found a note from his mother: "Supper at my place. You're a father."

Nobody would tell him if he was the father of a boy or a girl, they just laughed and said he'd find out when he went up to see for himself. Gus told his mother she made the best meat loaf in the world and her mashed spuds were enough to tempt the dead back to life. Mary Campbell knew he was flarching her, he'd been doing it since before he'd learned to talk, but she enjoyed his extravagant compliments. She didn't approve of much that he did, and she disapproved of more than was comfortable for her, but he had always been her sunny Sonny Boy and the whole family knew it.

Once Gus had packed away a huge supper, he went to the hospital. Kate looked like someone who had been running from the devil for hours on end—her face was pale, her eyes were dark and her voice was weak. But she was smiling, and she reached for him, so he cuddled her and asked how she was doing.

"I'm fine," she whispered, "and so is our daughter."

"A girl," he chuckled. "Who does she look like, you or me?"

"Neither. Both. Your mother a bit. My mother a bit."

"A real little mutt." He laughed.

"Would you take me down the hall to see her?"

"Madam, you are as good as on your way. I'll get a wheelchair, you look like someone who's been working damn hard for a long time."

They stood in front of the huge glass window and looked into the nursery. There were three newborns. Gus figured the one with the pink blanket was his. Her face was smaller than the palm of his hand.

"Isn't she gorgeous?" Kate sighed.

"Absolutely," he agreed, although he didn't think there was enough there to judge. "She's as bald as my dad," he teased. "Let's hope her jaw doesn't stick out like his."

"Oh, you stop that!" Kate laughed and slapped him lightly on the arm. "You *know* she's beautiful."

"Ssssh," he warned, "you're not supposed to brag or the boggards and ghoulies will hear and then you'll be sorry."

Marg and Hank arrived soon after with flowers and fresh fruit, then Karen and Olaf came in with fresh-baked buns and a meat and tatey pie for Gus's lunch the next day. When the nurse frowned and looked ready to tell them there were too many visitors, Gus took the opportunity to win some points with Karen. "I'm going to head off home," he said quickly, leaning over to kiss Kate's forehead. "I was too excited last night and I hardly slept a wink, so today I was dragging my tail at work. And I think this is probably a time when mothers and sisters count for more than the old man does."

"You catch up on your sleep," Kate agreed, and Karen smiled approvingly.

Gus took his meat and tatey pie and went home long enough to put it in the fridge, then he went down to the Domino. The houseman didn't need anyone to relieve him, so Gus sat in on the game and when he finally left he had more than two months' worth of pay in his pocket and just enough time to race home, get into his work clothes, pack the meat and tatey pie in his lunch kit and run to catch the crummy. The driver asked him about the baby and Gus told what he knew. When the driver asked the baby's name, Gus shrugged and laughed. "Her mother gets to choose," he said, sounding as if he was granting a huge favour. "I'll pick for the boys."

Marg and Karen couldn't believe how Gus was with the baby. Even before Kate and Cedar left the hospital, Gus was charming the nurses into showing him how to hold Cedar, how to burp her, how to carry her, how to change her diapers. He arrived for visiting hours with a milkshake for Kate, sat on the edge of the bed and visited with her until Karen and Olaf arrived, then he kissed Kate's cheek, smiled at everyone and went down to the nursery to visit Cedar. Gus got a green cotton gown and cap from the supply closet and even pulled a cotton mask over his nose and mouth. The nurses bent and twisted every regulation and rule, even showing Gus how to bathe her, then watching and smiling indulgently while he did it. "And is she my own wee hen," he crooned, "my own little pea in a pod, then? You're the image of our

Jennet, but there'll be nothing bad in life for you. Who knows, it may well be you're my Jen come back for another try."

When visiting hours were finished he left for the Domino Club. Except for the two nights he subbed for the houseman, Gus sat in on the games and sheared even the most skilled of sheep.

The day Marg took Kate and Cedar home from hospital they found a brand new made-in-England pram with oversized wheels parked in the small kitchen The card read: "For Cedar Campbell. Welcome home, baby girl." Kate was so pleased and touched that Marg felt like a cheapskate for noticing there was nothing, not so much as one wilting flower, for Cedar's mother.

Marg made supper and Gus came home to a house full of rich good smells. He grinned widely, kissed Kate on the cheek, kissed Marg on the forehead and bent over the pram to smile at his daughter. "And look who's come here to see you," he said softly. "Aren't you the little honey, and doesn't your daddy think you're wondrous. No, no," he warned, "no use twisting up your face and getting ready to pout to be picked up, your Da is filthy from work and won't put so much as a finger on you until he's had his bath. Patience, my girl, patience."

When Gus came back to the kitchen he smelled of soap and toothpaste. He went to the pram, picked up the baby and sat cuddling her even while he ate his supper.

"The doctor says you'll make her bones ache if you hold her too much," Marg warned. "He says she should only be held when she's being fed or she'll wind up spoiled."

"Is that what the doctor says?" he mocked gently. "You hear that, my babe? I'm supposed to put you down and ignore you. But the doctor, poor fool, is only used to ordinary everyday babbies, he's not had much experience with Campbell babbies, who everyone knows are much, *much* better than the other kind. Makes their bones ache, he says. Ah, but Campbell babbies don't have achey bones, and they aren't spoiled brats, either. Holding and cuddling and loving and pooching makes Campbell babbies' bones good and strong."

"You're making a stick to beat your own back with," Marg told him.

"Nobody," and the smile was gone from his face, "beats a Campbell."

When dessert was half done, Cedar began to squirm. Marg was

about to say something about aching bones, but before she could form the words, Gus laughed. "Oh, now, you just put a hold on that!" He shifted Cedar to his other arm and rocked her slightly, and the noise stopped. "You'll get your pie when your mam's finished hers. But first," he warned, "there's the meat, spuds and gravy to be had, not even a Campbell babby gets pie first. You eat up your dinner, then you get a sweetie. Hush, now, you can wait a bit, your poor wee mam needs some quiet time. Don't be greedy and don't be grabby, you've already got one person dancing at the end of your string, you don't need to make a slave of your momma, too." Marg held her tongue. Maybe he really was trying to take some of the burden off Kate.

Gus didn't go to the Domino Club that night. He cleared the table while Kate sat in the big chair and nursed the baby. He even dried the dishes Marg washed. And when the baby was fed, it was Gus who bathed her, spread Vaseline on her bum, dusted her with powder, then got her into fresh clothes and wrapped her in her blanket. But then, instead of putting her back in the pram the way the doctor had ordered and the way the baby book said, he lay on the third- or fourth-hand sofa with Cedar on his chest. While she slept, he listened to the radio, and he even managed to read the evening paper, holding it up awkwardly. Cedar lay belly down, snuggled against his chest, soothed by the sound of his heart. She breathed in the scent of him, she heard and felt his breathing, and like her mother and who knows how many other females, she fell under the spell of Gus Campbell.

At 9:30 Kate fed Cedar again, and Gus changed the diaper, then placed his daughter in her pram and covered her with a blanket. "You hush, now," he told her. "You give your poor momma a rest. This is your father talking to you. I expect good Campbell behaviour, Miss, and I'll accept nothing else, you hear?"

When Cedar wakened, yowling, four hours later, Gus was sound asleep and heard nothing. It was Kate who got up, went to the baby, changed her wet backside, then sat in the big chair in the tiny living room breast-feeding and looking out the window at the night-enshrouded neighbourhood. The late May moon was full and bright enough to illuminate the world with a pale glow. The first frogs were croaking, and down the road the neighbours' bulldog barked monotonously.

"A spot of tea?" Marg asked sleepily from the doorway.

"You're a darling," Kate said. "She starts to drink and I get so thirsty I could drain a river."

Gus slept through the second wake-up call from Cedar, too, but when his alarm went off he was instantly wide awake. He had the kettle boiling for tea by the time Marg came into the kitchen. "You go back to bed," he smiled widely. "I can fry me an egg and make a cuppa, I'm not helpless."

But Marg made him a good breakfast and made sure his lunch was packed and his two thermoses were full of hot coffee. Only when he had headed off to wait for the crummy did she go crawl into bed with Kate to catch a nap before Cedar let them know she was hungry, again.

Kate nursed the baby, Marg bathed her, and then she was put in her pram until it was time for her next feed. The book said that babies should only be fed every four hours, but Cedar seemed to think it should be more like every three hours. By the time Kate sat down to feed her again, Cedar was red-faced and screaming. Kate wept, but Marg held firm "It says," she reminded her younger sister, "that over-feeding is the most common cause of colic. We don't want her getting the colic, do we?"

And so the clock ruled and Cedar was held only during her scheduled feedings until Gus came home from work and had his bath. Then he picked up the baby and took her outside for a breath of fresh air.

"The book says to be careful of breezes," Marg warned. "She should only be outside between eleven and one, and then only on warm, still days."

"I'll keep that in mind," Gus said agreeably. But he walked the backyard, talking to the baby, holding her against his chest, the movement of his body lulling her, the sound of his heartbeat soothing her.

After supper, once Cedar had been nursed, burped and changed, Gus shocked Marg and terrified Kate by dressing the baby in a knitted suit, wrapping her in a blanket and putting her in a cardboard box in the carrier of his bike. "We're going to visit with the Campbells," he laughed.

"Good God!" Marg blurted. "If you have an accident, she's dead."

"Well, then, I'd best not have one," he agreed, and he swung his leg over the bar and pedalled off down the road.

"You've married an insane man."

"He's crazy, all right." Kate was scared, but ready to defend Gus to the entire world. "Crazy about that baby."

Marg loved her sister too much to say anything, such as too bad he isn't as crazy about you, he might treat you better. And yet, she had to admit that Gus was behaving better with his newborn infant than many men would have. Most men would volunteer to have both hands amputated without anesthetic rather than change a diaper, and while they might look into a pram or a cradle, few would reach in, pick up an infant and rock it calm. Men who could skillfully and gently handle newborn spaniel puppies, could even dock their tails without sicking up, wouldn't dare to bathe a baby. It was hard to put her finger on what it was about Gus and his behaviour that made Marg's stomach twist. Something just wasn't right, and whatever that something was, it had to do with the casual, almost indifferent way he treated the woman who had as good as handed her life to him. It was as if Kate could have been any woman at all, any incubator.

Gus made it safely to his parents' home, which he still thought of as his own. He parked his bike at the back door and went into the kitchen, where Mary was just finishing the dishes. "I'll do that," he smiled at his mother. "You get acquainted with your granddaughter."

Mary Campbell sat on the closest chair and unwrapped Cedar. She checked her over from head to toe, even taking off the diaper and having a good look at the tiny backside. "She's well built," she acknowledged, nodding approval. "Straight bones, no birthmarks, and good long legs."

"The best," Gus agreed. "She reminds me of our Jen."

"Jen was more blondy at this age, and she had a good cap of hair. This one is as bald as a wee pig." Mary Campbell was smiling. "She has the look of our Jen around the eyes, no doubt of that, and that's Jen's own wee cheeky mouth."

Colin Campbell came into the kitchen. "What's that you've got, then?"

"This is a baldie. This is a wee bare-bum baldie." Mary tickled Cedar's belly, then walked her fingers up her tiny chest to tickle her under the chin. Cedar's lips twitched. "Ah, see, and she's listening to the angels," she crooned.

"It's gas," Colin pretended to argue. He turned to Gus. "How did you get her here?"

"Carrier of my bike."

"Probably bounced her and jounced her into a case of colic," said Colin, but he was smiling, stroking Cedar's cheek with his thick finger. She stretched, then looked around, turned her face to Colin and smiled widely. "Well, and would you look at that!" he blurted. "That was'nae gas, the lass knows me."

Mary touched Colin's leg gently. "We were saying how much she looks like our Jen."

"Pray to God and the saints she does better with her life." Colin's face darkened. Cedar yawned, and stretched again. "Well, and you're a scrawny mite," he decided. "But you'll do, girl."

"Listen to you," Mary teased. "She'll more than just 'do.' She'll do *fine*."

"Is this what all the fuss has been about?" Ewen brought his tea into the kitchen and went to get a refill. "She's got your stamp on her, for sure, Gus," he laughed. "So much for your claim she isn't yours."

Gus glared, but wisely let it pass. The only person who had ever got the better of Ewen either verbally or physically was old Colin.

"You're like a plucked chicken," Ewen told the baby. "Or a wee skinned rabbit ready for the pot. It's a good thing your grandma's got hold of you or we might stuff you up with onion, throw in some carrots and spuds and put you in the oven."

Cedar stuffed her thumb in her mouth and closed her eyes. Mary put the clothes back on the baby, gently removing her thumb from her mouth as she pulled the sleeve of the knitted suit down over the little hand. "Here, here," she warned, "and you'll be so bucktoothed you'll be able to eat apples through a picket fence. And we aren't having babbies with big fat deformed thumbs, either."

When Gus got home he was full of scones and home-canned raspberry jam and he had so much tea in him he practically sloshed. "Cedar was good as gold," he told Kate. "She did you proud, behaved herself and won them all over. We should take her to see your mom and da tomorrow after supper. We could walk over to my parents' and borrow the car. Or," he smiled at her, patting her bum, "I could hurry over after supper, while you're getting ready, bring the car here and pick you up the same as if you were a movie star, or a princess. Which you are, my princess. Two princesses, I have."

"That would be lovely," Kate said, realizing she was desperate to get out of the house.

Only Marg wondered, and she kept it to herself, why Gus hadn't taken Kate along that night, on Cedar's first visit to his family.

Marg stayed with them a week. Two evenings after she'd gone, Gus played with the baby, bathed her, got her into clean dry clothes. Then, while Kate was nursing her, he put on his jacket and left, ostensibly for the Domino Club. "See if I can make a bit of cash," he said, patting Kate's head. "She's going to need a crib before long."

"But—"

"And *you*," he grinned, "are going to need a bigger house. The rellies are filling this one with baby gifts. Don't wait up for me, you need your sleep so you can make good rich milk. I'll be home as soon as I can, hopefully with a dollar or two."

Gus wasn't home when Cedar demanded her midnight feed, but when Kate wakened for the four o'clock one, he was in bed beside her, and she thought he was asleep. She didn't know he'd only just made it into bed. In the morning, when she wakened and went sleepily into the kitchen to start his breakfast, there was a few dollars' worth of change on the table. She thought it was his pay for relieving the houseman. She didn't know anything about the money he won at poker.

The next place they moved to was bigger and had more of a yard to it. The place after that even Marg called decent sized, with a big living room, a cozy kitchen and two bedrooms. A back porch ran the width of the house, and it had a bathroom at the end of it and room for the washing machine. The walls were solid from floor to waist, then windows up to the ceiling. Kate told everyone she blessed the place a dozen times a day—she could do her wash without catching a chill, she could hang her clothes on the line without having to put on her coat and hat, and she had a place to store all their shoes, gumboots, overcoats and bumbershoots.

"Listen to you," Marg teased, "making poetry about a glorified back porch." And she chanted, "Shoes, gumboots, overcoats and bumbershoots . . ."

"Souvenirs," Kate joined the rhythm of the chant, "knick-knacks, folderol and bric-a-brac."

"You're both crazy," Gus said. "I'd best leave here before I wind up daft as well." And he was gone, seemingly to the Domino Club.

Marg came to visit often, and sometimes Hank came with her. The nights he did, Gus stayed home and they drank tea, played cards or checkers and listened to music on the radio. Gus would take Kate by the hand and dance her around the kitchen, showing off his most intricate steps, sometimes counting softly so Kate could learn to follow him. Two or three songs later, he would escort Kate to her chair and dance with Marg. That always spurred Hank to action. When the song was over Hank would dance with Marg, and if he had no fancy steps or complicated moves, he was still a good dancer. Hank didn't talk much, he wasn't overly fond of card games and a bit of tea went a long way for him, but he smiled and did what he considered to be his family duty.

Hank preferred to stay home and work in his garden, or head off into the bush with his rifle. He invited Gus to go deer hunting with him, but Gus shook his head and looked embarrassed. "Can't do it," he admitted. "I shot a deer once. But when I got to it, it wasn't dead. I vow to God it was crying. Saddest noise I ever heard in my life. Now fishing, that's a different story. I could show you some fine spots if you're interested. And grouse and pheasant, I can do that and not be bothered. It's just the deer I can't manage."

"I enjoy fishing," Hank nodded. "We'll do that, then."

And sometimes they did, and got along well together. Hank noticed that Gus had no trouble eating deer meat, which they all called government mutton, and sometimes wondered about the streak of supposed soft-heartedness, because Gus didn't seem to show it for anyone or anything else.

Cedar's first birthday was the occasion for a family get-together, and both the Larsons and the Campbells gathered at Kate's house for supper. Kate had her figure back again and her eyes sparkled, even after a full day of cooking and getting ready for the crowd. Karen brought food, Marg brought food, Mary Campbell brought food, and there were four different cakes, each with a single candle. Cedar sat in her high chair and squealed excitedly, all her favourite people around her at one time.

Not a month later, with no family mob to smile approval or go on about how obvious it was that Gus adored his baby, there was another birthday party. Gus wore a bright red paper hat and sang Happy Birthday to Bev Callahan, Sheila's daughter. He'd bought a panda bear for Cedar and he bought another for Bev. He'd blown up balloons for Cedar, and he did the same for Bev. The Callahans had already held their family party and had not invited Gus, which was fine with him. He went over with his party after the rest of them had gone home, and it was no skin off his nose that little Bev fell sound asleep shortly after he arrived. His show of paternal love was more for Sheila than anyone else.

Sheila's second child was born fifteen months later. By then Kate was pregnant again and Gus was carrying on more or less openly with Bridget Riley. Sheila's second daughter was named Janet, and Gus bought a bed for Bev so that Janet could have the crib. Sheila bragged to a totally unimpressed family of Callahans that Gus had bought three sets of sheets and pillowcases as well as two blankets and a quilt. Her relatives looked at each other and shook their heads, wondering how they had managed to turn out such a fool. Yes, Sheila got money from Gus every second week, and yes, it was far more than any other dizzy bizum got for her bastard children, but still and all, couldn't she see what was as plain as the nose on her face?

By the time Kate's son was born, she and Sheila were probably the only ones in town who weren't talking about the fact that Bridget Riley was not only in the picture but practically filling it.

Kate sat in the rocking chair breastfeeding Rory and watching out the window as snow drifted from a dark, clouded sky. The walkway to the house was covered an inch thick, and the road showed only a couple of ruts where the occasional car had passed without stopping. When Rory was full and burped and asleep again, Kate put him in the pram, then went into Cedar's room. She was still sleeping in her crib but her new single bed was set up, and made, and waiting for her to get used to the idea of sleeping in it. In the afternoons, when it was time for her nap, Kate put her on the bed and lay with her until she drifted off. By the time Rory outgrew the pram and needed the crib, the transition would be made. And now was as good a time as any to help it along. Kate lifted Cedar from the crib, moved her to the single bed, slid her between the sheets, then lay beside her, staring dry-eyed at the wall.

When she wakened and got up to start breakfast, snow was still falling but the footprints on the sidewalk were dark, and she knew Gus hadn't been home long. He was in their bed and he looked to be asleep, but she knew he wasn't.

"Will there be work with this snow?" she asked.

"Probably not, but I'd best get up and go wait for the crummy, just in case." He pretended to yawn. Kate nodded and went to the kitchen to make coffee, cook bacon and eggs, and pack a lunch. She felt as if she was packing up her own laughter and putting it in with the sandwiches and cake.

Gus headed off in his work clothes, carrying his caulk boots over his shoulder, his lunch kit in his hand. An hour later he was back. "No sign of the crummy," he said, shrugging, as if it didn't matter whether he worked or not, made wages or not.

He spent an hour making a sled and another hour playing on it with Cedar. When she was red-faced with cold and starting to shiver, he took her home and plunked her in a warm bathtub. Then they ate the lunch that Kate had packed. At naptime Gus lay down in Cedar's bed with her. She slept for an hour and a half, and Gus slept until Kate wakened him for supper.

After supper he sat in the rocking chair with Rory on one knee and Cedar on the other. He sang to them, he rocked them, he even let Cedar hold the baby. When Rory began to fuss, Gus handed him off to Kate and took Cedar for another bath, kneeling on the floor beside the tub, his shirtsleeves rolled up, guiding the boat he had made for her. "Look out, now," he teased, "she'll run you over if you don't get out of the way. That's it, slither down in the water, won't matter if you get your hair wet or your face splashed, just don't get run over."

When the children were settled, Gus went out to shovel off the walkway. The snow had stopped by then and the stars showed clearly in the cold night sky. Gus cleared the walkway and the front steps and spread ashes on them so nobody would slip. "Best go see if anyone's done my mom's steps," he said easily, smiling and hauling on his warm knitted cap.

Kate just nodded and made herself smile. She knew Mary Campbell's steps were clean and ashed and probably salted as well. And she knew Gus knew she knew. But if Kate wasn't much interested in making things easier for Gus by pretending, she had every intention of making things easier for herself. She wasn't even twenty-three years old and already she felt as if she was worn to a tiny nub.

Gus walked to Sheila Callahan's place and made a sled for Bev, but she was too sleepy to go for a ride in it so he supervised her bath and played tugboats and ducks with her. "Come on, then," he said, "let's sing our Jennet to sleep and give Mom a rest, shall we then?"

He rocked them, put them to bed, rubbed their backs and whispered to them. When they were both asleep he went into the kitchen to spark Sheila, but she wasn't as friendly as she had been. "What's wrong, then?" he asked, looking wounded.

"Nothing."

"Well, then." He tried to put his arm around her.

"Don't," she said. "No more of that, Gus. No more. Not ever."

"What?"

"We're done," she told him.

He stared at her, his face set, his eyes narrowed. Then he laughed.

"Your loss, lady, not mine," he said, and reached for his sweater and jacket.

Not three-quarters of an hour later he was in Bridget Riley's bed, doing his best to drive her crazy, to prove that there wasn't a better lover within a three-day search. And while he revelled, and Bridget twisted under him, panting and moaning, he told himself Sheila Callahan would regret the day she'd sent him packing. She'd beg for it before he offered it to her.

He didn't go to see Sheila for almost two weeks, and when he did go over, Gordon Bridges was already there, sitting at the kitchen table in his sock feet, drinking tea and eating butter tarts, Bev on his lap with crayons and a brand-new colouring book.

"No home of your own to go to, then?" Gus challenged.

"Oh, I've a home to go to," Gord answered, his smile mocking. "I've a house, and if I didn't want to be there I could be on my boat. Plenty of places I could be. I just happen to like it here, is all."

"Pandering another man's daughter."

"Gus, stop it," Sheila said, frightened.

"Trying to get close to the mother, are you? Play with the kitten to catch the cat?"

"Gus. Please. I told you, it's done. It's done forever."

"It's not done as long as my two daughters are alive. I'll come to see them whenever I've a mind to, and not you nor the imps of hell will get in my way."

"Go away, Gus, please."

"You hear me, Gordon Bridges?"

Gordon laughed. "Oh, I hear you well enough."

"Don't get in my way, then."

Gus lifted Bev from Gordon's lap and hugged her. "And are you a good girl, then? Are you your daddy's love?"

And of course she was. But when he left, she didn't cry. She went back to her crayons and the new colouring book. Gus glared, but said nothing.

Gordon Bridges left three hours later, and Gus got him as he went around the corner of the house. The length of two-by-four connected across Gordon's shoulders, stunning him and knocking him to the ground. Before he could get his feet under him, Gus was standing astraddle, swinging the length of fir again and again on the ribs, the shoulders, the hips, the legs, but not on the head or face.

"Just you remember," he said repeatedly. "Just you bloody well remember."

Gordon Bridges remembered. He had to wait two weeks for the bruises to begin to fade and the swelling to disappear, then he had to wait another week until he could move normally again, but within a month he was as fit as ever. He waited outside the Domino Club, watching and biding his time. Finally, early one morning, Gus left the club alone.

"Well." Gordon stepped from the shadows. "You told me to remember."

Nobody saw the fight but they all saw the bruises. Those who knew Gus vowed he had won the fight, those who sided with Gordon said obviously he had won. Neither of the two brawlers ever said anything one way or the other. But Gordon continued to visit with Sheila and Gus saw less and less of Bev and Janet. Eventually a half-civilized arrangement was agreed to: Gus would let Sheila know when he was going over, and she made sure she and Gordon stayed in the living room, leaving the kitchen to Gus and the girls.

When Gordon Bridges and Sheila Callahan got married, they moved into Gordon's house, a big two-storey place overlooking the sea.

"You can come see the girls," Gordon told Gus, "and I won't interfere, but I remind you, they live in *my* house now."

"Shove your house up your arse," Gus raged.

He stayed away until prawn season was open and Gordon was off working round the clock. Then he went to visit his girls, and he blamed Gordon for the fact that Janet barely remembered him and Bev talked and chattered on about Unca Gord until Gus's teeth were on edge. Even more, he blamed Gordon for the change in Sheila's attitude.

First he tried teasing, because it often worked. "What are you saving it for? You know how good it was for us, you know it was the best."

"Not the best," she corrected. "There was never any affection from you, Gus, just the other."

"The other had you coming back for more for a good long time!"

She laughed softly. "Well, of course. If a person has only known oatmeal it might seem like a real meal. But just let that person taste good roast beef and see how eager they are to go back to the oatmeal."

"Bitch."

Still, every two weeks Sheila got a money order in the mail. Kate knew nothing about it. All of Gus Campbell's official pay went to his wife and children; he paid for his blow-bys with the money he made at the Domino Club. Sheila put the money in a savings account. She knew Gordon would only remain quiet as long as he was the one supporting the family. "When I married you," he told her, "I married them, too. I won't make any demands, but I would like it if they had my name."

"We'll see," Sheila stalled. "Let's not kick up a fuss. Let things calm down a bit."

Gus was having trouble with Bridget Riley. "I might be willing to share you with your wife," she hissed, "but I'll be damned to hell if I'll share you with Sheila Bridges. Best you decide what you want, little boy, or you'll wind up with bugger nothing!"

"Bridget, you know better than that."

"You can bet your bottom dollar I know better. And now, so do you."

It took a fair bit of flarching to get past her anger and hard-headedness, but Gus, as the whole town said, had a way with women. He even managed, while reassuring Bridget, to convince Kate that he was settling down and becoming a stable family man. Kate wanted to believe life had taken a turn for the better. Yes, it wasn't always easy living with

Gus, but you probably couldn't find a more devoted father in the entire town. He came home from work, got cleaned up and took both children for a walk before supper, giving Kate plenty of time and space to get things ready without having to worry about little faces getting in the way of pots of hot water. And after supper, while Kate cleared up, he took them out into the garden and let them dig with big soup spoons while he spaded the spring-warmed earth. "That's a good man," he'd say, and Rory would smile happily, flinging dirt with his spoon. "You work on that and get it all soft and ready and then we'll plant us some nice lettuce or maybe some radishes. And you," he said, turning his charm on Cedar, "you're going to be one of the best gardeners in town, you've got the touch."

The children were in bed and falling asleep by eight and Gus was off to the Domino Club. Somehow, and Kate wasn't sure how, his other interests had fallen away. Oh, he still went trout fishing, but usually only on the weekends, and there were no more volunteer fire department meetings. Just about the time she would start to get fed up with spending every evening alone, Gus would leave five or ten dollars on the table for her to put in their special account, and right away Kate would feel guilty. He worked so hard for so little and seldom a word of complaint.

The first time Gus back-handed her, Kate was so surprised she could do nothing more than stare, slack-jawed with shock, looking stupid and vacant-eyed.

"How dare you!" she blurted.

"How dare I? How dare I, missus? This is how I dare." And he did it again.

"Gus! Stop it! Dear God, what have I done?"

"Shut up, Kate, I'm warning you. I've had enough of your bellyaching and jawboning. Just shut the hell up and leave me be."

He didn't go to the Domino that night. He went to bed early and slept so soundly he didn't even notice that Kate had spent the night on the chesterfield in the living room. He went to the Domino the following night, or at least that's where he said he was going, and when he came home, he found Kate sleeping on the couch. She woke up as she hit the floor.

"Gus!"

"You've got a goddamn bed, woman, and you'll sleep in it."

The next afternoon, while the children napped, Kate soaked in a deep tub of almost hot water and looked sadly at the bruises on her arms and legs. Irregularly shaped, almost but not quite round, the marks were spots where Gus had gripped her with his strong fingers. Even the inside of her thighs felt battered, and while she couldn't say the ache inside her was a pain, it was a dull ache, and she knew it was from the rough way he'd thumped at her, banged into her, not so much taking her as using her with no sign of love or even sexual desire, just using her, as much a punishment as a slap in the face. She felt degraded, and the worst of it was, it wasn't something you could talk about to anybody, not even your sister. If it wasn't for the fact they were married, she would have considered it to be rape. But how could a man rape his wife? She'd never heard of such a thing. It didn't occur to her that she hadn't heard of it because nobody else could bring herself to talk about it, either.

TWO

Cedar fully expected to love school. She'd heard all about it from Neal Sutherland, who lived next door with his father Art and his younger brother Sam. Art was older than any of the other dads. He had grey hair with white streaks in it and lines in his face, but he was tall, and obviously very strong. When he rolled up his sleeves, his muscles stood out along the sides of his arms, and if he reached for something they moved smooth as snakes in long, damp grass. Sometimes when he was mowing the lawn he took his shirt off and worked in his singlet, the hair on his chest showing white but his muscles bulging across his back. He had so many muscles he almost looked as if he had breasts, like a woman. Art Sutherland had got his muscles the honest way—not in the mines and not on the logging slopes, but at the foundry. His hands were square and so callused that the palms looked yellow. Uncle Forrest teased that Art had got sick and tired of having to pay good money for gloves that lasted no time at all, and had grown his own.

Neal and Sam's mother was a small, softly curving young woman with dark, curly hair and big brown eyes. When people who didn't know her saw her with Art, they sometimes thought he was her father, and when they learned differently, they went tsk tsk with their tongues against their teeth. Tsk tsk. Too much age difference, they whispered to each other, there's no good ever comes of that. The young get on better with other young, the older should stick to the older. Cradle robber, they said, tsk tsk, and there'll be wigs on the green for sure because of it. Alice lived with Art and the two boys like a normal family until midwinter, and then something awful happened. Cedar didn't know exactly what it was except that on a Sunday, almost at noon, a car had stopped in front of the Sutherland place and a man much younger than Art had got out and moved to the front door. Not five minutes later he had come hurtling back out, falling down the stairs, sliding on his back, his head hitting the concrete walkway. Stunned, he tried to get to his feet but Art went at him and beat on him until the neighbours on the other side got sick, the man jumped the fence and the woman ran in the house to call the police. The neighbour tried to help the young man and Art went back into the house—to wait for the cops, they thought. But then a new uproar kicked off, and Alice's clothes started to tumble out the front bedroom window. Dresses and skirts, blouses and sweaters, lace-trimmed underwear and more pairs of shoes than any one person needed. And then Alice herself came out the window and landed in the snow, her face swollen, cut and bleeding even before she landed. She got up and tried to run, one shoe off and one shoe on, just like in the nursery rhyme, but Art came down the front steps like a bull going through a flimsy gate, and he had her by the throat with one hand, slapping her face over and over and over again with the other. The man from the other side tried to stop it but Art cold-cocked him and finally it was Gus went over the fence to put a stop to it.

"She's had enough, Art," he said clearly. "And your boys are screaming."

"Never enough. The bitch! The two-timing floozie bitch!"

"Your sons need you, man."

"You getting in the middle of this?" Art challenged.

"Not me. If they were two-timing you they deserve it. But the wee boys don't. Look at them. Whatever she might or might not be, she's their mommy."

Art let go and Alice fell in a miserable heap on the snowy ground, her face pouring blood. Kate made a move to go to her but Gus stopped her with no more than a threatening look. Art went back up the stairs to Neal and Sam, sat on the threshold of the open front door and pulled the little boys to him, cuddling them and talking softly. Far off down the road, the wail of sirens sounded thin and angry.

"If they take me off, will you watch my boys?" Art asked, so calm it seemed impossible that he was in any way connected to all the crying and sobbing, the puking sounds coming from the young man.

"Take them to my place right now if you want."

"Might do that. I thank you, Gus."

Sam cried but Neal sniffed and nodded and tried hard to be a man, like his father wanted. The ambulance took the young man and Alice off to the hospital, and the police took Art down to the pokey and kept him overnight. Monday morning at ten they were all in court. The judge let Art out on bail, ordered him to come back for his trial and told him what day to show up. Art agreed, signed a few papers and went back to his house on the city bus.

Alice's clothes and shoes were still in the snow. Art picked them up and stuffed them, soaking wet, into boxes, the same ones that had held their belongings when they moved into the house the previous year, the ones he'd kept in the basement in case he ever decided to sell the house and move. He carried the boxes to the young man's car, stuffed them in the back seat and left them there. Kate offered to wash the clothes and dry them on the indoor lines in the basement, but Art said no and Kate wasn't about to press the subject.

The young man showed up in a police car with two constables, who stood guard while he got in his car, started it up and drove away. Art watched from the front porch, his face impassive. He looked at the constables and gave them a quick nod of recognition.

"Don't worry, boys," he told them gently. "Nothing else is coming down."

They nodded back, got in their car and drove off.

When Art went back to court he was fined twenty-five dollars and ordered to keep the peace. Two weeks later he was back in court about something totally different, and the next day Alice was on the road outside what had once been her home, wailing and screaming, "They're my sons, too! This is wrong! I'm their *mother!*" and Sam, who didn't go to school yet, was standing in the doorway, sobbing and calling for her. Art picked up the boy, little more than a baby, and tried to calm him, but Sammy wailed and screeched, leaning away from his father and reaching for Alice, and screamed Momma, Momma, until Art couldn't stand another minute of it. He walked to the road and handed Sam to Alice, let her hold her baby, cuddle him and sob helplessly. Nobody else heard what got said there on the road, but later, when

Alice and the young man were living together in a little house on the other side of town, the car would arrive on Friday nights, and both boys would run out to it, climb into the back seat and ride off, grinning happily. They were back again Sunday evening and tumbled out of the car still grinning, racing for their father's house, ready to be swooped up in those heavily muscled arms, the hands that could pummel, bruise and rip flesh, even break bones, gentle with them, the eyes as they watched the car drive away hard as pebbles under thick eyebrows lowered in a frown.

"Nobody I'd want mad at me," Gus said in a voice that was almost a sigh. "That man can love deep, but he can hate even deeper."

"He did right." Kate didn't even try to hide her bitterness. "All he was doing was trying to protect his family."

"Protect it? He damn near killed her!"

"His children. Protect them from trash." She turned away, eyes burning with the jealous wish that she, too, was larded with muscle, with huge hands capable of breaking noses, cheekbones, anything if it would keep the children safe.

With everything Neal had told her about school, Cedar expected to enjoy every minute of it. Her first day taught her otherwise. She found out you couldn't leave whenever you felt like it. She also found out that it does no good at all to argue with the teacher. Even the new pencils and crayons didn't make up for having to sit on a hard chair at a big table with five other kids when what she wanted to do was go home, change the new clothes she had been told to keep clean, get into something she could play in, and go outside where the sun was shining, the breeze smelled of ripe fruit, and she could get a drink or go to the bathroom without having to tell the entire class about it. The water at home came from a well but the water here came from somewhere else—it was flat, and tasted of metal pipes, and she didn't like it one little bit.

She asked Neal about it on the way home and he shrugged. "Ya get used to it," he told her. "Or ya take drinks from home."

That night at supper she told her parents about having to stay.

"Yes," Kate nodded. "That's the rule."

"Who made that rule?" Cedar hoped she could meet this person, maybe even get the rule changed. When she found out that wasn't possible, she was indignant. "As if that's fair!" she blurted. "They should

at least have . . ." But Kate was smiling in that way that meant she wanted to laugh, and Gus was nodding, agreeing with her, but already
laughing. "Well, their water *stinks,*" she told them. "Makes you want to
puke."

Kate found a small jar with a tight-fitting lid, and Cedar filled it
with well water and took it to school along with her little bottle of milk
and her sandwich. "See?" Kate tried to put some of the glow back on
school. "It's just like a little picnic."

But it wasn't, because the only place you could eat your lunch was
at your seat. No going out onto the playground with it, no leaving the
school grounds, and that was another thing that wasn't fair, because
just the other side of the fence there was a vacant lot with a big chest-
nut tree in front, and she could have eaten her lunch there, all by herself.

"There's good reasons for some rules," Gus told her. "That big
fence didn't use to be there, nor the big gate, either. And kids did leave
the school grounds. But then one time a girl didn't go back after lunch,
and the school thought she'd played hooky. The next day, when school
opened, the police were there." He took Cedar's face in his big rough
hands and looked her in the eyes. "That girl got stolen," he said grave-
ly, "and what's worse, she wound up killed."

"Oh!" Cedar whispered.

"And her dad just about went crazy. So they put up the fence and
brought in that new rule."

To think that someone could be stolen. To think that someone
would go where kids were sure to be, the school, and then swipe a girl.
Cedar could understand swiping candy—sometimes Neal stole some
and shared with her; other times she gave him some pennies from her
jar and he bought it for her and she shared with him and with Sam. She
could understand why someone had swiped Tommy Cranshaw's pregnant collie, because not only was she a beautiful dog, her tummy was
full of what everyone said were purebred puppies. But to steal a kid?
And then to kill that kid? If you wanted one bad enough to swipe it,
why wouldn't you take real good care of it? She tried to ask at least
some of the questions, but nobody wanted to talk about any part of it
so she didn't learn a thing.

Cedar learned to read quickly, thanks to Kate's help with the alphabet. They sat at the table after supper while Gus was playing with Rory

and giving him his bath. Kate drew the letters and Cedar copied them. When the other kids her age were still learning the alphabet song, Cedar was already sounding out small words. By the time the others got to small words, Cedar and two other girls were able to sound out bigger ones, and even read sentences. One of those girls was Beryl Campbell, and at first she and Cedar thought they were cousins. Gus shook his head. "No relation to us. Different Campbells altogether." That was confusing—same name but not cousins, especially when Linda Lewis was a cousin and she didn't even have the same name.

"No, but she's a cousin. Twice over." Gus got a piece of paper and a pencil. He drew a picture of a tree, and started to write names on it. "See, on Linda's mom's side, they're McNabs. Grandma McNab was born a Campbell, but changed her name when she got married. And over here, on the Lewis side . . . See, again, a Campbell, my own cousin Blanche. So both her mom and her dad are related to us. So she's a Lewis, yes, but she's your cousin."

"It's very confusing," Kate said gently, "but after a while it will start to make sense. If you like, we can keep a list of who is and who isn't related."

But there were other aunties and uncles, not even family ones. Auntie Inger, who was an auntie only because she'd been Grandma Larson's best friend for more than forty years, and Auntie Martha, who had come from the same place in Scotland as Grandma Campbell. John Riley was Uncle John because Daddy said so, and John's sister Bridget was Auntie Bridey for the same reason. The whole idea of family became amorphous, the boundaries opening and closing in odd ways, like it was Auntie Martha, but her husband was Mr. Agnew, not Uncle at all. By grade three she had decided, with the help of the Sunday school class she attended only briefly, that if Eve was *everybody's* mother and Adam was *everybody's* father, then go back far enough and *everybody* was a cousin. It made everything so much easier. Auntie Inger's grandchildren were Cedar's cousins not only because their grandma was her auntie, but just because. And sooner or later everyone was her cousin—even, as Auntie Marg laughingly agreed, Haille Selassie, the Lion of Judah. But not, according to Gus, the kids who lived with Uncle Ewen. "No bloody kin of ours!" Gus half shouted. "Just because Ewen's got no pride is no reason the rest of us should lose ours."

"Ewen's happy," Kate said mildly.

"Ewen's been wandering around sniffing after other men's leavings since he was seventeen and thought he was in love with Allie McCarthy whose husband worked in the coal pits."

Cedar didn't understand the first thing about whatever it was Gus was shouting about, and she didn't understand why Kate started laughing, or why she said, "Other men's leavings?" as if it meant something other than what it said. Most of all she didn't understand why Gus suddenly swung an open-handed slap that caught Kate on the side of the face and knocked her into the wall.

"Oh," Kate gasped. Then she straightened, one hand to her face, her eyes glittering, but not with tears. "Oh, that's nice, Gus. Very nice."

"Get another if you keep it up," he warned.

"Stop crying, Cedar, it doesn't matter. Come on, now. There's a girl." Kate wiped Cedar's eyes with her apron. "See what you've done?" she asked gently. "Scared the wits out of her, you have."

"Cedar, you stop that," Gus ordered.

Cedar started crying again, her sobs deep and phlegmy.

"I said stop it, or I'll give you something to cry about."

"Come on, honey bun, let's go to your room for a little while." Kate led her away and Gus got his jacket and left.

Kate had no way of knowing that the slap had little to do with what she had said, or hinted, or left unsaid. The slap came from the frustrations Gus felt at work, his suspicion that other men snickered whenever the talk turned to his not-the-least-bit-secret bed hopping. It came from the ongoing tension with Bridey, it came from as far back as Gordon Bridges and the terrible fight Gus could no longer convince himself he had won. All it would have taken, he knew, was one more punch. Not a haymaker, not even a solid wallop, just a punch. Gordon had been standing, bent at the waist, head down, his arms hanging heavily and uselessly, his lungs heaving, heaving for breath. He was incapable of defending himself, incapable of attacking. Gordon Bridges was finished, blood pouring from his nose, his mouth, a cut above his eyebrow. And if Gus had thrown just one punch, he would surely have flattened him. But he didn't throw it. He said, "Go, now." And Gordon turned and went, lurching, staggering, his legs like wet noodles. Several times he bounced against the side of the building. Gus watched him go, knowing but not admitting that he had failed to throw that final punch because he couldn't do it. He couldn't even muster the strength to clench his fists, let alone swing a roundhouse.

When Gordon Bridges was out of sight, Gus had turned and made his way along the sidewalk, moving slowly, feeling sick to his stomach. When he got to the bridge, it seemed to stretch for miles. He wasn't afraid of falling off, pitching over the side to the ravine far below. He just didn't want to pass out on the bridge, where he might be seen. He particularly didn't want to be seen by the local constabulary.

So he walked down the slope, pushed his way through the weeds and brush to the underside of the bridge. There he slumped to the dry ground and leaned against the cold concrete abutment. After a while he slid himself down and lay on his side, his knees drawn up to relieve the pain in his guts. He gagged and choked, but nothing would come up. The dizziness grew worse, and he felt almost like weeping. He closed his eyes and slept for three hours, then wakened stiff and cold, feeling guilty—or something. He didn't know what he had to feel guilty about, so it must have been something else. For a long time he had told himself that he had won that fight. But lately he wasn't sure he had.

"Why aren't Uncle Ewen's kids my cousins?" Cedar was trying to understand what had happened.

"Because they had a different dad than him. They were already here before he even met their mom."

"But he said they *all* got married."

"That's what Uncle Ewen said, but that's not how it works."

"Why doesn't Daddy like Patience? He says I should call her Patience, not Auntie Patience."

"Well, your daddy didn't want Uncle Ewen to marry her, is all. He'll get over it once he gets used to the idea."

"Grandpa didn't want them to get married, either."

"No, he didn't. But when little Rosie was born your grandfather came around quickly enough. And so will your dad."

"Grandpa says she's the Black Rosie. Daddy said she's a half-breed. What's half-breed?"

"Why don't we wait until some other time to tackle that one. It's very complicated."

"You can see the mark of his fingers on your face."

"Yes, well, we all leave our mark one way or the other, don't we.

There's your brother howling for his bath and his bedtime. We'd better go before he yells the house down around our ears."

It wasn't Rory brought the house down, though. It was Gus when he got home. He ranted and raved, he yelled and hollered, and made out it was all Kate's fault for being saucy. Rory woke up wailing, then Cedar woke up and started to cry, and still Gus vented, pounding his fist on the tabletop, warning Kate she was within an inch of getting a hiding, telling them all to either shut up or get the hell out and leave him in peace.

The next day Uncle Forrest came with his truck and moved Kate and the two children out of the house. They took their clothes, they took their beds, they took most of the kitchen stuff, but they left everything in the living room. When Gus came home from work the house was cold, there was no supper, and there was only the sofa to sleep on.

Instead, he rode his bike over to his mother's place. "She's gone," he said. "She took my kids with her."

Colin got up, reaching for his smoking kit. "It's been longer coming than I thought it would."

"She'll be back. With her tail between her legs."

"Well, someone's tail should be tamed, for sure." Colin went out onto the porch, settled himself in his chair, turned on his little radio and rolled a cigarette.

"Have you eaten?" Mary Campbell asked.

"No, ma'am, I haven't." Gus sighed. "House was cold. Barely enough hot water for a bath. Bloody shock, it was."

"Sit yourself at the table, then, I'll fix you something."

Gus was beginning to realize what Kate had done. "If I go get my kids, will you watch them while I'm at work?" He expected instant agreement—Mary Campbell was soft on kids, especially her grandchildren.

"No," his mother said quietly. "I'll not help you deprive them of their rightful mama. They grew in her body, Gus, not yours."

Gus couldn't believe his ears. If he had been anywhere else, he'd have sworn a blue streak, but he knew if he swore in his mother's kitchen he'd be out on his ear with a thick lip in less time than it would take a cat to switch its tail.

"Use the time to think, Angus. You're too fast with your hands and tongue and not fast enough with your loyalty. And if you go out to the

Larsons' place with blood in your eye there's three big boys out there, any one of whom could use you to clean the chimney. They'll not stand by and watch you slap their sister around as if she was a stray dog."

"Mam," he pleaded.

She put a plate of warmed-up supper in front of him and shook her head. "I don't know where you learned that, my boy. In all the years I've lived with your dad, through good times and bad, not once has he lifted his hand to me. Where I come from, other women wouldn't stand for it. I mind one neighbour put bruises on his poor wife. The very next day, when he came home from work, all the women in the neighbour- hood were waiting for him with lengths of wood, bits of broomstick, even a brick or two. Beat him and beat him good, then told him if he did it again, there'd be more beatings for him. Here? Well, all I can say is there's not enough women like that. More's the pity."

But she let Gus sleep in his old bed, packed his lunch for him, got up and made his breakfast, and saw him off to work.

"Kick his arse," Colin suggested.

"He's our son. I can't put him out in the rain."

"He always could flarch his way around you."

"And listen to who's talking." She pinched him, but not hard. "You and your flarching, that's where he gets it. If it wasn't for that flarching I'd have married Barry McLean and been living in that big house on top of the hill."

Cedar had to change schools, and she didn't like that. There was just too much to have to get used to, and the worst of it was she had to take the school bus there and back. She missed Neal and Sam, she missed Beryl and Linda, she missed her neighbourhood, and after a while she missed her dad, too. On the other hand, she loved living with Grandma and Grandpa Larson.

This wasn't town, with sidewalks and roads dividing everything up like the slices in a pie. This was bigger, freer and as much hers as anybody else's. People here had chickens, some people had pigs or cows, and everybody had dogs. Uncle Hugh lived just up the road with his wife Georgina, and their sons Steve and Piers, and their daughter Karen, who was called Little Karen to distinguish her from not only Grandma Larson, but also her other grandma, Karen Fogarty.

"My world," Uncle Hugh joked, "is filled with Karens. It's even my wife's real name."

"No," Cedar breathed, as if something magical was being disclosed.

"Her full name is Karen Georgina."

"What's my full name?"

"Cedar fulla beans Campbell. Cedar can-a-soup Campbell."

"You!"

She darted at him but he got out of her way easily, then scooped her up and sat her on his shoulders, her legs dangling down either side of his neck, her feet bumping his chest. He jumped up and down, and Cedar started laughing. "If you get any taller your legs will be down at my belly. And the next you know they'll be long enough to touch the ground."

Grandma Karen had two flocks of chickens, one for laying, the other for meat. The laying rooster was cranky and jittery and as apt as not to go for your face when you went to gather eggs, but the meat rooster was a big, slow-moving thing who didn't mind if you picked him up and carried him around like a baby. He had feathers all the way down his legs and even on his three-toed feet. Cedar called him Mr. Britches and made sure she had some grain in her hand when she went to visit. "That child," Grandpa Olaf smiled. "She'll be out hand-feeding cougars next. She sees an animal and has to make friends."

Cedar even made friends with the big scar-headed black and tan mutt of a dog who lived at the neighbouring dairy farm. Nobody knew what kind of dog he was supposed to be, he'd been bought for two bits at a farm auction in Chemainus when he was just a puppy. But whatever he was, he was big. And he could fight like a tiger. Uncle Forrest had Cedar half convinced the reason the dog had a short tail was the missing part had been bitten off by a bear, but Uncle Wade laughed when she asked him and said it was called "docking" and it had been done when he was born.

"Why do they do that?"

"So the bears *can't* grab them by the tail." Wade looked totally serious, so of course Cedar believed him.

She was ready to believe just about anything her uncles told her. But what other people told her was suspect. For example, there was the matter of what they were taught in school. And, just as importantly, what they weren't taught.

"No," she breathed, not in disbelief, but in protest.

"Yes," Grandpa Larson said. "The shaft ran from under the main street of town, under the ocean and over to that little island there. It's about sixty percent number one anthracite, and what they should have done was start a new workings over there, but no, that would have cost them a few cents startup money so they just kept following the seam of coal. When the explosion happened, it started a fire, and the company was afraid the fire would follow the coal seam to the big deposits on the island, so they flooded the tunnel with seawater. Just flooded it. An entire shift of men." He shook his head, and his tone changed. "Oh, but it was a glorious funeral. Even though there were no bodies brought out, the company picked up the tab. Big monument. A chunk of coal, no less. Had it on a wagon with bunting and union jacks and the pipe band and all."

"You give over," Grandma Karen said softly, "You'll turn her into as big a communist as yourself and the boys."

"Oh, I hope so," Olaf said. "I do most sincerely hope so.

"Nah, nah," he said. She was sitting on the back of his big chair, one leg on either side of his neck, her feet resting on his chest, brushing what was left of his hair. "Nah, they might make a fuss over him, might have given him the title Lord Dunsmuir and put in the paper that he was a fine man. But the truth of it is he was a mean, miserly old bastard whose money was drenched in the blood of honest workers."

"Oh, no," Grandma mourned, "and what kind of marks will they give her if she puts *that* on an exam paper at school? You'll have them failing her."

"Shot them down like dogs in the street," he said. "Right across the creek over there, on the road leading to Company Town. Opened fire on unarmed men, they did. Women and children right behind them. And they just shot them. Shot the men. Killed them."

"Olaf. Please. That's no kind of story for a child."

"No? But other children got to *see* it."

Some evenings, some wonderful warm evenings, with the scent of the fir and cedars ripe, and the sound of the frogs like an accompaniment, Grandpa Olaf would sit in his chair on the porch, with both Cedar and Rory on his lap, their hair still damp from their baths, their feet in clean socks, their pyjamas on and maybe a bit of a blanket over them, and he would sing. "The workers' flag is crimson red with blood of martyrs cruelly shed . . . When freedom's inspiration through the workers' blood shall run, there can be no power greater anywhere beneath the sun . . . It is we who plowed the prairies, built the cities where they trade, dug the mines and built the workshops, endless miles of railroad laid . . ."

"Oh, my," Grandma Karen sighed, "and listen to yourself. What kind of songs are those for youngsters to learn?"

"You teach them your kind of prayers, I'll teach them mine," he said. "These are the best kinds of songs for youngsters. If they learn them early enough nobody will ever put his foot on their neck."

Uncle Forrest took Cedar with him when he went fishing. He showed her the best place to cast her worm-baited hook. "The fish are really on the other side of the creek. But if we go over there, they'll hear the rocks rattling and come over here. So we sit here and cast our lines over there. Got to be smarter than the fish."

The first few times she went, she got skunked. And then, without any warning, something had her hook and was trying to take it away. Uncle Forrest moved over behind her. "Let him tire himself out before you try to bring him in. That's it, see how he has to take a rest? When he's resting like that, quick as you can, you take as many turns on the reel as possible. That's it. Okay, he's starting to fight again, just let him do it, that's it, he can't keep it up forever."

She caught another one before they headed home. The second one wasn't as big as the first, but it was as big as any of the ones Uncle Forrest caught.

"Look what we have for supper," Uncle Forrest bragged. "And see this big one? Well, it was Cedar Campbell caught that one."

Grandma Larson was suitably impressed, and so was Grandpa when he got home. "Won't be a fish left in that creek if Cedar keeps going fishing," he teased.

It felt good to sit at the table at suppertime and watch as Grandpa Olaf carefully slit the trout down the back and from the vent to the tail, then lifted with quick movements and the bottom side of the fish was lying, boneless, on the plate. A fast flip and the skeleton was out completely, looking like something in the funny papers, where the cat eats the fish down to the spine and ribs. He cut each half into three pieces and there was some of the big one for everyone. Cedar didn't say anything but she personally thought the smaller ones tasted better. Nobody else seemed to think so, though, and Rory could hardly get enough.

"Spuds, too," Kate told him. "And your carrots. Then if you're still hungry, you can have more fish."

There were other things to do, too. Berry picking, and if you got enough of them there would be pie, with everyone saying how good it was, how lucky they were Cedar could pick berries and Grandma would make pie. Cedar wanted to go hunting, too, but none of the uncles would take her, not even Uncle Hugh.

When school let out she was allowed to go swimming in the creek if she could find someone to take her who could swim well, and who promised to keep an eye out for her. She had been hoping her mother would take her, but that idea went by the wayside when Kate got a job at the TruckStop diner. She worked from two in the afternoon through to midnight, when the place closed. Sometimes Cedar rode her bike down the highway and ate supper sitting at the TruckStop counter, watching her mother smiling and joking, refilling coffee mugs or taking orders and writing them on the little pad she carried. "With fries," she'd ask, "or mashed?"

Cedar was allowed to choose from the menu, the same as if she was a customer. She could have anything she wanted. Mostly she ordered the liver and onions because they didn't get that any more. Grandpa Olaf wouldn't allow it, unless it was deer liver. "I've seen how they raise beef animals and that's all I'm going to say." But at the TruckStop, the cook knew Cedar liked calf liver and made sure she got an adult helping of it, with hardly any spuds or veg because there's a limit to how much a kid's stomach can hold. Sometimes he gave her such a good helping of it she had no room for dessert, but she didn't mind, there was always cake at Grandma Larson's house. Cake and pie and sometimes Grandma's special pudding. "Too many eggs," she'd pretend to complain, "they're just piling up on me, I'll have to do something with them, or they'll all go bad and start to smell." Then she would wink at Cedar and ask, "Is there someone here who would run up to the farm and ask if they have two spare quarts of rich milk? Tell them to put it on the bill." When Cedar repeated that to the farmer, he laughed and made sure both quarts were rich with cream. Sometimes he added a pint jar to the string bag and asked Cedar to please tell her grandma he needed some help getting rid of all the cream and would she please be a true friend and use up some of it for him. "The cows, you see, can get very insulted if they think we don't use what they give us."

She didn't catch on for quite a while that no money ever changed hands. The farmer got paid in venison, usually the kind that arrived well after dark, by the back door.

At the TruckStop they had a Wurlitzer jukebox. Cedar thought it was just about the most beautiful, magical thing she'd ever seen, with bubbles running through its coloured glass tubes. And the music that came out! Sounded lots better than when it came from the radio. Sometimes, riding her bike home from the diner, she'd sing the songs she'd heard, even though she didn't sound anything like those singers. "See them tumblin' along, pledging their love to the ground, lonely but free I'll be found, driftin' along with the tumblin' tumbleweed . . ." She had to ask what tumbleweed was, then ask why there wasn't any where they lived. "Too wet here," Uncle Forrest told her. "It only rolls around like that looking for a place to spread seeds and grow. Here, it would just take root right away, because of the good rich soil and the good rain. Down there, you see," he winked at her, "the poor buggers live on sand and bake in the sun."

"Like the desert? Like in the movies?"

"Exactly. And those fancy shirts? Well, they're just for show in the movies, they don't really wear them all the time. Nor ride around on a horse strumming a guitar, either. You couldn't really do that, no more than you could ride your bike and play the fiddle."

She didn't care. She'd have a shirt like that. She'd have lots of shirts like that. And guns and holsters, too, like the Cross Draw Kid.

She asked the big kids if she could tag along swimming with them and they smiled and said of course she could. One of them, Chuck McKellar, even stopped off at the place long enough to tell Grandma Karen that he'd keep an eye on Cedar. "I won't let her dive or jump off the rocks until she's a real good swimmer, I promise," he said, and Grandma Karen thanked him and gave him a big piece of apple pie.

"Anytime you need a guard dog," he teased, "give me a yell—your gran makes damn good pie."

At the beginning of the school holidays, Cedar had only been able to dog paddle, but by the time school went back in again, she was swimming properly. Chuck would yell to her and she'd run across the big rock, grab his hand and leap with him into the deep part of the creek. The first few times she was scared stiff and once she even peed. She was starting to learn to swim underwater, but once school started up again, that was the end of that.

Cedar was so unhappy about starting school that Kate said she could bring Rory with her and have supper at the TruckStop. Rory didn't want liver and onions, and he didn't want meat loaf, either. He wanted fish and chips.

"That's all he ever eats," Cedar laughed, "every chance he gets."

"It's good," Rory insisted. "I like the fish better'n I like the chips, though." The cook heard that, and when Rory's plate came there were three big pieces of deep-fried cod and only four or five fries.

"He spoiled us," Cedar told him as she looked at her plate of liver and onions with only a dab of mashed potatoes.

"That looks good." Gus slid onto the stool next to her.

"Daddy!" she screamed, and her supper was forgotten. She would have cuddled him all night, but then Kate came over, her face pale.

"I'll have the liver, please, ma'am," Gus smiled. "And a take-out bag for these kids as well."

Cedar was stuffed with liver and onions and visiting happily with Gus when Uncle Wade arrived to take them home. He looked long and hard at Gus, who looked just as long and just as hard back.

"Time to go," Wade said firmly, lifting Rory to his shoulder.

"Daddy?" Cedar said uncertainly.

"Off you go with your uncle," Gus smiled at her. "And no crying. I'll talk to your mommy and we'll figure out a time and a place for us to see each other again." He kissed her and patted her head.

"Oh, no," Grandma Karen mourned. "Oh dear God, please." But when Gus wanted to be charming there was nobody more skilled at it than he, and by Christmas, Kate had weakened to the point that she was taking both children to work on Friday night and turning them over to Gus, who borrowed Ewen's car for the occasion. Gus drove Cedar and Rory to his parents' house, where a bedroom was waiting for them. Late Sunday afternoon he drove them back to Olaf and Karen's place, let them out at the gate, then sat watching as they raced up the driveway, making no move to escort them to the door.

By Easter the kids were helping Kate pile boxes of clothing and their beds and mattresses into the back of the pickup. Karen watched, dry-eyed, keeping her opinion to herself, and Olaf refused to lift anything. "I won't help you make this mistake," he told Kate. "You're setting yourself up for more misery."

But Cedar had wept for her father and Rory had joined her, not because he had any special affection for Gus but because he couldn't stand to see his sister crying. Any resolve Kate might have had was washed away by the tears, and Gus had made promises. "I've prayed every night for the chance to prove to you that I've learned my lesson." Kate stuffed down the suspicion that she was hearing something he had memorized, something he was saying for effect and not because his heart insisted.

Cedar switched back to her old school and found herself ahead of the other kids. She enjoyed that, and she ended the school year on a high note, fully expecting to go back after summer holidays and continue to shine. But two weeks after school ended, they were moving again.

The new place was smaller, with no basement and no big add-on room for the washing machine. It stood on the small back porch, and to run it, Kate had to bring the cord through the back window and plug it into the outlet in the kitchen. There was no roof on the porch, and the washer had to be covered with a big piece of canvas to protect it from the rain.

The two bedrooms were side by side, there was no living room, and the couch barely fit in the main room. The big chair was in the bigger bedroom, between the bed and the wall, and on nights when Kate found it impossible to sleep she sat there with a blanket over her knees, looking out the window at the glow from the pit.

The pit had been a valley with a creek running through and trout eager for the hook, but the sawmills needed somewhere to dump their hog fuel and sawdust. Truckload by truckload the mess piled up in the valley. The creek ran clean until it vanished under the heaps of chopped and shredded wood fibre, and when it reappeared at the far side, the water was dark brown and so full of cedar oil that it killed the fish. More than a mile long and at least three miles wide, the pit was a wasteland, devoid of vegetation, abandoned by birds and animals alike.

At some point someone had set the mess on fire. Nobody knew

who or why or even how, but the results were long-lived. For years the fire smouldered, eating tunnels under the hard-packed surface, digging deeper in the rainy season and coming back up again in the dry season, searching for oxygen like it was a live creature. Every once in a while the surface of the heaps collapsed, sparks showered, flames darted up, and the living menace danced wildly across the dry ground, leaving black tracks behind it. Cedar hated the times when the fire burst through. She was certain it would make its way to the bush, set the berry thickets on fire, attack the willows and alders, leap from cedar to fir, attach itself to the porch, take the house, the furniture, consume, consume, consume.

Gus told Cedar she'd get the hiding of her life if she went past the creek behind the house. She could go just about anywhere else she wanted, but even a hint of her being near the pits was enough for her to feel the leather belt across her butt. The warnings were dire—and unnecessary. The place gave her the utter creeps, even from the safety of the back porch. But Gus seemed to like to repeat his threats. "You remember, now, the fire is the least of your worries, you'll have me and my belt to deal with."

When she protested that she never went there, didn't want to go there, and wouldn't go no matter who teased or tempted her, she got no approval, no pat on the head, just a sideways look, and: "You just make sure, you hear."

Sometimes the bigger kids, especially the boys and the tough girls, would ride their bikes across the surface of the pit, yodelling and yelling, pedaling frantically, daring each other to ride closer to the vent holes where the smoke rose. Cedar watched, her stomach tight, her neck stiff, waiting for what she felt was sure to happen. She could see it so clearly, even feel the heat waiting just under the weather-hardened crust.

Part of her envied those boys and those tough girls. Part of her wanted to rear up on her heels and spit in the eye of the world. But she knew what would come down if she tried, and the price was too high. She'd felt that belt, felt those callused hands against the tender skin of her backside, heard the voice roughen and harden, seen the face change in a flash, and it was too much to dare. "Oh, our Cedar," Kate would brag, "she bends over backward to be good. She's so easy to get along with, she wouldn't say boo to a goose."

Cedar missed the old house, she missed living with Grandpa Olaf and Grandma Karen, she missed both her old schools, she missed Neal Sutherland and his little brother Sam. She felt cheated. Gus hadn't said anything about moving to this place where the air always smelled faintly of burning wood and sometimes was blue-hazed with smoke. He'd talked about how wonderful it would be if they could all be together again, in the old house, with its back yard and the familiar walk to school, reminded her how much fun she'd had playing with Neal. There had been no talk then of this strange place, miles from town, even more miles from Grandma Karen and Grandpa Olaf. Cedar couldn't figure out what they were doing out here, with no car of their own, the closest bus stop two miles away, and no possible way Kate could hold down a job, especially shift work.

No problem for Gus, though. All he had to do was stand beside the road, sipping coffee from the lid of his metal thermos, smoking casually, waiting for the crummy to come up the road on its way to the slope. He actually had more time to get ready in the morning and got home earlier at night, and presented this as a big benefit to them all. "I'm home more," he grinned. "Makes it nice." And they all nodded.

As part of the family togetherness, he dug up the abandoned garden in the side yard, then wheelbarrowed load after load of reeking pig manure from the hog farm just up the road a ways. He dug the foul muck in, went back for more, dug that in, then planted rows of parsnips, carrots, even big yellow Swede turnips. He planted lettuce and green onions, he planted corn and set out a row of cabbages, then he hauled more wheelbarrow loads of sawdust from the hell pit and lay it thickly between the rows to smother any weeds. His spud patch was separate because, he said, pig muck would make them grow with scabby skins. "And in the fall," he planned aloud, "I'll dig in more pig muck, mix it thick with the sawdust, turn it all in and let it rot all winter. Be good for it," he nodded, as if he was discussing a lifelong dream, as if he had yearned all his life to be a farmer.

And every evening after the sun went down and the dishes were done, Cedar stood with the hose, watering the rows of vegetables. "Soak 'em good," Gus told her. "Let them drink all night and then they won't burn out during the day."

The creek wasn't deep enough to swim, but they could at least splash around and cool off a bit. Rory loved it, but Cedar longed for the swimming hole, the rocks from which they used to jump into the deep water. Sometimes she would lie down in the creek, the water barely covering her belly, her head propped on a rock, and she would try hard to remember how it had felt, with the big kids agreeing to keep an eye on her, and the boulders so hot under her feet, the sudden shock as the cold water covered her face and head. Her feeling of having been cheated grew and grew.

The other kids seemed like foreigners, and she knew they thought of her the same way. It took weeks before any of them even acknowledged her presence, and then it was just a nod of the head as they rode their bikes past the front fence. That whole summer felt so off-kilter she was glad when it was time to go back to school—at least there would be something to do.

On the first day of school, the bus was almost full when Cedar got on, and only the front seats were empty. She didn't mind. She didn't know anyone anyway, and had no best friend to sit with and giggle and share secrets known by everyone else.

"You the new girl?" the driver asked.

"Yes, sir."

"Well, those who don't behave on this bus get put off and made to walk home."

"Yes, sir."

The school looked like a house. It was set well back from the road and surrounded by open fields. To start the new school year, the tradition was to go outside to pick the fruit that was ripe and ready on the trees. Some of the trees were already bare, and the teacher told them they were transparent apple trees. The plum trees still had some plums, but most of them had fallen or been pulled off and eaten by ravens. The cherries were long gone. The pears weren't ripe yet, nor were the walnuts or hazelnuts. But there were plenty of ripe apples, and some of the boys climbed the trees and tossed apples down to other boys, who caught them skillfully. The girls got to hold the bags in which the apples were placed.

Everyone got an apple to eat, and the teacher said she would take the rest of the apples to the hospital so that the sick people would be cheered up and have something nice and fresh for a snack. Cedar couldn't imagine a sick person even wanting an apple, let alone pulling herself back from the brink of death and actually eating one. She resented not being allowed to climb the trees, and she let the other girls hold the bags. When the teacher noticed her, standing bagless and slightly apart from the group of chattering girls, she smiled and clapped her hands. "Maybe our new girl would like a chance to help," she suggested. The girls turned and looked at Cedar, who wished the turf would open beneath her feet. She shook her head jerkily. "It's OK, someone else can have my turn," she blurted.

"Well, that's very nice of you, my dear. Isn't that a kind and neighbourly thing to do, girls? The new girl is giving up her turn so someone else can have more time as a helper."

Cedar could have wept. One new student in the entire school this year and the teacher couldn't remember her name. Called her "the new girl" as if she hadn't even been alive the day before school started, but had sprung into existence on the bus.

They took the apples into the school and washed them, then sat quietly while the teacher read aloud, and Cedar was suddenly in Camelot with Arthur and his knights. She could have stayed there all day. But suddenly it was lunchtime, and no sooner had they finished than the bus came to take them home. "You'll have a full day tomorrow," the teacher said, as if promising them a treat. "Today was just registration."

Cedar sat in the front seat on the way home, while all the other kids bunched together in the back. When the driver stopped near her house, she got out and stood to one side, waiting for the bus to pull away before she crossed the road. She was amazed when several other kids hurried off the bus behind her. They hadn't got on at her stop that morning. Cedar knew who they were—the Lamberts, who lived just down the road. Most of them were boys, but there was one tough girl, a year older than Cedar, with butter blond hair and strangely squinty blue eyes, named Betty.

"What's your name, new girl?"

"Cedar."

"Cedar? That's a tree like a weed! We cut down cedars and chop 'em up for firewood." The boys laughed, and they all moved closer.

Cedar knew there was going to be a fight, and she knew she didn't have much chance. She'd seen these kids riding their bikes, whooping and hollering, heading down the surface of the pit, daring the fire. She'd seen how the other girls had behaved that morning at school, making way for Betty, being sure not to bump into her or block her way.

If it would have done any good at all, Cedar would have crumpled to the gravel and cried. She was so scared she thought she might pee, or burst.

"I don't want trouble," she quavered.

"She don't want trouble," Betty mocked. "She don't want trouble. Well, you got trouble, little weed, you got lots of trouble." And she moved forward, obviously ready to pound the snot out of Cedar.

All of a sudden Cedar swung. Her fist caught Betty right in the nose and blood gushed onto Betty's jacket. Cedar swung again, her fist landed again, and the brothers surged forward, not to pound on Cedar but to grab Betty, pull her away, haul out their hankies and hold them against gore, and Cedar was running, one foot after the other, moving faster than she had ever moved before, tearing across the road and through the grass, hurtling toward the little house.

She burst into the kitchen weeping.

"Cedar! Baby, what's wrong?" And she was safe in Kate's arms.

"Betty!" she blurted. "She wanted to fight. She and her brothers tried to beat me up. And she got hurt!"

Kate let Cedar cry for a while, then took her to the little pantry and washed her face with cold water. "There, there," she soothed. "There, there now."

Kate made tea in the Brown Betty pot and sweetened a cup of it for Cedar. Just as Cedar was starting to relax a bit, a car drove up to the house and a deeply tanned woman in jeans and man's work shirt got out and headed purposefully for the door. Betty's brothers sat in the back seat looking as if they wished they were somewhere else.

"Oh no," Cedar wailed. "It's Mrs. Lambert! Betty's mom," and the tears flowed again.

But Kate had had enough of the waterworks. "Oh, stop it!" she snapped. "Weepy won't help." She resisted the impulse to give her daughter a crack on the ear. She'd been canning all day, fruit from the farm across the road. Now she wished that she had bought the fruit from the Lambert farm, it might have put them in a better frame of mind. And anyway she was on the verge of cabin fever, stuck way up this country road, so far from the bus stop you prac-tically needed to hire safari guides to get down there. She had enjoyed working—enjoyed, too, having her own money in her pocket.

Kate opened the door before Sis Lambert had a chance to knock. The two women looked at each other and nodded, as if they had known each other for a century.

"Kids are fighting."

"I know. Cedar told me."

"My husband Bob took Betty to the hospital. He figures she's got a broken nose."

"Oh my God. Listen, why don't you come on in, have some tea."

"You sure?" Kate stepped aside and Sis walked into the kitchen and sat down at the table as if she'd been there a thousand times before. She looked at Cedar and blinked. "She's about half the size I expected."

Kate poured tea and they sat and talked, but not about the fight. Sis said she'd seen Kate walking down the road with Rory, pulling him in a wagon. Kate said she must have been on her way to catch the bus to go shopping—it was so far to the bus stop that Rory couldn't walk all the way. "I suppose the rain will put an end to that." She shook her head. Sis said she did her shopping mid-week, and if Kate wanted, she could ride into town with her.

Kate turned to Cedar. "You might take some cookies out to the boys."

Just about the last thing Cedar wanted to do was go near those tough boys, but she got off her chair and went out to the car with the tin of cookies. The boys stared at her, ready for anything. Wordlessly she held out the tin, and equally wordlessly they rolled down the window and took two each.

"Our mom?" the brown-haired one asked.

"Having tea with my mom."

"You sure hurt Betty," the white-haired one glared.

"She wanted to beat me up." Cedar didn't feel as calm as her voice sounded. "And you know it."

"Blood all over everything," said the white-haired one, reaching for another cookie. "Chuck had to run home and get Dad to come and get her."

"Never saw anyone bleed like that," Chuck agreed. "You sure swatted her."

"I don't want to fight," Cedar said desperately. "I just don't want
to be beat up, is all. I only hit her because she was going to beat me
up."

"Sure did hit her."

"And you guys were on her side."

"We wouldn't have ganged up on you." Chuck sounded insulted.
Cedar almost believed him, but she wasn't sure, and anyway she knew
that Buster, the whitey-blond one, would have jumped in if he'd had a
chance.

Sis walked up to the car and Cedar stepped back, feeling trapped.
What if Sis lost her temper and got Cedar between that car full of boys
and the house?

"Who started it?" Sis asked. Cedar froze, unable to speak. "You
deaf?" But Sis was grinning.

"We started it," Sandy said. It was the first time he'd said anything,
and both Chuck and Buster looked at him. They didn't seem angry that
he'd as good as squealed, they seemed to be considering what he had
said and wondering why he had said it. "We were going to back Betty
up," Sandy continued, "but we never got a chance. She just . . ." His
voice trailed off, and he looked down at the knees of his faded jeans.

"Well," Sis sighed, "there you have it. This is the end of it, you
hear?" The boys nodded. "Cedar's smaller than the bunch of you, she's
younger than you are, she's new here, and you should know better than
to gang up on someone. And you." She looked hard at Cedar. "You
watch it with that fist of yours, you hear?"

Cedar nodded, still unable to speak. Sis got in the car and drove off
without another word to Cedar, but her mouth was going, and the boys
in the back seat looked worried.

"If there's a next time," Kate told her, peeling potatoes for supper,
"you do what you did today, but add a few kicks, as well. Mostly the
knee, okay? You hear me? Knees and shins, and run like hell."

"I don't want to fight," Cedar insisted.

"Sometimes a person has no choice," Kate said quietly.

But the fight began to fade from Cedar's mind, as if it had happened a long time ago to someone else.

When Gus got home from work, Kate told him what she knew while
Gus rolled cigarettes and put them in his little metal candy tin. When

the tin was full, he walked over to Cedar and looked at her fist. "Got some nice cuts and bruises there," he smiled. "Little souvenir, to remind you who won."

"Gus . . ." Kate's voice was sad.

"Hush up, woman," Gus grinned. "This is Campbell business."

After supper he told Cedar to put on her play clothes. Then he took her out behind the house, where nobody could see what they were doing. "Make a fist," he told her. She did, and he shook his head gently. "Not like that, my bonny girl, you'd bust your thumb if you punched someone with that wee thing. Here, like this. See, you make a hammer out of it. Fold your thumb along the goink, like that. Make the knuckles straight and even. See how mine is? That's it. Now the thing of it is, if you aim for their nose, all you'll hit will be the tip of it and all that'll do is make 'em mad. You aim for the back of their head and go *through* their nose to get there. Just like you did today. Understand?"

Cedar felt sick. She didn't want to do it. But Gus was so approving, so pleased, and she would pull off her own skin to keep him that way. So she nodded, and fixed her fist the way he said.

"Good," he smiled. He held up one hand, palm toward her. "Now punch my hand." She did, and he nodded, then winked. "And now punch the back of my hand. Don't worry, you won't hurt me. The back of my hand, now, hard as you can."

She lay in bed that night with two sore hands, wondering how Gus could get his hands punched so hard so many times and not get hurt. She wanted to cry. She wanted to sob and blubber and convince him and everyone else in the world that she was nothing but a gutless sissy. Then they might leave her alone, pass her by, ignore her in their contempt. But she knew they wouldn't. They would all pack up and go at her. Gus was right when he said there were only two kinds of people in the world: those many who got their arses kicked and those few who did the kicking.

She could hear the rise and fall of their voices in the other bedroom, Kate explaining something, her voice gentle, pleading, Gus laughing harshly, his voice rumbling, telling her about Campbells being arse kickers and never, not ever, being the ones to offer their arses to be kicked.

Finally she fell asleep, and when she wakened it was daylight, and her hands weren't sore any more. She could smell bacon, hear Gus and

Kate talking softly in the kitchen. The fuss of the previous day seemed unimportant now, something already over and done with.

Betty wasn't on the bus that day, wasn't at school for several days, and when she did come back, both her eyes were black and blue and her nose swollen, the nostrils packed with gauze. "I'll get you," she promised. She sounded as if she had the worst cold anybody had ever had.

Cedar would have laughed if she wasn't so scared. Had she actually done that? "You leave me alone," she answered. "I don't want trouble but if you start it, well, I'm not scared of you."

And suddenly, she wasn't. What could Betty do? Beat her up? So what? Gus was proud of her, and anything was worth the feeling of safety when he patted her on the head and told her she was learning. Every night they went out behind the house and he showed her how to block a punch, how to jab, how to move her head out of the way of a punch while at the same time driving an uppercut, short and hard. He made her a punching bag out of an old sack filled with dry sawdust, and gave her a pair of his work gloves to wear when she was practising. "Don't want to wear holes in your skin on that rough sack." He swooped her up and spun her around, both of them laughing.

The third week he hung a small sack from a tree branch. "Let's see you kick it."

"It's awful high."

"So you jump and then kick. Like this," and he demonstrated. "Now, I'll hold your waist, you jump as high as you can, and then kick that bloody sack as hard as you can."

He taught her front kick, side kick and even how to kick straight behind her. He taught her that if someone grabbed her from behind she should stomp on their foot and kick their knee. He showed her how to grab someone by the wrist, yank their arm straight and kick into their armpit. "That'll knock their shoulder out of its socket," he explained, "or you can haul their arm ahead and sideways and kick their elbow and break it."

"How did you learn all this?"

"Uncle Ewen showed me some, Uncle Tamas showed me some. Now I'm showing you. And when Rory's older, you and me both will show him. Nobody hits on a Campbell and goes home unmarked."

"Oh, Gus," Kate sighed.

"Oh, shut up," he laughed, winking at Cedar.

Kate detested every minute Gus spent teaching Cedar how to fight. She didn't want her daughter turning into some kind of pugilist. She could well understand the need to stand up for yourself, could even understand schoolyard politics. She had, after all, been the one to tell Cedar to fight back, stand her ground, not allow others to intimidate her. This other, this was something else, something so unfamiliar it seemed weird. But she didn't want to argue with Gus, and she certainly didn't want to go past protest to a fight. Things were tense enough lately.

THREE

The garden was finished. The spuds were stored in the shed, the carrots in a box of sand, the beans in jars, the squash and vegetable marrow stacked, the corn sliced from the cob and packed in jars. Kate had made a big crock of sauerkraut. Gus had brought over more pig manure and dug it into the garden plot. The garden was higher now than the ground around it, and he had roped it off so nobody would walk across it and compact the soil again.

There was more than enough wood for winter, sacks of coal were stacked beside the woodshed. And as the evenings closed in earlier each night, Gus grew increasingly bored. Some nights he sat playing solitaire until Kate thought she would go mad with the sound of the cards slap, slap, slapping on the wooden table. There wasn't even enough light left after supper for him to head up to the nearby lake to try for some trout.

And one night, dark before the dishes were done, he put on his jacket, went to the door and said, "Be back in a while." Kate listened to him go with a knot in her stomach, heard the door of the lean-to creak, heard it creak again, then heard him get on his bike, the fender rattling slightly. She watched from the window as the bike bounced over the rough ground, the beam of his headlamp bobbling as he went. His tail light flared and dimmed, flared and dimmed, with each sweep of the pedals.

Kate sighed deeply. When she turned away from the window, Cedar was looking right at her, eyes wide and apprehensive.

"Is the homework done?" Kate smiled.

"Yes. Want to check it?"

"I'd love to. And we'll get Rory set up here with a piece of paper and a pencil, and when I've checked your work, we'll teach him some of his letters. How would that be?"

"OK." Cedar sounded relieved, as if she had been waiting all her life for the chance to be a teacher. "And his colours, he's not very good with his colours."

When Rory protested that he didn't want to learn any more, Kate made cocoa, then read to them from *Alice in Wonderland*. Cedar loved the sound of her mother's voice, loved how the change of tone signalled when she was reading descriptions or reading conversation. It was better than the radio because there was no static cutting across the words, no fading out of the signal. Cedar felt as if she could sit on the big sofa forever, sipping cocoa and listening to Kate.

"I think maybe Rory needs his pyjamas."

"No," he protested. "More story."

"I'll read some more when you've got your pyjamas on," Kate promised. "But my bum is getting sore sitting here. Let's go into your bedroom and I can sit on the bed with my back against the wall."

Rory was asleep in less than ten minutes. Kate smiled down at him, then at Cedar. "What say to another cup of cocoa," she said brightly, "and then you can read to me for a change."

Cedar fell asleep propped up on pillows with the book in her lap. Kate sat quietly, smoking a cigarette, holding it with fingers that looked steady but felt as if they were trembling. The unwinding had started.

Part of her had expected it all along, but another part of her was filled with disappointment and dread. She had hoped it would be better this time—Gus wasn't being forced into anything, wasn't being hammered by his father's fists into something he didn't want. He had come courting with a smile on his lips and honey in his voice, full of promises, hopes, wishes, dreams, and she had dared to believe that everything would be better because this time he *wanted* it.

She finished her cigarette and took the book from Cedar's lap. She moved two of the pillows, eased the child's head down gently and covered her with the handmade quilt. Then she sat down at the kitchen table, feeling numb. After a while her hand reached for the deck of cards and she began a game of solitaire, the cards slap, slap, slapping on the wooden tabletop.

Gus rode his bike to the Domino Club and walked in as casually as if he'd been going every night, as if it hadn't been more than six months since his last visit. Bridget looked up and saw him, and smiled widely. To Gus, that smile of welcome meant he'd won. To Bridget, Gus's coming into the club meant she had won. John Riley just blinked, smothering the urge to sigh deeply.

The rift between Gus and Bridget had started in bed, after a particularly athletic and satisfying hour of sex. Gus lay on his back, his arm under Bridget's neck, her head on his shoulder. "It's nice," he said, softly, "not having to get up and leave. Nice to wake up in the morning and see you."

"Mmm . . ." She was falling asleep, and her face was so soft he smiled.

"I could move my stuff in."

Her eyes snapped open.

"I could just tell the crummy driver to pick me up at the corner here."

"No." She shook her head. "Not here."

Gus misunderstood. "Well, then, we could find a place of our own."

"No. I don't want to live full time with you."

He was amazed. "Why not?"

"You're a man who wants what he hasn't got. As long as I have you on the side, you'll be here. As soon as I have you full time, I won't hardly have you at all."

"We'd be a good team," he wheedled. "I could work the card table every night, save the cost of a tableman, put it back into the business."

"It's not your business to put anything back into. It's mine and John's. You want a club, you build your own. Maybe set up a mah-jong palace for the Chinee."

"Pangini room," he corrected. "They bet everything they own in pan."

"Ah, but they're the only ones know the rules," she laughed. "They'd skin you."

"Not me they wouldn't," he yawned. "I been playing pan since I was, oh, fifteen or so. The old fart got me a job in the pits with him. Bloody pits! There was a winch kid working the line next to mine. Well, they called him a winch kid but he was as old as my da. They never did pay the Chinee a man's wages, nor treat them like men, either. We got to talking, then got to riding home together in the jitney, and next thing you know he invites me to the pan game. The old fart was some hot about it. He doesn't think they're really human, said I might as well be playing games and betting my money with a dog or a rooster. He was so loud about it I set my mind on learning, just to put one up his nose." He laughed. "We could be a team," he coaxed, "put on another room, then those who didn't want to sit with the Chinee wouldn't have to. Run a pan game. I'd deal it, they expect the dealer to take a percentage of each game. We could do it."

"You could do it," she corrected, "when you've got your own place built. You could even build it close to Chinatown. Skin them in their own backyard so they wouldn't have far to walk back."

He dropped it that night. But he brought it up again, trying to act like it was all a pie in the sky, a game, nothing to take seriously. And Bridget played the same game with him, right up until the night she stopped playing. "Stop nagging me," she said, smiling, not sounding the least bit angry. "I'm not moving in with you. You aren't moving in with me. And we will never, not in any way at all, be partners."

"Hey . . ." He tried a soothing tone.

"There's a lot in it for you, and bugger-all for me that I can see. If you want to buy your own place, go ahead. Just stop nagging, because I won't budge, Gus. I know you. I grew up with a da like you, and I learned early. Sweet as honey on your tongue right up until they've got you where they want you and then you're just another old boot, to be worn once in a while when they see fit, and left to gather dust in the corner the rest of the time."

"Great opinion you've got of me!"

Bridget's smile was gone now. "You're a good roll in the sheets, Gus, but you're nothing to build dreams on, and less to build a future with. You think I don't know about the others? Your wife, poor bitch, might prefer to be deluded, but my mother told me to always make sure I knew which side my bread was buttered on, and to make sure it was my own butter."

"Oh, fuck your mother!"

She laughed, and for a wild moment he considered giving her a good crack alongside the face. Instead, he got dressed and left. He sulked at home for several days, then borrowed Ewen's car and drove out to where he had heard Kate was working. That the kids were there was a bonus.

Gus sat in on a poker game, took the pot twice, then stood up to leave. "Morning comes early," he said, as if apologizing, "and the boss is a slave driver."

"That's right, Campbell," someone groused. "Sit down, take the money and leave before we get a chance to win any of it back."

"You be here tomorrow night," Gus grinned, "and you can try to do exactly that," and he grabbed his jacket, waved happily, and left. Bridget felt as if someone had poured a glass of cold water over her head.

Kate was in bed when he got home, but he knew she wasn't asleep. He washed up, then crawled into bed beside her.

"Went to the Domino Club."

She didn't answer.

"Won ten bucks. It's on the table, and it's for you—don't spend it on the kids, this is for you."

"Gus—"

"John Riley said I could have my part-time job back," he lied. "It might make the difference between this dinky place and something with more room."

He curled around her back and pulled her against his body, then kissed the back of her neck. "Nighty-night," he yawned. "Sleep soundly."

Kate was awake most of the night, and she wasn't sure why. Over and over she told herself that she was being silly, that it couldn't be the start of the same old thing. He'd come home at a decent hour, he'd put money on the table, he didn't smell of beer or perfume or sex, and he wasn't flarching her for sex either, he'd been loving and gentle. So why was she lying here with a big lump where her stomach ought to be? She didn't spend the ten dollars. She put it aside and said nothing to anyone about where she had hidden it. You just never know.

On Wednesdays, Kate went into town with Sis Lambert to do the shopping. Sometimes Rory stayed behind at the Lambert farm and tagged along with Bob while he did his chores. Bob didn't talk much, but each time he had a job to do he did it slowly enough that Rory could see, step by step—how to check the oil in the tractor, where and how to add the top-up, how to slip a small piece of wood under the hammer before pulling a nail, how to set the staples in the posts so the fence wire would stay tight. And Rory got to do things, too. Rory oiled the gate hinges, snipped blackberry runners, brushed the cows, and it was Rory who put down milk for the barn cat. Bob Lambert even showed Rory how to wash the cows' udders with warm water and a slightly soapy cloth. The cows enjoyed the attention, and not one of them made a move to kick or butt the boy. He felt useful, he felt important and he adored Bob, who never yelled or grabbed his arm or shoved him out of the way. Rory so enjoyed his time with Bob that when he started school, he kicked up a fuss every Wednesday, insisting that he had an earache or a sore throat, or he felt pukey, or anything to stay home so he could go to the farm. Kate knew the illnesses were invented, but without a word to Gus about it, she just didn't bother getting Rory ready for school on Wednesdays. If Rory wanted his Wednesdays so much, he probably needed them. Cedar buttoned her lip as well. She might get impatient with Rory, even consider him a sucky baby and a total chicken to boot, but she didn't want Kate wearing fingermarks on her face again, didn't want to waken hearing her mother sobbing bitterly in the next room. So she said nothing about Wednesdays, and rode off to school feeling righteous—and also feeling cheated, because nobody gave *her* any time off school.

Meanwhile, Kate and Sis carried out their Wednesday ritual, stopping first at the library, then at the grocery store. Usually they were finished in time to go to the TipTop for lunch. Sis invariably ordered a Denver sandwich with fries, Kate preferred to work her way down the menu, trying something different each time.

Sometimes Cedar would stand with her head back for long minutes, watching the huge vees of migrating geese as they honked their way south, and she would marvel at the ever-changing formation and wonder how their steady call sounded so clear and so close when the birds themselves were miles high, so far away they seemed like golf ball-sized black lumps against the pearl grey of the sky. Kate had told her where the birds were coming from and where they were going, and Cedar had looked it up in the big atlas at school. She had to believe Kate, who had told her that scientists banded the legs of geese and tracked the migrations. But the thought of birds flying such unimaginable distances challenged her concepts of time and space. Most amazing, to her, was that the birds knew where they were going. Little teeny heads, little teeny brains, and they could remember all that. She could hardly remember how to get back to the old neighbourhood, and look how much bigger her brain was than theirs.

"Are they the only birds that do that?"

"Almost all birds migrate," Kate said. She was standing out on the porch doing the wash, feeding clothes from the agitator tub through the wringer, to fall into the rinse tub on the other side. Cedar was helping. She had a toilet plunger, which they didn't need for the toilet because what they had was an outhouse, and she was using it to pump the washed clothes up and down, up and down in the cold rinse water, taking out the soap residue. They used the plunger because it was too cold to roll up your sleeve and use your hand. They were both wearing jackets, and their faces were turning red in the stiff breeze.

"Really?"

"They fly south for the winter. Then in the springtime, they come back up here again. We'll watch this year, maybe mark it on the calendar when we see the first robin, or the first hummingbird."

"Little tiny hummingbirds fly that far?"

"And then turn around and come back again."

"Oh, wow. Anything else?"

"Some butterflies."

Cedar laughed. "Uncle Hugh says, 'Pull the other leg, that one's getting too long.'"

"I'm not pulling your leg. It's true."

That was even more unbelievable than the geese finding their way over thousands of miles. Bugs! It must be something other than brains—bugs' heads were so small they couldn't have much brain at all.

"So how do they know where to go?"

"Instinct."

"What's that?"

"Instinct is—well, it's something you just know. Like when Rory was a baby, and he started to crawl, and nobody had to teach him how to do it? Then later, he learned to stand up."

Cedar nodded, remembering.

"And you can take, say, a baby chick, and you can put it in with a whole bunch of baby turkeys, but that chick will grow up to be a chicken. Turkeys don't eat worms, but that chicken will. A turkey hen makes a kind of a peep peep chick chick noise, but that chicken will cluck and cackle like a hen is supposed to, because that's her instinct. They've taken eggs from one kind of bird and put them into a nest with eggs of another kind of bird, and that adopted baby bird hatched and was fed and cared for and raised by the foster parents, but when it was time for it to sing, it sang its own song. Instinct. Mind you," she added, "they've done the same thing in other experiments and the baby birds of one kind learned to sing the song of the other kind, and when they had baby birds of their own, they taught them the song their adoptive parent birds taught them. And wouldn't that be something, a sparrow singing the same song as a junco!"

So much to think about. A big world full of things to ponder. Cedar used the handle of the plunger to fish the towels out of the cold water, one at a time, so Kate could feed them through the wringer. And when the towels were done, she moved out of the way because the sheets had to be folded exactly a certain way or they wouldn't go through the wringer properly, they might even get ripped.

"Don't stand there," Kate said sharply. "Use your eyes and use your head."

"What?" Cedar was frightened. Kate sounded angry, but what had she done wrong?

"Look at the wringer, then look at where you're standing. If anything at all goes wrong, say if the sheet goes through the wringer the wrong way, or has a twist or lump in it and goes through too thick, the wringer will balk, then the pressure bar will snap, and when that happens, this jigger whaps sideways and takes the whole top of the wringer attachment with it, releasing the rollers. And if that happens and you're standing where you're standing, you're going to get it smack on the side of the head and that will be the end of you."

Cedar moved quickly, not understanding but responding to her mother's tone of voice.

"Look," Kate said, and she hit the pressure release bar. It happened just the way she had said. And sure enough, when the whole clattering process was finished, there was the metal, right where Cedar's head had been.

"I didn't know," she blurted.

"My fault," Kate agreed. "I should have shown you a long time ago. Get Rory and we'll do it again for him. You can hit the pressure release bar if you'd like."

And what other dangers lurked? Well, you could step on a rusty nail and get tetanus and maybe they'd have to cut off your foot, or even your whole leg. Or you could get scratched on old barbed wire. Or you could fall and smash your head or get hit by a car or tumble down the stairs or . . .

"If you're going over to that hog farm again," Kate said firmly, "you watch out for the sows with piglets, because if a grown pig ever bites you she'll take a hunk of meat. You wouldn't look as good with only one cheek of your bum left."

"I don't go in the pens, I only go down the aisles."

"Well, you wear your old clothes and your gumboots, and when you get home you be sure to wash all the pig muck off those boots. The smell of that place is bad enough already, I don't need you bringing more stink home to make it worse." Kate shook her head. "I have to tell you I have never before in my life encountered anybody as fond of pigs as you are. A person would think your nose would tell you what they really are."

But the stench didn't bother Cedar enough to keep her away from the hog farm. She was fascinated by the huge sows, intimidated by the mammoth boars and charmed by the piglets, which squealed and yelled and chased each other, fighting and snapping, and were always eager for food. Cedar would pick a gunny sack full of grass and clover and hold handfuls of greens through the slats for the babies to eat. She went to the abandoned orchard and picked windfall crabapples and took them to the pigs.

After a while Joe Conrad, the owner of the farm, asked if she'd like a part-time job. "Twenty-five cents an hour," he offered, "and what you do is drag this wagon along the aisle and fill the feed troughs."

"How much do I give them?"

"Fill the trough, they'll clean 'er up."

Kate rolled her eyes when Cedar asked her. Her first thought was to say no, but there was the matter of the twenty-five cents an hour. It took an hour each night—that meant almost two dollars a week, nothing to sneeze at and a good lesson for Cedar about work, money, responsibility and earning your keep. "But pigs," she whispered to Gus, "I wish it was something like—oh, I don't know. But pigs!"

"She'll rot her teeth right out of her head if she buys nothing but candy with that money."

"Oh, no worry there. I've already talked to her about it. She gets to keep fifty cents a week, the rest of it goes in a bank account."

"Ah, and I'll make a Scotswoman out of you yet," he teased, his hands stroking her belly, her thighs, his breath warm on her neck. "And when they ask you, 'Do you have Scots in you?' you can say, 'Oh, a wee bit from time to time,'" and he laughed, sliding gently into her, and she thought she would give anything to keep him this loving, this nice.

Frost was forming on the grass, and the mud in the walkways between the pens was cold. Cedar could feel it right through her gumboots and thick winter socks. She had to haul as hard as she could to get the wagon to move through the guck, and she was horrified at the thought of slipping and falling in the mess.

Just ahead of her there was an awful commotion, piglets squealing and screaming, a sow oinking and bellowing, Joe hollering and poking his stick between the thick slats of the pen. "Bitch!" he hollered, and something about bacon, and "your last chance." Cedar hurried, leaving the heavy wagon behind her. The first thing she saw was a newborn piglet, buried in mud, flailing weakly, more dead than alive. The sow was at the other end of the pen, grabbing other piglets in her mouth, tossing them, biting them, slaughtering them. Cedar had been warned more times than she could count, not just by Kate but by the farmer himself, but she shoved her hand and entire arm between the slats, grabbed the piglet by one hind leg and hauled it out of the awful mire. She had no sooner got her arm back out of the pen than the sow charged, her eyes slits, her body shaking with fury.

"Jesus!" Joe yelled.

"I got the piglet!" Cedar yelled back.

"Good girl. But that damn sow is crazy. Come on." And he grabbed her hand and hurried her away from the pen.

"It's freezing cold," Cedar worried, "and filthy dirty."

"Tell you what, you take her into the utility shed and clean her up, and I'll get Ted to finish the feeding. I've got to deal with that sow before she kills someone."

Cedar went to the shed, dragged a basin of warm water in front of the glowing woodstove, put the limp piglet in the water and washed the filth off its little body. She had never held a newborn pig before. The feel of its skin was a shock—it was so much like people's skin. In fact, the piglet looked a lot like Rory had when he was small, except for the feet and the head, and the bit of a tail. Cedar felt the hooves, still soft, and stroked the skin, then wrapped the piglet in a clean rag and put it in a box near the stove while she changed the water in the basin. This water was much warmer, and she laid the baby on its back, holding its head in her hand. The belly button was still dirty, so she took the bar of strong yellow soap, and lathered it on the pink-skinned belly. "There, there," she crooned, "there there."

She heard the rifle shot. Goodbye sow, hello pork roast. Usually the thought of butchering made her cringe—she hadn't eaten bacon since she started her job at the hog farm—but this time it seemed somehow right—that's what you get, you miserable old bitch.

Joe brought in three other piglets and put them on the floor. "All the others are dead," he said, "Four out of fourteen, that's poor return." Then he looked at the squirming piglet and smiled. "You've got a touch, girl. I was sure that thing would die."

The next time Joe came in, four piglets were snuggled together in the box beside the woodstove. "Here," he grinned, holding out a baby bottle full of something thick and yellow. "You're in charge of feeding pigs, aren't you?"

"What is that stuff?"

"It's called colostrum. See if you can get at least two ounces into each piglet. They need this to get their stomachs working properly."

She had no trouble at all getting the baby pigs to feed. And when they'd sucked down their two ounces, she rubbed their bellies, then put them back in the warm box.

The sow was hanging by her back legs from the big hooks in the slaughter shed, her belly slit wide open and her guts in a big washtub. Cedar stared. Ordinarily she avoided the shed, turned away from any sign of the butchering process, but not today.

"Why did she kill her babies?" she asked, almost afraid to hear the answer.

"Don't know," said Joe's son Ted, who was waiting to be told when he was to leave the farm and go to air force pilots' school. "It happens, and more often than you'd believe. The sow goes nuts, is all. And if they do it once, they'll do it again. We had one old girl who had been a great mom for about two or three years and suddenly, no warning, she just up and ate each of them as fast as they came out. Munch munch, the whole damn litter. Next litter, she tried the same thing, only this time we were right there, and we scooped them out as they came. When she'd had them all, we gave her time to calm down and put one of them in to nurse. She tore it apart. And she'd have just kept doing it."

"What happened to the babies?"

"Bottle-raised them," he winked. "Just like you're going to do with these ones."

She was up a half hour earlier in the morning now, racing over to the hog farm to bottle-feed the piglets, then racing back home to get out of her work gear, have a fast wash and get ready for school. No sooner was she home from school than it was the same thing—off with the good clothes, on with the grubbies, and over to check on her charges.

"At least you haven't brought them home and put them in your bed to keep them warm at night," Kate laughed.

By the time they were a week old, the piglets could slurp milk from a tin dish, and they were easier to take care of. They stayed in the utility shed, on a bed of clean rags and newspapers, and their milk dish was refilled regularly. Bit by bit Cedar added pig mash to the milk, and one night she introduced them to slops. Ted emptied all the household scraps and leftovers into a big tin trough, and each evening at about the time the cafés were closing, he wedged the trough into the bed of his pickup and drove it into town. There he made the rounds, tossing in the unsellable vegetables from the produce stores, the discard eggs and scraps from the butcher, the milk and whey the dairy couldn't use, the stale bread from the bakery. He then drove the whole ghastly mess back and emptied it into a big tin tub that sat on a wood-burning stove behind the utility shed. By morning the swill was thoroughly cooked. Ted thickened it with mash, added a measure of silage and then poured it into the feed troughs by the bucketful, still steaming.

Before the silage was added, Cedar pulled off some of the liquid stew and added it to the swill she fed the piglets. At first they were puzzled—they were used to milk—but one taste and they were frantic for more, pushing and shoving, planting their pointy little feet into the basin. "What a pack of pigs," Cedar laughed. "Just look at you's—a bunch a swine!"

She didn't like to think about the fact that the sow's guts and lungs had gone into the swill stew.

"Cannibals," Kate shuddered, when Cedar told her. "God, raising food is a dirty job."

But she didn't say no when the hog farmer sent half the sow's liver home with Cedar, and she certainly didn't complain when, after hanging in the cooler room for two weeks, the sow was butchered and Ted carried over a big roast and enough pork chops for two meals. "Really appreciate you letting Cedar work with us," he grinned. "She pulled those piglets through when otherwise they probably wouldn't have made it. She's good."

"How did you do it?" Kate asked Cedar that night, after Rory was in bed and Gus had ridden his bike down to the Domino Club.

"Just petted them. Stroked them lots, talked to them. They need lots of that or they get puny."

"Well, there you have it," Kate smiled. "We all need love."

"Are we having roast sow for supper tomorrow?"

"No, we'll have the roast on Sunday. But tomorrow night we're having chops. With crabapple sauce."

"Mashed spuds with chopped onion?"

"If that's how you want them. After all, you're why we got the chops."

"Pig girl, pig girl, pig girl," Betty chanted. "Oink oink, oink," and several other girls joined the chant. Cedar wanted to yell at them, or hit Betty again, but she couldn't take on all the girls at once. Worse, she couldn't make them like her.

In May, Ted left the farm for pilots' school and Joe had to hire someone to take his place. Cedar was afraid the new guy, a spotty-faced teenager named Harry, would wind up doing her job, too. But Harry wasn't keen on pigs or farming—or, it seemed, on work. As the days lengthened, so did the number of hours Cedar put in. She not only grained the pigs, she washed the concrete floor of the slaughter shed and disinfected the buckets, tubs and slop-cooking gear.

"Show you something?" Joe asked, grinning. He led the way to the new building, opened the door and gestured for her to go inside. The floor was concrete and sloped to a wide trough in the middle. In three places there were galvanized tubs, with hoses running from them. The hoses were fastened to a metal bar, and each had what looked like a baby bottle nipple on the end. "What do you think?" Joe grinned. "Pretty good, eh?"

She could see how it worked. One thing led to another thing that fitted something else. "Why, that's wonderful!" she blurted. "And you figured it out by yourself!"

He laughed, and nodded. "There's one hitch," he warned. "See if you can figure out what it is."

Cedar stared at the riggins, moved forward to touch, to feel, to examine. "If a piglet pulls the nipple off a hose," she said slowly, "the whole tub of milk will drain onto the floor."

"You got it."

"We could use that same kind of glue that sticks linoleum to the floor."

He stared at her, then shook his head. "Let's try it," he agreed. "The only thing is, it'll make it harder to clean the hoses."

"If we only try it with a couple?"

"Worth a try."

They cut the glued-on nipples off the ends of the hoses, but by then, between the two of them, they had figured out a way to use a twist of copper wire around the base of the nipple where it fit over the hose. They put orphan or reject piglets in the nursery, they took surplus piglets from large litters, they took the runts and the weak, and the losses dropped drastically. Joe went to a stock auction and came home with ten week-old black and pink piglets, scrawnier than any of the ones he raised—but, he said, from good bloodlines. He introduced them to the feeder nipples in the nursery and they slurped, gorging themselves, frantic for more, more and then more.

"Gonna pay for itself in no time flat," Joe bragged. "Gonna make things a lot easier."

By the time school let out for the summer, Cedar was working four hours a day at the hog farm. One Wednesday she drove into town with

Sis and Kate and took some money out of her bank account. They went into the store with her, but let her pick out her bike all by herself. The man from the bike store lifted the bright red CCM into the bed of the pickup and Cedar got a crick in her neck riding home, gazing out the back window, admiring her purchase.

The next afternoon, immediately after she had finished her stint at the hog farm, she raced off on her bike, headed up to the lake with her towel, a bag lunch and a book.

"You goof off up there and drown yourself," Gus warned at suppertime, "and you don't need to come crying to me about it."

"If I drown I won't be able to cry."

Rory nagged that he wanted to go too, but Kate told him to put a sock in it. "You can't swim anyway."

"But you could use Daddy's bike," Cedar said to her. "Rory could ride on the bar. I'd take your towels and stuff in my carrier."

Kate didn't answer, but on the weekend Gus came home with a spare bicycle seat, drilled a hole through the bar on his bike, installed the spare seat, and told Rory if he put his toes in the whirling spokes he'd get such a hiding he'd have blisters where his bum used to be. And the next afternoon, Kate and Rory headed up to the lake with Cedar.

It was one of the nicest days Cedar could remember. She hadn't realized how well her mother could swim. Kate taught her to dive off the log, and Cedar kept an eye on Rory while Kate swam out farther than Cedar would ever have dared go, as far out as the big boys went.

"Come on," Cedar said to Rory. "Lie on your belly, put your face in the water and blow bubbles."

"Not my face," he protested.

"Well, your mouth, then. Mouth and nose, and blow bubbles."

Kate lay on her back in the clear lake water, watching the clouds, listening to the noises the ducks made as they took off and landed in the bay. She wanted to lie there forever, water lapping at her cheeks, feeling light and carefree. She wasn't even thirty years old, yet she felt she might be getting as hard-nosed as her sister Marg, especially when it came to Gus. How was she ever going to live to be as old as her mother? Thirty years seemed older than she ought to be. Thirty seemed like the end of the world. Thirty meant she had two children playing in the shallows, waiting for her, demanding she return and not just stay out here, alone and at peace, and let time stop. Thirty was a dirty trick someone had played on her.

Cedar knew something wasn't right at home. Gus said things, but didn't seem to mean them. He smiled and laughed, but there was an edge to his voice, and Kate grew quieter and quieter, especially when Gus was home. What Cedar could not know was that Bridget Riley had nothing to do with it. She was as puzzled as Kate. Gus showed up at the Domino Club nearly every night, stayed an hour or two and left with money in his pockets. She had no more idea than Kate did about where Gus went or who he was visiting.

The fact was, Gus wasn't visiting anyone. When he left the club he got on his bike, extra seat and all, and pedalled his way back to the little house. He was working hard and making good wages, and at least once a week he made sure he left a few dollars on the table for Kate. The garden was in and doing well, the kids were doing well, even Kate looked more relaxed and happier than she had in a long time. But in spite of all that, things were not going well at all. Even Gus couldn't have said what it was inside him that was starting to ravel, or at just what moment it all fell apart.

Cedar was woken up in the middle of the night by a loud crash, followed by her mother's voice. "Leave me alone!" she was crying. "What is wrong with you? There's no reason to act like this!"

"I'm surrounded by leeches!" Gus's voice, raging. "Take, take, take, and never give a damn thing!"

"You're crazy! The whole place revolves around you, what you want, what you need. We eat the food you like, we have supper at the best time for you. You, you, you, that's all you ever think of!"

"You bitch!" Cedar had never heard Gus sound like this before, as if he was choking. Then she heard the sound of fists against flesh, and Kate wasn't yelling words any more, she was just crying and gasping.

As Cedar headed for the kitchen, Rory came out of his room, screaming and they both got to the kitchen in time to see the big carving knife leave Gus's hand, fly through the air, glittering wickedly, and sink into the wall not four inches from Kate's face.

For a moment there was silence. Then Cedar found her voice. "Daddy!" she screeched. "Stop it!"

"Momma!" Rory ran to Kate.

She looked at him, dazed, but as Cedar watched, Kate shook her head and her face cleared. She grabbed Rory and raced for the door. Gus stood shaking, staring after them. Cedar started for the door but her father grabbed her arm. "You stay here," he murmured, "You sit on that chair and be quiet."

She sat. She made sure she was quiet. She had to pee. Gus paced the kitchen, his lips white, the outer corners faintly tinged with blue. After what felt like hours, he sat down and rolled a smoke. He leaned his elbows on the table and put his head in his hands, his cigarette in his lips, smoke wreathing his bent head.

"Go find her," he said dully. "Tell her to come back."

"I don't know where she is."

"Go find her, I said."

Cedar grabbed her jacket and ran outside, with no idea where she was going. She supposed she must look like a loony, barefoot, and wearing pyjamas, with a jacket over to keep her warm. The grass was thick with dew and her feet and pyjama legs were soaked before she got to the road. She dismissed the possibility that Kate had gone to the hog farm simply because she didn't know Joe and she would hesitate to go to a place where there was no woman. Maybe she'd gone to Lamberts' place. Ought to be able to tell easily enough—they went to bed early, so if there was a light on, something or someone had wakened them.

The lights were on in both the living room and the kitchen at the Lamberts' house. Cedar opened the gate and padded to the back door. Sis Lambert's big black Lab came out from under the back porch and barked a few times, but not as if she meant it. Cedar knocked on the door, and the light over the porch clicked on.

"Are you all right, dear?" Sis asked through the still-closed door.

"Is my mom here?"

"Yes, she is. Are you all right?"

"My dad wants her to come home."

"No, dear, she can't go home tonight. And he's not to come here. Bob phoned the police."

"Can I stay here, too?" Cedar was shivering with cold, and with nerves and fear.

"No. If you stay here, he'll be down for sure."

"But he'll be mad," Cedar sobbed. She had never felt so helpless. "Please let me stay."

"He'll be even madder if you stay here. I'll get your mom."

"Cedar, honey." Kate's voice was thin, and trembling.

"Momma? Momma, let me in?"

"I can't let you in, Cedar. If you come in here there's nothing will keep Gus on the other side of the door."

"He's not with me, Momma!" Cedar howled. "It's only me!"

"Bob's got his gun out. He phoned the police. But if you don't go home, your dad won't care how many guns or how many police. You go home and he'll be fine. Just do what we say and everything will be fine."

"Momma, please."

"Be a good girl, now. Be my big girl. You know your dad isn't going to hurt you. You're his sun in the sky. You go home, there's a good girl."

Cedar stared at the door, heard her mother's words without understanding them. Then, sniffling and sobbing, she went down the stairs. She stood a few moments, feeling as if she had no idea where she was. The dog moved to her and nuzzled her hand, and she stroked its head absently. Then she walked back toward the little house where the knife was stuck in the wall. She had no idea what else she could do. She was beginning to feel she didn't even know what was happening, had no idea what was going on. She didn't know that white-faced, white-lipped stranger with the big googly eyes. He looked like her daddy, but he wasn't her daddy—he was the knife-chucker, a demon who had taken over her real daddy's body. It didn't matter that Gus would never hurt her, because Gus wasn't in control any more, just the demon.

She sat down to rest on the big white rock outside her house. Far down the road she could see a flashing red light approaching. Maybe if she waited until the cops were at Lamberts', she could go back then, and if Sis still wouldn't let her in the house maybe the cops would let her go to jail or something until the demon was gone.

"What you doin' sittin' here?" Gus asked, and Cedar nearly jumped out of her skin.

"She won't come." Cedar tightened her belly muscles so she wouldn't pee herself, tightened her bum so she wouldn't skitter like a frightened cat. "I told her what you said and she said no."

"What else?" A match flared as he lit another cigarette. The flashing red light was closer. Gus cleared his throat and spat. "She do that?"

"Bob's got his gun." Cedar didn't know where that came from, but once she said it she felt like it was probably true, and she hoped it would keep Gus from going to get Kate.

"What a bunch of chicken-livered assholes," he whispered. "Guns and cops and total bullshit and none of it is any of their business."

Gus bent down and scooped Cedar up and carried her into the house. He washed her face with a cold, wet cloth, and Cedar thought he looked like himself again. He smiled at her. "You stop crying. You stop, now, or you'll make yourself sick. There's nothing for a wee girl to worry her pretty head about. Here, get into dry pyjamas. You just go climb into bed, the sandman will be here soon and then you'll sleep."

But she didn't. She lay in bed shivering, feeling like she was about to puke. Her feet were so cold she thought they would never be warm again, and her stomach was cold, too, like there was a huge snowball right behind her belly button.

She heard the police come up the back steps in their big boots, heard their polite knock, then heard the door open. "Come on in, fellas," Gus said easily. "Sorry to bring you out this time of night."

"What's the story here, sir?" a deep voice asked.

"Well, here's the truth of it. The wife and I had an argument, then she went hysterical. Grabbed my son, got him screeching and wailing, and took off with him. I sent my daughter looking for them, she says they're down at the neighbours' place and the wife has them all in a dither, too. Seems they've got a gun out and they wouldn't let the kid in and so she's all upset, came home in a right state."

"What's this about a knife?"

"A knife?"

"Your wife says you tried to knife her."

"She says I *what?*" Gus sounded flabbergasted.

"She says you threw a knife at her."

"Threw a knife? Me??" Gus sighed and Cedar could see him, in her mind's eye, shaking his head slowly. "Jesus," he breathed, "don't they have doctors for this kind of thing?"

"Did you throw a knife?"

"I never did no such thing."

"There's a mark in the wall. Right here."

"Oh, that." Gus paused for a moment. Then he laughed. "She did that herself last weekend. I came home real late, around three in the morning, and I didn't have both feet in the house and she was on about it again. See, I work the odd night at the Domino to make some extra money for her and the kids, and she makes out like I'm running around on her. When I told her to shut the hell up, well—you can see the mark in the wall."

"Story we got was you threw the knife at her head tonight."

"And you believe that? Damn it, man, *think,* will you! Off she goes, crazy as a bedbug, and I send the kid after her, and the kid finds her. Now if you were a mother and someone was chucking knives and had murder in his heart, would you send an eleven-year-old kid back there? They wouldn't even let the poor wee thing in down there!"

Cedar wanted to jump out of bed, run into the kitchen and tell them it was lies, all lies, he had *so* thrown the knife, he did *so* try to kill her momma, but then she felt the snowball in her belly and thought about how she had stood outside shivering while her own mother talked to her through a locked door and refused to let her in. But Rory had been inside. Rory was safe. Maybe it was only Rory who mattered to Kate.

And then Gus was standing in her doorway. "Are you awake, sweetheart?"

"Yes."

"Come talk to these nice men, just for a few minutes." He picked her up gently and carried her into the kitchen.

The cops were big, and they stared at her as if trying to read something written on her face.

"Did you see what happened tonight?" one of them asked her.

"No—" A sob escaped her throat. "All I did was hear Rory crying. And I came out here and Momma was running away with him."

"Did you see a knife get thrown?" Cedar didn't even hesitate before shaking her head. "No," she said, "there was nothing like that." She started to cry. "My dad told me to go get her, but she wouldn't come and they wouldn't let me in."

Gus patted her back, pulled out his hanky and wiped her nose. Cedar wrapped her arms around his neck and cried on his shoulder.

"Jesus Christ." Gus sounded as if he was going to cry, too. "What's a guy to do? Look at this girl! Her own goddamn mother turning her away."

Cedar cried until she was dizzy. Her dad and the cops kept talking but their voices faded in and out, in and out. And then faded out.

Kate hadn't slept, of course. She lay on the sofa in Sis Lambert's living room with Rory sleeping beside her, the two of them squeezed together uncomfortably. She'd tried to get him to sleep by himself, in two chairs pushed together, but he was clingier than usual, which was probably only to be expected, and she wasn't in any shape to go through it all with him. She was glad when it was light, and the farm demanded attention. Gladder still when she could phone Marg and tell her what had happened, what might still be happening.

Marg didn't say anything, but Kate knew she was angry about Cedar being sent back to the house with Gus. Hank didn't say anything either, he just opened the door to the back seat and told Rory to get in. Rory didn't want to sit in the back, he wanted to sit up front, and he said so. Hank just stood quietly until Rory began to slow down a bit, then Hank told him it was the back seat or shanks' pony. Kate told Rory to get in the back, Rory started to cry and Hank took off his wide leather belt. "I can give you a reason to cry," he offered. Rory shut up. Kate hurried into the back seat, and Rory, sniffling, clambered in with her and climbed up into Kate's lap as if he was still a toddler.

When they pulled out of Sis and Bob's driveway, there was Wade in his pickup, and he had his hunting rifle in the gun rack he'd fastened to the back of the truck. Kate wanted to tell him to put the thing under the seat, out of sight, but Hank just waved and didn't stop, even though she'd asked him to.

"But he's got a *gun!*" she protested to Marg.

"Kate, you let other people handle this. I know you think you know how to handle Gus, but look what it got you when you tried. You set each other off like gas and matches. Don't even *talk* to him today. You're so upset your voice sounds like sand in a porcelain sink, it could drive the fillings out of a person's teeth. He hears you and he's going to be mad immediately."

"If he sees a gun he'll get angry and he'll start in right away and then . . ."

"Shut up, Kate, for Christ's sweet sake, will you? You aren't thinking clearly. You're a wreck. You look like you've been dragged backwards through a firethorn hedge, you sound like you're halfway to hysterics, and you couldn't think clearly if the man offered you a silver dollar to do it."

They drove to the shabby little house and parked. Kate stayed where she was, just as Marg had told her to, with Rory on her lap, cling-ing to her and on the brink of tears. Well, she didn't blame him. She was close to breaking down herself. What if Gus got angry, what if he lost his famous Campbell temper and went mesachie on them?

Instead, he carried Cedar from the house, then stood holding her, still asleep, until Marg got into the front seat. He passed Cedar to Marg, then went back to the house to help Hank and Wade stuff clothes into pillowcases and put them in the back of the pickup.

As they drove off, Gus waved, as easily as if they were off for noth-ing more than a weekend visit.

Cedar half wakened as they drove over the bumpy ground between the house and the road. "Easy my darling, easy," Marg soothed. "Auntie's here, Auntie's got you, and I'm not going to let you go. You're a darling, and you can just go back to sleep, again, there's a good one."

"They wouldn't let me in," Cedar said clearly. "They said go away."

"Ah, but I didn't say that, did I? You're not going to get away from me. I've got you for as long as you need to be got."

They put Cedar to bed in what had been Hugh's room, and she slept until suppertime. Karen looked in on her every hour or so, and each time she returned with a worried frown. "She's still asleep and she's drenched with sweat," she told them. "I think she might need a doctor." She said it so many times that Forrest telephoned old Forbes, and whatever else you might say about the old butcher, he was there lickety-split. He watched from the doorway for a few minutes, then went in and sat on the edge of the bed, his fingers on the pulse in Cedar's wrist. She didn't waken, not even when he lifted her eyelid and shone a little light inside.

"Did she receive a blow to the head?" he asked.

"No," Kate said firmly. Then her confidence faded. "I don't think so," she added.

Cedar wakened as old Forbes felt for lumps on her head. She opened her eyes and looked at him calmly.

"Hi, doll," he grinned at her. "I'm Dr. Forbes."

"I'm Cedar Campbell," she answered drowsily.

"So they tell me you're eleven. Is that true?"

"Yessir," she yawned.

"Did you get a bump on the head of any kind last night?"

"Nossir," she blurted, her eyes widening. "He never hit me or anything."

"You didn't fall down, or . . ."

"Nossir."

"Do you know why you're sweating?"

"No."

"Well, you are. But you don't have any fever. Do you think you can wake up?"

"I *am* awake," she slurred.

"But not wide awake, huh?" He teased her gently, but she only grunted. "Well, the thing of it is, your grandma has a wonderful supper made, and she'd like it if you'd get up and eat some of it for her. Think you can do that?"

Cedar didn't answer, she just sat up, yawning, and moved her feet so that she was sitting on the side of the bed, legs dangling. She swayed, and old Forbes put his arm around her shoulder. "Maybe I can help a bit."

"I have to pee," she said clearly.

"Oh, well, you'll have to do that on your own. But I can get you to the bathroom door."

He did, and then he waited for her to come back out again. "So could you sit on a chair for me? Let me test your reflexes and all?"

She sat on the chair and he tapped her knees with his little rubber hammer, tapped her elbow, even tapped at the back of her neck. He checked her ears, he looked down her throat, he lifted her arm and then let go of it. Cedar yawned, and her arm slowly sank down again.

"Would you have supper with us, Doctor?" Karen asked.

"Madam, I have been praying to the good lord above that you would say exactly those blessed words. I would *love* to have supper with you," and he smiled, as if he didn't know full well which Campbell connection he was dealing with, as if he didn't know they knew about poor dead Janet and the hows and whys of it all.

Cedar picked at her food, and seemed to have trouble swallowing. Twice she as good as nodded off again.

"Can you eat your meat?" old Forbes asked.

"No," she said, eyes focused on nothing much at all.

"Well, have your spuds and gravy, then, would you?"

She didn't answer, but she did eat her mashed potatoes and her garden beans. She didn't touch her roast venison, she didn't touch the salad, she didn't want dessert, but she did drink two big glasses of milk.

"She's falling asleep again." Wade's voice was tight with anger. "What's wrong with her?"

"Shock," old Forbes said bluntly, taking more venison, more spuds, more gravy and a slice of Karen's homemade bread. "I have no idea what went on and I'm not asking, but this child is shocky if ever I've seen it, and I've seen my share."

"What does that mean?" Olaf spoke for the first time. He sounded fine, but he looked as if he was ready to rip the moon out of the sky and throw it at someone.

"It means something has happened and she doesn't like it here with us any more. And she can't go somewhere else physically, so she's gone somewhere else in her head."

Predictably enough, Kate started to cry. And when Kate began to cry, of course Rory did, too.

Olaf looked at Kate as if he'd never seen her before. "Stop that. It isn't helping anyone. And if you can't stop, take that boy and go to another room."

Kate left the table, looking as if she'd been slapped, and she took Rory with her. Once away from the table, Rory stopped crying, and when he said he wanted to go outside to play on the swing hanging from the cherry tree, Kate nodded. She sat in the living room, listening to the voices from the table, feeling hungry enough to eat a horse and chase the rider, knowing that if she went back to the table she'd start weeping again.

"Is she nuts?" Wade asked.

"No, young Larson, she's not nuts. Few are, actually. This is one of the healthiest choices she could have made."

"Healthy?" Wade sounded as if his heart was cracking in two right there at the table with the venison roast on the platter in front of him. "Oh, Jesus, Doc, look at her! She's as good as asleep again. Sitting at the table, eyes wide open, but you can tell from the look on her face . . ."

"But she isn't screaming." Old Forbes sounded happy, as if he was delivering the next best to greatest news possible. "She isn't pitching fits on the floor, she isn't running off down the road, she hasn't jumped off the train trestle into the river and she hasn't taken an axe to anyone. Shocky people have been known to do any or all of that, and worse.

She's just sitting there as quiet and polite as possible, hiding inside herself, giving herself time to heal. Mrs. Larson, I am not a man given to extravagant praises, and I've eaten at many a table in my time, but you are, without doubt, one of the finest cooks I've met. This, uh," he chuckled softly, "this government mutton is better than any prime rib of beef I've had. And your gravy could give lessons in any dining room in the city."

"We eat at this time every night." Olaf amazed everyone except himself when he spoke. "Any time you're out this way, just come by. We've always room for another at the table. Even if you aren't out this way, if you've a mind, come by."

"Next Sunday it's chicken," Karen said. "That's mostly how we do it. One Sunday we have a big roast, the next it's a nice plump hen. I keep my meat birds in a pen by themselves, and every day they get a nice feed of parsley."

"And milk," Marg added. "Mother buys the to-be-chucked milk from the dairy, curdles it and gives that to her birds, too."

"And what may I bring next Sunday? Some wine, perhaps?"

"We don't drink," Olaf said gently.

"Some of us do," Wade corrected him. "Me, Hank, Marg, Kate . . . It's just you and Mom took the pledge."

"I took no pledge," Olaf laughed. "I just don't like the taste of the stuff."

"I'm Temperance," Karen said proudly. "And you'd be better off if you were, too. So you'll come, then?"

"I would be delighted," old Forbes answered. "And not to worry about this child. Just make sure she eats. Right now she can hardly be bothered. You notice she only wants things she can put in her mouth and swallow without much chewing? That's fine, she won't suffer from malnutrition around here! Let her sleep for the next day, but on Tuesday morning, whether she helps you or not, get her up and dressed and outside. Maybe by then you can actually take her by the hand and coax her to take a walk with you."

"Jesus Christ!" Wade sounded as if he was going to cry. "This isn't fair. This isn't right! She's a good kid, she deserves better than . . ."

"I can tell you love her," old Forbes said, sounding as if he was nodding his head. "And I know how upset you must be to see her like this. But I can promise you, she'll come out of it. I can't say when, but I can tell you she will. And the best way you can help her is to be very quiet and calm around her, sit her on your knee, talk to her about nice things, maybe—oh, I don't know, would you know anybody with kittens, perhaps, or puppies? Take her to see them. Take her to the river, put her in the water to swim. Get her an ice cream. Tell her you love her."

"We have strawberry shortcake for dessert," Karen said softly, her eyes wide and glistening with tears. "And all the whipped cream a body would want. Would anyone like any?"

"Yes, please." Cedar focused her eyes.

Kate got up and went back to the table. She sat beside Cedar and then reached for her hand. Cedar turned her head, looked at Kate, then pulled her hand away and reached for her glass of milk. She ate her strawberry shortcake and whipped cream, then she was as good as gone again.

Wade got up from his chair, went around to Cedar, and leaned toward her. "If you put your arms around my neck, sweet darling, I'll carry you back to bed."

Cedar swivelled on her chair and put her arms around Wade's neck, and he lifted her easily.

"And wasn't that a great supper your grandma made for us? I'm sure I'm going to wake up in the middle of the night and hear a piece of that shortcake calling 'Wade . . . Wade . . . I'm waiting . . .' And I'll have to get up and come down here and dive into it, to keep it from whining. What do you think?"

"Wake me up, I'll dive too," she mumbled.

Kate might as well have handed her life over to other people for a while. Marg said it was stupid to go looking for a house of her own when Olaf and Karen had made it plain that there was plenty of room with them. "Besides," she said reasonably, "you'll be looking for a job and this way you don't have to worry about finding babysitters or transportation to get them here."

"No," Karen told Rory. "You'll have a room to yourself. Cedar can stay where she is, your mother can have Forrest's room, and you can have your Auntie Marg's old room."

"But I'll get scared."

"And you'll get over it," Wade said firmly. "You're growing up, and nothing you can do about it. You might be able to keep on acting like a baby, but you aren't one and never will be again."

"I don't like you!" Rory yelled.

"Well, that's fine. No law says you have to. Too bad, though, because I'm getting ready to go trout fishing and I was going to invite you. But nobody should have to spend time with someone they don't like, so maybe I'll just go on my own."

Rory went with him, and Wade kept him out until it was dead dark. By then Rory was so tired he could have slept on the point of a pin and there was no fuss about him moving into Marg's room.

FOUR

The café had changed hands and the name was changed, but Kate got a job there almost immediately. It was called Mom's now, although the owner wasn't anybody's momma but a Greek man named Nick whose last name had so many letters in it that it sounded like he was coughing when he introduced himself. The menu was the same, the customers the same, the prices the same, and Kate got paid on time, in full, every two weeks. They could call the place whatever they wanted, it made no difference to her.

She rode one of the bikes there, usually Cedar's red CCM, and went by way of the footpath rather than along the highway. She wore her jeans and carried her freshly washed, starched, ironed uniform in a brown paper bag, then changed in the women's washroom when she got to work. At night she avoided the footpath and went home along the highway. She could turn right without having to cross the lanes of traffic, and the visibility was much better than the path through the bush.

On Mondays she helped Karen with the laundry, on Tuesday she did most of the ironing, Wednesdays it was floors, Thursdays windows and dusting, Friday was garden weeding, Saturday grocery shopping with the car, and Sunday there was always a big dinner to cook.

Cedar remembered none of it, from the terrible night when the cops finally left and she cried and cried in Gus's arms, until the moment when she was floating on her back in the river and Aunt Marg was coming up out of the water next to her, tapping her on the shoulder. Cedar rolled onto her belly, thinking she was dreaming, thinking she must be in bed, just coming awake.

"Lunchtime," Aunt Marg grinned. "They've been hollering for you, but I guess you had water in your ears."

They swam back together, and Cedar got up on the rocks first. She reached back for Aunt Marg's hand and helped her out, and then for some reason, Marg didn't let go of her hand as they walked over to where the others had spread out lunch on a red tablecloth. Kate was there, and Rory too. They were all there, everyone you'd expect— Grandma and Grandpa, Aunt Marg and Uncle Hank, Uncle Hugh and Georgina with their kids, Uncle Wade and Jean, who was pregnant and wearing a man's shirt over her belly. Uncle Forrest, drinking beer and flirting with a red-headed woman, and two of Uncle Hank's sisters. But not Cedar's father. Not Gus.

"I hollered for you half a dozen times," Kate said, "and I figured if you weren't answering, maybe you wanted me to eat your lunch for you."

"I didn't hear you," Cedar answered, and suddenly her hands and feet were too big, she felt clumsy and stupid.

"Water in her ears," Aunt Marg laughed, poking Cedar in the ribs. "Better than water on the brain, right?" Cedar thought maybe she did have water on the brain. Or had she dreamed the whole thing—her parents fighting, Gus throwing the knife, Kate fleeing with Rory and refusing to let her into the Lamberts' house? Cedar took a second helping of potato salad, and a few slices of Karen's homemade potted meat. She ate slowly, paying little or no attention to the conversations going on around her. Then she got her towel and spread it on the bank, near the willow thicket, where she could lie with the sun on her body, but her head and face in shade.

"How's she doing?" Hugh asked.

"She seems better," Kate answered. "Quiet, though. Hardly speaks unless someone speaks to her first."

"What you going to do about school?"

"Send her, of course!"

"Sure she'll be okay? If she goes spacey, the other kids will pick on her something awful."

"Nobody will pick on her," Marg laughed. "Spacey or not, she's Gus Campbell's daughter. Even half-asleep she can make them sorry they ever thought of picking on her."

"Some pretty rough kids at that school."

"Hughie, my dear, when it comes to tough kids, our Cedar is one of the toughest. If she was a boy, we'd be chipping in to pay gym fees and trainer's wages and aiming her toward the Golden Gloves or something."

"She wouldn't do very well," Forrest said sourly. "They won't let you fight with your boots and elbows. She's a right dirty fighter, is Cedar."

Nobody said anything. Lying apart from them on the bank, Cedar listened to them talk and realized that she did remember something else. She remembered the fight. Forrest was the only one of them who had seen it, and he hadn't said much. Cedar had seen the look on his face, she knew what he thought. But he'd only been there at the end of it, he hadn't seen the whole thing.

She had been coming down the road on the rattly wreck of a bike that had been Wade's, because Kate had her new red one, and she heard Rory crying. The sound came from the footpath and she didn't hesitate one little bit—Rory wasn't just snivelling or trying to get his own way, he was sobbing.

Two boys had Rory on the ground and they were holding his face over a mud puddle. "Drink it or drown!" they were yelling. "Drink it or drown, you sucker!"

Rory was coughing and choking. "Don't," he begged as he struggled, "please don't."

They were so intent on their bullying they didn't hear the rattletrap until it was as good as on top of them. Cedar slammed into one of the boys with the bike. Then she jumped off the bike and started in on the other boy, a flurry of hard punches, and when he turned to run, a field-goal kick to the family jewels that sent him face down on the path, puking.

The first boy was back on his feet and starting to run when she got him with a hard rabbit chop to the back of the neck. He fell and she put the boots to him, kicking him everywhere she could reach.

"Here, you kids, stop this!" someone yelled.

Cedar whirled, still in a fury, ignoring the almost-but-not-quite familiar voice. She went back to the boy who was puking and gave him another kick where the first one had landed. He screamed, so she kicked him again. "Leave my brother alone!" she yelled. "Just leave him alone, you hear me?"

Then someone had her by the elbows, pulling her back, pinning her so all she could do was flail uselessly.

She looked over her shoulder, and up. "Uncle?" she faltered.

Forrest looked down at her and—she saw fear in his face—but why would he be afraid of her? She was half his size.

"Calm down, girl. They've had enough. Rory," he said to the sobbing boy, "you get that bike and bring it to the roadway with you."

"I can't!" Rory wailed.

Forrest turned on him. "Get up off your ass and do what you're told, damn it!" he snapped. "Don't give me any of your guff, get the goddamn bike!"

He waited a moment to make sure Rory's tormentors were going to be able to get themselves home, then followed Rory and Cedar to the road. Rory was still sobbing when he got there with the bike. Forrest didn't say a word to him, just opened the trunk of his car, threw the bike in, then opened the back door for Rory.

"Can't I sit in the front?"

"Get in."

Two of Cedar's knuckles were swollen and one of her fingers was stiff, but Uncle Forrest grabbed it and pulled it straight out, then let it go again, and after that it was much better. "Don't hit 'em on the head like that," he growled. "Dumb move to hit on the head."

The father of one of the boys came over after supper. "What kind of dirty fighting bullshit is going on?" he yelled. "My boy's been to the Emergency, he's swollen up like a soccer ball and can't pee without a rubber tube! He says it was one of you did it."

"I did it," said Cedar. "He was picking on my brother. And if he doesn't leave him alone I'll whip him *real* good next time."

"Who in hell is this wildcat?"

"Why, that's young Killer Campbell," Wade laughed. "Gus and Kate's daughter."

"She's as crazy as her lunatic father."

Cedar could remember the fight as clearly as if it had happened that day. She even knew what she ought to have done different, what would have been more effective. She just didn't know where to put it in her memory—obviously somewhere between falling asleep in Gus's arms and waking up in the river, but where? How long ago was it, and how much time had she missed, anyway?

She yawned. The grass was soft beneath her, she could see the silver ribbon of river sliding away to her left, could hear the cousins laughing and playing tag, could hear the adults talking together. The river was a solid thing, shiny where the sun glinted on it. She felt as if it was tugging her, gently, lovingly, trying to get her to just roll and roll and roll until she was in it, part of it. But she didn't want to slide into it—the cold would wake her up. It was so much nicer just to lie here in the hot sun, and drift into sleep.

Kate knew everyone took her for a fool. She didn't blame them—she took herself for one. At least nobody yammered at her, or lectured her, or warned her, or said you make your bed this time, don't call me to get you out again.

It was just that she missed him so much. He was so familiar to her, the smell of him, the touch of him, the little noises he made when he slept, little sounds of contentment, almost as if he was humming a tune. Yes, he had a hair-trigger temper. For that matter, so did Cedar, and Kate wasn't about to walk out on her! Yes, he was stiff-necked and hard-headed, just like each and every one of her brothers. Even her dad, in his own quiet way, was as stubborn as a stone.

And Gus had stood there, in her own mother's kitchen, and shook his head as if he couldn't quite believe what he was hearing. "For crying in the night, Katie," he'd said, sounding as if someone was twisting his knackers in a noose, "You know full well if I'd been going to throw a knife into your face it would still be stuck there."

"You threw it!" she shrieked.

"Oh, Katie, Katie, Katie," he said, sighing deeply. "I'm not about to argue with you. I'm sure you believe what you're saying. It's all right, really it is."

For days she thought she might well be mad. A knife had been thrown, there was a mark in the wall as proof. She would have bet her eternal soul it was Gus who threw that knife. At her. And he looked so sincere, so baffled, so hurt, he sounded so heartbroken, and patient, even indulgent, everything about him suggesting that, well, a knife might well have been thrown, but not by him, and certainly not at her. More than that he refused to say. A gentleman never tells, he intimated.

The first few times he came over it was to pick up the kids and take them to visit with his parents. He took them on Friday, after school and supper, and brought them back on Sunday morning with a brown bag full of Mary Campbell's scones and eccles cakes. He brought more money than anyone expected, to outfit the kids for school. He got Rory a new bike for his birthday and brought over a truckload of firewood.

He was polite, he asked for little, he ignored the hard looks from Kate's brothers and the distrust plain on the faces of Marg and Karen. He acted as if he knew something they didn't know; as if this big secret was so important that if he ever shared it with them they'd see everything his way.

Kate was lonely. Surrounded by family, up to her ears in customers at Mom's, people talking to her, talking at her, talking around her until she began to feel like she had a good idea what it had been like in the Tower of Babel—and still she was lonely. She'd be busy, almost too busy, taking orders, carrying trays to the tables, refilling coffee cups, smiling and smiling, and it would wash over her like a tidal wave—a feeling of desperation so strong she could almost taste it. At those times she wanted to scream, to throw the plates of food at the wall and yell at everyone to stop talking and leave her be. And then that urge to strike out would pass and all she wanted to do was sit down on the floor and sob until the huge lump in her chest dissolved.

She was thirty-one years old, for God's sake, and living her life as if she was fifty. She wasn't even Catholic and here she was, as good as a nun, Sister Mary Dreary 'n' Grim, rising in the morning, making sure the kids had eaten and dressed themselves properly, hugging them and sending them off to the school bus, then helping Karen with the housework, sometimes managing a short nap before it was time to get ready and ride to Mom's and work until closing time feeding people. And then after Mom's she came home to a house that was dark except for the one light still on in the kitchen. She would make a pot of tea, sit with her feet up on a second chair and read the evening newspaper Olaf always set out on the table for her. She didn't eat anything—she had already been assailed by more food scents than she could tolerate, and she was too tired. Once in a while Rory would waken while she was still reading the paper, and he would come downstairs to sit on her knee for a while and snuggle. But not Cedar. There didn't seem to be many snuggles left in Cedar, certainly not for Kate. The thought of it, just the thought of it, made Kate want to scream "I'm sorry!" until her tongue was frayed. She wanted to grab her daughter and yell it in her face again. "I knew he would never hurt you, don't you understand? If you'd stayed, he'd have come down that road after you, 'Not my daughter you don't, you bitch!' and not even Bob's gun would have stopped him. He'd have let himself get blown apart, or he might have killed us all!"

But why dredge it up again? She'd tried to tell her at the time, and look what had happened. She was as cool as a stranger and now she was having these episodes when she wasn't quite tuned in. Old Forbes called it dissociation, said it would wear off and told them not to pressure her. Well, at least he hadn't said it was nothing to worry about. Anyway, Cedar was distant with Gus, too, not just with Kate. It made you wonder if she was distant with herself.

And so Kate, who had once lived in a family of four, wound up as half of a family of two—just her and Rory. There was no way she could lie to herself. She knew what had happened, what she had been forced to do, and she knew it would lie there between her and Cedar forever. There was only one person that Kate wanted to talk to about all this. She couldn't talk to Karen, not even to Marg, they'd look at her as if she was crazy. No, the only person who would listen, and actually hear, was Gus. Not just because he was so focussed on Cedar and what was best for her, but because he was bending himself into a pretzel trying to be gentle, trying to be easy to get along with, behaving through what she thought of as his courtship manner. She knew it wouldn't last but she longed to bask in the warmth. For a while at least she would have someone to listen, to understand, to share with her the feeling that they were skirting the edges of the very pit of hell. Someone who knew what she meant when she said she was lonely, and frightened of being lonely forever.

And one night, as she came off work, he was there outside Mom's, leaning against the wall, smoking a cigarette. "And will you please talk with me, Kate?" he asked. "There's much needs settled between us."

She knew the smart thing would be to go back inside and get Nick, and she knew what everyone would say if she went with Gus. But she walked with him and let him push both their bikes, and they talked and talked. He listened to her, she listened to him, and when he started clowning around with the bikes, one on each side of him, pretending the bikes were racing and heading for a collision, just being silly like a big kid, she had to laugh. "Christ, Kate, but life is a grey goddamn place without you," he said, and she understood exactly what he meant.

She didn't say anything then, but looking back on it later she decided that that was the moment she had made her decision. Sometimes she thought Gus wanted to move them as far away from Sis and Bob as he could, but if that was his intention, he didn't mention it. And she didn't understand why, if that was the case, he had moved practically into the Larsons' back yard in his attempt to avoid them. But that's what he did. He found a house just down the highway from Mom's.

Gus showed her the house before he made a decision. It was big, and if anybody ever got around to finishing it, it could be very nice. "I hope it's not drafty and damp," she said hesitantly, but Gus made no assurances, he just waited. Finally she nodded. It would do. The windows were big, just what you needed on the coast, where winter light was as scarce as rocking horse shit.

Gus and his brothers moved their furniture in. He hired a woman to spend an entire day scrubbing walls and floors, cleaning windows inside and out, scrubbing shelves and lining them with new shelf paper. All Kate had to do was move her clothes, the kids' clothes, the bicycles, fishing rods, sports gear and precious knick-knacks, like Rory's collections of rocks and fungi.

Nobody called her a fool. Nobody said any of the things she knew full well they were thinking. Olaf sighed when she told him, but even he didn't protest. She waved from Ewen's new pickup and they waved back, but not one of them was smiling—including Kate. She knew everyone took her for a fool, and she didn't blame them.

The big window in their bedroom looked out on the orchard. The trees were small, only four or five years old, but when the cold released its grip and the spring days coaxed them, the young trees blossomed, and Kate could lie in bed and look out on them and feel like the Queen herself. If she happened to wake up at night, she felt so safe snuggled against Gus, feeling the warmth of his skin, the bulk of his presence, that she drifted gently back to sleep.

He got himself off to work every morning, and the kids slept until Cedar's alarm went off. Then they got up, had breakfast, got dressed and ready to leave, and by then Kate was awake enough to go down to the kitchen to check them over, kiss them and tell them to have a good day. After they left to get the school bus, she could go back to bed for a couple more hours, or she could get on with the housework, and still have several hours before she had to leave for work.

She bought bulbs and got them in the ground in time for the springtime show. She spaded and weeded and spaded and weeded again until there was a garden plot, small but adequate. She planted flowering shrubs even though she had planted others in other places and had to leave them behind. She made casseroles for her family's supper and baked bread for them, leaving it cooling on the racks. She baked cakes and cookies, then she soaked in a nice hot bath and got ready for work at Mom's. That's where she was when the kids and Gus got home to a kitchen rich with the smell of baking, and a casserole ready to heat for supper.

On Friday nights Gus came straight home, shucked off his work clothes, had a fast bath, got dressed in clean jeans and shirt, then went to Mom's to meet the kids for supper. Sometimes Kate would act like she didn't know them, taking their orders all businesslike and professional. Gus would flirt with her and the kids would play along, Cedar very serious as if she almost believed the act, Rory giggling and grinning in that way he had, which Gus said was proof the boy should never play poker. Other times Kate knew they wanted the other scenario—Momma, Momma, Momma, as if they were laying claim to her, letting the customers know she was theirs.

The owner, Nick, had some strange ideas, but it was his nickel, after all. He'd decided the place would be more appealing if all the tables were round. That made it hard for Kate to move quickly with trays loaded with full glasses and plates of food. Round tables apparently came in queer sizes and customers wound up packed tightly between them, leaving no space for the workers. All three of the waitresses had complained to Nick about it. But he just grunted, shook his head and sipped from his tiny glass of something the Liquor Control Board would have had a fit about, because the place wasn't licensed for booze.

One of the waitresses quit after that, but Nick didn't hire anyone to replace her. Kate and the others had to work harder than ever with no increase in pay. Finally, unwilling and scared for her job, Kate approached him. "We're run off our feet," she said, her throat dry. "And that means we can't give the customers the service they expect. And if they don't get service, they'll go somewhere else." Nick just stared at her. "If they go somewhere else, that's lost business, which means lost profit."

"So?" He sipped from his little glass and licked his lips. "What idea you have?"

"Rush hour relief!" she blurted. "Teenagers will work for less per hour than an adult will, and they'd come in for two or three hours instead of a full shift. Between six and seven-thirty it gets too rushed for Georgina and I to do it properly on our own . . ." Her voice trailed off as he stared at her. She couldn't tell what he was thinking.

"You handle it," he said finally. "I don' know nobody."

Kate took a piece of paper and wrote Part Time Help Wanted—Good Job for Teenager, and put the sign in the window.

"Your girl not work?" Nick asked.

"She's too young," Kate answered. "In a year or so, though."

He went out back to smoke one of his fat, stinky cigars. Kate imagined he was gazing out over the miles of Douglas fir and red cedar, wondering how in hell he had ever wound up in this wild place. As far as she knew, Greece was covered from one end to the other with picturesque villages and people who drank liquor that smelled like turpentine while dancing ankle-deep in broken glass. A far cry from this place!

"You know about ordering?" he asked Kate in the kitchen.

"No."

"I show." He took a grease-spotted clipboard from the shelf under the sink. "See? Names of suppliers. This one produce, this one beef—see? You need, you phone, two-day delivery," and he put the clipboard back and walked away.

Nick told her to show the teenager what to do, and Kate did. The first two or three nights the girl was shy and awkward, but once she had survived the Friday night madness she settled in, and inside of two weeks she was smiling widely, even bantering with some of the regulars.

Kate told Nick they should hire a second teenager part-time to pearl dive for two hours a night. Nick grunted, sipped, and reached for a new stinky cigar. But later on he nodded, and Carol was hired. When she had worked her way through the worst of the dish pile, she moved to the other sink, washed lettuce, peeled cucumbers and helped tear and chop things for the salads. The cooks nodded their thanks to Kate and kept moving.

"Why flowers?" Nick grumbled.

"Because the place looks shabby," Kate told him. "Look at the other restaurants when you drive out to work tomorrow. They've got lawns, they've got flowers, they've even got rose bushes. What do we have here? Gravel. Long grass full of weeds."

"Spend, spend, spend," he grumbled.

"Spend means business and business means profit," she answered sharply. "Profit means you can go home to Greece for a visit." He scowled.

A local boy came by after school to mow the grass, hang baskets of begonias and petunias, rake the gravel and pull weeds. And one Sunday, without even mentioning it to Nick, Kate had Gus come down and replace the rotting porch steps.

"If someone falls and breaks a leg," she told Nick, "it's going to cost you more than your trip back to Greece. And if I had my way, I'd hire Gus to extend the bit of a porch, run a wide one along the front and around the side, then put tables out there so people could eat outside."

"And be chewed up by mosquitoes," he growled.

Kate burst out laughing, knowing his game now—devil's advocate, eternal curmudgeon. "And stung by wasps, and bitten by spiders, maybe even attacked by rabid dogs."

"Goddamn fine idea," the cook yelled. "Maybe if you kill off some of the customers we'll get a break back here."

"This goddamn woman," Nick yelled back, "she making me bankrupt. She boss me around so bad maybe I make her manager. *Then* I go visit Greece."

But he was eyeing the front of the café, already picturing how it might look with the wraparound porch.

Mom's got busier by the week. Carol began spending all her time on vegetable preparations, and they hired another dishwasher. When Gus was off for fire season he was bored half out of his skull, and one day he showed up at the café. Without talking to Kate about it, he spoke with Nick, and the next thing she knew, there he was with an apron over his jeans, serving tables the same as if he was trained to do it. "Yes, sir," he smiled, "we've got the best hamburgers you'll find this side of Hamburg, the best frankfurters outside of Frankfurt, and better fish'n'chips than England because our fish is so fresh it's still flopping around when it goes in the batter." And, "No, sir," shaking his head sadly, "no liquor licence yet—you know how they are at the Liquor Control Board, they don't have any fun and don't want anyone else to have it, either. But we've got a homemade lemonade that will pucker you right up, comes with crushed ice and a free refill."

Kate felt dizzy with happiness. The kids were home for the summer and they all got up at ten or even later, and while breakfast cooked, Kate packed lunches for Rory and Cedar. They all ate together, then it was yard work or berry picking or just sitting on the back steps talking.

Then Cedar and Rory would ride off to the creek on their bikes. They weren't supposed to go there, but the game warden knew them, knew they were better brought up than to light a campfire or toss a cigarette butt into a patch of dried moss. In return for his selectively blind eye, the neighbourhood kids made sure they stayed near the bridge, where the gravel banks were wide and they couldn't really be said to be in the bush.

One hot day followed another. The fields, usually green all year, turned yellow, and the leaves on the trees dried and fell to the ground. The creek shrank until there was no swimming in it, just wading and splashing. Then one morning they wakened and smelled evergreen smoke, and they knew immediately that the bush was on fire somewhere. They were out of bed in a flash. "There," Kate pointed. "See?"

"Oh, sweet Christ in heaven," Gus breathed.

They turned on the radio and learned that the fire was on the far side of Big Lake, a good fifty miles away. But by noon there was more than the smell—there was smoke in the air. Two days later, the first of the bugs arrived.

Nobody had seen them before. Even the loggers who worked the upper slopes and had seen all manner of weird insect hadn't seen these hard-shelled stinkers. The foul things clung to the screen doors and reeked, and when they were crushed they sent off a nauseating stench. They didn't bite anyone or do much of anything except find a place to settle, and then they stayed there, smelling awful. No use spraying them with DDT—they stank worse dead then they did alive, and no birds the least bit interested in eating them.

The outdoor porch at Mom's stood empty. Truck drivers would stop for a sandwich and a glass of cold lemonade, and before they got back in their trucks they'd take a broom to the front of the truck, sweeping the stinkbugs off so their radiators wouldn't get plugged.

Gus and Kate's brothers, men who ordinarily worked in the bush as fallers and buckers and hookers and chokermen, joined the fire crews and went out to do what they could to stop the blaze. Time after time the fire crowned, raced faster than anyone could believe, wiped out ravines and gullies once thick with trees. Crews were forced to head for safety, crammed into crummies with men clinging to the backs and sides, their faces chalky with dust, grime and soot, their eyes wide with fear as the flames chased them. One crummy, trapped when the fire claimed a wooden bridge across a small river, drove right into the lake and the men waded in up to their chins, ducking their heads under the water, soaking hankies and holding them over their noses and mouths.

The congregations of every church met morning, afternoon and evening to pray for divine help, and for all anyone knew, that was what did the trick. At ten o'clock one night the sky was clear, the angry red glow visible along the horizon to the west and north, the half moon barely showing through the smoke, the stars obscured. At three in the morning people were jerked awake by the crashing of thunder so loud the windows rattled, and lightning so bright that when they looked out the windows, they could see the orchard bathed in ghostly blue light.

When the rain started it was almost as scary as the threat of the fire. No pitter patter, no drizzle, no introductory gentle shower, just a sudden, furious swishing sound as tons and tons of water droplets hurtled down from the sky. At nine the next morning it was still coming down like billy-be-damned. The clouds hung low, the thunder rumbled, water ran off the hard-packed earth in rivulets and creeklets, which ran into ditches and eroded gardens and made dips in the road into huge puddles.

The smoke was thicker that night, but the red glow was noticeably quieter. By the third night of the downpour the forestry department dared to give some of the fire crews a twenty-four-hour rest break. By the time the rain stopped ten days later, the fire was as good as out. "Best of all," Gus grinned, "the damn bugs are gone."

The Larson adults and kids gathered at the river for a picnic. The water was almost back to its winter level, and the small inlet where the little kids waded and splashed was full. But the inlet was calm, protected by the arm of rock jutting into the current, and in the deeper water they could sit on the big inner tube and paddle around without stubbing their toes.

All the uncles looked tired, the fingers and palms of their hands grimy with soot. The black had got under their nails, too, and no amount of scrubbing was going to get it off. They teased each other that they might just as well have stayed in the mines. The men were back at work, but not logging. They were cleaning up after the blaze, rebuilding the logging roads, most of which were littered with half-burned fallen trees, some of which had been chewed up by machinery or blown with explosives in vain attempts to construct fireblocks. Gus looked as tired as any of them, lying on his belly, yawning often and making little jokes about none of them having sense enough to get the hell up and go home to bed. "We're like a pack of bloody zombies," he told them, "more dead than alive and too witless to lie down and rot."

"Doesn't take many fourteen-hour days to teach a guy just how much the union has won for us," Wade agreed.

"God, get a sock," Forrest yawned. "He'll be singing 'Solidarity Forever' next."

"The workers' flag is crimson red," Wade yelled suddenly, "with blood of martyrs cruelly shed."

And then Gus was on his feet, one fist raised, his face wreathed in a smile. "From Stalingrad to Moscow Square, we'll keep the red flag flying there," he sang, his voice rich and full.

All the uncles joined in, laughing and reaching for more beer. "Off to the salt mines we must go."

"Oh, honestly." Aunt Marg tugged at Hank's hand. "You're all a bunch of kids."

Cedar was walking along the riverbank, picking salmonberries and eating them, looking over at the clowns on the rock and laughing softly to herself. She was halfway to the sandbar, where the river narrowed and the current ran strong, where even the uncles didn't go swimming because of the big rocks jumbled there, marked by spumes of white water.

And then she heard Rory yelling. Nobody else seemed to hear it. She looked for him and finally saw him, scrambling from the little cove, stumbling over the hot rocks, yelling and pointing and trying to get someone's attention. The other little kids were out of the water, on the bank, some of them crying. And out on the river, where they shouldn't be even at the best of times, Karen and Sam, uncle Hugh's preschoolers, were clinging to an inner tube, their eyes wide with terror, mouths open and wailing.

Cedar never remembered kicking off her sneakers, although Aunt Marg found them later, a step apart, right where Cedar had been picking berries. She dove in and cut through the water, arms stroking, legs kicking strongly, swimming with the current at a slight diagonal, fighting the water that pulled her straight down. She was willing to go down the river, but not without the tube, not without those two ridiculous goddamn kids.

She was surprised at how quickly she got to them. She fought to act calm and to smile as if it was all wonderful fun. "Hang on, now. We're going to have a bit of a ride." She began pushing the tube back toward the sandbar, straining, kicking fiercely, struggling to keep the tube away from the area where there was a deep, dark undertow and a pile of big slippery rocks.

During a few dreadful moments, she thought they had missed the sandbar completely. Twice the water shoved her against hidden boulders and she bashed her shin against something sharp. But then there was Hugh, jumping into the river and reaching for the tube, and Gus behind him, white-faced. Cedar's hands slipped off the tube and she was pulled underwater. The current banged her against something. She saw a lacework of rusty fender, and then felt someone grab her by the hair.

Gus hauled her out of the water and sat on the sandbar holding her. "Oh my poor baby, oh my God I thought I was losing you," he sobbed, not caring whether the uncles saw him bawling, and he couldn't seem to get his feet under him to stand up.

"I've got her," Olaf said quietly, and he helped Cedar to her feet. "Here, Forrest, carry this girl back, she's hurt her leg." Then he helped Gus to his feet. "Dear God," he said, shaking his head. "You've raised a wonder."

Cedar wakened slowly and heard somebody moaning. She didn't know she was the one making the noise.

"It's okay, darling," Auntie Marg said softly. "You're fine. You're in bed, in the hospital, and all you have to do is sleep."

"My leg is sore."

"I bet it is! You should see the crud Dr. Forbes got out of it. Chunks of bark, bits of wood, and he said to tell you he got enough hamburger out of it to do him for two suppers and a lunch."

"My back hurts."

"You're the technicolour kid right now. Bruises? Goodness me."

"Karen and Sam?"

"They think you took them for a fun ride down the river to the sandbar."

"Is there something I can rinse my mouth with?"

"Bottom of a canary cage?" Marg guessed.

"Dead canary, too."

There was a brand new toothbrush and a new tube of toothpaste. She brushed and spat, spat again, then rinsed with water and shook her head. "Maybe bigger than a dead canary. Can I have some tea?"

"Dr. Forbes says you can have anything you want any time you want it."

The first cup of tea came back up again, but the second cup stayed down and Cedar felt as if she was back in her skin again, not floating halfway to the ceiling any more. "Oh, look!" she said, not realizing that she was panting. "Flowers!"

"Those ones are from Karen and Sam. See the card? They wrote it themselves."

Cedar didn't see Auntie Marg press the buzzer, but a nurse came in. She took Cedar's pulse and noted her rapid breathing, the film of sweat on her upper lip and the frantic look in her eyes.

"Cedar," she said, "look at me, dear. That's it. Now think about what I ask you. Does your leg hurt?"

"Yes." Cedar realized it did hurt. It hurt like hell.

"This will fix it." A needle slid into her arm and two minutes later she was floating, smiling, and her leg was a million miles away.

Then it was morning and Auntie Marg was gone. The head of the bed was down, her leg was thumping in tune with her heartbeat, echoing painfully from under the thick padding of gauze and bandage. She tried to sit up but couldn't, because her leg was higher than she was, suspended from a contraption that hadn't been there earlier. Cedar felt tears slickering down her face. She wanted to sob and howl. How did they expect her to eat anything, or drink her tea, or do anything at all when she couldn't even sit up? Was she supposed to lie flat on her back and have tea, just pour some on her face and lick off what she could?

"Here we go, darling, let's go up in the world and see what's on that tray."

"I don't feel well."

"I expect not." The nurse looked at the tray and her lip twisted. "Let's get rid of that slop, shall we? I'll get you a nice basin of warm water and a clean cloth and towel, and you can have yourself a little freshen-up, brush your teeth and attack your hair. When you look better you'll feel better, and then we can have something appetizing for breakfast."

The nurse helped her, and it wasn't just her hands and face got washed, she managed a good bedbath, got a clean gown, even had her bedding changed, and then, blessedly, another shot in the arm. As the cottony calm won out over the throbbing in her leg, her new breakfast tray arrived. Scrambled eggs, fresh toast and coffee that smelled so good she almost hated to drink it. She wasn't used to coffee and she didn't like the taste of it all that much, but the smell was like a promise of much better things in the offing.

"Would you like a glass of milk?" the nurse asked.

Cedar smiled and shook her head. The very thought of it was enough to make her shudder. She could imagine only too clearly what it would do to the remnants of the birdcage still stuck in the back of her throat. Ah, but the little glass of orange juice was something else.

"Someone here to see you."

Cedar opened her eyes. The breakfast tray was gone, sunlight came through the window at a different angle, and Kate stood there smiling at her.

"Momma." Cedar tried to smile but her lips felt ready to crack.

"Auntie Marg says you woke up after I left last night. My luck, eh?"

"Were you here?"

"Oh, yes, darling, you bet I was. For hours. It seemed forever! And then your dad said I should go home, get some rest, let the others know how you were doing, and by then I was so dead beat I did. And *then* you wake up!" She leaned over and kissed Cedar on the cheek.

The leg took its own sweet time healing. As good as he was, Forbes hadn't been able to get out all the slivers and bits. The leg swelled and spat out pus and bits of bark, wood and dirt. Cedar's backside was sore from injections of antibiotics. Her face broke out in red spots, her temperature went up and down, and she fretted because she was stuck in bed while everyone else was getting ready to go back to school.

When the leg had been quiet for five days and the oozing had stopped completely, Forbes said she could go home. "But at the first sign of any oozing or swelling, you get her back to me," he warned. "I don't want any infection building up in there. If it gets into the bone we're in deep shit."

"Come on, darling," Gus said, picking her up gently. "Look what I got to take you home."

It wasn't a new car by a long shot, but the back seat was roomy and they sat her in it sideways, with pillows to cushion her leg.

Rory was waiting for them on the front porch, practically ready to jump out of his skin with excitement. He held the door open for Gus to carry Cedar inside and set her up on the sofa in front of the big window. When all the fussing and adjusting of pillows was done, when her leg, heavy with bandages, was propped up comfortably and Kate had gone to make tea, Rory sat on the sofa and put his arms around her. "I was scared," he whispered. "I cried for you."

"I cried, too," she admitted.

"Does it hurt bad?"

"Real bad sometimes. And it's ugly."

"Poor you," he said, patting her arm, "poor little you."

She went back to school on crutches. Every kid had heard one or more versions of the incident and they stared curiously. A few seemed to think she'd just been showing off and got what she deserved. But as the leg healed and the crutches were replaced with a wooden cane, other events pushed the incident into the background. Uncle Wade and Aunt Jean had a baby girl they called Donna and Aunt Marg came up pregnant again, and this time she made it past the third month and started to dare to hope. Rory was accepted on the neighbourhood soccer team and Gus stopped acting as if the boy was a disappointment. He even set up a goal in the back yard and helped Rory practise. "Left foot, too, son," he encouraged. "If you're two-footed you're twice as effective. That's the way, good man, way to be."

Christmas came and went, New Year's was finished, Valentine's Day made its brief appearance, and St. Pat's day was coming closer with each tick of the clock. Cedar only needed her cane when she was tired, and the shine on the new skin on her leg began to fade, although it was still an odd purply-red colour. Sometimes the toes on that foot felt cold, and sometimes she needed one of the pink pills to numb the pain, but as March stormed itself into April and the first bulbs began to sprout, the leg stopped throbbing. By May, when Aunt Marg's baby boy was born, Cedar was walking with only a slight trace of a limp, and could ride her bike without hurting herself.

"Oh, wow," she breathed, looking into the buggy. "He's beautiful."

Auntie Marg agreed happily. "He's just about as gorgeous as you were when you were born. Not quite, but almost. You were the most beautiful baby I have ever seen in my life." Marg hugged her and squeezed hard, whispering, "I was so jealous of your mother! I wanted you for my own."

"I love you, Auntie Marg," Cedar said. "More than anybody or anything in the world."

His name was Anthony, but everyone called him Tony, or Tony-Oh. He had enough thick black hair for three babies, and eyes as deep brown as a spaniel pup. All Cedar wanted to do was sit and hold him, marvel at his little fingers and toes, his tiny bits of soft nail, the curve of his eyebrows, his lashes like spiders on his cheeks when he slept.

"If you don't put him down," Grandma Karen teased, "he'll grow up shaped like your arms. You'll spoil him so bad nobody will want him around."

"Do you want to hold him for a while?"

"Of course I do." Karen took him, sat in the rocking chair. "Oh, little man," she crooned, "you have no idea how happy you've made your momma. Even if I didn't love you for yourself, I'd love you for what you've given her."

"You'd better have another one real soon," Hank said, "because that's the only way you or I will get any chance at all to hold them."

"I'm up for it," Auntie Marg laughed. "But are you, old man?"

"You know what they say, the older the bull, the stiffer the horn."

"Hank! There are children present."

"What children? You must mean the baby, because the only people

I see here are three of those Larson women." He winked at Cedar. "That'll fix 'em," he added.

Kate welcomed the springtime. Not only did the warmer weather seem to be doing wonders for Cedar's leg, but now they weren't all cooped up in the house together getting cabin fever. And best of all, she could start working in the garden.

Ewen Campbell collected several loads of well-rotted cow muck from the dairy and brought it over in his pickup, and Kate dug it into the soil, already planning her rows of lettuce, beans, peas, chard and marrow. On Saturday, when Gus drove them into town to do grocery shopping, she got him to stop at the nursery and she bought more bulbs, day lilies and iris corms, most of them already showing fresh green growth. "If I dared," she said, looking at the boxes of bulbs, the display of rose bushes, clematis and grapevines, "I'd go hog wild here, but—"

"You'd turn the place into a jungle," he agreed.

The kids helped her put the groceries away, and then she had to rush off to work. She cleaned up, changed her clothes and hurried out to where Gus was waiting in the car, the engine running.

"Sometimes time just gets away on a person," she said.

"It does that," he agreed absently.

Kate didn't try to get his attention. It was nice to have the car. It was handy when she was late for work, but it had been a godsend in the dead of winter. No more trudging home, hoping you wouldn't pee down your own leg, no more crunch crunch of frozen snow and earth beneath your feet, no more slipping in the slush or on the ice. Just out the door of Mom's and into the car, with the heater going and Gus grinning. "Hey, babe," he'd tease, "wanna go check out the gravel pit?" And sometimes they did, necking like kids, their breath fogging the windows, both of them on the verge of giggles the whole time.

Saturday night at Mom's was busy. They'd pushed the old Wurlitzer into a corner, out of the way, to make room for Alison McCann and her guitar. Only nineteen years old and she could play better than anyone you'd hear on the radio, everything from ballads to rock and jazz, and if she was feeling particularly in the mood, she'd give them fifteen minutes or so of Spanish music, wild, gypsy-sounding rhythms.

Nick paid Alison good money for her Saturday night music, but Kate figured it was still less than a quarter of what she brought them in extra business. "And you couldn't buy publicity like that," she told him.

"Ah, if I pay her more there won't be money to hire someone else for Friday night," Nick grumbled.

"You're an odd one," she told him, and he laughed.

She didn't think she'd said anything funny, but you never knew with Nick. Kate had been surprised and moved by his concern when Cedar was in hospital, showing up in her room with piping hot meals, doing everything he could to tempt her appetite. "Try this, little miss, a special sauce from my home, made with lemon grass, not lemon juice. Best food for hurt leg." He'd put off his trip to Greece, saying that he couldn't relax and enjoy anything until he knew Kate's daughter was all right. "Heart like a Greek!" he said of Cedar's heroism. "Scared from nothing."

"Greek my arse," said Gus. "She's a Campbell, is all."

"No, the blood of Diana the Huntress, swift and brave."

"Horse shite, it's good Scots blood in her veins."

"And maybe," Kate dared, "a good dash of Scandihoovian as well. Vikings."

They had a liquor licence now, and Nick was planning to add on to the dining area as soon as the weather cleared enough for the back part of the roof to be removed. "My luck," he grumbled, "take it off, snow fall again. Or rain for three weeks. Never good luck."

"Listen to you! You were born with a horseshoe in your teeth," Kate teased.

"Shoe in teeth?" And when she tried to explain, he shook his head and laughed. "You're an odd one," he said, heading back to the kitchen.

Gus was waiting in the car when she got off work, slumped behind the wheel, smoking a cigarette, looking far too innocent.

"So," he said, "I was thinking about what you said about wisteria vines and spring bulbs and such, and about time passing, and I got to thinking of all the damn money we're throwing down a rat hole by rent-ing, so I went to see the landlord."

"Oh God, Gus, don't tell me we're moving."

"Only if you want to." He grinned. "Or we can go see him tomorrow, the two of us, and sign the paper. Have it lawyerized and all on Monday, then sit back like the cats who wiped out the flock of canaries and wait for the mortgage papers to arrive."

"What?"

"I told you," he laughed. "Stick with me, babe, and I'll set you up in the biggest tarpaper shack on the outskirts of town."

Such a difference those few bits of paper made. Not renting any more, but buying. Not a short-term life, but something safer.

At last Kate could dare to buy her rose bushes, to buy three pots of clematis. The only reason she couldn't put them right in the ground was that Gus and his brothers were putting new siding on the house.

Rory was busy going from uncle to uncle with the box of nails, refilling the little pouches on their work aprons, taking them cold beers and hot coffees, fetching and carrying while they asked him about soccer, and was it true he had been picked as best novice goalie, telling him they were proud of him.

The siding was on in just a day, and the two-by-fours laid for the big front porch. By evening the next day the porch was nailed in place and the shingles were hammered down, and they sat out there with bottles of beer, their bellies full of venison steaks and oven-browned spuds.

The next morning Kate planted the clematis. "They don't look like much right now," she said, "but give them a year or two and they'll be a glory."

Now that it was their place, Gus could take a chain saw to the small cedars in the back. He dropped them, trimmed off the branches, cut them to length, stripped off the bark and then, with Cedar helping, dragged them to where he had holes dug and waiting. Cedar and Rory held each post upright while Gus jammed rocks in the hole, checked that the post was straight, then poured in concrete he had mixed himself. "Give her a few days to firm up," he told them, wiping his balding head with his work hanky, "and next week we can run crossbars." He pointed and drew an invisible line in mid-air. "When they're spiked in firmly, we can run some others back to the roofline there. Then, when the posts and all are in place, we'll get your mother those grapevines she's always dreaming of, and they'll grow up the posts and across the poles to the roof, and we'll have ourselves a little arbour."

Things were going so well that even Mary Campbell began to relax and to believe, once in a while, that things would continue to get better. Back on track, his brothers said, finally got it together and got back on track. The only trouble with getting on track is that you can go off the rails without warning.

Cedar and Rory had been down at the creek, fishing for trout. They had plenty for a meal, three for him and two for her, and they were on their way back home when they heard Gus shouting and yelling, heard Kate sobbing. Rory stopped dead, clutching the string of fish as if it was the only thing keeping him from falling through the earth to the hobs of hell. Cedar ran, limping slightly but making good time.

He was hitting her, knocking her back and forth on the porch, swinging easily, his open hand cracking against her skin again and again. "Behind my back, knew bloody well, sneak around like an egg-sucking dog!"

"Stop it!" Cedar screamed, pelting toward the house. Gus didn't even turn his head.

Cedar grabbed at a hammer lying on the chopping block and threw it as hard as she could. It slammed into the new siding, just missing Gus's head. He stopped and whirled around.

"Leave her alone!" Cedar yelled, leaping from the path to the porch. "What's the matter with you?"

"Mind your own bloody business!"

"It is my business, she's my mother." Cedar threw herself in between Gus and Kate.

"Get the hell out of my way, you're as bad as she is."

"How can that be? You're the one keeps saying I'm all Campbell."

Kate was still sobbing, thick, phlegmy gasps of grief. "Oh God, Gus, all we did was have a pot of tea and talk."

"And I can just hear it now, talking behind my back, gossiping about me."

"We didn't talk about you at all!"

"I bet. I just bloody bet."

"Please, Gus, don't do this, please. I haven't done anything wrong."

"Two-faced bitch."

Cedar's anger grew, not just at Gus but at Kate, too, grovelling, crying, begging.

"Will you fuckin' listen to your fuckin' self!" Cedar exploded, using a word she had never spoken before. "Who the fuck do you think you are?"

"You watch your mouth, little bitch!"

"Or what? You'll hit me? Go ahead. Big brave yahoo beating on a woman who hasn't done anything but kiss your backside. You want to hit me? Do it, then, if it makes you feel big and—"

He hit her hard. She saw it coming and didn't even try to get out of the way. The back of his hand slammed the side of her face and she could only think, it's true, you do see stars. She tasted blood, and the pain was something she could have held in her hand. She wanted to stay on her feet and stare him down, but her legs wouldn't hold her. She sank to the porch, stubbornly refusing to fall flat, holding herself up with her arms, blood pouring from her mouth onto the new planks.

"Oh my God," Gus whispered. "Jesus Christ, Kate, get the car! No! You phone Forbes, I'll get the car. Oh Jesus, what have I done?"

Rory knelt down beside her, his eyes round, his face pale. He held a towel to Cedar's mouth to catch the blood. "Can you stand up?" he asked. She nodded. Rory helped her to her feet and she was surprised to realize that he was almost as tall as she was. He put his arm around her waist. "Come on," he urged, "let the old bugger drive you to hospital."

"Fucker," she managed.

"One day I'll kick the shit out of him," Rory promised, "and when I do, I'll kick his balls in for you."

"Deal."

Forbes didn't say a word to Gus, but he took a few seconds to assure Rory that Cedar would be fine. "I'll put her to sleep," he explained, "and then go in and fix the damage. You can wait in the staff lounge if you want."

"Can I watch?"

"If you faint you're on your own, we'll be too busy to look after you."

Rory didn't faint. He sat on a high stool well out of everyone's way, swathed in sterile garb, face covered by a mask. The bonnet on his head was too big and slipped sideways like a jaunty beret, but all he cared about was his sister, out colder than a clam, stuff running through tubes into her arms, other stuff running through other tubes into her nostrils. He wouldn't have believed that anyone's mouth could open up that wide, or that Forbes could actually work in there, and when they cut along Cedar's jawbone he was fascinated by the sight of the skin rolling back.

Finally Forbes stepped back from the table and a nurse wiped his face.

"We're done," he breathed. Then he looked over at Rory. "Well, old man, you ready for a bowl of soup and a cup of tea?"

"Is she going to live?" Rory whispered.

"Yes, she is. She'll have a little scar, but it's not going to show, and if I do say so myself, I've done a job that the finest plastic surgeon in the country would envy. Come on, now, and I'll show you how to get out of all this goddamn stuff."

Gus was pacing in the waiting room and hurried over to Forbes when he saw him. "Is she all right? Can I see her?"

"Go home, Mr. Campbell," Forbes said distantly. "She won't be awake until tomorrow morning. You've done enough for today. Just go home and leave the child alone."

"You self-righteous old fart," Gus gritted. "Come on, Rory."

"The boy stays here," Forbes said. "He's in shock. I'll keep him overnight."

"There's nothing wrong with him."

"I'm his physician and I say he needs to stay here overnight."

Rory didn't mind at all. There were comic books lying around on bookshelves and little tables, and a big television set in what they called the day room. He had soup and crackers in the cafeteria with Forbes, he asked questions about what he'd seen and he got answers, and they let him sit beside Cedar's bed for a while. She was snoring, and he grinned at the prospect of being able to tease her about that. He and Dr. Forbes played some checkers.

Then Grandpa and Grandma Campbell came in, and Rory was afraid. Grandpa looked like he was going to beat the living shit out of somebody. And Grandma Campbell bent over Cedar, stroked her face and said something in a language Rory didn't know. She looked at Grandpa as if she was mad at him, but she also reached over and took his hand. He nodded and lifted his hand to kiss the back of hers.

"Were you there?" he asked, not looking at Rory.

"No, sir. I got there after he hit her."

"You didnae see him?"

"I saw, but not from close. I was in the yard and they were on the porch."

"Your mam says he'd been whaling on her, too."

"She was bleeding," Rory agreed. "Split lip, and blood from her nose."

Grandma Campbell spoke again in whatever language it was, and again the old man nodded. Rory sat back in his chair, waiting, watching, expecting somebody to do something.

When Marg got there, at a full run, she found Dr. Forbes sitting on the side of the bed assigned to Rory, playing Chinese checkers with him and sharing a box of Cracker Jack.

"Good Lord, Marg," he smiled, "slow yourself down. A woman of your advanced age shouldn't rip around like a youngster."

"Is she going to live?"

"Oh, my heavens, yes, she's going to go home tomorrow. She's just here to sleep off the anaesthetic. There was a broken blood vessel, and a crack in the jaw, down near the chin, here." He pointed to the spot on a small model skeleton he had brought in for Rory. "I stitched everything up so fine that I've nearly dislocated my own neck from patting myself on the back. Sit down, woman, I'll find us some tea. And if you need to cry, why, young Rory here is an excellent shoulder."

Marg sank into the stuffed armchair beside the bed and clasped her hands over her belly. That should have been her child, the one lying in bed with one side of her face swollen up like a pumpkin. Why was it the ones who could have them so easily took so little care of them? How many times had she tried to convince Kate that her best move in life would be to turn her back on crazy Gus, have the baby and give it to Marg and Hank to raise, get on with her life, wait until someone sane and kind and responsible came along? But no, don't listen to anyone, Kate, do it your own stupid way, bumbling and fumbling and reeling from one terrible episode to the next. And now this.

Cedar moaned, and reached up to touch her swollen face. Marg leaned over to take her hand. "Easy baby. Don't touch that, you'll hurt yourself."

Cedar opened her eyes, managed to focus on Marg, then attempted a smile. "Hi," she whispered.

"Hey, Cedar," Rory piped up. "I'm over here in the next bed. Dr. Forbes gave me a model skeleton. His name is Billy Bones."

"Hey, Roar." Cedar tried to sit up. "Oh, Jesus Christ almighty," she groaned.

"Boy, he got me a good one, eh."

"Why didn't you duck?"

"Silly goose."

"What?"

"Duck, goose. Get it?"

Marg and Hank and Tony-Oh took Cedar home the next afternoon, with a small bottle of pills and an appointment to see Forbes again in four days. Kate met them at the door, her eyes streaming tears, finger marks on her face and a nasty bruise on her arm.

Cedar shook her head slowly. "Momma," she sighed, "this is nuts. Look at you."

"Look at *you*. You got the worst of it."

Cedar laughed bitterly. "But I asked for it, didn't I?"

She sat down, staring at nothing. Marg and Hank looked around, and Kate shook her head, answering the unspoken question: no, Gus wasn't there.

"He didn't come back from the hospital," she whispered. "I don't know where he is."

"Momma, what was it all about? Who was he yelling about?"

"Sis and Bob stopped by," Kate said bleakly. "They were on their way down-island to the stock auction so they left early to have time for a bit of a visit."

Kate went to put on the kettle for tea, but Marg and Hank said they had to get back.

Rory took Billy Bones to his room and hung him from the ceiling. "Hey, Billy," he whispered. "How are all those bones of yours?"

"What in the name of heaven is that?" Kate asked from the door.

"Billy Bones," Rory laughed. "Dr. Forbes gave him to me. Every bone Billy has, I have. So do you. And Cedar. Everybody has all these bones. And look." He held out his hand, then clenched it. "See?" He turned to the skeleton and took its little plastic arm, moved it, then carefully, slowly, he turned the finger bones in, making a sort-of fist. "Great, eh?"

"Well, it's certainly different."

"He's going to give me a book, too. When Cedar goes to see him.

It's got pictures in it—bones, and muscles, and things like livers and lungs and where they are in your body. But I asked, and he said they don't have any picture of where your soul is. They don't know where it is. They never found one yet." He stared at the skeleton, then looked at his mother, and she could see in his eyes that something had changed, he wasn't the little boy he'd been the day before. "I would have thought," he said carefully, "your soul would, like, be either in or very near your heart."

Kate went back to work the next day. Nobody asked any questions and she didn't offer any explanations. The red finger marks had faded, but not completely, there was still a faint pink blush on her cheeks. The bruises on her arms could have come from anything—bumping furniture, trying to move something too big and heavy, a piece of stove wood falling from the pile—but nobody believed for a moment that any such thing had happened. They knew. If the women hadn't worn marks like that themselves, their mothers had, or their sisters or daughters. The men might not have left marks like that, but their fathers, brothers or uncles had, or their friends, or sons. If Nick had an opinion, he kept it to himself.

The second night she was at work, Gus's brothers Rod and Bruce came in, sat at the counter and ordered coffee and pie. Kate served them, suddenly tense and frightened. But they smiled at her. Bruce even winked, and he held out the car keys.

"Here, hen," he said, his Scots accent burring his words. "Ye'll need these, I've no doubt."

"Not tae worry," Rod burst out. "Ye'll get his pay packet." And he blushed and became suddenly fascinated by the pastry on his pie.

"Why is it," she asked, as if there was only one important question in the world, "that every one of you talk like heather hoppers, except him?"

Bruce shrugged, and Rod shook his head and finally tasted his pie. "Not sae guid as mam's," he said quietly. "Nowheres near."

It was easier this time. They didn't have to pack their stuff, they didn't have to move, there was no changing schools, no uproar, no dislocation. Marg helped Kate pack Gus's clothes into boxes and Hank drove them to Colin and Mary's house. The women sat in the car while Hank unloaded the boxes. There was no sign of Gus. Mary came to the doorway and stared at Marg and Kate for a moment. Then she walked down the porch steps. Marg and Kate got out of the car, and Mary put her arms around Kate.

"Easy on, hen," she said, "Ye're nae alone in this."

"Thank you."

"And how is our Cedar?"

"She's fine." Marg reached out and touched Mary's arm. "It looked much worse than it was."

"Ye must be a verra honest woman, Margaret Larson, because ye canna lie worth shite," Mary laughed harshly. She touched Marg's belly. "That bairn will be here in nae mair than three days," she predicted, "and there's a right rare surprise waiting for ye."

"What." Marg went pale.

"Och, it's naething bad! It's wonderful, it is. Would I lie tae ye? Now ye're tae stay in touch, and I want tae see my granddaughter. He'll nae be here," she hastened to add, "but her grandfeyther and I need tae see her. And the wee lad, too."

As soon as Gus's things were out of the house, Kate started to make it her own. She started in the bedroom, moving the bed so she could see out the window. She took out the bit of carpet she had never liked and she spent days sanding and scrubbing the floor. Then she waxed it and buffed it until it took on a deep gleam.

"Gonna move the carpet back in?" Cedar asked.

"I like it better this way."

"Me, too," her daughter agreed.

Hank and Marg drove Cedar and Rory to their grandparents' house and dropped them off at the front gate, then they drove Kate down to the Motor Vehicle Branch to take her driver's test. When they went back to pick up the kids, Kate was driving, smiling proudly. Cedar and Rory got in the back seat with a bag of scones and tea biscuits. "Here," said Cedar, reaching over the seat to hand Kate some money. "Gran says this is yours."

"I can't take her money!"

"It's not from her exactly. And don't turn it down, you'll insult her and she'll get all stiff-necked again."

"Is that why she wanted to see you?"

"She said it was Campbell stuff," Rory laughed. "Private Campbell stuff."

"Oh dear God," Marg muttered. "The secrets of the bloody universe, no less."

"Hush," Kate giggled, whispering. "They'll get all stiff-necked."

FIVE

The surprise Mary Campbell had predicted was a seven-pound, three-ounce girl they named Susannah. And another, smaller girl who looked nothing like her twin and whom they called Mary Christine, ostensibly after Hank's mother.

"How anyone could overlook a fireball like that is beyond me," old Forbes laughed. "I think I'll pack it in and retire. If it wasn't for the tiny size of her, I'd say this child was a year old and impatient to taste all life has to offer."

Susannah was as beautiful as Tony-Oh, with thick, curly dark hair and huge dark eyes. Chris was like a cat, slender, wiry and alert. Susannah was placid, Chris was a going concern. Susannah liked to be held close and cuddled, Chris wanted to be held so she could watch everything. When Susannah was still snuggling contentedly, Chris was standing on Hank's knee, balancing by gripping his fingers, stepping from tiny foot to tiny foot, always on the go, always on the move. "She's even bouncing in her sleep," he laughed. "I'm going to need another job just to buy shoes. Once she starts walking she'll wear them out as fast as I can bring them home."

When school let out, Cedar applied for a job at Mom's. Kate tried to talk her out of it, but Cedar was stubborn. "It's no harder than any other job I could get. I'm damned if I want to be bent over picking strawberries, then early spuds, then peas, then beans, then more spuds and just for a break I get to stand up and pick raspberries? And at the end of a ten-hour day I've made less than I can make in four hours at Mom's? I think not!"

"But—"

"Momma, I'm only taking a summer job, I'm not getting married to the damn place."

"Don't swear, Cedar, please. It's just that I want . . . more . . . for you."

"It's a summer job, not a lifetime career. Someone is going to get that job, and it might as well be me."

"But we can't just leave Rory alone."

"Why not? When I was his age I was looking after myself *and* him. You fuss him too much. No wonder he was such a whiney, snivelly little kid."

"He'll be lonely."

"Then he can go out to the highway, flag down the bus and ride it down to Grandma Larson's. Or Auntie Marg's. He can babysit Tony-Oh and give her a break."

Kate gave in to Cedar for the same reasons she had so often given in to Gus—the harder you tried to change their minds, the more stubborn they got.

Nick put Cedar on the early shift. The place wasn't as busy and the tips weren't as good, but there would only be a half hour between the time Kate left and Cedar got home. Rory was more than capable of looking after himself for that brief time. Besides, Cedar would get off early enough to play softball at the park or go swimming in the river.

Sometimes Marg and the girls went to the river with Cedar and Rory. Susannah sat in her stroller and Tony played with his pail and shovel near the water. Marg sat with Chrissie in the warm shallows. No use putting Suzie in, she wasn't yet ready for it, didn't even like her bath. While Suzie hummed and made ga-ga-goo-goo at the salmonberry leaves and the clouds in the sky, at the people swimming and splashing, Chrissie kicked her legs and splashed.

Hank liked to go to the river after work, slip off his dirty clothes and dive in in his boxer shorts. As soon as Tony realized his dad was out there in the big water, he would stand up, his sturdy little legs planted like trees, and hold out his arms and yell "Da! Da!" until Hank swam back to shore.

"You ready?"

"Yes! Yet's go!"

And Hank swam back out, Tony riding on his shoulders, clutching Hank's curly hair in his fists.

Cedar would take a turn holding Chrissie while Marg swam. She laid her in water just deep enough for her to float and swished her through the water, supporting her by holding one hand under her head.

Sometimes when Marg watched Hank and all the kids, she couldn't think of one single thing that would make life better than it was at that moment. She didn't know what filled her with more pleasure, the sight of Hank with his son, or the sight of Cedar so completely focussed on Chris. Cedar dropped her hard protective shell at those times. Her body relaxed and there was no smart talk, no self-deprecating jokes; she was just a kid, suntanned and laughing.

Some evenings they had potato salad, garden salad and cold cuts, some nights it was chicken roasted in the oven, then cooled and sliced. Once in a while Hank would haul on his jeans and drive off for fish and chips. Often they filled up on egg or salmon sandwiches and bean salad. If Chris started to fuss, and it was almost always she who fussed, Cedar would put a little dab of salmon on the baby's tongue and let her suck at it, enjoying the taste. Only when Marg was full, and relaxed and ready would she take the squirming baby, lean up against an arbutus tree and nurse her right there on the riverbank. The two babies were completely different even in the way they suckled. Susannah nursed slowly, gently, contentedly. Chrissie went at it like a terrier with a rat and God help you if you tried to separate her and her milk before she was ready. She slurped and smacked, she wriggled and butted her head like a calf. "You watch yourself," Marg warned, "or you'll wind up with a rubber nipple and a glass bottle." And by the end of July, she had to carry out the threat. She had braced herself for a fuss, but you'd think the child hadn't even noticed the change. She slurped greedily, eagerly, so intense that sometimes she had to let go of the nipple for a moment and gasp for breath.

After the picnic dinners no one let Marg do anything but hold a baby and feed her. The other three did the cleanup and packed the car. Once home, Marg sat in her big chair with the footstool, and Rory did the washing up while Cedar hung towels, blankets and sandy bathing suits on the line. When Tony and the girls were asleep, the rest of them had tea and dessert.

"I'm spoiled rotten," Marg would say.

"Stinking rotten," the others would agree, and then Rory would get his and Cedar's towels and swim suits off the line and Hank would drive them home.

Before they fell asleep, Marg snuggled close to Hank, rubbing her cheek against the fur on his chest. "Was there ever a more wonderful summer?"

Kate wasn't finding the summer very wonderful. She hardly saw Cedar, and there were few trips to the river. She came home from work hot, tired and sweaty, made a cup of tea and took it with her to the bathroom. The bathwater relaxed her but the heat of it made her sweat even more, and a couple of times when she got out of the tub she felt dizzy. She tried a cool bath but didn't like it, and vowed she'd just have to be more careful, get out more slowly. A second cup of tea and she took it to bed with her, sat propped up by pillows, feeling the night breeze through the half-open window. She might read the newspaper, or an article or two in a magazine, she might open a novel and try to lose herself in it, and sometimes she wakened in the morning still propped on the pillows, her book on her lap.

She would hear the water running from the outside tap, and knew that Cedar had the soaker hose on, drenching the roots of the plants in the garden. Some mornings when she got up, both kids were in the garden, picking beans or peas or baby beets. Other times there were bowls of berries set out on the counters. Kate would make coffee and take it out onto the porch, sit in the wicker armchair sipping it and smoking cigarettes, yawning often, putting off the moment when she would have to take off her thin cotton nightgown and put on some clothes, kickstart the day and get on with her life. She didn't even know what time Cedar wakened in the morning, let alone what time she went to sleep at night, and then there she'd be some mornings, maybe coming back from the creek with a few trout, or heading for the kitchen with more berries.

"How are you today?" Kate would ask.

"Fine, and yourself?" Cedar answered. Always the same—fine, and yourself. The kind of thing you said to a casual acquaintance encountered on the street.

Other mornings, most mornings, Cedar was already gone before Kate wakened. Oh, there'd be those few minutes at shift change when they would see each other, and smile, speak casually about things of little importance, but then Cedar would be off, climbing onto her bike to rush home, change her clothes and whip down to the highway with Rory, to catch the bus for the fifteen-minute ride to Marg's place.

The shelves in the basement were filling with jars of peas, jars of beans, jars of pickles—sweet ones, dills, mustard and bread and butter. There were jars of berries, even jars of plums picked from their own trees. Smaller jars of canned trout, of salmon caught by Tamas or Gordon and brought to them, jars of venison caught out of season by Hugh or Wade, by Forrest or Bruce. When Karen did in the last year's laying hens she shared them with her daughters, "in-law and outlaw," she laughed. They too wound up in jars, breasts and legs stuffed into a quart sealer, the rest of the scrawny things boiled into soup stock, which was also canned for winter. Laying hens had no meat worth mentioning on them, you needed the heavier breeds for that, but there was enough for sandwiches, perhaps enough for a stew. Marg was on at her to save up for a freezer, insisted it was way lots easier to spread berries on cookie sheets, freeze them, then put them in plastic bags. She insisted, too, that meat frozen was different from but as good as meat jarred. The cost of it was something to worry about too, and God knows no one was standing out on the street corner handing out free canning jars, and the doing of it, especially on a wood burner, turned the whole house into an oven.

In mid-August Nick shoved in his oar and changed the direction of more lives than his own. He called a staff meeting and told them all that Kate was now officially the manager.

"She tell you something, same as if I tell you," he lectured, like the father he never had been.

"Me?" she blurted.

"You," he nodded. "Only person can tell you no is me. And I won't be here, I go to Greece, see my mother before she's die." He laughed. "Just don't you go fire this Cedar girl, she's good worker."

Funny he would say that. It was Kate's first thought when she realized he was serious about her promotion.

She came off the floor, of course, and hired one of the Dolan boys as a replacement. At first she felt as if she was going to drown in paperwork. How did they run things like logging camps and pulp mills if there was all this go-round with a café that was moving toward being a real restaurant? Shifts to figure out, days off to figure out, hours worked to keep track of, overtime if any, ensure the cooks never ran short of anything—it just went on and on and on, and gradually she realized that Nick had been doing more than walking around smoking his cigar or sipping his little glass of turpentine-smelling liquor. There were so many details to keep on top of—little things like whispering softly to a waiter that he should go change his jacket, something had spilled on it. But there were some real satisfactions to it, too, because once Nick had headed off, Kate arranged with the laundry to do all the uniforms so the waitresses didn't have to take theirs home with them and wash and iron the damn things themselves.

"If you want to do a touch-up on them," she said, pouring coffee for them, "that's fine. We'll set up an ironing board and everything in the freezer room. And I'd like to know how you feel about those gorpy little hats."

"Get rid of them," someone laughed. "They look like doilies or something."

It was nice not to have to take any part of work home with her. No need to take the uniforms, just drop them in the hamper when she changed into her going-home clothes, and next day she could get a clean starched one.

Except there were the creases needed ironed out where they'd been folded, and one day she stood watching as the waitresses wielded the iron, taking turns, one by one, talking and teasing softly.

"This is nuts!" Kate blurted.

They looked up at her and Hazel grinned as if she already knew what was going to be said.

"It costs twenty-five cents a uniform to get them cleaned, starched and pressed." Kate was thinking out loud, needing to hear the idea as it hatched. "We pay a set fee every month to rent the damn things, then pay to get them picked up, cleaned and dropped off again, and then there's all this tiddle-widdle around the ironing board and . . ." She shook her head, as if to shake loose an idea. "Employment Standards say we either provide uniforms or pay for . . ."

"I've got two pair of black slacks," Hazel agreed, "and several white blouses."

"We could take the laundry bill and divide it, to cover wear and tear, I suppose." Kate looked at Georgina. "What do you think?"

"I think it would be a *lot* more comfortable. I mean, I know these things have to be starched or they'll go limp as a hanky in no time, but the starch bothers me, especially at the waist And the underarms," she admitted, "I've got a rash that itches like crazy."

"Let's think about it."

"No," Hazel laughed. "We could think until next year and still not know unless we tried."

"Is that okay with everyone?"

"I don't have black slacks, but I've got a couple of dresses that would be okay."

"Yes, I don't usually wear slacks," someone else said. "Especially not when it's hot like this."

"Just nothing low-cut or . . . revealing." Kate didn't want to say the word *tacky*. She didn't have to—they nodded. "What about the guys? Couldn't they wear white shirts instead of looking like busboys or East Indian servants?"

One change led to another. The tablecloths with identical patterns were replaced with white ones, the matching red-and-white-checked curtains came down as well and weren't replaced at all.

"So you can see the sunsets better," Kate told the customers. "Might as well enjoy them, they're the best in the world."

The changes at work changed the routines at home. Kate gave a set of keys to the senior cook so that he could open up in the morning, get the grills ready for the breakfast rush, and she changed Hazel's job description to assistant manager so that she could keep an eye on the place until Kate got there to handle the big push at dinnertime. She thought of cutting Cedar's hours to encourage her to enjoy more of her summer, actually have some holidays, but in the end it was easier to leave things alone. She knew the balloon would go up and she wasn't ready to get into it with someone as stubborn as her own daughter.

"Well, at least I see more of you this way," she said, trying to make light of it.

"Maybe too much," Cedar laughed. "Hard to believe my mom is my boss!"

Kate watched the way Cedar moved among the tables, serving meals, smiling, chatting with the customers, and felt she was looking at herself. No doubt about it, the girl knew her job and wasn't afraid of work. If it was anybody else's kid, Kate realized, there would have been no hesitation about keeping her busy, no thought of laying her off and sending her swimming.

"She's a good worker," she told Marg. She didn't think to say the same thing to Cedar.

Miss Grayse sat behind her desk, watching intently as the students bent over their test papers, some writing furiously, others frowning, nibbling the ends of their ballpoint pens, a few looking lost and worried. Miss Grayse never gave warning that a test was in the offing. Sometimes she would go for months without even so much as a review, other times she dropped tests on them two or three times in a row. There were no makeups—if you weren't there on a test day, you didn't write the test. She had the reputation of being the toughest teacher in the school. She also had the reputation of being the best teacher in the school.

Cedar checked her paper and figured she had most of the questions right, but she wasn't sure how. How can a person know the answers and have absolutely no recollection of studying the material? The day and date had been chalked in yellow on the top of the board. It was Thursday the seventeenth, but she couldn't remember Monday, Tuesday or Wednesday. But if Miss Grayse wrote Thursday the seventeenth, that's what it was—period.

Cedar handed in her test. "May I leave the room?" she asked quietly.

"Are you feeling well? You look pale."

"I'm fine." Cedar waited.

Miss Grayse nodded, and Cedar left the room. She stood in the hallway, looking around. She was willing to swear on a Bible she'd never seen this hallway, these lockers, the class photos lining the walls of the entryway. But she knew her way to the washroom and, when she got there she almost, but not quite, recognized it. Was that because all washrooms looked the same? A row of basins against a mirrored wall, a tile floor, a line of stalls with doors that locked, dispensers for paper towels and tampons, a scent that was a blend of deodorant pucks and liquid green soap in the squirters.

She went into a stall and sat on the toilet. Seventeenth of what? Where had she gotten the plaid skirt, the white blouse, the yellow pullover?

She lowered her head, remembering that you were supposed to put your head between your knees if you thought you were going to faint. She felt dizzy, heard a strange whooshing roar in her ears. When it subsided, she was cold and her skin felt clammy. She had a sensation that time had passed, and she could hear people talking, water running in the basins, stall doors opening and closing. She sat there until the buzzer sounded and the jane emptied, then got off the loo and rearranged her clothes carefully. She looked at herself in the long mirror while rinsing her hands. Pale as chalk, eyes dark-rimmed, she'd be a good model for a ghoulie. She patted cold water on her face, then soaked some paper towels and pressed them to the back of her neck. The door opened. Miss Grayse came in, looking concerned.

"Are you all right, Cedar?"

"I thought I was," Cedar answered slowly. "But now I don't think I am."

"Are you ill?"

"No. Just . . . tired, I guess. Or—maybe today is Feeble Day, and I've been elected the school feeb."

"I think you should lie down in the nurse's room for a bit. I'll go with you."

The nurse's room was warm, but Cedar was glad of the blanket over her. She laid her head on the soft pillow, and when the swooshing and roaring started again in her ears, she could close her eyes and wait for the odd feeling of falling to pass.

She could remember. Of course she could. She could remember lots of stuff. She could remember that other people had their own agendas and that silence, too, could be deception.

"Didn't want to say anything to you until we were sure about things," Kate had said. Translation: "It's none of your business and you'll do what you're told."

"I've smartened up a lot, learned a hard lesson the hard way, and I want to apologize to both you kids," Gus had said. Translation: only Christ knew.

She remembered feeling shock, feeling cold as ice, and then suddenly she was so angry she scared herself, and the words came pouring out of her. You fuckin' fool, you never learn, do you, crazier'n hell the pair of you, count me out this time, he can damn well kill you and see if I'll try to stop him, lay so much as a hand on Rory or me and I'll kill you.

And then she was finishing an exam paper, answering questions she couldn't remember studying for, and now she was here, on this silly little cot, in a warm little room, feeling as if she was freezing.

And then she was on the school bus, her binder and book on her lap. The other students on the bus were chatting with each other, laughing, planning their weekend, and outside, the moving-past world was winter-struck, the leaves gone, only the bare bones of trees left, skeletons like Billy Bones. The rocks were rimed white and the dark clouds sat low, wisps of fog weaving aimlessly.

The bus stopped at the junior high school, the doors opened, frigid air blasted in and the first of the new passengers trooped on. Rory hurried down the aisle and slid into the empty seat next to Cedar. "Christ, it's as cold as a well-digger's arse out there. I thought my fingers were going to turn to icicles."

"How come you have to wait outside?"

"Huh?" He looked surprised. "Because of that big fight last week, when they almost wrecked the gym, and they decided to lock us out as soon as school is over. Don't you remember?"

"Oh, right. I guess I just thought they'd see how bitch-miserable it is and—"

"Them? They don't care if we die as long as we do it quietly."

The bus was warming up again, the heater on full bore, and still Cedar shivered.

Their classmate Marjory Peel slid into the seat in front of them. "Sure is cold, isn't it? You think it's gonna snow?"

Cedar shrugged.

"You still working weekends at Mom's?"

"Yeah."

"You like it?"

"I guess so. It's a job. Pay's good."

"You're lucky. You got just about everything, I guess." Marjory lived with her mom and her aunt, no sign of a dad or stepdad. "I mean, you do good in school, you got your job, and your dad is so much fun."

Cedar felt Rory stiffen and she leaned against him, making it seem as if the movement of the bus had pushed her against him.

"Yeah?"

"Yeah, I miss him. We saw a lot of him for a while, but I guess it's your guys's turn now."

"Turn for what?" Rory muttered. "Getting yelled at? Getting hit?"

"Your dad?" Marjory laughed.

"He's teasing you. Rory's got the most oddball sense of humour of anyone you'll ever meet. You have to know him really well to know when he's joking."

"Tell your dad hi from me, will you?" Cedar nodded. Damned if she was going to get sucked into whatever Marjory Dipshit Peel had in mind for them.

"Maybe I should put in an application for a job at Mom's," Marjory chatted on. Cedar said nothing. "It could be real nice and all. Like a family thing, you know."

"Family?" Rory frowned. "How d'you figure?"

"Well, I mean we're almost like sisters and brother, aren't we? Well, stepsisters and stepbrother."

"Our stop's next," Cedar said. She and Rory got up and went to the front of the bus.

"What was she talking about?" Rory asked, as the bus pulled away.

"Stop it, Rory," Cedar snapped. "You know full well."

"No," he said. "I don't."

Cedar could have slapped him. He knew. He was just doing that same thing Kate did, that refusing to face up to reality thing.

Kate didn't try to explain to anybody why she'd let Gus come back, and nobody asked her anything. That was the oddest and in some ways the most awful part of the whole mess—it was as if they had expected it all along. Except Cedar, who had exploded. Gus had said it was just another Campbell crisis. "Nothing to worry about, she's said everything she's got to say, and now it's over and done with." It was true that since then, Cedar had made no scenes.

But had there ever been a mother who didn't worry that she might have destroyed something in her child? Something about Cedar felt not quite right. "Mood swings," Gus said. "It's a family thing. The whole damn bunch of us, up one minute, down the next. It's just the way we are."

After Gus had been back for three or four months, his extra-good behaviour was wearing thin. There were more and more trips to the Domino Club, and he said he had joined the volunteer fire crew again.

But this time, Kate didn't care. He could come or he could go, no skin off her nose, as long as he kept his fists to himself, left the kids alone when he got proddy. Mood swings? Bratty temper tantrums, more like it. She wished she had figured it out earlier on, she'd have saved a lake of tears. You didn't really have to give him what he thought he wanted, you just had to look as if you were.

But just when Kate was beginning to realize that she could handle Gus, as long as she didn't require anything from him, not even responsibility or companionship, who should walk into Mom's but someone she hadn't thought of forever.

"For crying in the night!" said the tall, incredibly handsome man in uniform. "Are you Cedar's mom?"

Kate laughed. "That's how the world knows me. Do I know you?"

"Not really. I'm Ted Conrad. Cedar used to work on my dad's farm."

"You're a pilot."

"Yes, ma'am." He slid onto a stool at the counter. "How's Cedar?"

"Wonderful. Doing well in high school, works here on weekends, fulfilling every promise we saw in her when she was little."

"Great kid," he agreed.

Ted was back the next day, and the next, and Kate knew she was asking for a three-oh-three bullet between the eyes but she didn't give the first part of a damn. One night he offered her a ride home, and even though she had her own car, she said yes, and they went down to the viewpoint to sit in his rented car with the radio playing, looking out over the ocean and talking, until she realized with a start how late it was.

The next night there was no question that she would leave with him, and there was less talking, especially after the first kiss. He was on leave, and she was taking leave of her senses, but she'd be sane again when his holiday was ended and he had gone.

Why did she have to defy the odds? Maybe it just made everything that much more exciting, a bit more spit in your eye. What's sauce for the goose is sauce for the gander. Tit for tat, eye for eye and take that, you bugger.

Gus grinned from ear to ear and said there wasn't an invention made by man or mouse that could defeat the Campbell men. "Ah, it'll be a sneaky wee thing," he laughed, "creeping around rubber barriers and swimming through all that goo."

Kate laughed too, but for very different reasons. The satisfaction she felt was enormous.

Cedar half wakened. She heard Gus speaking softly and Kate whimpering and gasping. She was as good as back to sleep again when Kate yelped. Cedar sat up, her pulse racing. If the bastard was back in his mean streak again, there would be hell to pay. But when she listened to the voices, it sounded like Kate was terrified and Gus was consoling her.

Then she heard Aunt Marg's voice, so she got out of bed and stood listening for long minutes. When she heard her parents' bedroom door opening, she stepped into the hallway. Gus was walking toward the stairs, carrying a blood-smeared towel. He was weeping.

"What's wrong?"

"Nothing to worry about. Go back to bed, your Auntie Marg will look after things."

There was no point worrying about it. Nobody was going to tell her anything.

Kate took a week off work and Gus stayed home to care for her. One afternoon he drove into town and came back with a lovely azalea that the florist had assured him could be planted outside when spring arrived. Cedar did the housework and prepared supper every evening, and Rory helped with cleanup. They did their homework sitting at opposite ends of the kitchen table, listening to the rise and fall of Gus's voice in the bedroom. He read the paper to Kate, he played crib with her, he escorted her to and from the bathroom. He seemed ready to do everything but breathe for her, and if she'd asked, he might have done that, too.

Even Karen Larson began to reconsider her low opinion of Gus Campbell. One afternoon when she and Olaf drove out to see Kate, they found Gus busy folding the laundry, and not the least bit embarrassed to be caught doing "women's work." He made tea and brought it to the bedroom with a plate of his mother's scones and a little jar of homemade raspberry jam.

"I could have done that," Karen said.

"I know. But there's little enough I can do for her," he answered, and Karen could see his grief clinging to him like a jockey on his horse. He could not be consoled.

The only person who wasn't the least bit impressed by his sorrow was Big Jake.

"You don't seem to get it," Gus said, his body tense, his voice tight. "That was my kid!"

She handed him a beer and opened one for herself. "Gus, you've spent so much of your life flarching other people you don't even know when you're flarching yourself."

"What?"

"You've got two kids already, and what do you do for them? Most of the time you either treat them like people you hardly know, or you ignore them totally. You want what you don't have. And this baby's gone beyond anyone's reach, so you want it more than anything else. If it had lived, it would have been the same damn story. You'd have fussed over it like crazy as long as it was small, and once it was old enough that it couldn't walk under the table without bumping its head, you'd have slid away."

"That's a hell of a thing to say!"

"It's true, Gus. The little ones don't judge, they don't have opinions, they don't find us inadequate or foolish or spiteful or anything other than bloody wonderful. By the time they get big enough to read the newspaper without help, they're people like everyone else and they know just how weak and two-faced we all are. And all of a sudden they aren't so much fun."

"I thought you were my friend."

"No need to change your mind about that. I like you, Gus, even though you'll probably never do anything except a variation on stuff you've already done."

"Jesus, woman. You're hard."

"No, I'm not. Let's make us a deal—you bullshit your friends and I'll bullshit my friends and neither of us will bullshit each other."

The Kate who went back to work was not the same Kate who had wakened a few weeks earlier with violent cramps and a sticky warmth between her legs. The Kate who went back to work was quieter, and yet somehow younger. She had lost more than a pregnancy, and in the losing had gained permission to be her age. She was only thirty-five years old and she didn't have to be as settled and sure as her mother was.

Before the weather was warm enough to move her azalea outside, Gus was busy sparking someone else. This time Kate didn't feel insecure, or inadequate, or angry. That was just how it was, how he was, how he would always be. She knew Gus, and she had learned that just as a hoe handle could cause blisters that eventually became protective callus, so an oft-repeated behaviour could rub, rub, rub, rub until heart and soul were toughened and sheathed. And that a person could get to the point where she just didn't give a good rat's ass any more.

Cedar couldn't remember much of what went on at home. At school she had a few puzzling gaps, and there were no gaps at all when it came to her job. She loved it. She was good at it. She knew she wouldn't spend her life at it, but for now she put the most into it and got the most out of it that she could. Given her choice, she'd have worked every night of the week, but push had come to shove. Kate had it set in her mind that Cedar would only work weekends, and it had taken an incredible effort to stretch the weekend in Kate's mind to include Sundays.

"But Mom," Cedar said, not arguing or nagging, "I get my homework done during the day, and if I don't finish it on Saturday before work, I do it Sunday for sure. And I sleep in both mornings and I'm done working at ten on Sunday nights. And I could sure use the money."

"What for?" Kate snapped. She knew Cedar was right and that she was cut off at the pass, but she wouldn't fold that easily.

"Because I'm as Scotch as any of the Campbells," Cedar teased. "Because every time Grandma Campbell sees me, she tells me over and over to be sure I can always pay my own way in the world and not wind up beholden to anyone. Because I want to buy a fire truck."

"A fire truck. Why would you—" And Kate realized she'd been had. She laughed, turned to face Cedar full on, and resisted the impulse to grab her and hug her. "You!" she laughed again. "You're as big a tease as your Aunt Marg. A fire truck!" And then they were both laughing, and for a moment Kate could pretend things were always this easy, this loving between herself and the stranger who was her daughter.

All the kids at school were talking about Janet Bridges' car accident. Gordon was out fishing and Janet had climbed out her bedroom window, sneaked off and joined up with some fast kids who were tooling around, drinking beer and being silly on a back road up past the lakes. The driver wasn't as experienced as he liked to think, especially when it came to dirt roads instead of streets and highways, and he had lost control on a hairpin turn. The car had left the logging road and rolled down a rocky embankment.

The rescue squad had used the Jaws of Life to chop the car in pieces and get Janet out, still alive, but barely. She was air-evacuated to the big hospital in the city and was actually on the operating table by the time a cop went around to the house and thumped on the door.

They said Janet was on the critical list, they said Beverly was in shock, they said Sheila was out of it, they said Gordon had wept for two hours. They said a lot, and some of it was true. What they didn't say, because they didn't know, was that Gus Campbell went out to his woodshed and screamed. And screamed and screamed and screamed. Rory and Cedar heard the screaming and ran to the shed, where Gus stood with his fists clenched at his sides, his head back, his face red, the cords in his neck standing out like metal rods, and his eyes streaming tears. "What's the matter?" they asked, and just to stir the pot and spread the misery around, he told them.

"And now," he wailed, "now what? Him as what's not her dad is over there sitting by her bedside holding her hand, and me as what is her dad is here, as if I had no entitlement."

"Poor you, eh?" Cedar said, and she walked away, in the direction of the pathway leading to the creek, Rory hurrying after her. When they got back, Gus was gone and so was the car. Cedar did her bit of homework, had a bath and went to bed, but Rory waited up for Kate.

"And he said he was her dad," he quavered. "He was real upset, and crying and yelling and everything."

"Don't worry about it, dear." Kate's voice was gentle but her eyes were hard. "It's just more dramatics for the benefit of the onlookers."

"Is he? Her dad?"

"What's her name?" Kate stroked Rory's hair. "Is it Campbell, like yours? No, it's not. She's called Janet Bridges, isn't she? Well, then. There you have it."

"But he said—"

"And now I'm saying." She kissed him between his dark eyebrows. "Now you give yourself a break, just let go of it."

Gus went on a bender that lasted the worst part of a week, and when he finally showed up again he was bleary-eyed and hungover. But his clothes were clean, so Kate knew that he hadn't been sleeping under a bridge. He walked in the back door and stood in the kitchen, looking owly and defiant.

"Don't ask," he challenged.

"I won't," she said indifferently.

"It's none of your business, anyway."

"I'm sure you're right," Kate nodded, without looking up from her ironing.

"I'm not answerable to you. You're not my mother."

"I know that, Gus, and have done for years now."

"Feeling snotty, aren't you?"

"Me?" She slipped a blouse onto a hanger. "I'm just carrying on with what I was doing before you came in the door. I've ironed the blouse and now I'm going to press the slacks."

"Don't get fresh, you hear?"

"Don't raise your hand to me, Gus." Her voice was pleasant, almost offhand, as if she was passing the time of day with one of her customers. "And don't bully me, either. If you've got a hangover, there are aspirin in the bathroom. If you need to catch up on your sleep, you know where the bedroom is. But don't bother taking it out on me."

"That's one helluva fine welcome home!" he shouted.

Kate didn't even bother answering.

When Cedar and Rory got home from school he was asleep, and he slept through their supper and evening routine. He was awake when Kate got home, sitting at the kitchen table eating a toasted fried egg sandwich and drinking a glass of milk.

"I've got something to tell you," he said.

"I don't want to hear it."

"Well, you're going to hear it."

"I've already heard enough, thank you. You just about scared the shit out of those kids, standing in the woodshed howling like a gutshot dog. And as if that wasn't enough, you had to tell them about Sheila Callahan and your bastard children."

Gus slammed his fist on the table. "Don't you call those children bastards!"

"Then you rip off in the car," she continued, as if he hadn't spoken, "and have yourself a public display, get good and drunk and stay that way for days, and when you're not drinking, you're in Bridget Riley's bed. After which you come home and try to pick a fight with me. That's enough. I don't want to hear the when and where, nor the why and how. Leave me out of it, and the children too."

"Don't you bloody well lecture me on how to live my life." There was no avoiding a go-round with him. When Gus got a hair across his arse like this, nothing anyone could do or say would keep him from getting the uproar he seemed to need. So she sat quietly while he yelled that she had ice water in her veins instead of blood, and how bitter it was for a man to be denied visits with his own blood children. He shouted as many hurting things as he could dredge up, and finally, when she'd had enough, she hit back. She threw in his face the secret she had thought she would carry to her grave.

That shut him up. He sat and stared at her, his face white, and for a moment she was sure he would fly across the table and kill her. But there he sat, slack-jawed and wordless.

Kate walked out of the room, drew herself a hot bath and sat there until the water calmed her down enough to sleep. When she went to bed, Gus was still sitting at the table, only now, he was drinking whiskey instead of milk. In the morning he was gone, and when she got home from work that night, he was asleep in their bed.

Kate Larson Campbell spent the night on the couch, and the next day she moved her things into the spare bedroom. Nobody said a thing about it.

The summer Cedar finished grade eleven, Kate leapt recklessly and wholeheartedly into an affair with Ted Conrad. Even before he arrived to spend his annual leave getting the farm ready to sell, Kate knew she was going to dive into the whirling sensations and wallow in the touch, taste, smell and sight of him. She didn't care if the whole world found out and tattooed a scarlet *A* on her forehead She didn't care if Marg called her a fool, or if her brothers thought her a slut and a whore, she didn't even care if her mother and father heard about it.

The flower shop sent someone over to Mom's on Kate's birthday, and the basket of flowering plants sat in a place of honour atop the partition between the licensed dining room and the old café. Kate hid the card in Cedar's baby book. For Christmas there was a basket with fruit, cheeses and fancy sausages—easy to take that home and let everyone think it was by way of being a thank-you from work. The card that came with that went into Rory's baby book. And she knew, because he told her on the phone, that the V-neck vest she'd knitted for him was exactly what he needed in the dreadful cold of an Ontario winter, and, he said, each time he put it on he felt her arms around him. Kate hadn't told him about the miscarriage, she hadn't even told him she'd got caught pregnant. She didn't want to put pressure of any kind on him.

"Who gets all these socks you knit?" Rory demanded. "How come I never get any?"

"You want some socks? I'll knit some for you."

"Nah, it's okay. I just wondered."

"Well, there's the hospital auxiliary, and the Salvation Army, and . . ."

That was the only part of living a lie that bothered her—how easily the people she loved the most trusted her and swallowed her lies without question.

She knitted Rory a vest, then made a sweater for Cedar. She knitted winter pullovers for each of Marg's kids, a vest for Olaf and a cardigan for Karen. But mostly she knitted socks. She sat on a chair with her feet up, knitting and wondering how Ted was. She wondered what his apartment was like, and whether he made breakfast in the morning or just grabbed a coffee and drove to the base to eat in the mess hall.

She knew to the day when he would arrive, and she knew when and where he'd be sitting in his dad's car, waiting for her. After work she got in her own car and drove from Mom's parking lot down the highway, past the turnoff to her own place and on to the viewpoint. And there it was, the big old car with the faded paint job. She parked her car and there he was, smiling, wrapping his arms around her, kissing her, the two of them laughing, both of them talking at once.

She would gladly have stayed until starvation set in. But finally, reluctantly, she left him and drove home, hardly aware of where she was or what she was doing. She went straight to bed—no knitting, no tea, and fell asleep so fast it was like the flip of a light switch, plunging the room into darkness.

She couldn't believe that nobody noticed. She felt as if his kisses must glow on her skin, his touch leave golden tracks. After school let out for the summer, Cedar worked every evening and Kate worried that some evening she might be sitting watching TV or reading a book, waiting for Kate. But Cedar was always in bed, her light out.

Gus wasn't going to find out. They weren't officially separated, but he was busy being Gus and they seldom saw each other. When they did, they were so polite they may as well have been strangers. And that was fine with her.

Six weeks. She would have six weeks with him, and she would gorge herself, storing up memories, sensations, treasures to pull out later and relive, because after this the rest of the year was going to seem cold and hollow and very very dry.

Rory was working for the summer, too, in a day job—babysitting for Marg and Hank's kids. Marg had gone back to work part-time and Hank had brought home a wading pool, and about all Rory had to do was play in the water with the kids until they got cranky, then put them down for an afternoon nap. While they slept, he could laze around, and when they wakened, it was juice and snack time. Then it was back out to the wading pool with them, until Marg came home. Some days he ate supper with them, other days he rode his bike home and fixed something for himself. Often he went to the river and swam with the other kids until the light was fading and the mosquitoes appeared in hordes, then he went down to Mom's for hamburger and fries or fish and chips. Nick had offered him a job as busboy, but Rory turned it down. "Next year," he smiled. "I'm not ready yet. I like my summers."

Most mornings Kate hurried through her chores and then piled into the car with Cedar and drove to Marg's to pick up Rory and the kids and go to the river. Most days Ted was already there, lying on his towel, soaking up the sunshine, pretending it was sheer accident that they had wound up at the same place again.

"How come you don't go swimming at the lake up by the farm?" Cedar asked.

You could tell Ted hadn't spent much time around little kids. He wasn't easy with them. He didn't mind them, but he seemed to think they were like everyone else, only smaller.

He was good with the older ones, though. He and Cedar would race down the rock, yodelling and yelling, and dive into the river and swim as far as they could underwater. The first few times they did it, Ted got farther from the bank than Cedar did. She took it as a challenge, and pushed herself until she could swim almost to the other bank.

Other mornings, Kate caught up on her sleep, barely waking up in time to take Rory and his bike to Marg's place. And several times she got up before anyone else and left a note on the table, something like "Had to go to town," so Rory would get himself to Marg's. But she did not go to town. She went up to the farm, where Ted was picking away steadily but slowly, trying to talk Joe Conrad into retiring.

Joe wasn't of a mind to do it, though. He saw no reason at all to put good farmland on the market so some weasel could buy it and start building peas-in-a-pod subdivision houses. "Look," he said, pointing, and his proof was there for anybody who knew how the place had looked only a few years ago. The evergreens were gone, and what had been bush was changed forever. Neighbourhoods spread down the slope, and from the sawdust pit on, all you could see were roofs—red ones, green ones, black ones, grey ones, roofs made of cedar shingles, shakes, asphalt tiles, one after the other, with small patches of green lawn, and straight black lines that were streets. "Look at that. You think anyone else is going to farm this place? The price of land being what it is now?"

Bob and Sis Lambert still lived in their big old house, but they had sold off all but ten acres of their farm. Sis had put on weight, and she had the first sprinklings of grey in her hair. "And damn those electric guitars! When it was just Chuck twanging away, it was okay— Bob fixed up a room in the basement, soundproofed it as best he could. But then, wouldn't you know it, Buster had to get himself one, too. Then Sandy decided he was going to be a drummer. Listen, that did it. Don't laugh, I mean it! Jesus Aitch, two guitars with the amps turned up to max and a full set of drums hammering away. So Bob and I double-insulated the creamery house and fixed up the wiring, then banished them. Then their friends started to show up with *their* instruments. My God, half the time I don't know whose kid is coming down the walkway." The boys were out of school now, but still living at home. "Why not, where else will they get a setup like this? Room and board at the family discount, plus a place to make their uproar."

Sis knew all about Kate and Ted. She'd caught on the first time she saw Kate's car going up the road.

"Who am I to criticize?" she said. "God knows you hung in longer than I would have. Does the crazy bugger know?"

Kate shrugged. "I hardly even see him."

"Christ, what a loss, eh?"

"You got it."

"Well, at least you snagged yourself a good-looking one. He's flogging a dead horse, though, if he thinks he's going to get old Joe retired and sitting on the porch of the Silver Threads Old Folks Retreat. That old bugger is going to die with his hogs or not at all."

Joe had his hunches about what was going on, too, but he kept them to himself. Sometimes he asked Kate how Cedar was, and if there was any chance she'd come to see him—just for a visit, mind you.

"I like that girl," he said. "I used to pretend she was mine. There she'd be, not much bigger than the piglets herself, going from pen to pen as if there wasn't any stink or mud or poop or anything, and she'd pour in that grain mix so carefully, she knew spilling it was like throwing money into the ditch. And good with the piglets! I swear she understood every oink and grunt they made." He looked at his son. "Now Ted did his work, always did his work, and he did it well. But he didn't love those pigs like she did. He didn't ever just stand there watching them, talking to them as if they understood every word."

"Dad, you're talking about pigs. You've seen one, you've seen them all. And smelled them, too. You're right, I couldn't wait to get the hell off the farm!"

"See how it is in life? There you were, and you could have had it all at any time. But you didn't want it. And there was Cedar, and she'd have given anything for it. Maybe I'll just up and change my will, leave the farm to her."

"Fine by me," Ted laughed. "I've told you right out, you die and leave this to me and the place'll be sold so fast you won't have time to roll over in your grave!"

Kate wondered what Ted's life was like in Ontario, at the base, where he fit in and felt comfortable. Here he was out of his element. She couldn't begin to imagine him working in the pulp mill, or running small planes, or flying firewatch for the forest service. He was a jet pilot, it was what he had always wanted to be.

It seemed natural to suggest to the kids that they come up to the farm with her one afternoon. "Ted's invited us." How easily she handled lies, deceptions, half-truths! "You used to practically live there," she reminded Cedar. "You and your piglets."

"I think I'll pass," Rory said. "I'd sooner go to the town dump and chase seagulls than stand in the stink of a pack of pigs."

Cedar got out of the car grinning, and went over to hug old Joe Conrad as easily as if she'd seen him the day before.

"Hey, girl! How's Gramps's favourite?"

"I missed you."

"Me or the pigs?"

"You more than the pigs."

"Come see them," he said, and they walked off to the farrowing shed together.

"And hello to you, too." Ted shook his head. "Those two. Are you sure they aren't blood-related?"

As the magic days and nights passed, Kate found herself almost looking forward to the time when Ted would catch his flight to the city and go back to what she thought of as his real life. That way she could get back to her real life. She was busy every minute. Sometimes when she was lying in the bathtub or kneeling in the dirt weeding her garden, it seemed to her that life would be more manageable if she only saw him after work for a few hours of stolen pleasure. The other parts of it, the visits to the farm, the supposedly accidental encounters at the beach, were just too much work. The fact was they had next to nothing in common. She wondered why she had been more in danger of falling in love when he was miles and months away than she was now, with him right here. Is that why she had chosen to get involved with Ted— because she knew he wasn't staying forever, or even for very long? Had she chosen him because he was perfectly safe?

Cedar enjoyed her visits to the hog farm. It was more like coming home than anything—more, even, than biking down the highway after work, parking the bike at the back porch and going into the kitchen. That wasn't home, that was Kate and Gus's home, which was no home at all. The hog farm was home, because the very air was loose and easy, not tight with that feeling that the other shoe could fall at any moment, the balloon go up, all hell bust loose, over a big thing or nothing much at all. She didn't have to watch every word, she didn't have to be careful, she didn't even have to look at the little house where she could still see the knife quivering after it had stuck in the wall, inches from Kate's head. That house was gone, replaced by a three-bedroom split-level with a big picture window.

"What do you think of this?" Gramps dropped a magazine in her lap. "Think it would be worthwhile?"

She read the article, her uneasiness growing with each paragraph. The old man sat on the steps, smoking cigarettes and waiting for her reaction.

"My God." She shook her head. "Apart from the fact it would cost an arm and a leg to set yourself up this way, what in hell kind of life is that for the pig?"

"I don't think they're worried about the pig."

"One thing about it, there'd be enough equipment and gear to get Ted interested, then maybe he'd consider taking over. But how good is it for their feet, living on heavy mesh, up off the floor like that? You'd think their toes would, like, poke in and—you know?"

"Easier to keep them clean."

"Yeah, sure, according to this you just waltz from pen to pen with a high-pressure hose and blast the turds through the mesh and on to the honey bucket. Sure, it would work, but—"

"Like a factory," he sighed. "One of those assembly lines."

Cedar looked around at the pens, most of them empty now, the numbers reduced to what Gramps could manage now that he was older and increasingly frail. "If you switched over to this, on this acreage, you could probably run, oh, what do you think, a couple of thousand sows? Mind you, the place would be covered with big sheds, like aircraft hangars, and you'd spend all your time indoors, but if a person was to go into a pork factory—" She put the magazine aside. "I guess you wouldn't call it farming any more, right? I kind of like the part about the automatic feeders, though."

He laughed. "No need to have little kids shovin' wheelbarrows between the rows."

"What I'd do," Cedar dared, "is move the sows one by one over into the empty pens, then you could get in with the tractor and clean out the ones they've been using. Put down some sawdust, let them air out. Then you could do it all again. Keep moving them, into pens that have been cleaned and dried, give the flooring a chance to repair itself."

"You think we could move them? They might be feisty."

"We could do it. Make them a walkway between the middle pens, send 'em where the kid went with the wheelbarrow, with pens on either side to keep them from taking off. We could order a few truckloads of sawdust from the cedar mill, stockpile it."

"Good idea. Want to?"

"You want to?"

"If you do."

Ted reacted as if they were both crazier'n bedbugs, but that didn't bother Gramps any more than it bothered Cedar.

When Ted went to climb up on the tractor to move sawdust into the pens at the far side, Gramps stopped him. "Best let Cedar learn how," he suggested. "She'll have to do it after you've gone back to be a paid assassin again."

"If they're paying me to be an assassin they aren't getting their money's worth—I haven't killed anyone yet. Haven't even had the chance to blow up an orphanage or send a rocket into a hospital."

"Oh, just hang tight, son, you'll get your chance."

Cedar had fun learning the tractor. She spent several days taking sawdust from one side of the pile and dumping it over on the other side, pushing the pile from where it had been to where it was before she moved it back to where it used to be. When she could do it, and do it without getting so nervous she thought she might barf, she started taking sawdust down to the long-empty pens and dumping it in until it was a foot deep. As each pen was ready, she and Gramps moved a sow into it. It was easy, all they had to do was make sure they gave the sow enough time and space that she thought it was her idea to heave herself over and investigate the new area.

Some nights when Cedar went off shift at Mom's, Ted would be waiting to drive her over to Gramps's. She'd have a tea and natter with him, then go to bed in the spare room, get up farm-early in the morning and clean pens or move sawdust or check piglets or help a farrowing sow, until it was time for Ted to take her back to the house to get ready to go to Mom's again. Her days off were spent at the hog farm, and she made no secret of the fact that those were her favourite times of all.

"Jeez, we hardly even see you any more," Rory groused.

"Well, come on over sometime. It's great. I'll show you how to run the tractor."

"Maybe." But he didn't. He didn't fit into Cedar's chosen world any more than she fit into the world he shared with Old Doc Forbes, and he knew it.

Ted finally headed back to the city, and his absence had little impact on Cedar's life. Granted, it wasn't as easy to get over to the farm. Gramps had offered to come and pick her up but she didn't want him driving at night—as daylight faded he was apt to stumble just walking from the house to the shed, along a path he'd known for years. God knows what would happen if he drove in the dark along a highway that was almost always choked with traffic.

There are no problems, however, only challenges—that's what Grandma Campbell always said whenever something was trying its best to go wrong. For example there was the 10:30 bus into town, and she didn't mind if Gramps met her there and drove the few miles to the farm. For sure she'd have to figure out something else, but for now, it would do.

And school was waiting, with the necessary runaround to get ready. She needed new clothes, she needed new shoes, she needed her school supplies, and it would be nice to have a pack to carry them in.

"I'm going in camp," Gus announced.

They looked at him like people who were caught flat-footed when the graven image in the corner began to speak in tongues.

"Well, why not?" He sounded defiant, even though nobody had said a word against the idea. "I can make better money there." He waited, but still nobody spoke.

It was one of Kate's days off and she'd made pot roast, with the spuds and vegetables cooked around it, the kitchen full of aromas guaranteed to make a person drool.

"Pass the gravy, please," Rory said.

"Is that all you've got to say?" Gus challenged.

For a moment something sparked in Rory's eyes, but then he smiled. "Sounds like you've thought it all out," he said soothingly.

"Damn right I have."

"Then I guess that's all there is to it, Dad. You know the ins and outs and you've thought it out, right?"

"That's all there is to it," Gus agreed, but his tone wasn't the least bit agreeable. They all knew it wouldn't take much for him to pitch a fit and jump into the middle of it, work it out so the real reason he was going in camp was that his wife was a nag, his kids were a pain in the ass and it was the only way a man could get any peace.

"When are they going back in?" Cedar asked, not really giving the first part of a hoot one way or the other. "Fire season's still on, isn't it?"

"It's on but it won't be for much longer. I can go in with the first crew, check everything out, get everything set up for when the real work starts. It's lower wages for that, of course, but I might as well get paid for painting the cookshack as sit on Unemployment Enjoyment watching my toenails grow."

Nobody pointed out that he hadn't been around anyway, that he had ostensibly spent his fire season time at the Domino Club. That was part of the game they all played, and even if the rules had never been spoken aloud, they were observed and followed, because to break the rules was to bring down the roof.

"I suppose you'll need extra work clothes," said Kate, passing a platter of vegetables to Cedar. "And plenty of socks, too. I can get you some when I go to town."

"I guess I can buy my own socks. I guess I can do that much."

Cedar and Rory had been back in school for more than two weeks when Gus headed into camp. In other houses, where other men were heading off, there were farewell suppers and family nights out, there were special cakes, or plans being made for everyone to go down to the dock and wave goodbye as the camp boat headed off. But not at the Campbells'. Kate drove Gus to his mother's house the night before he left, then went home to sit in a nice tub of water and read a few pages before going to her own room.

Life with Gus in camp wasn't all that different from life with Gus at home, since he hadn't been around much anyway. All too often his presence had brought fear, pain or both, and nobody missed that at all.

Kate couldn't say life was perfect, but compared to some periods in her life, this one was fine by her. She supposed she was lucky that Cedar had stayed in school, aimed at finishing grade twelve and graduating. So many other girls made it to grade ten and then swanned away, thinking their job at Mom's or whatever was a lot more fun, and proof of overnight adult status. Some aimed higher and got jobs at the Bay selling perfume or shoes, or working in the camera shop. They said they were "in retail," which meant they worked for minimum wage—less than they would have earned as waitresses.

Cedar could easily have been one of those girls. She could have quit school, got a job, left home, given it all up for a place of her own. So Kate told herself she was silly and selfish to feel so cut off from Cedar when she stayed the weekend at the hog farm instead of coming home. She was home again on Monday after school, wasn't she?

But the weekends were the times Kate actually had a chance to see her. And now the sows got to spend more time with her than her own mother did! And besides, Rory shouldn't be alone so much. He was perfectly capable of doing for himself, and she left casseroles for him to heat up, and he often biked down to Mom's to have supper or to visit with her during her break. But a young boy—well, not young, really, but a boy—could easily get in trouble if he was left alone so long every day.

Not that he did, mind you. No trouble of that nature, touch wood and thank God. He seemed content with his own company. Sometimes he went over to Marg's place and Hank would drive him home, no question about that. Other times he caught the highway bus and went to visit old Doc Forbes, and Forbes drove him home in plenty of time for bed. Once she asked Rory what they talked about, and Rory laughed and said they'd done bones and muscles and were into veins and arteries. Well, ask a silly question and you get a silly answer.

Both she and Ted knew that their affair, or whatever it was, had changed. They had talked about it, but neither of them had any answers. Maybe it was the distance between them, or another case of nothing lasts forever. It was like sitting down to a great big turkey dinner that you'd been looking forward to for days and prepared for by skipping breakfast and lunch, and there it was, perfectly wonderful, and you ate and ate and ate, and then suddenly you didn't want another bite. But you couldn't just pick up the carcass with all that meat clinging to it and toss it to the dog! Especially when you didn't even have a dog.

So they hadn't called it off, and Kate wondered if they had both put on the brakes for the same reason—not slowing down was too dangerous, would demand too much. Ted was a military pilot, so he went where the air force sent him, and she had no intention of tucking her kids under her arms and following him from place to place. What if he got posted to a small town where the snow piled up higher than the bottom of the windows and you had to plug your car in at night? What would she do all day, sit around and wait for the man to get home? Who would she talk to? And she could just about imagine what it would be like living with two West Coast kids who had got ripped out of their homes and plunked down in the middle of a blizzard. She could hear Rory—"You're kidding, right?" And Cedar! The up and down of that was easy—Cedar would simply refuse to go. The thought of that was like a skewer in Kate's heart. She was so insecure in and about her relationship with her daughter that she couldn't bear the prospect of being rejected, flat out and for all the world to see.

Nick was busy with architects and designers. Things were going so well at Mom's that he had decided to start up a second restaurant. The north end of town was opening up and more and more people were moving in, all of them needing a place to go for a good meal and a few drinks—maybe, if Nick had his way, even a dance or two. The guy he'd hired to look at his plans had told him that was a bad idea, Too much space taken up and no cash coming from it, and besides that, dancing happened in the hard bars—the young people liked noise and crowds and music that thumped and banged and pounded. "Ah," Nick argued, "but the world is full of older people who like to dance." If Nick went ahead with his idea anyway, Kate knew, it was going to bring about big changes in her life. He had asked her to take over Mom's full time and on her own.

Cedar was just about ready to find a way to grow wings, so she could fly to and from school rather than taking the bus, where that dreary Marjory Peel clung to her like a limpet to a rock.

"We haven't seen your dad for a long time."

"He's in camp."

"In camp?" The dozey thing sounded as if she'd never heard of it.

"Yeah, in camp."

"We didn't know. He didn't say. Will he be gone long?"

"They're in six weeks, then out two, until the snow shuts them down."

"Can you write to them?"

"I don't know."

"You mean you don't write to him?"

"Do you work for the cops or are you writing a book?"

"Beg pardon?"

"Why all the questions? What do you care if I write to him or not."

"It's called conversation, Cedar." Marjory did her best to look adult and sophisticated, instead of dumpy and pug-nosed and poking around in other people's business. "It's called being friendly."

"Why are you trying so hard to be friendly?"

"I told you, because we're almost siblings."

"My ass," Cedar laughed. "You're not a Campbell, nor a Larson, either. Or don't you know your own name?"

"Yes, I know my name," Marjory hissed. "My name is Peel. And my father's name was Steve, and we're descended from John Peel, the guy in the song."

"Nothing to brag about," Rory laughed. "Bloody murderer."

You'd think things like that would slow her down, but no, not her. She was back a few afternoons later, hanging around with that strange smile, part determined, part hesitant. "My mom says maybe you and I could get along better if I told you how it is we're almost sisters."

"I don't need any explanation from you, or your mother. You think I don't know my dad dinks your mom? And your aunt? Both at the same time, for all I know. They're not special. They're on a very long list. My dad has probably dinked half the women in town."

"Yeah," Rory agreed, "and if you're not careful you'll be on the list, too."

"Don't be such a dirty-mouthed little child." Marjory was back to being oh so lofty and sophisticated. "He would never do that. Anyway," and she fought back with the few tiny weapons she had, "I call him Dad and he calls me—"

"My bonny lassie."

Marjory gaped.

Cedar shrugged. "He calls all his girls that. Probably because he's had so many he can't remember our names."

"God, you're mean."

"It's called truth, dear." Cedar did such a good imitation of poor Marjory putting on airs that even Marjory recognized it. "You really should try it sometime."

That kept Marjory away for almost a week, and then there she was again, smile and all, insinuating herself, not knowing or not caring that most of the kids on the bus couldn't wait for the next installment so they could take it home and share it with their parents, and they would all have a good laugh. That was what Cedar couldn't forgive. They would be laughing at her, too. Trust Gus to spread himself around and think no one would notice. Trust him not to care whether Cedar wound up as part of the comedy show, same as if she was being a goof herself.

Janet Bridges was back in school, still recovering from the accident. She got around in a wheelchair, although she could feel her legs a bit and the physiotherapist had said she might walk again some day. But you couldn't feel sorry for someone who refused to feel sorry for herself. Give her that much, Cedar thought, she's got guts. She had even gone from class to class to talk about drinking and driving.

"Your half-sister is very brave," Marjory said sweetly.

Cedar looked up from her paperback novel. She had hoped John Peel's however-many-times-great granddaughter would take the hint and keep her trap shut. So much for hope.

"Janet Bridges. Going to classes and talking about being crippled and all. You must feel proud that she's your half-sister."

Cedar almost put her foot in it. She almost said don't be silly, or fall on your lip, or I don't know what you're talking about, you fool. But she knew. Even if she couldn't quite remember the screaming meemie in the woodshed, something clicked inside her head and she knew exactly what Pain-in-the-Jaw Peel was saying. So she shrugged, as if the whole thing was unimportant.

"You mean you aren't proud of her?"

"What's to be proud of?" Cedar spoke with more scorn than she felt. It was that spiteful little smile, that burning shove-this-up-your-nose look in her eyes. "She was jackassing around in a car with a bunch of boozers, and she got tabbed."

"I'm not sure, if circumstances were different," Marjory said prissily, "that I'd be able to roll my chair into a classroom and talk about being disabled. She even admitted herself that she'd done a stupid, stupid thing. That takes courage, Cedar, real courage."

"Yeah? Well, what do you expect?" Cedar aimed for the tenderest bull's-eye. "She's a Campbell. We wouldn't expect anything less of her."

"Maybe she knows people are gossiping," Rory suggested as they walked home from the bus stop. "Maybe all this hanging around on the bus and making sure everyone sees her talking to us, all this yap yap about almost being a sister, maybe she's trying to ram it down their damn throats and choke 'em on it."

"Does it bother you?" Cedar asked.

"Sure it does. You think I like knowing that half the damn town expects me to be just like him? And the other half don't expect it but won't be surprised if it happens. Every time the asshole pulls another stunt, people I hardly know come up and talk to me, as if they think I'm the grand source of the latest dirt."

"It's them laughing that ticks me off."

"So maybe it gripes Marjory, too."

"She's a spiteful cow."

"Maybe not. I mean, think about it. Her mom *and* her aunt?"

Cedar did think about it. But not much and not for long. She had her own worries, and whatever was stuck in Marjory's throat was Marjory's problem.

And so she was caught off guard when the very next morning they had no sooner boarded the bus than Rory went up to Marjory, sitting with her nose in the air as if she was alone on the bus, and said clearly, "Hi, sis. How's things?"

Cedar showed no reaction at all. If Rory wanted to laugh and gossip and talk and hee haw with Marjory, fine. The world was full of paperback novels and she already had a reputation for being a bookworm.

The funny thing was, the minute Rory started being palsy-walsy with Marjory, all the yip about Gus stopped. No more how's your dad, no more gee he's a nice guy, no more have you heard from him. There weren't even any more digs about the Bridges girls.

With Gus in camp, the tension in the house was as good as gone. There was no need to keep a part of yourself always on guard, just in case. And two nights during the week, on Kate's days off, they had the kind of sit-down-together family supper everyone else in town probably had all the time. Sometimes Kate invited Auntie Marg and Uncle Hank and the kids, and everyone had a ball, talking and joking, everyone passing stuff to everyone else and the little kids excited and laughing. Other nights it would be turnabout and off they'd go to Auntie Marg's for supper, driving up to the house with a big fresh-baked cake or a couple of pies. Cedar and Rory would scoop up the carpet creepers and take them into their bedroom to play tickle-and-laugh.

"More, more!" Chrissie demanded, trying to climb up Cedar's leg.

"More? Okay, come on," and Cedar took the tiny wrists in her hands and lifted so that Chris could step up her belly and chest, almost to her chin, then flip herself over into a backward somersault between Cedar's arms.

"Again!"

"You sure?"

"More."

Now that Cedar knew what she knew about Beverly and Janet, it was so obvious that she felt silly for not having caught on sooner. Both of them had Gus Campbell's stamp on them. Both of them looked more like Cedar and Rory than Chrissie did, or even Suzie for that matter. They might carry Gordon Bridges' name, but that was all. Cedar wondered if they knew about her and Rory. She wondered how many other kids with different names had the stamp. And if any of *them* knew.

Cedar figured Rory was probably bored stiff, but he played with Tony's trucks and cars, steering carefully around the blocks Suzie was stacking up then knocking over again, a jumble of red, blue, green and yellow squares and rectangles. Every now and again Cedar wondered just how smart—or not—Suzie was. Weren't kids supposed to try out all kinds of stuff, learning and sampling? At the rate she was going, Suzie might be stacking blocks and toppling them when she was forty-seven.

"I'n sittin' on you knee," Chris announced.

"*I'm,*" Cedar corrected her. "Watch my mouth. Mmmmm. See, you do it with your lips shut. Mmmm. When you do *N* you do it with your teeth."

"I'm sittin' on you knee."

"And I bet you think you're going to gobble down all my dinner, too."

"Here." Chris handed Cedar a toy car. "You do."

"You do it." Cedar sat on the floor, beside Suzie. "We're going to do blocks."

And like that, Chrissie was into the car game with Tony. Rory moved over to sit near Suzie. She smiled at him. He patted his knee and she plunked herself between his legs, leaning back against him.

"What did you do today?" Rory asked.

"I washed my dolly's hair. And I played with the dog. I threw a ball and she brought it to me."

"Did you chase the ball?"

"I sat on the step. The dog chased the ball."

"How high can you count today?"

"One, two, free, four, five, six, sebben."

"Eight."

"One, two, free, four, five, six, sebben, eight."

"Nine, ten, eleven, a dozen." Chrissie called.

"Twelb."

"A dozen."

"Twelb!" Suzie shouted angrily. "Twelb, Kissie!"

"Twelve *is* a dozen." Rory soothed.

Cedar went into the kitchen to see if she could help and wound up mashing and creaming the spuds.

"Of course it's mostly house plants at this time of year," Marg was saying, "and a few bouquets. About all I'll be doing is answering the phone or filling orders and delivering them. But it's a nice break."

"And the kids?"

"Mom and Dad twisted my rubber arm. I had checked out some babysitters and had just about decided on one, and I mentioned it to Mom, and she nearly pulled out every shred of my hair. I mean, I had thought they'd be—well, when you get older you've *done* your babysitting. But no. And Dad! My God, he was worse than Mom. Then Hank's mom got into it—I was expecting them to start wrist-twisting, winner takes all."

Suzie sat in the booster chair Uncle Hank had made for her, and she let everyone know she wanted a dozen green beans, a dozen bites of spud, a dozen bites of meat loaf.

"Rory says twelb is a dozen," she announced.

"I said first," Chris reminded her. "I said dozen, you said twelb. You *shouted* twelb."

"I did not."

"You did so."

"Did *not!*"

"Only a little holler, eh Suzie," Rory said, and the tantrum was averted.

"She lies." Chrissie sat on Cedar's knee, and, ignoring her own plate, ate from the bigger one. "Suzie tells lies, don't she Tony."

"Shut up," Tony glared. "Just shut up, Chrissie."

"You'd better all three shut up," Auntie Marg said calmly, "or I'm going to rip out your liver and hit you on the bum with it."

"Ouch!" Rory laughed. "Oh, poor bum."

"I've never seen such competition," Marg sighed. "It's unending."

"It's because they're twins," said Rory, sounding as sure of himself as one of the adults. "They're doing some incredible research on twins, identical and fraternal. Even twins who were given up for adoption at birth and went to two different families—there they are, and they're both, like, soccer players with red bikes and a dog they call Buster, or whatever. I read about two guys in Sweden who were like that—even got married on the same day, to blond women who both had the same name."

"Well, yeah, they'd be blond if they were in Sweden, wouldn't they?" Hank teased.

"And then there are others who are total opposites. As if they'd had to spend so much time together before they were born that they got sick of the sight and sound of each other."

"Anyway," Chrissie nagged. "She tattletales."

Marg turned to Kate. "I used to think you were nuts. I'd think my God, if I had two gorgeous kids like that, just see if I'd get a job."

They both laughed.

Grandma Campbell was more involved, too, now that Gus was out of the picture. Maybe she felt as tense and as uneasy with him as the rest of them, always bracing herself for the next stunt. "Come see me more often," she said to Cedar. "I enjoy your company. We'll have us a wee Scrupach. Ye'll be on yer ain soon, and there's things ye should know."

Cedar accepted the invitation.

"It's the spirit, the energy," Mary Campbell explained. "There's more, too, but a wee bit at a time is better learned than tae much at once . . . when ye've finished your tea, see, the leaves make a pattern. So what I do is swirl, and I do it widdershins or counter-clockwise. And what that is, see, is that in *this* world, if ye've a choice of which way tae go, pick the right, all the time. Go with the clock, see. But Scrupach isn'ae of this world, so I do it otherwise. Four times I do it. For the directions, you see. Then I tip it up, so, and set it on its saucer so the last of the tea drains out. And in a bit, a wee bit time, we'll go on to the next." She smiled and patted Cedar's hand. "So, have ye plans yet, for when ye've finished school?"

"Well, Gramps—that's Mr. Conrad—says I can live at his place. The bus route goes up there now and it's way lots closer to town. I'd like that, I like helping with the pigs and such. And I guess—just a job, you know, the best I can find. It'll depend on how much it pays. You know me and money, I'll take the best paying, even if it's mucky."

"If ye've a mind to go on, university or teacher's college or whatever, there's money set aside for it."

"Thank you. I thought of that, Grandma, but . . . it's not what I want to do. I could do it, my marks are good enough, but I'm not like Rory. He knows he's going because he wants to be a doctor. I don't. Nor a lawyer, either. No use going if it isn't for something."

"There's nae young man in the picture?"

"Me?" Cedar laughed. "No, Grandma, that's about the last thing on my list."

"I had a sister like that," Mary confided. "Said the mere thought of it made her feel ill. And she never did, either." She turned the cup right way round on the saucer, and looked in it.

"Busy," she said. "Verra busy." Mary took something from her apron pocket, held it in her left hand and pressed the hand to her chest, above her heart. Then she put her right hand over the cup and examined Cedar's face. "The past is called Annwn, and that's always a confusion. It's the time we've been learning, picking our way." She spoke so softly Cedar had to lean forward and concentrate on hearing. "And the future is Ceugant, and to find her we have to be able to see our way through the past, understand at least that there has been a struggle, and, hopefully, understand what it was about. And the here and now, is Gwynedd, and she's pure, and waiting for us to live our lives properly, and well. If we do, the future will be calm, and fine, and fulfilling." She paused. "So tell me what some of the past anger is about."

"Oh," Cedar said, "same as everyone else, I guess."

"There's naething, *naething* at all about you that is the same as everyone else," Mary Campbell said sternly. "So that's one place ye've to do a lot of work, my darling, sorting out the past. It's like mucking out the basement trying to find what causes that wee bit of an off smell that taints the rest of the house. It might only be a wee dead mousie in a corner, but until ye find it and pitch it, there'll be that wee bit smell."

For some reason Cedar burst into tears. She couldn't have said why—it sure as hell wasn't the thought of the little dead mousie in the corner!—but on she wept, and Mary sat quietly and let her do it.

Cedar began to visit her grandparents regularly, and sometimes she spent the night. Colin always smiled when he saw her coming, and at suppertime he'd sit at the head of the table and look almost smug. He called her hen, or ma wee henny, and when he asked her about school she knew he was honestly interested, not just filling the silence. After supper Cedar insisted on doing the washing up, and Mary would pour tea for herself and Colin, then sit and smile.

"I could well be the Queen of England," Mary said. "Just taking my ease and letting my muscles go slack."

"T' hell with the bloody English," the old man would snap. "Bein' queen of that lot would be a step down in life for ye."

Uncle Gordon taught Cedar how to rattle two spoons together in time to the music he played on his button accordion. Sometimes Tamas would play his fiddle, and every now and again, if they were lucky, Uncle Ewen would show up with Aunt Patience and the kids and he'd play his harmonica, which he could make sound like just about anything you'd care to name. His train whistle was so good you almost expected a freight to come down the hallway and through the living room.

Grandma Campbell gave Cedar a small notebook in which she'd marked the symbols of Ogham, the ancient alphabet of the Scots. "They're the twigs from the branches of the tree of life, see?" After that, she began tucking little messages in with Cedar's lunch—pencil lines on a piece of paper, or little trails of jam on the top of her sandwich, or icing designs on a piece of cake. After a while Cedar began to find ways to leave messages of her own, scratching with her fingernails on the bar of soap in the bathroom or arranging a few toothpicks on the tablecloth.

When Mary decided she was going to do Scrupach, the men left the house, no questions asked. The signal was in the kind of tea Mary used. If she took tea bags out of the cannister, the others came to the table to have a cup or two and some scones with jam. But if it was leaf tea, stored in the lovely green can with the tight-fitting top, the men reached for their jackets and caps.

"I'll be off for a wee bit," Colin would say, as if it was all his idea in the first place. "Get me a wee breath of air."

"I'll come with you, Da," Tamas would say, and off they'd go.

Gus got out of camp for his two-week break and walked in the back door to the kitchen with a grin on his face. "Hey, hey, hey," he laughed, going directly to the sink and putting in a wet, squirming sack. "Caught fresh this morning," he bragged. "Two apiece, we can have them for supper."

But their lives weren't on his schedule any more. Cedar didn't even know he was out of camp until he'd been back for almost three full days, because she went to the farm after school on Fridays and was gone all weekend. Rory was busing on the weekends and went to work as soon as he had gone home from school, showered and changed into black trousers, white shirt and clip-on bow tie.

"Who are you?" Gus teased.

"Maître d' in training," Rory smiled, and anyone would have thought that it came easily, that there was no fear lurking behind the smile, that Gus had never taken a belt to him and beaten him until he couldn't stand up.

Gus held on to his smile. He'd be damned if he let anyone know he was disappointed. He cooked the crab, then shelled it and very carefully removed every scrap of meat. He put it in a dish in the fridge and took the shells to the garden to bury them in the tomato bed. Then he got in his car and drove to the Domino Club. He got into a poker game but didn't stay long enough to do anything except break even.

"Getting old," he laughed, "too bloody tired to concentrate."

"They work your arse off in camp, that's for sure," someone agreed.

"You've been there, right?" someone else chimed in, and they all laughed—everyone had been there at one time or another.

Rory and Kate were back from work when he got home again. They ate some of the crab and pronounced it delicious, but he could tell they were both as tired as he'd made himself out to be.

"You're sure it's not a bit much for him?" he asked Kate.

"I told him," she said, "the first sign it was too much, he'd be out of a job. You've heard him harping on about it, and we've had busboys younger than him. Not that I felt easy about them, either, but . . ."

"You promise your mam that you'll let her know if it gets too much and I'll go along with it." Gus poured three cups of tea, a man among equals, calm and reasonable. "But I want a true promise, not just hot air over your gums."

"I promise," Rory said readily. He was safe—nothing about the job was too much for him.

"Good man. Your mother's worked damn hard to raise you and your sister, and of course she worries. She's entitled. It's one of the few benefits a woman gets for being a mother. If she tells me she thinks you're looking worn out or sick, well, she's the judge of it."

Rory rinsed his cup, then headed for his room. Gus and Kate sat at the table for a while, neither of them looking at the other. Finally Gus rose, cleared the teapot and cups and took it all to the sink. He was rinsing the cups when he heard Kate stand up.

"You're my wife," he said, turning to look at her. She stood, one hand on the back of the chair, suddenly tense and stiff. Gus looked toward the stairs and Kate blanched, struck by the image of Gus in a fury, and Rory getting caught up in the middle of it. "He thinks he's well on his way to being a man," Gus smirked.

"Oh God," Kate breathed.

She was ashamed to admit how much she enjoyed her time with Gus that night, in spite of her feelings about him. Physically they worked, and worked well. He was a good lover and he knew her body better than she did. But emotionally she still needed to lock herself away. She was open and relaxed with Ted, but the physical part—face it, the sex was increasingly same old, same old. With Gus, where she wasn't the least bit safe, there was no predictability, no threat of boredom. Was the element of constant danger the spice of their lovemaking? After Gus fell asleep, Kate performed a small act of defiance by going down the hall to the room she now thought of as her own.

Under her tough exterior, Cedar walked softly when Gus was around. She blamed herself, couldn't understand why she had little or no trouble with anyone else and so much trouble with him. She'd heard people say, over and over, "Same old Gus," and "He'll never change," and "Oh well, more of the same." But she could remember a time before the slaps, the whacks, the sudden kicks to the backside. She could remember when he was her daddy and she was his queen of the world. So if he hadn't changed, if he was the same old Gus, then what had she done, how had she changed, and why couldn't she get along with him? What did she do that made him grab her by the arm so hard it left bruises, what look on her face or tone in her voice had earned her a swollen ear and welts on her back? And worse. Much worse. But she didn't want to think about that, so she tucked it away, wherever "away" was, along with everything else she had chosen to overlook or forget or stuff into a dusty trunk. Or a Pandora's box.

Maybe two weeks off wasn't long enough for him to get shirty, or maybe she walked so carefully that she didn't annoy him. Whatever the reason, when Gus went back into camp, she didn't have a mark on her anywhere. Just as surprising, Rory didn't either.

He headed back to work with his canvas duffel bags stuffed with clean clothes, plus a heavy cardboard box crammed with reading material. Tucked in with the books was what he said was a little portable radio. "Probably won't pull in much but static. But sometimes even static sounds good compared to the burping and farting of the rest of the guys in the bunkhouse." No need to let them know he'd diverted a bit of his poker winnings and got himself the best shortwave he could find. What they didn't know wouldn't hurt them, and anyway that money had never been part of the household funds. Not that household, anyway.

SIX

By Christmastime, reality had begun to set in for Cedar. Only six more months and she'd be finished school. So what, pray tell, was she going to do? She had to do something! Gramps had already made it abundantly clear that there would be no argument about her paying rent. "Damn it, girl, you earn your keep four and five times over with the help you give me and the work you do. If you're going to be bullheaded and argue with me, or if you think you can fool me by slipping money into my bank account, well, the up and down of that will be you won't be staying here."

Even so, she had to think seriously about getting a full-time job, as well paid as possible. She knew it wouldn't take much on her part to get a job as deckhand on Uncle Ewen's boat, he'd as much as said so. But when you're out on a boat, you aren't home on the farm. She could waitress—she had experience and knew she'd get a good reference from Nick—but she'd done that, thank you. Still, it was something to fall back on if nothing else came to mind. How much easier it all looked for boys, who could have just about any job they wanted. Who had decided that the job choices for girls would be limited? Cedar could think of a lot of jobs that wouldn't be easy for her, because however strong she might be, however athletic she might be, her strength couldn't even begin to approach the sheer physical power of some guys. Mind you, a lot of men had to say the same thing! No way she was going to be able to work as a heavy-duty mechanic, for instance. She wouldn't even be able to lug around the tool kit, for a start. No chance of being a swamper on a brewery truck, because if anyone rolled a keg of beer onto her shoulder, she'd crumple. She might be able to run a chainsaw for a couple of hours, but she would never, ever be able to run it eight and ten hours a day, five and six days a week, good weather and bad, up and down slopes, in any or all kinds of weather. Nor could most guys. Besides which, the mountain slopes were thick with whiskey jacks and everyone knew those beautiful, cheeky gray jays were the souls of dead loggers, and most of them fallers.

But how much sheer raw strength did a person need to sit in the cab of a truck taking freight up and down the highway? She wasn't old enough to drive a bus, you had to be twenty-five to get a job like that, but as long as she didn't make herself look like a fool by applying for a job where she'd have to unload refrigerators or pianos, sofas or heavy chunks and hunks of machine parts, she didn't see why a job like that should be out of the question. She'd just have to get the special permits.

But there was an ad in the paper, and all you needed to be was eighteen and tall enough that your feet reached the pedals. And have the registration fee. Well, she had the fee, her legs were long, and the course ran in the evenings, so why not give it a try? Luckily Gus was in camp, which might well mean that God was on her side, providing a very wet but unusually mild winter, and the bush hadn't yet been shut down for snow.

By the time the snow did close things down, Cedar's driving course was so much a part of the household routine that when Gus came home there was no reason, nor even any excuse, for him to pitch a fit. He shook his head as if he thought she was half out of her mind, but he didn't say anything against it.

First she got her vacuum brakes permit, then she forked over more money and got her air brakes. In a way, it was like buying your job. Except she didn't have the job yet, nor even the application form.

What she did have was Easter exams, and they were bloody awful. She thought she had her schoolwork aced—the last thing she'd expected was to feel as if she was sweating blood. She knew she hadn't failed, but passing was a lot harder than she'd expected, and year-ends would be even worse, everyone knew that.

Winter darkness was slowly releasing its hold on them, each evening lasted just that vital little bit longer. The depression that accompanied the gloomy shroud of cloud and fog lifted, and people began to head into their gardens, digging out weeds and grass clumps, cleaning up the mess of last year's blown leaves. Those who hadn't already dug out the corn stalks and disposed of them did so and lectured themselves on how this year, sure as sure can be, they would get rid of them when they harvested the corn, maybe drive them up to the dairy herd, give them a treat.

Kate didn't plan much by way of a garden. She was too busy to even think of the hours and hours of work required to do the canning and preserving, and anyway, there was enough jam put away to last them another two years, not to forget the fruit. But fresh salad was always welcome, and you might just as well put in some beets, some beans and some tomatoes, because nothing you bought was nearly as good. And while you were at it you might as well put in chard, green onions and a few marrow.

Cedar helped Kate and Rory get the garden ready, and on the weekends she worked with Gramps, moving tractor buckets of composted pig mulch, which they euphemistically called "black soil." They dumped it, then dug it into the already rich ground, and finally wrestled with the rototiller.

"It would help," Cedar grunted, sweat sticking her shirt to her back, "if you'd had someone come in and tame this wild bugger before you tried to put it to work."

"Tame that? Hey, that's wilder than any stud horse running loose on the prairie," he laughed. "I think it was invented by a chiropractor. You do an hour's work with it, then spend ten hours paying him to slide your spine back into place."

She dug the neglected flower beds that had once flourished along the fence in front of the house. More black soil, and the bulbs, even though they had been disturbed by the digging, responded with brave growth. If anything, the work she did encouraged them, broke up the congested clumps and gave the plants some room to grow. She looked at the iris bed and decided it was just going to have to tough it out the way it was, she'd wait until fall before doing much of anything with it. The corms were a solid carpet of yellowish brown crawling in all directions, the flat green spears looking like swords, or daggers.

The window boxes hadn't been used in years. Cedar emptied out the chickweed-infested dirt and replaced it with a mix of pig muck and potting soil, then planted fuchsia and trailing begonia. She'd have done more, but things grew too fast for her to keep up and the best she could do was draw a rough map of what was where, what grew first, what replaced it later. She could see where her autumn was going to go!

Cedar didn't wait for school to let out before she started campaigning for a job. She dipped into her depleted savings and went to an office on Main Street, where a middle-aged woman asked questions, took information, then wrote up a resume.

"Heaven's sake!" Kate said. "I'd hire you myself! She makes you sound like the best thing since sliced bread. Which you are, and always have been, but now everyone will know it."

Everyone might know it, but the only reply she got was from the potato chip company. It wasn't exactly what she'd had in mind, but, she told herself, it would give her driving experience for her resume, and besides that, potato chips didn't weigh very much. Irv, the man who interviewed her looked doubtful.

"I don't know," he said bluntly. "Never hired a girl before."

"I can drive. And I can lift boxes."

"Yeah? There's invoices, too, you know. That can get complicated. And lifting one box is one thing, lifting boxes all day long is something else."

"Like on the farm." Cedar smiled, pretty sure she wasn't acting nervous. "Only on the farm it's either feedbags or straw bales."

She knew Irv didn't want to hire her, but she didn't know that the wages he offered her were significantly lower than a male driver could make almost anywhere else, and the company had been left high and dry any number of times when their drivers landed union jobs elsewhere. Cedar was inexperienced, but so were most of the men who had delivered cartons of chips.

"When can you start?"

"When do you want me?" She still had two weeks of school, but she wasn't going to give up this job just for the chance to put on a gorpy dress and get her picture taken with the rest of the graduating class.

"Yesterday," Irv said. Cedar didn't blink an eye. Exams were behind her, what remained was mostly social, and she wanted the job.

The truck wasn't very big and it had vacuum brakes, so she knew she could handle it. That helped. She wasn't sure what she would have done if she had shown up ready to go in jeans, shirt and work boots and been confronted with a real rig. It was one thing to drive with an instructor at the dual controls, it was another to know she was on her own as soon as she turned on the key.

Irv had coffee ready. He gestured for her to get a cup, then he showed her the paperwork. "You keep track of where you've been, where you've still got to go. That's your responsibility, not mine. If you run out of chips, just come on home to daddy and you can have more."

"Good enough." She washed out her mug, feeling as if the coffee might come hurtling back up again. If it did she would somehow hide it from Irv. No need for him to know her nervousness had turned into something like sheer terror.

By noon she felt as if she'd been driving potato chips around all her life. She started at the far end of her route and worked her way corner store by gas station, back to the carrier yard.

"Chip lady. Just tell me how many you need and I guarantee you'll get them."

And when she'd carted in what a person asked for, she got the signature on the delivery slip and she got the money, for which she exchanged a receipt. Some of them didn't pay cash, they had accounts that they settled once a month. It wasn't complicated. It was all down there on paper, easy to see, easy to check.

She ate her sandwich in the truck and worked through her lunch break, and by 1:30 she was back at the yard to reload her truck. She handed over the paperwork and the money and made sure she got the signatures where they belonged. Not that she didn't trust Irv, but mistakes happen unless you make sure they can't.

One sack of chips weighs nothing. A dozen of them start to add up. A cardboard crate of them is a load, and by quitting time the muscles in her arms were stretched.

"You still think you're the one for the job?" Irv asked.

"Did I make any mistakes?" she grinned. If he was going to act like the master curmudgeon of all time, she was going to act like the most cheerful sad-ass in the world.

"Not worn to a nub?"

"Probably will be by this time tomorrow. You were right about that part of the job. I don't know how it happens—the first crate weighs nothing at all, the last dozen or so have boulders in them."

He surprised her by smiling. "Oughta get the scientists working on it. They could stay busy for the most part of a month figuring out how that happens. You could figure it out quicker, though. Add up how many of them you delivered and how many you had to load into the truck, then multiply by the weight of the crate and that's how many tons you moved today."

"Right," she agreed. "And figure, too, that when you're walking with them you spend about half the time on only one leg."

"Then there's up and down stairs."

"Thank God I'm not delivering pianos, eh?"

"Christ, and I've done that," he moaned. "Bloody near wrecked myself. Can't even stand to hear piano music on the radio now."

She rode her bike back to the farm and by the time she got there she was feeling fine. But she was glad to see her bed when she got to it, and the house could have fallen on her head and not wakened her. Even so, she heard the click before the clock radio started playing, and she was wide awake and ready to go.

Day two was like day one, day three like day two, and when she finally got her two days off, she was ready for them. Her arms were swollen and her thighs were tight. She'd bought herself a pair of leather roping gloves because the edges of the big cardboard boxes scratched and scraped her hands.

On Saturday they weaned piglets, moving them from the pens they shared with their mothers to bigger pens with piglets from other litters. The piglets squealed, the sows roared, the boars got themselves bent out of shape and one cantankerous pink terror even tried ramming his pen apart in his eagerness to save the entire herd from danger. The whole thing seemed funny to Cedar and Gramps, but the neighbours must have thought they were in the midst of wholesale slaughter.

"If I smell like you smell," Gramps teased, "then I need a bath."

"And if I smell like you smell," Cedar answered, "we both need to be buried."

"Doesn't take much. Just a tad of pig shit on this one's little hooves, and a touch of it on this one's rump—and of course there's always one or two let fly with a full load down the leg of your jeans. Pretty soon, you have enough swine shite on you that a sow wouldn't want to stand downwind."

"The smell of money. This is the *real* filthy lucre."

"It's their fear sweat that really stinks. You could fuss over them for an hour or two a day from the time they're born, they could know you as well as they know any of their littermates, and as soon as you go to pick them up and their feet leave the ground, they go hysterical."

Cedar got the first bath and enjoyed every drop of it. When Gramps was finished and dressed, Cedar put her clothes and his through the wash immediately.

"Now, you could have waited." He shook his head. "Don't you know when enough is enough?"

"You want those jeans sitting out there stinking up the place? Dirty old man."

The jeans were hanging on the line when she and Gramps left the place to go into town for fish and chips and a movie. "I could drive you out to see your mother tomorrow," Gramps offered.

"I'll phone her," Cedar promised. "But it's a working day for her, she'll sleep late and . . ." She shrugged. "See, I come by it honestly."

Alison McCann was waiting tables at the fish and chips shop. The place was packed, and the air was thick with the smell of bubbling grease, raw fish, cooking fish, and strong brown malt vinegar. Alison's face was red and the fine curls at her hairline were damp with sweat, but she was smiling, and when she saw Cedar her skin flushed even redder.

"I thought you were making music at Mom's."

"I was until a few months ago, but there weren't enough hours, and I needed more money. Isn't it hell how life gets in the way of living it the way we want?"

"But you're still playing?"

"Definitely. When I finish here I whip down to Cherry Lane—it's licensed until one in the morning so I get in a couple of hours there. And I have a few students during the day on weekends, but I haven't managed any during the week. I guess all the guitar players are in school then."

"Busy woman."

"You want coffee, tea, milk or pop with your order?"

"Cold pop." Cedar looked at Gramps, who nodded. "Two Orange Crush, please."

The food was perfect—hot and crisp, and they ate until they couldn't swallow another bite. Cedar reached for the bill, but Gramps beat her to it.

"Don't argue with me," he said.

"Okay, but I get the show. And the popcorn."

"I get the popcorn."

"I get the popcorn."

"Okay, I get the chocolate bars."

Alison was busy clearing a big table when they left, so she didn't see the wave Cedar gave her.

By September Cedar's arms and legs no longer ached. She could move crates of chips for a regular eight-hour shift then put in an hour or two of overtime and not feel as if she was about to fall on her face. As she grew stronger she could do the work more quickly, and Irv expanded her route. She knew she ought to hold out for a raise but something inside her refused to give him the satisfaction of having her ask. He didn't volunteer any increase in wages, so Cedar continued to work hard, to be pleasant, but she made a mark on the minus side of her mental scorecard.

Three weeks before Christmas she came home from work to find Gramps sitting in the living room, lights not turned on, smoking a home-rolled cigarette and staring at the faded pattern on the rug. He looked so bad she couldn't even ask him what was wrong, and when he held out a single sheet of paper without saying a word, she was flooded with anxiety.

She read the notice but her brain refused to deal with any part of it. "What does it mean?" she asked stupidly.

"It means we're sewered," he answered, his voice dull. "It means the muckety-mucks who made a fortune turning a sawdust heap into Grassy Knoll Heights don't want the sight or sound of pigs to lower the property values. It means the butt-diving bloodsuckers are going to make it impossible for us to keep on doing what we were doing long before they showed up with their jerry-built overpriced rabbit hutch-es!" Tears slipped down his wrinkled face.

"We'll get a lawyer."

"I've already phoned three of them. They all said the same thing. We can spend every dime we've got and they'll still win. We can hold out to the very limit and they'll just come with the sheriff and shift us. We're sewered," he repeated, sobbing. "The bastards!"

Cedar sat on the arm of the sofa and rolled a cigarette for him and one for herself. "There's got to be some way to come out of this without losing everything." Her voice was calm, but inside her the Campbell rage was growing. They'd pay. One way or another, sooner or later, the whole lot of them was going to wind up wishing they'd made some very different choices in life.

For days it seemed as if the old man was going to drown in heartbreak. He stopped eating, he paced the house at night and he developed dark bruise-like pouches under his eyes. He managed only the bare minimum care of the pigs. After a few days he headed off to the city by himself. He was gone three days, and came back looking more grim-faced than ever. When he told Cedar he'd seen a lawyer she nodded, but when he told her the name of the lawyer she shook her head.

"That guy costs a fortune, Gramps," she protested. "Yeah, his name's in the paper all the time, and yeah he's won some spectacular cases, but by the time you pay his bill—"

"Nothing to worry about there." He forced a smile. "He's set me a fixed fee, five hundred bucks. They take some kind of oath to do so much stuff 'pro bono'—for the good of something or other. He's gonna get in touch with the lawyers who work for the development company. All's I gotta do is go see those bastards in town."

Gramps seemed better after that visit, though he was still obviously heartbroken and spent much of his time just walking around his place, looking at things. She knew he was preparing to say goodbye, knew there was so much of his life attached to each of the buildings, each of the posts and poles and pens and sheds that leaving was almost like losing his life.

But on Christmas morning he was showered, dressed in clean dress pants and a white shirt, shoes shined and a smile on his face. "Merry Christmas, Cedar," he said when she came down. "Your Grandma Larson wants us at her place for breakfast at nine."

"Okay." She handed him a package. "Merry Christmas, Gramps."

"For me?" He seemed surprised. "Thank you."

He opened the gaily wrapped box, lifted out the watch, and just stared at it. Without any prompting, he turned the watch over and read the inscription. "Thank you," he repeated. "This is more than an old fool like me deserves."

Cedar poured a cup of coffee and drank it sleepily, almost wishing they could find a way to get out of the family breakfast, but the hour or two of peace and quiet would never compensate for the repercussions. Fortified by the coffee, she hauled on her work clothes and went outside to do the morning chores. The roofs of the buildings were white with frost and the metal fencing and gates looked lovely, the rust covered by frozen crystals. She used the tractor to lift the big vat of warm mash and drove down the centre aisle of the pens, stopping regularly to lower the vat and bucket out breakfast for the grunting, shoving, snuffling hogs.

An hour later the chores were done, Cedar was showered and in clean jeans and shirt, and, unusual for him, Gramps had graciously allowed her to drive his car.

"Turn left here," he said quietly.

"Left?" She laughed. "Don't you know where Grandma Larson lives?"

"Turn left," he repeated, tapping his fingers on the dashboard. His nails were clean and trimmed short, but still very much the nails of a hard-working man, so thick they looked more like claws, or horns, and they were yellowed by cigarettes and, she supposed, by age. She wondered if nails were like ivory. His looked like the keys on an old piano. His knuckles were huge and his fingers thick. Years of lifting, hauling, heaving, shoving were written on his hands.

"Left again, up ahead."

"Where are we going, for crying in the night?" She checked her own watch. "We'll be late."

"We won't be late. This is only going to take a few minutes."

She made the turn, then drove in puzzled silence while Gramps tapped his fingers and grinned. So the old fart had a surprise up his sleeve, did he. Whatever it was, it had changed his mood—he was back from the land of the living dead, as perky as a three-year-old kid.

"Right, down that gravel road."

"I figure we're about ten miles out of town, up between Green and Hampton Lakes," Cedar said. Gramps nodded. "We could have come straight here on the highway, so why the round-about mystery?"

"Because I'm an old man and I like to do things my own way."

"Well, you'd better do something real fast, because we're just about out of road here."

"We're fine."

"Been this way before, have you?"

"Just around that bend there . . ."

Just around the bend the heavily treed bush ended and the clearing began. The gravel road had become a one-vehicle-wide track that led up a slight slope to a large old house.

Gramps was out of the car almost before it stopped, hurrying toward the front door. Cedar followed him. On the doorknob was a small green and red ribbon from which hung an envelope with "Cedar" written on it.

"Go ahead," Gramps giggled. "Open 'er up."

She read the words over and over but she couldn't understand their meaning.

"I told 'em I'd fight until hell froze if they didn't deal fair and square," Gramps crowed. "Asked 'em how much they thought their fancy damn subdivision was going to be worth when the news got spread round that it was built on a sawdust pit that was prob'ly still burnin' away somewhere underneath. Told 'em I was going to bring in a high-priced lawyer from the city, gonna check out all their permits and such, gonna look for conflict of interest and I don't know what all. I raised hell, I did."

"And what does it all mean?"

"It means that we've got six and a half months to get ourselves set up and move the pigs into that barn, with pens coming out off it all the way around. It means we wind up with twice as much land and just about double the size of house and enough cash to hire a few strong backs to do the worst of the work. And it means Merry Christmas and Happy New Year, Cedar, she's all in your name."

"*Mine?* But Gramps—"

"You're welcome. Now drive like hell or we'll be late at your Grandma Larson's and I don't want to miss out on one single pancake. You're a good cook but your pancakes don't hold a candle to your grandma's."

The family gaped when Cedar showed them the sheaf of papers and told them what was on them.

"You musta done more than just yell at them," Grandpa Larson guessed.

"Got me a tame shark," Gramps admitted. "Sent him into the swamp aheada me. He'd already talked to the real money, the ones who pull the strings that make the wooden-headed dolls dance. These guys here are small-time, whatever they think of themselves. And the big money didn't want the bad publicity. Poor old man, been on his farm forty years, never any trouble, model citizen, forced into a life of cold porridge in a low-rent basement suite." The two old men laughed together.

"Jeez, Cedar," Wade said. "Maybe you can spot me a loan now that you're a big-time landowner and all."

"At least let us borrow the caddy once in a while," Hank winked.

Kate went out on the porch to smoke a cigarette and try to get some control over her emotions. She was glad for them, but she couldn't help but feel that Joe Conrad had stolen her daughter. It wasn't the money, it wasn't the value of the land and house, it was the very fact of them. He'd given Cedar exactly what she had always wanted, and that cut deeply into Kate's heart. If Cedar had worked double shifts for ten years she could only have come up with a down payment on the place, and then she would have had to work another ten or fifteen years to pay it off. It was the investment of an entire lifetime, and poof!—like that it was already hers. She had the papers in her hand, Merry Christmas for all the years of your life. Kate had been praying that Cedar would get over her love affair with pigs and with farming, maybe go to university. All right, so she didn't want to be a lawyer. There were other things—accountant or teacher or anything, but the local pig lady . . .

"What's wrong?" Marg said from behind her. She handed Kate a jacket, and Kate pulled it on, glad of its weight and warmth.

"Just me feeling like a bitch."

"His son's probably gonna raise holy old hell about this."

"Ted? He's never wanted any part of the farm."

"No, but he wouldn't have turned down the money."

"I suppose not. Nobody would."

"Then smarten up out here. You just said it yourself. Nobody would. So why should Cedar? It's exactly what she's always wanted."

"I know that!" Kate snapped. "That's what sticks in my throat, damn it! I'm her mother. If anyone's going to give her exactly what she always wanted, it should be me."

"You're right, you are feeling like a bitch," Marg said angrily. "The only thing that kid ever wanted from you is the one thing you won't give her—some peace and quiet. You've made one dumb mistake after another, and not only hasn't it worked out for you, it hasn't been much of a childhood for those kids. Sometimes, Kate, honest to God, I could just reach out and slap you."

"Yeah? Well, sometimes, Marg, I could reach up and slap myself. This is one of those times. That's why I came out here."

"If you people don't eat every single one of these pancakes," Karen yelled from the house, "I'll have to give them to Cedar for her pigs." Kate and Marg went back in. The children jammed in around the table, elbow to elbow, while the adults stood behind them with plates of food, eating and smiling, going to the warming oven for more. As well as the pancakes, Karen had old-fashioned sausages from Swenson's deli, real cured bacon and warmed-in-the-oven barbecued salmon tips. And a huge pot of her famous coffee.

"The best," Joe Conrad grinned. "The very best. If I wasn't afraid of your husband, madam, I'd ask you to marry me."

"Get in line," Dr. Forbes snapped in mock anger. "I've been trying to get this woman to wear a scarlet letter for years. She won't take me seriously. I don't know what old man Larson's got, but I doubt any of us can steal her away from him."

"Next year," Joe Conrad said, "we provide the sausage. You hear me, Cedar?"

"Yessir." She laughed. "Maybe we can walk it in the back door on all four feet, with its curly tail switching and its big ears flapping."

Kate made her voice sound happy and easy. "The way you are with those creatures, you won't even need a collar and leash. Just snap your fingers and it'll follow like an obedient old dog. You never saw such a kid for fussing with pigs," she told the others, and she and Gramps tried to outdo each other with stories of young Cedar and the piglets. But for all the smiles and chuckles, inwardly Kate was burning. For Christmas Cedar had given her a "family ring" with two stones, Cedar's and Rory's birthstones. It was a lovely present and it had probably cost more than the watches she'd given Joe Conrad and Rory, but that didn't matter one little bit because what Cedar had really given the old man was more than a watch or a ring or the most expensive bauble in the world. Kate was glad Gus had bowed out of the family breakfast and gone to see his parents instead, where he could have a drink or two without being treated as a pagan. If he were here now, she might just dump her pancakes on his head and snarl, "Now see what you've done!"

By springtime, most of the switchover was accomplished. The three-man crew that Cedar had hired had the new pens in place, each set up to allow free access to the straw-filled den in the barn, each sow with her own stall and outside pen, each boar set up similarly, the inside area smaller than the space given the sows because there had to be room for piglets. When the piglets were old enough to wean, they would be moved to other pens in the new addition to the barn, and their outdoor pen was big, with two feet of sawdust on the bottom and a feeding trough built close to the fence.

The house crew started on the top floor and worked their way down, room by room. They tore out the old carpeting, patched and smoothed the drywall, painted the walls and ceilings, sanded the floors and then covered them with four layers of Varathane. A plumber checked the pipes, replaced some worn taps and put something in the septic tank that was guaranteed to revitalize and energize the bacterial action. When the inside of the place was done, the same crew moved outside and fixed the porch and stairs, replaced some damaged boards, looked everywhere for dry rot or punkiness.

"Can't paint until it gets warmer," the crew chief told them. "Prob'ly be back to do that in mid-June. Got you marked in my book."

"Ah, yes, the book," sighed Joe. "Where would we be without it?"

The moving company took half a day to transfer the furniture from what they were already calling "the old place." Cedar and Joe spent two days unpacking and setting things up the way they wanted them.

"No stairs for me," Joe insisted. "I'm fine here, more than enough room for an old fart. Room after room—my God, whoever built this mausoleum musta got his wood for free."

Cedar's room was on the second floor. "My lord in heaven!" Kate yelped. "This is as big as my kitchen and living room combined."

"The foreman called it the master bedroom," Cedar laughed, "but there's no master here, just me."

"You'll need roller skates," Rory said. "Better set up some chairs so's you can stop for a rest on your way to the dresser."

"Yeah? Well, come see this." She grabbed him by the hand and dragged him down the hallway to a second bedroom. "See? Any time you want you can come out to visit and there's a room, just for you."

"He'll hardly ever be here," Kate snapped. "This place is miles from anywhere. How would he get to school, or to work?"

"I go to town every morning." Cedar said. "What's wrong, Mom?"

"Nothing!" But it was everything. Not even twenty years old and Cedar had a special bedroom set aside for her brother. Who did she think she was? Besides, she'd already had her daughter stolen, she wasn't about to stand by and watch her son get swiped, too.

"She's just worried you'll be exhausted by all the responsibility," Aunt Marg said soothingly. But even Marg didn't believe it. She couldn't imagine what was up with Kate, and she was tired of Kate's moods. Exhausted, even. "Your mother has always had an awful time with change," she reminded Cedar. "She always expects the worst."

Uncles from both sides of the family helped with the move. Cousins of all ages raced around exploring, and Chrissie had a minor fit when she saw Rory's bedroom.

"Where's mine?" she demanded.

"You can have whatever other one you want," Cedar told her.

"I want a *special* one."

"Whichever one you claim will be special," Cedar assured her, hiding her irritation. Chrissie was not improving with age. She had been a willful baby and now she was a stubborn brat. Apparently the only place in the universe that Chrissie would accept was the centre. Everyone thought Suzie was a bit too placid, but maybe there was something to be said for her after all. Suzie would be content to sleep on the floor with no pillow and only someone's overcoat for a blanket. But not Chrissie.

For a week and a half they lived in the new place and went to the old one to care for the pigs. Then the stock truck arrived, and they spent an entire weekend moving the pigs. The boars went first, because they were the hardest to handle. Of course they got to fighting in the back of the stock truck and arrived with cuts and scratches, torn ears and bloody faces. All of them were thoroughly enraged, and once they were in their pens they roared around, threatening to demolish the earth and all those who walked upon it.

The weaned piglets came next. Again the noise was incredible, but the switch was made easily. The truly hard part came when it was time to move the sows with litters. All of Sunday was devoured by that chore, and both Cedar and Joe went away with bruises. But when they sat down to Sunday night roast with Grandma and Grandpa Larson, the worst of the job was done. Cedar ate hugely, feeling as if she was about to fall asleep, not to waken for years.

The uncles organized the last of the moves. The old wood burner was shifted with the help of the tractor, brought to the new place and set up in the new firebrick-lined shed. The orphanage was in the same building so the runts and rejects would be warm there, and their area was set up even more efficiently than the one at the old place.

And one day, when Cedar came home from work, Joe was there to greet her, a grin on his face. "We're here," he laughed. "One hundred percent here. Your uncle Forrest even moved the manure pile here for us! Said he wasn't leaving those bloodsuckers anything at all, not even fertilizer for their fancy lawns."

Now all she had to do was find a way to feel at home.

It took Cedar the rest of the year to feel at home. But only she was aware of how strange the new place felt to her and how uncomfortable she was. Everybody else in her life heard only the up side of things, how cool the house was in the summertime, how easy it was to care for the pigs. They heard about the triumphs, the Best in Show at the fall fair, the good price for their pork. And true to his word, at Christmastime Gramps provided the sausage—and the bacon. He took two of his finest hogs to Swenson's for processing and paid for it with a share of the meat. Swenson said he rarely saw meat of that quality any more, and Gramps gave Cedar the credit, for letting the pigs roam outdoors instead of running a battery operation.

"Steady market," Gramps told Cedar at supper that night. "All's we got to do is keep turning out top quality, like you been doing."

"I was reading about those red Tamworths," Cedar said. "They're like the pig equivalent of a special breed beef animal. They grow slower, but in the end they're more solid-packed. Supposed to be real good foragers, too. Expensive, though."

"Well, you pay for what you get. Might be worth trying. I was kind of wondering about those Hungarian wild boar, they say they make one helluva tasty animal."

"They look like warthogs or something."

"Supposed to make a good lean bacon."

"Maybe. I'm not sure I want to free-range them in a big field, though, they look like they could jump any fence and run faster'n a racehorse."

Cedar brought out the tractor and a groundbreaker plow and started the garden plot. When the ground was turned and re-turned she took the rock-picker through, then hitched the big rotovator to the tractor and went over the area repeatedly. She moved mini-mountains of the old composted manure that had been transferred from the other place, and rotovated it until the garden plot was fine-soiled and rich with fertilizer.

And when the vegetable plot was ready, Cedar started planting her flowers. Gramps made window boxes and hanging cedar planters for fuchsia and trailing carnation, geranium and begonia. "Whoever lived here before was a good worker," he commented. "A good builder, and had no taste for pretty stuff at all."

When Ted arrived unannounced, Cedar went to greet him with a smile on her face. He looked at her as if he had never seen her before, as if something about her puzzled him beyond all belief.

"Cedar," he said quietly, "what in hell are you trying to do?"

"What do you mean?"

"He put this place in your name."

"Uh, yeah. He, he just—"

"Yeah. Right. He just. Jesus, woman." He shook his head. "As if the whole world didn't have enough to gossip about without you two adding fuel to the fire." And he walked past her and into the house.

Ted stayed for a week, and by the time he left Cedar felt black and blue. She wanted to sit down and weep, but the Campbell in her wouldn't allow it. She hurried home after work every night, refusing overtime and the extra money it brought, so she could turn out bang-up meals, and Ted ate them as if they were wet blotting paper—no sign of enjoyment, no thank you, just cold silence and hot glares. Joe noticed, but said nothing in front of Cedar.

Kate was relieved that Ted so obviously wasn't interested in sex, or even in much visiting or conversation. She was sure he had a bone in his throat because Cedar, not Ted, held the papers on the new place.

"I don't want the goddamn place!" he shouted when she broached the subject. "What in hell would I do with fifty acres of raw bush and a whack of pigs? It's not the money, damn it! Can't you understand she's got that old man convinced everything is going to be just pie-in-the-sky and fine, as if he shouldn't be taking it easy instead of putzing around with pigs!"

"But it was his idea."

"You might think so. For that matter he might think so. But I know better! She put the idea in his head, and don't try to tell me differently."

Kate shrugged. She wished they would all just leave her alone. She had no interest in defending Cedar, and less interest in trying to coax Ted out of his foul mood. All she had to do was say, "I'll talk to her, honey." All she had to do was reach out, take his hand and smile at him, saying, "Come on, don't ruin your vacation, this crazy idea will start to wear thin." But she said and did none of it. This was his fixation, his uproar, and if she opened her mouth it might well be to tell him exactly that.

Cedar wasn't at the house when the balloon went up. She was at work, driving from familiar stop to familiar stop on her route, chatting up the customers, taking the time to smile and tell a few jokes, even though her route had been extended again. She figured that if she ran, she could get it all done in an eight-hour shift with a proper half-hour lunch break and two coffee breaks. But she didn't take a lunch break. She ate her sandwiches in the truck, and her coffee came from a thermos, the red plastic cup held between her thighs as she drove.

When she got home that night for supper, Ted was gone and Gramps was coldly silent. She knew there had been some kind of go-round, and she waited as long as she could before she finally had to ask what had happened.

"We never could talk things over without getting into it. Not enough like his mother, that guy. Too much like his old man, I guess." He paused. "Ted's convinced I need to be put in an old folks' home. He says this is all too much for an old codger like me. He tells me the whole damn town is talking about it. How he'd know that when he's hiding out back east, I don't know, but he says everyone is saying that you 'n' me's shacked up and you're nothing but a gold digger out to strip me of every cent."

"Jesus, do you think that would be more fun than what we're really doing?" she asked. "I mean, would we be better off tryin' that than we are moving tons of pig shite around with the tractor?"

"Pig shite's clean alongside some of what he said. I set him down at the table and showed him what we got for the other place, showed him what it cost to set us up here, showed him how much of your money had gone into it, and showed him that there was money for him in the bank. He said he didn't know you'd been picking up the tab. I told him he was an ungrateful son of a bun who wouldn't even have a bloody inheritance if it wasn't for you. Then he got mad. Called me a bloody old fool and asked why I hadn't told him the real story sooner, and I got mad and told him it was none of his bloody business anyway. And then," he winked, "things got nasty and he left."

"Make it up with him, Gramps, please."

"Hell with it. Let him stew a bit. Old folks' home! I'm seventy-one years old and I come from long-lived people. My dad was ninety-six before they got him into a so-called home, and then he'd only go if they promised he could have an electric scooter so's he could get hisself to the pub every afternoon for a couple of cool ones. My granddad was ninety-eight when he died. Heart attack. Doing the polka, they said. When I'm ready for a rocking chair, I'll let you know. Then you can let him know."

"I'm looking around for a different job." She changed the subject blatantly, afraid Gramps would have his own heart attack, not from the polka but from sheer rage and insult.

"What's wrong with the job you've got?"

"My boss is a cheapskate," she snorted, and she told him about the longer route and the non-existent raise.

"Cheeky bugger," Gramps said. "Time to move on, for sure."

She didn't say a word to the twit in charge of the chips and trucks. Irv didn't have to know she had her name in at every possible place, from local delivery for a furniture store to hauling people with wheelchairs to their physio appointments.

When the call came it was from the gravel pit, not six miles from home. "Can you start on Monday?" Brendan asked. "Six in the morning, and we go until 4:30. It's a long day but you get time and a half after eight hours, which gives you two hours overtime every day, and if it goes past 5:30, you get double time. Union benefits all the way."

"See you Monday morning," Cedar said. "Thanks, cuz."

"No problem, cuz."

Brendan wasn't really a cousin, but his forebears and hers had taken the same boat to Montreal, then the same train to Vancouver, and by the time both the grandfathers were working in the same coal mine and both the grannies were steeling themselves to spend no more than one year in company housing, the bonds were forged—so strongly that two generations later it was "Cuz," and Brendan's two kids were calling Cedar "Auntie."

She told Irv on Wednesday, and had the satisfaction of watching his face as he absorbed the news. "Supposed to give two weeks' notice," he managed. "I could hold your last cheque."

"You could," she agreed, smiling. "And I could go to the Labour Relations Board."

"Why would you do that?"

"Come on, Irv, you know why. You'd have me sweating blood before you even thought of suggesting an extra ten cents an hour."

"I got expenses! There's an economic downturn, or haven't you heard?"

"Oh, I've heard. And I know I'm humping nearly double the amount I was when I started, seeing more customers than anyone else working here, and I bet I'm getting paid less than them."

He went pale, confirming her suspicions.

"It's a damn insult," she finished, "and you just cheapskated yourself out of the best bargain you've got."

"I'll give you a raise."

"No thanks."

The weekend was jam-packed with work, and Cedar and Gramps were both so tired by suppertime on Saturday that they agreed to settle for grilled cheese sandwiches. Even the thought of driving in for fish and chips was a bother, and neither of them felt like seeing a movie.

"We should get us one of those video players," Gramps said. "We could rent movies, pick us up three or four on a Friday night. Make our own popcorn. Sprawl in comfortable chairs. Not have to listen to everyone else crunching and burping and coughing."

"I'll check them out," Cedar promised. Once she'd pumped some food into herself, she could almost face the drive to the theatre, but Gramps had found an action adventure shoot-'em-up, blow-'em-up and bury-'em-deep on TV that was sure to be at least as funny as anything showing in town. She watched about half of it before she fell asleep on the sofa. Gramps woke her up when he was on his way to bed, and she stumbled up the stairs to her own room, kicked off her sneakers and lay on her bed, to rest a bit before undressing.

She wakened to the smell of coffee and cooking bacon.

"Shoulda called me sooner," she told Gramps.

"Anyone as falls asleep on that lumpy old sofa doesn't need wakened up in the morning. You been working too hard."

"Yeah, but I've got that new job now. No long drive to and from work, no mad traffic in town, no slave-driving boss. Better money, too. Way lots better. We'll be able to get ourselves set up real good with that feed conveyor system and that'll take a lot of the hump work out of it."

"We could get that conveyor system now if you weren't so damned bullheaded."

"Not without dipping into your legacy fund. And Ted is already mad enough about the farm, he doesn't need any more excuse."

"He'll get over that."

"Good. I hate to think of you two being on the outs."

"All's he has to do is get it through his head that I'm the dad and he's the kid. Been trying to boss me all his life."

Sunday was one of those magic spring days that make up for the winter fog and drizzle. In the window boxes the small green promises of begonias were already up, the yellow and pink squill was in flower and the anemone was flaunting itself proudly. In the iris beds green spears grew tall, some of them already showing the swellings that would be flower stalks. The lilies were a foot tall, the Oriental poppies were forming heads and the Californias were up. No flowers were showing yet, but there would be—like death and taxes, poppies were certain.

Gramps was on his knees, digging happily among the lilies, loosening the dirt, pulling out chickweed, humming a tune Cedar didn't recognize. The pens were cleaned, the weanlings had been moved and were raising hell in their new pen, and the sows, the depth of their maternal feelings fully expressed, lay on their sides in the late spring sunshine, ignoring the uproar. Out of sight, out of mind.

Cedar took a break from the tractor, stretching her legs, bending to get the crick out of her back. Maybe she'd just sit down and design a tractor seat that actually fit the human backside. Probably make a fortune and get letters of appreciation from every farmer in the country.

She lit a cigarette and inhaled deeply. Another half hour and she'd have the entire manure pile turned. She had seeded it liberally with Rot-It, and now all it needed was time and the occasional wetting down, and by autumn it would be fully composted. The landscaper in town wanted to buy as much as they and the pigs were able to turn out. Mixed with dirt it would make excellent topsoil. Cedar supposed that she and Gramps could handle that part of it, too, but no. There was a limit to how much work two people could handle without exhausting themselves.

And then a car came down the driveway. Dear God, no, please, not a pack of townies out for a Sabbath creep, come to see if they could let the children see the baby pigs. You'd think the place was a damn zoo, admittance free. The next thing they'd want a popcorn stand. Maybe she should make up some little baggies of pig food and sell them for a dollar each, let the dear little children have the joy of feeding the babies, make some money out of the pain in the butt.

But it wasn't townies. It was Alison McCann. She got out of the car and waved. "Hi," she called. "I needed some fertilizer for the garden and I thought why give the money to the store when I can get better quality out here? Not quite straight from the horse's mouth, mind you, but pretty much direct."

"You're in luck," said Cedar. "We got plenty." The passenger door opened and a little boy climbed out, and the sight of his distinctive curly blond hair and bright blue eyes might as well have been a hammer smacking Cedar between the eyes. Another bastard with Gus Campbell's stamp on him. Jesus, was the man sick in the head, or what? Alison wasn't all that much older than Cedar herself!

"What's his name?"

"Campbell McCann," Alison answered, daring to meet Cedar's gaze. "He's five."

"Gus give you any financial help?" No reason to beat around the bush.

"Sometimes. Not so much since I showed him the door, of course."

She shrugged, and surprised Cedar with a wide grin. "Same old story, eh?"

"Yeah. Hey, Cammy." Cedar held out her hand. "Would you like to see some brand new baby pigs?"

"Do they bite?"

"Nope. They don't bite and they feel like brand new human babies. All soft and smooth."

"Do they stink?"

"No. None of my pigs stink. Pigs try hard to be clean, you know."

"I don't know nothin' about pigs. We don't even got a dog."

"You don't?"

"Not a cat, not nothing. Landlord won't let us. We don't got a house, we only got a 'partment. I got a budgie bird, but . . ."

"Right, they're not much fun."

"You got a dog?"

"Not yet, but we're looking for one."

"You sure got you a big house. How big is your yard, anyway?"

"Huge."

She led him into the barn and showed him the hours-old piglets. He was afraid of the sow, even though all she did was lie on her side and grunt, but when Cedar lifted the runt of the litter and placed it in his hands, Campbell grinned.

"You're right!" he laughed happily. "They are soft. Can I show my mom?"

"Sure. Hold it safely, that's it, one hand under, one hand over, just like you're doing."

Alison made all the appropriate sounds of appreciation and watched fondly as Cam showed Gramps the piglet.

"I brought some garbage bags," she said.

"Tell you what," Cedar said without thinking. "Why don't you leave the bags where they are for now, and I'll bring you a pickup load this afternoon. We're going for dinner at my grandmother's place and you aren't much out of the way, shouldn't take more than ten minutes."

"Would you? That's wonderful!" she reached for her wallet and Cedar shook her head. "Well, of course you'll let me pay," Alison protested.

"Nah," Cedar laughed, "you know the rule, family doesn't pay."

With practically no urging at all, Alison stayed for lunch. "Let me help," she insisted. "It's only fair. My heavens, I'm getting free babysitting and a load of fertilizer, the least I can do is whip together some sandwiches and a salad. Just look at him out there. He's running in circles just for the fun of running."

"Nice kid," Cedar agreed. "Reminds me of my brother at the same age. Except Rory was kind of whiney. Small wonder, though. Mom as good as forced him to stay a baby. The old man was far too hard on him and mom was far too soft. It was like he was their battlefield or something. Dumb way to treat a kid if you ask me."

"He seems fine now."

"The best."

"Gus said he was going to university?"

"You bet he is! He's been waiting ever since Doc Forbes gave him a plastic skeleton to hang in his room."

"Going to have a family practitioner in the family?"

"My Grandmother and Grandfather Campbell don't know whether they should shit or steal third base. They've hated Doc Forbes for years and all of a sudden they have to swallow it because if it wasn't for him, Rory might be just another kid heading into the bush or onto the deck of a prawn boat."

They had lunch and then Cam sat on Cedar's knee while she finished the manure pile. He sat with his hands on the steering wheel, grinning widely. "When I'm bigger will you show me how to drive this thing?"

"You betcha. Have you working a full shift by the time you hit grade one. Then I'll retire, just sit in a chair on the porch and watch while you do it all."

"And will I live here?"

"If you're going to be doing all the work you'll have to live here. I'll put you in that upstairs bedroom—see the one I mean, see the way those windows at top are, with little peaks over each of them? The one in the middle there, that's the biggest of the upstairs rooms. We'll put you in there. Throw the dog blanket on the floor and you can sleep on that."

"Where will my mom sleep?"

"Under the back porch with the spiders."

"Nah! She don't like spiders."

"Well, I guess she'll have to sleep in the barn with the pigs."

The garden was in the back of Alison's parents' yard. Mrs. McCann watched as Gramps and Cedar pushed the black soil from the back of the pickup with a big snow-scoop-cum-pusher. From the look on her face Cedar knew that Mrs. McCann knew full well who Cam's father was, and felt very uncomfortable watching her grandson's half-sister laughing and letting the boy push the handle with her. Bad enough that the situation was what it was, there was something almost indecent about such easy friendship, The link should be ignored, swept under the carpet. Everyone should pretend it didn't exist.

Grandma Larson didn't mention the truck or any smell coming from it, and once Cedar had ducked into the bathroom with her plastic bag of clean clothes and washed up and changed, Grandma smiled and hugged her. "Goodness me," she said mildly, "I couldn't believe the state of you when you got here."

"I was delivering a load of you-know-what. You're lucky I left my sneakers outside."

"Your sneakers should be buried."

"Something smells absolutely glorious," Cedar hinted.

"Something will be glorious. We traded a big roast of that pork you gave us with the neighbour who raises turkeys, and it's big enough to feed us all and then some. Now there's something you should try. There's no comparison at all between what you get in the store and what they grow. You should set yourselves up and raise some of them, too."

"Can't," Gramps said flatly. "Turkeys 'n' pigs get the same kind of diseases. Bring in turkeys and we'll have problems. Bad enough losing a fifty-dollar turkey, but I'm not interested in losing a seven hundred-dollar breeding sow."

"My heavens, I had no idea a pig cost that much!" Grandma said.

"By the time they're ready to throw a litter, they do. You figure, you've been pouring the best of food into them for a year. Got to have a really healthy sow if you want good strong piglets."

"Did you know the US military uses pigs?" Rory said quietly. "To test their weapons. Pigs respond to wounds the very same way we do, so they shoot them with new-style bullets, blow them up with this or that or experiment with grenades. And then they use them to train field surgeons to get used to operating without proper anaesthetic."

"Biggest criminals in the world," Gramps agreed. "The only others as bad are the damn politicians that send 'em out to do to others. Sometimes I think about Ted and his airplane and I feel sick. He's trained to send rockets into targets. And somehow the targets always seem to be schools and hospitals."

"The turkey is ready," Karen said, changing the subject to everyone's relief. "Wade, can you get the bird out of the oven for me? It's that heavy it took the both of us to get it in."

"Clear the kitchen!" Wade called loudly. "Kids out or we won't have dinner."

Cedar lifted Chrissie and took her out on the porch, holding the door open for the other kids to tumble out after them.

"You like her best, don't you?" Sue said.

"Who best?"

"Chrissie. She's always the one you pick up like that."

"You think so, do you?" Cedar bent over, scooped Sue up and straightened, setting each kid on a hip. "You weren't near the big chair," she said, smiling and fibbing. "How could I scoop you from across the room?"

But Sue wasn't about to be flarched. "Is that really why?" She stared at Cedar, looking a lot like Grandma Larson.

"Darling," Cedar crooned. "I love you and Chrissie the same. Remember when you were smaller, and talking baby talk, and I'd say I love you both the same much? Well, I still do."

"I hope so," Chrissie piped, "It's not fair if you don't, you know."

"I was talkin' to her, not you!" Sue flared.

"I can talk if I want to."

"If you don't stop nagging each other I'll throw you both down the old well and nail the lid in place."

"Oh, sure," they chimed. "Sure you will."

The next morning, Cedar was at the gravel pit ten minutes before the shift started. "Hey, Cuz," she called, getting out of her pickup truck.

"Hey, Cuz," Brendan answered. He gestured with his thermos. "Got time for a splash?"

"Always."

"Don't say I never gave you anything." He handed her a brand new hard hat and she put it on, tipped back and a bit sideways. He grinned at her. "Don't let Compy see you workin' like that."

"Hey, I'm not working, I'm pouring coffee."

"Right." He pointed. "That's your truck over there. For now."

"Jesus, it's a monster."

"It's one of the smallest we've got. You get good with it and I might even move you to one of the big ones."

"I guess I should get in the beast and try 'er out."

"Nah, why do it on your time when you can do it on ours? We give what we call a two-hour training indoctrination." He winked. "Makes us look good with the union and with Compy." He pulled some papers from his pocket. "What you got to do right now is fill out this form. Application to the union. We take your initiation fee and dues out of your first cheque. You got a problem with that?"

"No. Hell, I even know two verses of 'Solidarity Forever'." She took his ballpoint and started filling in the form. The other workers began to arrive in twos and threes, and wandered over to have their pre-shift coffee and cigarette. "This is Cedar," said Brendan, "and once you jokers get your hats on your heads she'll be able to read your names." He turned to Cedar. "Except for this joker, he wrote his in Russian."

"Why not?" The hunk smiled. "Ain't this a bilingual country?"

Brendan laughed. "His name is, believe it or not, Ivan. Ivan the Bohunk."

"You're so stupid," Ivan answered easily. "A Russian isn't a Bohunk, a Bohunk is Polish or Ukrainian. You heather-hopping oatmeal savages don't know a thing."

"Hey, hey, hey," said Cedar. "Watch what you say. Don't you know that the best thing about being Scots is you don't have to be anything else?"

"Dear God in heaven." A middle-aged man with "Taffy" written on his hat shook his head. "That's two of them on the job. Check your pockets, make sure they haven't already skinned you."

Cedar and Brendan took the truck to the far side of the huge gravel pit, where there was plenty of room to manoeuvre. She felt as if she was trying to steer the Goodyear blimp.

"Nothing to be nervous about," Brendan told her. "Just ease yourself into it. Drive around a bit, do some backing up, make some turns, do a few three-points. When the butterflies stop, it'll be easy. They're geared to a fare-thee-well, the steering in 'em is easy, you've got more mirrors than the funhouse, and anyone who could tool that piece of shit of a chip truck through traffic can handle this one. All's you need to do is feel easy."

Three-quarters of an hour later, Cedar did feel easy. She felt more than easy. She felt as if the steering wheel grew out of the ends of her fingers. "This is great," she sighed. "As smooth as a piglet's skin."

"Good. Put you to work, then. She'll feel totally different with a load." He gave her a nudge. "I didn't tell you that before. It's how I keep you from getting intimidated."

"You bugger," she laughed.

He was right. With the truck loaded she was right back at square one. But this time it only took ten minutes to get the feel of things.

"So, what's the next thing you didn't tell me about?" She lit a cigarette and sighed. "Just so's I wouldn't be intimidated, of course."

"Now you're going to dump 'er." He lit his own cigarette and reached for his thermos. "First we have us a cuppa. I'll talk you through the routine a coupla times while we sip. This is the make 'er or break 'er, Cedar."

"Shit."

"Yeah. It's scary. What you're doing is shifting tons of gravel. And I mean tons of it! The truck's gonna lurch and there isn't bugger-nothing you can do to stop it. When it does, you're gonna feel total panic. I been doin' this for ten years and I still get that. You know when the car goes over a bump in the road, or you're on one'a those rides on the midway and your stomach jumps? Well, even this much later, that happens to me when I drop a load. Everyone feels it and if they say they don't you're talkin' to a liar."

Half an hour later, Cedar was on the job, and when she took her lunch break she was amazed to find that she was almost too tired to eat.

"What you got for sandwiches?" Ivan asked.

"Meat loaf."

"Trade you?" He held out a wax paper-wrapped sandwich. "My sister packs my lunch for me. She's a good person, but her idea of a sandwich is a piece of pita bread stuffed with sprouts and avocado and tomato."

"Here." She handed him her second sandwich.

"Hey, this is good. Your mom make the meat loaf?"

"I made the meat loaf. I don't live with my mom."

"Why not?"

"I've got my own place is why not."

"You're not married?"

"Not married, not engaged, not going steady, not dating, and not interested."

"What a waste. There oughta be a law against good-looking women disqualifying themselves. I got four sisters. Three of 'em got married young. The fourth, the sandwich maker, she won't even date guys. She went off to university, came out of it a social worker, has a job with the welfare, lives at home, packs my lunch when she does her own, and heads into the bush on days off, hiking and stuff. I tell her she's wasting her life and she tells me to mind my own business."

Cedar yawned and stretched. "What a day," she moaned. "I feel like I've been beat up."

"Tomorrow'll be rough, too, and after that, no sweat. What you got for dessert?"

"Chocolate cake."

"Want to trade?"

"No, but you can have mine. I'm too—"

"Yeah, first-day jitters. You make this chocolate cake, too?"

"Yeah."

"See, the girl of my dreams. How are you at ironing?"

"Never do it."

"Good. We definitely have got to get married."

"Right. I'll go pick up my ring on my way home from work."

She was early to bed and slept soundly, got up hungry and looking forward to her second day on the big truck. Gramps was still sleeping, and she closed the door to the kitchen so the sounds of breakfast wouldn't disturb him. Fortified with scrambled eggs and three cups of strong coffee, she headed out to the pigs. They grumbled, their schedule having changed because of her early starting time, but they'd be fine in a few days. Early breakfast was no hardship for them, and if it meant they had to have extra at lunch, she figured they'd adapt themselves. If there's one thing a pig likes to do, it's eat.

"Hey, Momma," she crooned to the big Tamworth sow, "you wait until I get home before you spew out those babies, you hear me? Good girl, good Rusty, yes, you are. Here." She pulled a potato from her pocket, slipped it to the sow. "Yes, Rusty likes her raw potatoes, don't you? Such a fine swine. You're Cedar's favourite, but don't tell the others."

Her second day was easier than the first, the third day easier still. By the end of the week she felt at home behind the wheel, taking loads from the gravel pit to the construction site. They were pushing a new highway through, so there would be months, probably a couple of years of work on this job alone. And all she had to do was back up to the loader, feel her stomach lurch as the fill was dumped into her truck, then drive from the pit to the worksite, feel her stomach lurch again as the load shifted, dump it where the foreman indicated and go back for another load. She drove with the driver's window rolled all the way down, the passenger's window partway down, Itzhak Perlman blaring from the stereo. She had her thermos, she had some small bottles of juice, she had a package of gum and some chocolate bars, she was all set up in the cab, at home as surely as if she'd been sitting in her own living room. Most days she ate in the truck, and only occasionally did she happen to be at the pit at lunchtime. Ivan teased her—there they were engaged to be married, he said, and he seldom saw her.

Rusty produced fifteen piglets, all healthy, all hungry. Cedar took four of them and put them in the orphanage, checked on them as soon as she got home from work, fussed them, rubbed their bellies, checked their formula, cleaned the nipples and made sure the feeder tubes were running easily. "Good babies," she said as they scrabbled at her feet, tame as puppies and just as eager for affection. "Good little Tammies. You'll be as fine as your momma if you keep on growing like this."

Instead of writing her name on her safety hat, she got a red cedar branch painted on it. Nobody said anything at work but a few days later Taffy showed up with a brand-new hat with a leek painted along the side, his name written on the stalk. Ivan got what he said was the Russian bear, and Brendan had the McKenzie tartan added to his.

"So you should come to the movies with me Saturday night," Ivan said. "We could go for dinner before and drinks after. Maybe do some dancing."

"No, thank you."

"Listen, I'll tell you what I told my sister. You're wasting your life.

You should start dating, get yourself involved, maybe even fall in love, fulfill your life."

"And I'll tell you what your sister was probably too polite to say. You have no idea about my life, it isn't any of your business." She did not smile or pretend to be kidding around. "I have a life, and it's a very full life. I don't need to get involved, I don't need to fall in love, and as for being fulfilled, how do you know I'm not?"

"Whoa!" He held up his hands. "Easy there."

"Certainly. And you do the same."

"All I did was invite you to a movie, I mean . . ."

"Have you invited any of the other drivers?"

"Why would I invite them?" he gaped.

"Think about it. You've known them a lot longer than you've known me, and you know them better than you'll ever know me. Now, I think I hear my truck calling."

Brendan intercepted her on her way to the truck.

"You okay?"

"I'm fine. Why would you ask?"

"Oh, you know how it is, born snoopy and got more so as I grew."

"I'm fine, Cuz. Won't interfere with my driving at all."

"You don't think you might be just a bit proddy about it?"

"Just a bit."

"Sometimes I hardly understand women at all. Other times they bloody well puzzle me."

"That's funny. You guys are real easy to figure out. Anything and everything revolves around your dingus."

He gawked.

"Jeez, Brendan, think it through. What did he really ask me?"

"To go to a movie, and have a meal."

"He doesn't need my eyes to see the movie, or my ears to hear it. If he wants to buy someone something to eat, the country is full of home-less people, any one of which would be damn glad to chow down on someone else's ticket. Has he ever asked you to a movie?"

"Why would he? I'm a guy, for Chrissakes."

"Yeah, so why did he ask me? Because when all the watching movies and eating and dancing is done, he wants to bounce on my bones."

"Christ, Cedar!"

"Think about it. Maybe ask Dixie about it."

"When Dix and I started going out it was because we liked each other."

"And if she'd refused when you asked, you'd have kept going out with her even if you weren't getting any?"

He stared, his face went red, he opened his mouth to say something, then he shut it again. Then he nodded. "I'll think about it," he promised. "There's something about it that really pisses me off, but I'll think about it."

Cedar thought about it, too. For days. On the surface she was just Cedar, doing all the things she was supposed to do, had to do or enjoyed doing. But inside, her brain was busy, pulling and prodding, poking and peering, and several times she thought she might be on the brink of something, but then it slid away and was hidden again, squirming out of sight, determined never, not ever, to be exposed.

Gramps met her as she drove up in the pickup. "You better come out to the barn."

"What's wrong?"

"You better come see."

The second Tamworth sow lay on her side, grunting contentedly, her newborn litter fighting with each other for a place at the milk bar. Cedar watched for a moment, then jerked with surprise. She reached down, picked up a piglet and tried to understand what she was seeing. Just behind the front shoulder was what looked like an extra leg—a back leg at that.

"I'll be damned. It was almost a Siamese twin, I guess."

"That's pretty much what the vet said," Gramps nodded. "She's going to drop by on her way home from work. Sometimes when they do in the piggy and investigate, they find the bones of the other one crammed inside. Other times the other one has just been eaten, or absorbed, or something, and there's no extra bones or anything."

"A five-legged pig. Does it work?"

"Doesn't seem to. It's not very big, though."

"Well, hello, Muffin." Cedar stroked the soft-skinned piglet. "Are you a good girl? Are you? Here, you go see if you can use that extra leg to kick the rest of those fat pigs away from the taps. You get yourself a good one. After supper I'll be back out and maybe give you a special snack from a bottle. Yes, got to make sure you get lots and lots of food, you've got an extra haunch to grow, right?"

"You gonna keep it?"

"Might as well. She wants to live as much as any of us do, I bet." She shrugged. "You never know, we might get a couple of extra rump roasts out of her, come butchering time."

But by butchering time, Muffin was sleeping on the porch and following Gramps around more faithfully than any dog. She was safe from the slaughtering knife for the rest of her natural life, however long that might prove to be.

"I don't know," the vet admitted. "I've never known a pig who got the chance to grow old. I'll check it out, though." When she phoned back two days later, she was laughing. "Would you believe about thirty-five years?"

"Thirty-five? I was thinking more like ten."

"Not too far out. You got the first quarter right."

Cedar could take any one of three routes to get home after work. The old highway took fifteen minutes, the new highway took twenty-five and what everyone called the back road took half an hour. But unlike the other two, the back road was a quiet drive through well-treed hills, along the side of the river, then back into the bush again. The animal shelter was two miles out of town along that road, and every few days Cedar stopped to see who was up for adoption. She thought she was looking for a pup and she thought she wanted something with either a lot of blue heeler or a lot of Australian sheepdog. Visit after visit she just shook her head, smiled and said, "I'll be back."

And then, as autumn moved shyly across the land, and the leaves began to dry and drift to the ground, there was exactly what she had not been looking for. The bitch was middle-aged, maybe six or seven. She wasn't any part heeler or sheepdog, she looked to be pretty much all Staffordshire bull terrier. Her ears had been docked off entirely, and her face, head and shoulders were criss-crossed with scars. Where other dogs whined eagerly or stood on their back legs begging for attention, this one sat quietly, not even looking at Cedar or the attendant.

"We don't know much about her," the attendant said. "She was muzzled and tied to a tree. Our vet says she's had several litters, and his guess is she was used for fighting until she got past her prime. All those scars, you know. Then she was left to die."

"She vicious?"

"Hasn't shown any sign of it, but she could be if she was used for fighting. There's a municipal bylaw that you can't have this kind of dog in town unless they're muzzled and you have a special licence."

"I live way out of town. I'll take her."

When they got home, Gramps stared and shook his head, but said nothing. Cedar walked the dog around the farm, talking quietly to her. She took her in the barn and the dog stiffened, muscles bulging, when she saw the pigs. "No." Cedar tugged the leash. Puzzled, the dog looked at Cedar, then looked at the pigs again. "No." Cedar led her through the barn, past the sows, past the boars, past the weanlings, and each time the dog stiffened, Cedar jerked the leash and said, "No." When they left the barn fifteen minutes later, the dog seemed indifferent to the sight and smell of pigs. And then she saw Muffin. She sat. She whined. She looked at Cedar, then at the pet pig, then at Cedar again. "Hey." Cedar hunkered down and stroked the ugly head. "Good dog. Yes, you are. Good, good dog. Oh, you're a fine one. Yes, you're as fine as silk, as good as gold, yes, yes."

The dog accepted the fussing, but did nothing to return the affection. She watched Muffin, watched Gramps, watched the pigs in their outdoor pens. When Cedar straightened and moved toward the house, the dog followed, the leash slack.

That night the dog lay on the rug beside Cedar's bed. Cedar reached down, rubbed the earless head, made soft sounds with her tongue against the roof of her mouth. The dog sat up. Cedar patted the bed. "Come on, then. Keep my feet warm." The dog climbed up on the bed and sat down stiffly and warily. "Good girl. Lie down." The dog obeyed, but did not relax. She lay beside Cedar almost shivering with anxiety. "Never been on a bed before? Hey, it's okay." Cedar stroked the dog, then settled herself for sleep. In the morning the dog was lying on the floor. When Cedar got up, the dog stood, and when Cedar was dressed and ready to go downstairs, the dog followed.

Cedar scrambled twice as many eggs for breakfast as usual and put down the extra for the dog. When she left for work with her lunch kit, there was an extra sandwich in it and the dog went with her. "Get you a safety harness for in the truck," Cedar promised.

"Anything happens, I don't need you lurching around in here like a guided missile."

"What's your dog's name?" Ivan asked. He was uneasy around the animal.

"Silk."

"Might be the ugliest dog I ever saw in my life."

"Probably is."

"She's wearing a muzzle. Does she bite?"

"Any dog will bite. But when this one does, she does a good job of it. So—better safe than sorry, right?"

Silk sat in the gravel truck, watching the world slip past. On her first trip she was alert and on guard, on her second she was more relaxed, and by the fifth trip of the day she was lying on the floor, her head on her front paws, eyes half closed.

The contract with the animal shelter specifically stated that Cedar would have the dog spayed. She waited two weeks before taking her to the clinic. "I want her to know us and feel safe before I get it done," she told the vet. "How's she going to feel if this stranger brings her somewhere and then she goes to sleep and wakes up hurting?"

"I think that's what they call over-identification," the vet teased. "She probably can't put two and two together in a situation like that. There's no evidence they're linear thinkers, you know."

"Still . . ."

"Fine by me. You've got three months to get it done before they're authorized to take the dog back. So until then, let's just give her a good checkover, make sure you haven't adopted a dog with a bad heart or an advanced case of emphysema or something. Leave the muzzle on this time, please. Even a gerbil can draw blood if it's nervous."

When the vet had finished examining Silk, she looked at Cedar and shook her head. "We have a problem. This bitch is pregnant."

"What?"

"She's pregnant. I'm amazed they didn't pick up on it at the shelter."

"Puppies?"

"Well, we can hope so, because the TV people will drive you nuts if she gives birth to a baby horse. If you schedule the spaying in the next couple of days, I can do it and abort the litter at the same time. If you wait much longer, it's too risky."

"No." Cedar stroked Silk's back. "No, I'll phone the shelter and tell them I'm going to let her have the puppies. Then I'll get her spayed, for sure. And make a contract with anyone who takes a pup that they'll have it neutered. It's not the puppies. It's that I don't want her to think she got dumped off here. I want her to trust me enough that when I leave her, she knows I'm going to come back for her."

When the pups were born, the vet came out to the farm to check on them. "I think it's safe to say," she said slowly, "these are what we in the profession call 'mixed breed.' We've got more than one dad in there."

"Oh, Silk," Cedar scolded, "you're such a whore."

Gramps wanted the long-eared male. By the time it was old enough to neuter, it seemed obvious that its father had been either a beagle or a basset. It was short-legged, long-bodied, long-eared and blunt-nosed.

"Looks like a bit of every dog in the world," Cedar teased.

Gramps laughed. "Looks like every dog in the world and he thinks he's a pig."

The pit bull-type pups went first, and then the long-haired husky-looking one. The black and tan short-hair was marked like a Rottweiler or Dobie, but built like Silk—broad-chested, compact and powerful. "She's a keeper," Cedar decided. "Hey, babe, you gonna stay at home with your momma? Well, give her a big kiss because you aren't going to see her for a couple of days. Come on, Silk, we're off to get you fixed."

"Don't even stop for gas," Gramps warned. "She might come in heat and be knocked up before the tank is full."

Campbell loved Keeper. He lugged her around until she got too heavy for him to carry, then he walked with his hand on her head. "We can't have dogs," he said for the umpteenth time. "The landlord is a grouch."

"Ah, but you can come here for the weekends and we've got three dogs. Silk is my dog, Muttly is Gramps's dog, and I guess, while you're here, Keeper is yours."

"I should live here all the time," he said. "You got a big big house. We don't. You got dogs. We don't. You got no landlord."

"There aren't any other kids for you to play with, you'd get lonely."

"Would not! I go to kindergarten, there's kids there. And I'd have Keeper. And Muffin. And Gramps. And you."

"And what about your mommy?"

"She could live here too. She could sleep with me."

"Is that so? You've got it all planned, do you?"

Gramps went to bed early that night and Campbell fell asleep on the couch in the living room. Alison carried him upstairs, to the guest room and put him to bed. But she didn't sleep with him. She tucked him in, then went down the hall to Cedar's room and walked in without knocking. "Could we talk?" she asked.

Alison and Campbell went back to their apartment the next afternoon, and Cedar slept lightly that night. She wakened early, and on her way home from work that day stopped briefly at Alison and Campbell's apartment. On Alison's next days off, they moved their few things to the big house—clothes and toys and budgie bird.

SEVEN

On Christmas morning, Campbell sat on the floor by the Christmas tree surrounded by wrapping paper, grinning widely, holding up Keeper's new collar. Gramps got two pictures of him, which later turned out to be the best he'd taken in five years. He got them enlarged and framed, and hung them on the living room wall.

Alison and Campbell were going to have Christmas dinner with the McCanns, and Cedar and Gramps were going to join the crowd at Grandma Larson's.

"We'll probably be back before you," Alison said. "Is there anything I can do to help when I get here?"

"Have a cold beer ready," Gramps said firmly. "Karen Larson is a wonderful cook with a heart of gold, but there won't be a drop to drink within an hour's walk."

"Oh, yes there will," Cedar said. "Just go see one of the uncles, they usually keep it hidden in their cars."

When they got home at nine, in the pitch black of a west coast winter night, the lights were on in the house. Cedar and Gramps walked into a warm, cinnamon-smelling kitchen and Alison handed each of them an open beer.

"See, your wish is my command."

"To your very good health," Cedar toasted.

They stood sipping beer and grinning foolishly, then Cedar slipped off her sneakers, shoved her feet into her black gumboots and went out to the barn. The feeders were half full and the pigs were stuffed, most of them settled for the night.

"See," Alison said from behind her, "I can figure out how to feed a few pigs."

"Thank you," Cedar said. "I appreciate it, really. But you don't have to, you know. It's not expected."

Alison came up beside her and took Cedar's hand in both of hers. "My kid is asleep in his own room with what he considers to be his dog sleeping on the bed with him. We've got more room than we've ever had. I could have worked my whole life away and never been able to set things up this well for him. You have to let me show my appreciation and you have to let us *live* here, not just . . . stay." She leaned over and kissed Cedar on the cheek. "Listen, if you want, I'll go to a lawyer and get a paper made up that says that I have no claim to any part of this. Like a prenuptial agreement without the nuptials or something."

"No need," Cedar said. "I just don't want you to feel that you have to . . . anything."

Gus was furious enough that he drove out to Cedar's farm for the first time. Even the bald top of his head was red, and his blue eyes flashed coldly.

"What in hell you trying to prove?" he shouted. "Just what in hell do you think you're doing, anyway? You got the whole goddamn town talking!"

"About what?" Cedar taunted him.

"You know damn fine well about what! They're killing theirselves laughing."

"They've been laughing at you for most of my life," she answered scornfully. "It never slowed you down any, why should it slow me down?"

"Do you know what they're saying?"

"I don't give the first part of a good fart what they're saying. Or not saying. Alison and Cam live here, now. And why not? After all, Cam's family, isn't he?"

"They're saying you 'n' her are queer for each other."

"So?"

"They're saying—" He choked with fury.

"Maybe they're making jokes about how you got there first and I picked up where you left off," she said calmly. "And how much Cam and I look alike."

"My own daughter!" He swung and Cedar ducked. And Silk had him by the wrist. She didn't break the skin, she didn't crush the bones, she didn't even growl. She just held him quietly by the wrist and did not let go.

"I wouldn't suggest you try that again." Cedar laughed. "You might piss her off."

"I'll shoot the bitch."

"No, Gus, you won't. You'll get in your car and get the hell off my place."

"I'm your father!"

"I know who you are. But you will not misbehave when you're in my home."

She snapped her fingers and Silk released her hold. Gus glared at the dog, then glared at Cedar. And finally he went wordlessly to his car, got in and drove off, his tires spitting gravel and mud.

"Easy, Silk," Cedar soothed. "Easy, girl."

"Who was that?" Gramps asked, coming out of the house.

"My esteemed paternal parent," Cedar replied. "As usual, Gus is a tad upset."

At the time of Gus's visit, the gossip was actually off the mark and it stayed that way for weeks. But by Easter, anything that the loose-lipped might have said was true.

"I was wondering," Alison said shyly, "and I know it's probably stupid, but . . . if I got you a ring, would you wear it?"

"Third finger left hand?" Cedar asked.

"Doesn't have to be *that*." Alison sat cross-legged on the bed, looking down at the quilt Grandma Larson had given Cedar for Christmas. "And if you don't want to, well, I'll understand. It's just . . ."

Cedar put her arms around Alison. "Why don't we go into town today and look around, see what they've got. But I have to tell you, I think I'd feel like a bit of a fool with something that looked too much like a wedding ring."

"I thought maybe a signet ring? Or a silver one, with Native designs on it, an eagle, maybe, or—?"

"We could wait until next weekend and go down to the city.

They've got some stores there that specialize in Haida jewellery and such."

They headed off on Friday night after work, leaving Gramps and Cam at home to look after the pigs. They stayed in a hotel with a bed the size of a baseball diamond and a bathroom fit for the Governor General. They visited the museum, and it was there, in the gift shop, that they found the rings. Alison gasped at the price, but Cedar just hip-butted her and laughed. "Nothing but the best," she bragged. "After all, I've got plastic." When they left, they not only had the rings, they each had a wide silver bracelet, intricately carved with First Nations designs. "I've never had anything this nice," Alison whispered.

"Know what I'm looking forward to?" Cedar asked. They were in bed, naked as the day they were born, sitting facing each other, the boxes open, the rings glittering in the lamplight. "I want to walk into the club some night and there you'll be, sitting on your stool, playing like an angel, and I'll sit down and order a beer, and just watch, feeling smug as hell, seeing the ring and the bracelet, and knowing. And there they'll be, scads of them, practically panting, and I'll be thinking, you're out of luck, you sad shit. You're out of luck!"

She kissed Alison and slid one of the rings onto her finger. Third finger, right hand. "Great idea," she said.

Alison reached for the other ring and put it on.

"And now—" Cedar took a bracelet and put it on Alison's left wrist. "Gotcha!"

"And I've got you!" Alison put the other bracelet on Cedar.

They got home early Sunday afternoon, with souvenir T-shirts for Gramps and Campbell, and a ring for Gramps—an adjustable one, because they didn't know his size and Cedar doubted any ring in the store was big enough to go over his knuckles.

He smiled shyly and slid the ring onto his baby finger. "I always wanted a pinky ring," he said, "but I figured my hands were too ugly."

Cedar wanted to protest, but the words got stuck in her throat. She hugged him instead and kissed his cheek.

They snugged into life together without even knowing how blessed they were. Cedar made her breakfast and packed her lunch kit, did barn chores and headed off to work in the morning while the others slept. Then Gramps and Campbell got up, and Gramps made oatmeal for their breakfast, serving it with whole milk from the dairy farm and brown sugar and cinnamon to sweeten it. They stacked their dishes beside the sink and trudged out to the barn to check on the pigs. The dogs followed them to the barn door, then sat and waited for them to re-emerge. Alison wakened later than the rest of them, in time to take Campbell to school. Sometimes she went back to bed when she got home, but most times she waited until late afternoon for her power nap. She saw her students at her mother's place in town, then picked up Cam after school and drove him home. She and Gramps started supper, except when she was too tired. On those days he ruled the kitchen and Cam peeled potatoes or made salad or measured rice for the cooker. When Cedar got home, she went to the barn. Cam had to go with her, of course. Often there were new piglets to examine, and sometimes she and Gramps had to decide which ones to move to the orphanage. Cam would sit with a piglet on his lap, holding a bottle, giggling as the baby grabbed it and slurped and sucked, squirming and dribbling milk:

They all ate together, then Cedar and Campbell did cleanup and Alison got ready for her job at Chuckles. She played there four nights a week, and on the weekends she was replaced by a three-piece band so that the customers could flail and lurch around the floor, drunkenly convinced they were dancing.

"The band asked if I wanted to play lead guitar with them, " Alison told Cedar, who sprawled on the bed, watching Alison get dressed for work. "It would mean quite a bit more money."

"What about a night off once in a while?"

"I could go to two nights a week, plus the weekends with the band. That would be four nights, same as now, but almost twice the pay."

"Sounds good."

"So you wouldn't mind?"

"Why would I mind? If you want to do it, great, and if you don't want to do it, that's great, too."

"I'd be working on your only nights off. They've been . . . kind of special . . . and . . ."

"But you'll still have nights off; and whatever night it is, it'll be special. All our time together is special. And nobody expects you to sit at home and play wifey."

So the routine changed, but only slightly, and if Alison enjoyed her work less, only she knew about it. Often her mind wandered, away from the blasting sound of the band and the few chords she played over and over. She dreamed of a different life, where she could not only teach classical but study with someone herself, someone who understood the nuances and wanted to talk about the things Alison found interesting. And however much she enjoyed Cedar's company, however much she felt content and safe, Alison was starting to realize that she wasn't that interested in talking about pigs or gravel pits.

"So," Mike said during their break, "are you completely exclusive with your girlfriend or would I have any chance at all?"

"Yes and no," she said without thinking, her cheeks hot.

"Damn. I was hoping you had an itch I could help scratch."

"You ever taken a good look at Cedar? You really think there'd be an itch?"

Mike laughed as if she'd said something outrageously funny. Alison smiled, as if she weren't ticked off enough to slash his tires, and several people watching them thought what good friends they were.

That night, as Alison was getting ready for bed, she thought about Mike's comment about an itch that needed to be scratched. She examined her reflection in the mirror, wondering if it showed. Was it her eyes? Is that what looked unsatisfied? How did he know, or was it a lucky guess?

She would have pulled out her own tongue before she would say a word about it to anyone, especially to Cedar, but the truth was, Cedar was less interested in sex than almost anyone Alison had ever met. In fact, Alison suspected Cedar might be just as happy and fulfilled just snuggling.

But Alison didn't have to tell her—Cedar knew their sex life was less than perfect. For some reason, after the first few months of their relationship, the whole sex thing started to seem ludicrous to her. The positions were awkward and probably looked ridiculous, and sometimes, as she stroked Alison to climax, Cedar felt detached, almost bored. Sometimes she thought she made love to Alison for no reason other than to have company, to ensure that Campbell would be there when she came home from work. It was a chore she did, like dishes or laundry, necessary and not unpleasant. Then again, if she was honest with herself, she knew that the kissing was wonderful, the holding and stroking was magical. It was just when they got to the point where Allie was passionate and throbbing, holding tight and straining for orgasm, that something in Cedar went *click* and shut off completely. She had the frightened feeling that the *click* wasn't supposed to happen, but she wasn't sure, and she didn't know who to ask.

Kate was one of the last to hear the gossip about Cedar and Alison. It came to her by way of Marg, who showed up one afternoon with the kids and a tray of lemon squares.

"We've maybe got a family problem," Marg said carefully.

"Oh, dear, what now?"

"It's Cedar."

"Cedar? What do you mean?" Kate's heart lurched, her throat tightened.

"No, no, she's fine. It's the gossip, it's spreading like wildfire. Haven't you been hearing it?"

"What gossip?"

"Well, think, Katie. Use your brain here." Marg was fast losing patience with Kate's seeming innocence, which was really a refusal to face the realities of life. "That Cedar is . . . involved . . . with Alison McCann. Hank even heard it from the guys at work."

"Alison and her son rent the upstairs, I know that."

"They don't just rent the upstairs, Katie. They live there. And Allie and Cedar are . . . well, the way people put it is that they're, you know, gearbox."

"A year ago people were saying she was shacked up with old man Conrad. I wish they'd get it straight!"

"This is no joke, Katie. They're wearing matching bracelets. Rings, too. They go everywhere together."

"Oh, fiddle."

"Did Gus tell you he went out there?"

"No."

"He did. And he told half the town. Had himself a rant and rave at the Domino Club. Did you see the bruise on his wrist?"

"Yes, he said it happened at work."

"It happened when that ugly dog of Cedar's grabbed him. That's what he was holding forth about. Wanted someone to go out and shoot it for him. Seems he and Cedar had an argument and the dog went for him."

"Remind me to buy some dog treats," Kate laughed. "What were they arguing about?"

"Come on, Katie."

Kate shook her head, trying to clear the humming noise from her head. Why did Cedar have to let it all flap in the wind, too scrappy even to attempt to keep things private? No, not Cedar, no way she'd be sneaking around at night, meeting someone at the viewpoint, never breathing a hint of it to anyone, even her closest friends. Here it is, out in the open, like it or lump it, and either way you can kiss my backside.

"Have you ever seen Alison's son?" Marg continued.

"I think I saw him when he was a baby. But I've hardly seen her lately, let alone the little guy. Why?"

"Do you know what she called him?"

"No."

"His name is Campbell McCann. Gorgeous little guy. Big blue eyes and a head full of curls. Soft, blond curls."

"Oh my God." Kate felt the blood drain from her face.

"So what they're saying is that Allie couldn't get an exclusive on the old one so she shacked up with the young one. They're saying she'd have gone after Rory except he was still in school."

"Oh my God." Kate said again. She laid her slice of lemon square back on her plate and absent-mindedly began wiping her sticky fingers on her cotton napkin, rubbing, rubbing, rubbing.

She tried to shrug it off, she tried to ignore it, she tried to make sense of it, and still the worm twisted in her guts.

"You okay, Mom?" Rory asked. They were sitting at the kitchen table drinking tea, unwinding after a busy Saturday night at Mom's.

"I'm fine."

"You don't look fine. You look like someone who hasn't had anywhere near enough sleep. You look like someone who's very worried about something."

"I'm fine," she insisted. She looked up into his calm gaze and knew she was seeing him as he would be when he was Dr. Campbell—concerned, interested, involved, able to see through evasions, denials and outright lies.

"It's Cedar."

"What about Cedar?"

"This gossip about her and Alison McCann."

"Who told you?"

"Auntie Marg. You *knew?*"

"What did Auntie Marg say?"

"She said everybody's talking about them. That they're . . . you know."

"Well, it's true. They are. They're—"

"Queer." Kate said it like a sob.

Rory nodded. "Gearbox, dyke, bull dagger, any number of put-downs."

"It's unnatural."

Rory laughed. "Mother, really. Have you never watched your own chickens? And why do you think they say 'horsing around'?"

"It's against everything! In the Bible it says—"

"Oh, stop it." Rory wasn't laughing any more. "As if the bloody Bible had anything to do with the way we've lived for years! Bad enough the old man is out there fracturing the ten commandments. What's your excuse?"

Kate was suddenly terrified. What if she and Ted hadn't been as careful as they had thought?

"That Bible, doesn't it say that those who condone the sin are as guilty as those who commit it? You've known for years the old bugger was up to his nose in adultery, and what have you done about it?"

"Certainly not condoned it."

"He lives here when he's not in camp. All cozy and family-like."

"We were talking about Cedar. Not about your father."

"Cedar works hard and she's good at her job. Cuz says she's one of the most reliable drivers he has. She doesn't owe anybody anything. She and Gramps have their pig farm on its feet. It's doing better all the time. She pays her taxes, in full and on time."

"But Rory—isn't it a sign of mental problems?"

He refilled their teacups, then tapped his finger on hers to remind her to sip it and calm herself. "In this family we should worry about mental problems?" he said gently. "Whatever anyone else thinks or says, whether it's the psychiatric association or the neighbour down the road, Cedar is family. And so is Campbell. He's a great little guy, and he and Cedar are good together. Gramps thinks the sun rises and sets on that kid. And Allie, well, she's a nice person. You used to be friendly, remember?"

"I didn't really know her. She played at Mom's, but . . ."

"She plays a good guitar, and she lives her life as best she can. I don't think her sex life is any of my business, and I know for sure my sister's sex life isn't."

"Don't talk like that!"

"What, sex? You can't spend the rest of your life pretending it doesn't exist. Cedar has a sex life. So do I—it isn't much, I grant you, but one can always hope."

"You're a kid, you're just a boy!"

"Yeah? How old were you when Cedar was born?"

"That wasn't the same. It isn't the same."

Kate tried to ignore the gossip, tried to mind her own business. She tried to concentrate on the positive things about Cedar and her life, and the harder she tried to get past what Marg had told her, the more it just leaped up and slapped her in the face. Rory spoke to Dr. Forbes, and between the two of them they gathered more articles and books than Kate would ever have time to read. But to Kate, none of it had to do with Cedar. Not Cedar! Not her firstborn and only daughter!

Finally, white-faced and sleep-deprived to the point of dizziness, Kate headed out to see Cedar. It was a Saturday morning, and the spring flowers were in bloom, the wild currant bushes glorious deep red against the blue-green of the bush, the salmonberries already forming, the alders blushed with new life.

Kate found Cedar sitting on the tractor, loading composted pig muck into the back of the pickup truck. Campbell was sitting on her knee, his hands on the steering wheel, his face turned up to hers, talking to her, and Cedar listened intently even as she worked. The sound of the tractor engine was loud enough to drown out the noise of Kate's car, which gave her time to catch her breath. They looked more alike than Cedar and Rory did!

Three astonishingly ugly dogs came barrelling toward the car, so Kate sat tight, waiting for someone to call them off. Campbell turned, looked at the car and said something, and Cedar looked, too. For a moment she locked eyes with Kate, and her face was absolutely expressionless, as if she was seeing a rock, or a tree, or someone she had never met. Then she smiled, a wide, easy smile, and turned off the tractor.

Campbell was first off the tractor, running toward the car, yelling at the dogs. "Back!" he screeched. "Sit!"

All three dogs stopped barking and sat down, their tails wagging. Kate got out of the car and waved at Cedar as she walked toward her.

"Hello," she called. "Is that all you've got to do on a lovely day like today?"

"I'm Campbell."

"Pleased to meet you, I'm sure." Kate forced herself to smile. He looked like Rory had at that age, except for the hair—Rory had the butter blond hair of the Larson family and Campbell's was almost white, like Gus and Cedar's had been. But they all had the same Scots-slanting eyes, the same long upper lip, the same kiss-my-arse manner that had been Cedar's and still was.

"This is a surprise." Cedar hugged Kate, kissed her cheek. "To what do we owe the honour of your visit, madam? Tell us, so we can do it again and have you back more often. Cammy, could you run on ahead and plug in the kettle for us?"

"You just want to ditch me, is all."

"Off you go, boy, or I'll rip off your head, reach down the hole and pull out your lungs and feed them to the pigs."

"You did that last week." He patted Cedar on the bum, then ran for the house.

As soon as he was out of sight, the smiles vanished. Kate and Cedar looked at each other for long, silent moments.

"He looks like Rory," Kate managed. "And moves like you. So it's true."

"What's true, Mother?" Cedar sounded as formal as if she were talking to the owner of the gravel company.

"What the gossip is saying. About him being your half-brother. Gus's boy."

"What else is the gossip saying?"

It was a challenge. Kate could either pick it up or leave it lie. "They're saying that you and that boy's mother are . . . deeply involved."

"That's a nice way of putting it," Cedar smiled. "You've got a way with words, sometimes. Who told you what 'they' were saying?"

"Your Aunt Marg. Uncle Hank overheard some gossip at work. You know what they're like, sitting in the crummy with nothing to do but work their jaws. Men are such gossips." Kate tried to laugh but managed only a faint smile.

"Yeah. Well, if they're talking about me they're leaving my friends alone. My mother taught me that. My mother always did know how to handle gossip."

"Your mother is a bit upset."

"Why would my mother be upset?"

"There are some pretty ugly words for it."

"There are ugly words for everything."

"You aren't making this easy, are you, Cedar?"

"What is it you want to know?"

"Is it true? Are you and Alison McCann . . . involved? Are you a couple?"

"Yes."

There it was, out in the open, squirming and twisting. For a horrible moment Kate was afraid she was going to puke. She wished she had stayed home, had never asked the question. Why had she asked, when she knew, the way she knew the sun set in the west, that Cedar would tell her the bald truth?

"I'm shocked. Upset. I don't know . . ."

Cedar watched the tractor, as if it might suddenly begin to tap dance.

"Is it an affair? Is it some kind of experiment?"

"We live together, Momma. We share a bedroom, we share a closet, we share a bed, we share the kid. She even insists on paying half the grocery bill."

"And the farm?"

"The farm is Gramps's and mine. Allie had a contract drawn up by a lawyer. A promise never to make any kind of claim. She insisted on it."

"And the boy?"

"His name is Campbell. For short we call him Cam or Cammy. He's Campbell Ewen McCann."

"And is he a suitcase, a little bit of baggage that accompanied her?" Kate snapped, "Or is he a real live person in your life?"

"Oh, he's real live all right. He's in my will as my heir. If I get buried under a load of gravel on Monday morning, all this is his, with Gramps running the show for as long as he can. After that, I've asked Cuz to look after things. It's all so complicated that I decided not to get killed until Cam's at least twenty-five and able to take over himself."

"And if you and Alison split up?"

"Campbell will still be in my life. I had a paper drawn up, too. I can't adopt Cam, for obvious reasons, but I've got legal rights, and in the event we split up, I get him every weekend and for half the summer holidays."

"I very much need a cup of tea," Kate blurted. She dabbed at her eyes. "I'm sorry, Cedar, this might take a bit of getting used to."

"I know, Momma. It's taken me a bit of getting used to, too."

They began walking toward the big house.

"Does Joe realize the situation?"

"Oh, he realizes it fully. His only regret is that he was hoping I'd hook up with someone and have a few babies for him to fuss over and spoil."

"And will you?"

Cedar laughed, a genuine chortle. "I don't know. I wasn't pining for the chance before Allie came along, why would it suddenly move to the top of my list?"

"I understand your father was out here, raising hell."

"When isn't he?"

"Your dog bit him."

"No, she didn't bite. She just clamped on. He was all set to get rangytang and throw his weight around, and Silk took objection. Didn't you, old girl? It'll take more than Gus Campbell to get away with that kind of trashy behaviour, right?"

"When your Auntie Marg told me that part, I promised I'd get dog treats for her." Kate nudged her in the ribs. "They're in the car."

Cedar smiled. "He's really angry, Momma."

"Well, he's back in camp, now. Let him take it out on them."

"Did he raise any trouble with you?"

"Didn't say a word about it. But then, he wouldn't. He might have to admit Campbell got his name honestly."

Alison was still sleeping, but Gramps had made tea and set out a carrot cake. Campbell brought the sugar bowl and the carton of cream to the table, then held his hands out to Cedar, who looked at them, kissed the back of each, and nodded.

"I have to keep my hands real clean," Campbell said to Kate. "Because I help with the food. Cedar says nobody wants pig poop in the soup. Or dog smell on their sammiches."

"Good idea," Kate agreed, reaching out and ruffling his hair. "When Cedar was little she had to always keep her hands clean, too. We didn't have pigs, but she could always find something to get into."

"Was she a nice kid?"

"She was the nicest girl you could ever meet. The next time I come out I'll bring some pictures of her."

"You're looking tired, missus," Gramps said, pulling out a chair for her.

"I'm a bit short of sleep," Kate admitted. "Spring fever, I think. Your body feels dead tired but your brain just will not turn off."

"When that happens, I get up and get myself a good stiff shot of whiskey," Gramps winked. "Why, sometimes I'm so tired by seven o'clock at night I have to have a couple of shots."

"Maybe I'll have to try that."

Halfway through their second cup of tea, Alison appeared in the doorway to the kitchen in a nightgown and a terrycloth robe. She saw Kate and stopped dead, her face suddenly pale.

"Good morning, Allie," Kate said pleasantly. "I hope I didn't waken you. The dogs set up a terrible row when I arrived. Probably because I've been such a stranger around here, they didn't know me."

"No," Alison managed. "No, I didn't hear . . . anything."

"Tea, love?" Cedar stood up. "I'll put it on, it'll be ready in no time."

"Thank you. I'd love some tea."

"They only let me have a little bit," Campbell complained. "Mine's mostly milk."

"Oh, that's how I take it, too, look." Kate held out her cup. "I always add milk to mine. Now, Cedar, she likes hers weak, no milk or cream, lots of sugar. And Rory, he likes his the same way. But I like milk in mine."

"Do you sugar yours?"

"Oh, you just bet I do. Here, try."

"Yours is sweeter. It's good."

"Try a bit of sugar, then. Just a bit, see? Tell you what, my favourite way is to have it with honey. I get my honey from a woman who works with me. She has her own bees. I'll get a small jar for you, and you can try that in your tea."

"They say it stunts my growth."

"I know. That's just what grown-ups say because they're so cheap they want all the tea for themselves." Kate winked at him. "Next time I come I'll bring honey. And the pictures. And bones for the dogs." She looked up at Allie and smiled as if there was no reason in the world for either of them to feel awkward with each other. "You should sit down, dear, Cedar can get your tea for you."

Halfway down the bush road to the highway, Kate pulled the car to the side and turned off the motor. She put her hands over her face and sobbed. "Damn, damn, damn!" she moaned.

The following Saturday she was back, with honey for Campbell, bones for the dogs and two picture albums. "There, see? That's our Cedar when she was brand new."

"Who's that with her?"

"That's her daddy. Gus Campbell."

"And who's that in the next one?"

"That's her grandpa, Colin Campbell."

"Everybody's called Campbell. My name is Campbell, too. But my first name, not my other one."

"I know. Campbell Ewen McCann, right? Well, you see this big guy here? That's Cedar's uncle Ewen. His first name is the same as your middle name. And it's Rory's name, too. Rory Ewen Campbell."

"Did he roar?"

"No. He was a very quiet baby. But his granddaddy, that's old Colin, had a brother named Rory. And when Rory was born his grandpa wanted him to have that name because the other Rory, the one who still lives in Scotland, he didn't have any boys, just girls."

"Is that Cedar's dad, too?"

"Yes."

"And who's *that?*"

"That's Cedar when she was the same age you are now. Well, maybe a bit older, that was taken on her first day of school. Maybe your first day of grade one I'll come out with my camera and take your picture, too. See, she's got all her new schoolbooks and everything. Of course she's also got a look on her to sour the milk. She didn't want to go to school."

"I want to go to school. I already go, but only to kindergarten. Grade one you get to learn to read."

"It's very hard to learn to read. But Cedar caught on fast. Rory, too. I expect you'll catch on fast, too. You seem very clever. Or are you just trying to fool an old woman?" She nudged him in the ribs, and he giggled.

"You're not old," he said. "My Grandma McCann is old. She says she's old because my momma was the tail of the cow."

"Who's my dad?" Campbell asked at supper. "The other kids have dads. Why don't I?"

"You have a dad," Alison said calmly. She had been prepared for years for this very moment. "I've told you about him."

"So where'd he go?"

"He had things he had to do. Work he had to do."

"Other dads don't."

"That's because our situation is what people call 'unique'. That means it's special."

"Tell me about him."

"What else do you need to know? I told you he's very tall, and very very strong, and he has curly blond hair like yours, lots and lots of it, even more than you have. And he's a real good singer, and he can tap dance."

"How big is he?" He wasn't ready to let go of it. "As big as Gramps?"

"Bigger."

"You know how big my uncle Hank is?" Cedar intervened, going to Alison's rescue. "Well, your dad is as big as he is."

"How come some of the kids say I've got no dad?"

"Are they stupid or something?" Gramps said suddenly. "Didn't their moms tell them the truth? Think of the pigs. If we never put the sow with the boar, would we get piglets?"

"Course not. You have to have one of each to make baby pigs."

"Well, people are the same. Everyone has a dad. Even I had a dad! Cedar has one, your mom had one, and you've got one. Those kids say you don't have a dad because they don't know where babies come from."

"Where do they?"

"We're not going to talk about it at the supper table. It's private. You and I will talk about it after supper. Now get back to your plate, boy, there's cheesecake for dessert."

Later, when Campbell was in the tub and Cedar was rinsing his hair, he brought it up again.

"Cedar?" He took the cloth from his face and held it over his little dingus. "Do you know about babies?"

"Yes."

"Are you going to get one?"

"I don't know. I don't think so. Why?"

"Gramps told me." He looked so serious, so much like Rory. "About men and women and how they make babies. And you got no man to be a dad for you. And Gramps is too old and I'm not a man yet. So how would you?"

"Well, I guess I'd have to go shopping. Look around until I saw a guy I thought would make a good baby. I'd want him to be very healthy, and very nice. I think I'd want a smart one so the kid would be smart, too. What do you think?"

"And then what? Would you marry him?"

"I'm not sure I'd want to do that. You don't have to be married to make a baby, you know that."

"What if he wanted to be a real dad to his baby?"

"Ah. I see where this is going. Well, maybe I wouldn't even tell him. Maybe I'd want to have my kid all to myself, and not share him."

He shook his head. "That's not fair. If I was a dad I'd want to see my kid. Once in a while, anyway."

"I'll remember that. If the time ever comes, which it probably won't. Did you get your smelly little feet clean?"

"My feet don't smell. Gramps says noses smell, feet run. Except in backwards land, and then noses run and feet smell. In backwards land you do everything the other way."

"Right. I guess in backwards land if you wanted clean feet, you'd have to wash your face."

When Cedar went downstairs after putting Campbell to bed, Gramps had coffee ready. She poured herself a mug and took it to the living room.

"How'd the talk go?" she asked.

"Fine. He'd figured out most of it already. They're getting wiser a lot younger. I bet I was nine before I wanted to put it together. Ted was probably seven. This one's not going to be six for another month and a half. Keeps on this way, they'll have to explain it to them as they slide out into the world."

"He asked me if I was going to get a baby." She laughed.

"I've wondered that myself, from time to time. Be a shame in some ways if you didn't, but it wouldn't be no surprise. Even before Alison I wondered if you'd ever hook up with anyone."

"There's no part of it interests me," she said frankly. "I don't believe the happily ever after part and I'm not interested in the fighting and nagging part."

"Doesn't have to be that way. Wife and I didn't do much of that. Course, she was a lot easier to get along with than you are. Or me, for that matter."

"I wish I'd known her."

"Yeah, I wish you had. She was an angel come to earth. I miss her. Every day there's something I see, or hear, and I want to turn around and have her be there, so I can share it and . . . Damn commercials! You know, they start off the movie with the breaks spread out pretty well, then they've got you hooked and the closer you get to the end of the movie, the quicker they come."

Gus went apoplectic when he came out of camp and found out that Kate was going to visit Cedar almost every Saturday.

"If you had any idea at all of what's going on out there," he raged, "you wouldn't set foot in that place!"

"Cedar is my daughter. And that's all I need to know. "

"You don't have the first clue what—"

"I've never been as dim as you thought, Gus. I'm fully aware of the situation, fully aware of the relationship, and I know, too, what's written on Cammy's face for the whole world to see. So don't tell me I don't have the first clue."

It stopped him, but only for a moment.

"You stay away from that place, you hear?"

"You are my husband," Kate said coolly, "but not my master. I'll see my daughter any time I want. If I want to sit at a table and have tea with Cedar and Alison, that's none of your business. If I want to sit with Cammy on my knee and look at old photos, it's no skin off your nose."

"Damn it, woman!"

"Stop it, Gus, you're making yourself look foolish again."

Gus took his anger to his mother, expecting her to agree with him that it was all a terrible, terrible thing.

"It's none of your business," she said calmly. "I had a sister said the mere thought of having a man squirm on top of her was enough to make her lose her last meal. She didn't spend her life living alone."

"Mother!" Gus couldn't believe his ears.

"Oh, indeed," Mary laughed. "Listen to you. So righteous. So morally superior. Next I suppose ye'll be telling me it's unnatural. There's other things go against nature, my boy, and you're guilty of several of them yourself. You haven't mentioned a few facts in this situation. You haven't mentioned you should be doing far more for that wee lad than ye've ever done, and ye don't even recognize your own jealousy when it jumps up and bites you on the airse. That's all it is, my boy, is jealousy. Allie McCann wouldn't gie ye the time'a day, now, and why should she, puir fool? If it was anybody else, or at least if it was someone ye'd not already got close to and then been ignored by, ye'd laugh. Och, ye'd say, listen to the fuils, as if the Campbells had ever been made to live by the same rules as other folk. Ye can just stop this wee fitty ye've been having."

"And stop your gob, as well," Colin put in loudly from his chair on the porch. "Tellin' the entire scabby bunch at the Domino Club that the dog lunged at ye! Might as well have invited 'em all to go along and see ye mek a fuil of yerself! Ye've been flap-jawing as if your tongue was fastened in the middle and wigglin' at both ends."

"Nobody's business but Cedar's, anyway," Tamas rumbled from where he was sitting on the porch with his father.

"Listen to the lot of you! You mean to tell me you approve of this?"

"I wasnae asked for my approval," Colin said. "Now if it's disapproval you want to hear, ask me how I feel about a McCann boy wi' no da' of his own."

Gus came close to shoving back his chair, getting to his feet and telling them all to go to hell. But the look on his mother's face stopped him. If he did any of that, she would close her door to him. Currents were flowing that Gus didn't recognize. Somehow there was something that they all understood, but that had escaped him completely.

"I expected better, is all," he said weakly.

"Och!" Mary Campbell scoffed.

"Aye," Colin agreed.

EIGHT

Campbell was in grade two when Alison told Cedar she thought one of them should have a baby.

"Come again?" Cedar stared at Allie as if she had begun to talk old Gaelic.

"I think we should have a baby."

"Why?"

"It isn't good for any kid to grow up the only child."

"He's done fine with it so far. Even if you got pregnant tonight—and small chance of that, you have to admit," but the joke failed totally, "he'd be eight years old when the next one came. When it was eight, he'd be sixteen and bored with having a small sib tagging along."

"Rory has never been bored with Tony or Suzie or Chris."

"They're his cousins. He doesn't have to live with them."

"He might as well, he sees so much of them. He goes to all of Tony's soccer games—"

"Only when he's home, Allie."

"Well, of course only when he's home!" Allie snapped. "You know, just about the only thing about you that makes me mad is the way you refuse to take anything seriously!"

"Are you mad at me?"

"I'm getting livid."

"Maybe we should put the conversation on hold, then. Try again sometime when we aren't both tired."

"Tired. I am so sick of hearing the word tired!"

"There isn't any law says a person can only discuss things at," Cedar checked the clock, "one-thirty in the morning, you know. Couldn't we have talked about it at, say, noon?"

"I hadn't made up my mind then. And anyway, all of this is just another way to deflect the discussion."

"Oh, now it's a discussion. Well, tell you what, you make coffee while I have a pee, and wash up, and then we'll discuss."

"Wash up? What, you're going to take a shower instead of—"

Cedar winked. "I've got you all over my face. How in hell do you expect me to carry on a sane conversation when every breath I take smells of you? It makes me dizzy, it makes me drunk, it makes me—" and she pretended to faint, flopping on the bed, her eyes rolling.

It worked. Alison giggled, her anger dissolved. She bent forward and kissed Cedar, then she was out of bed and heading for the door. "I'll make real coffee, it won't take any longer than boiling the kettle for instant."

Cedar got out of bed, peed and washed up, put on a clean T-shirt and brushed her hair. How could you have a real discussion when you looked as if you had a bird's nest on your head? The faint scent of Allie came to her when she used the brush, and she half grinned. Not just her face and hands, not just her chin and throat, even her hair. But the stickiness was gone, and she could move her mouth without feeling as if her skin was going to crack. There were things about sex that were really just too funny for words. Things nobody talked about or wrote about, things like waking up in the morning and the first sight of yourself you get, your face has little whitish flecks stuck to it, where your lover's fluids have dried. Things like your eyebrows getting stuck and matted and twisted, and rumpled, if eyebrows can rumple. Sometimes it was almost offensive, this after-mess, as if lovemaking should not leave signs and stains and evidence, as if such a nice thing should not leave such gross debris.

Finally they were settled, fortified with coffee and cigarettes.

"So," said Cedar. "When did you first start thinking about this?"

"The first time was when Cammy was about two years old. He was up, and walking, and had perfected such charming phrases as No, I won't, and Shu' up, and he was doing endearing things like flinging himself onto the lawn and having a fit. I realized he was growing up, and I thought how much I was going to miss having a baby around."

"But you didn't have another one."

"I didn't have the money, the time or the place. We were in a one-bedroom basement suite and I was so broke all the time I even considered going on welfare."

"You should have."

"There's never been a McCann on welfare," Allie said prissily. "Every now and again, I'd get this craving. But it would pass."

"Maybe it will pass again." Cedar stifled a yawn. Allie would pitch all kinds of fits if she yawned right now, and the thought of Allie angry again was like a rock in Cedar's stomach.

"Well, it hasn't. I want it more and more all the time."

"Do you have someone picked out?" No way in hell would Cedar be using her mouth on Allie if she was dinking some guy. She'd cut off her lips and pull out her tongue first.

"Well . . ." Allie sipped her coffee and took her time puffing on her cigarette, drawing it out as if she were thinking deeply.

To Cedar's shock, she realized that she didn't believe what she was seeing. This was a very good actress doing an excellent performance. Allie must have been thinking and planning for a very long time.

"There's the fertility clinic in the city. They have a list of sperm donors, and you pick one. You never see the guy and he never sees you."

"I understand the process," said Cedar. "We use it with the pigs when we want to introduce a new bloodline."

"It's expensive, but it's one way. Or we can pick some guy we know and use a turkey baster."

Cedar laughed, she couldn't help it. The image of Allie impregnating herself with the baster, squeezing its bright yellow rubber bulb, cracked her up.

Allie laughed too. "If we did it that way, I thought we could ask Rory if he'd help us."

"Rory?" Cedar jerked upright.

"Well, why not? Then the baby would look like Campbell, and you. It would be almost like it was really *us.*"

"Jesus Christ almighty."

"And they'd be related."

"They sure would be. They'd not only be half-brothers, they'd be—what, bloody cousins as well? One's dad is the others' granddad. What would that make them to each other? It boggles the mind."

"We wouldn't have to tell them that part of it." Alison reached for another cigarette. "I'll buy you a pack tomorrow," she promised.

"You owe me a carton by now."

"Oh, listen to you."

"No, I'm not going to listen to me. Nobody else does."

"I'll get more coffee. Give you time to think a bit."

Cedar thought about how she was usually the one who got the coffee, did the up-and-down-the-stairs thing. She didn't like this part of herself that surfaced sometimes, like the corbie of doom, telling the truth as the corbie always did, but telling it in such a way it seemed ugly. It was true, though. The only times Alison did the wide-smile go-for-coffee was when she wanted something. The same with the bath. More times than enough, Cedar would climb the stairs, start the bath water, add the bubble bath or the scented crystals, and all Allie had to do was get herself into it and soak. It was Cedar who made the little snack and left it where Allie would find it when she came in from work, Cedar who picked the nicest flowers and put them in a vase on Allie's dresser. Unless Alison wanted something, like a trip to the city. Then it was breakfast in bed with smiles and kisses and Cedar arranging to trade overtime for the shifts off, even though it cost her money. A helluva price to pay for scrambled eggs and toast.

Shut up, corbie, it's more than scrambled eggs and toast, there's coffee and jam too, and of course the trip to the city, excellent Chinese food, shopping, concerts.

Ah, the corbie squawked, you need the city to go shopping for jeans and T-shirts. Oh my, yes. And work boots, mustn't forget the work boots. After all, they were ten dollars cheaper than they would have been right here at home and it only cost you gas, flex time, hotel costs and meals to save all that money. Such a bargain, my dear. Run the pig farm that way and you'll be belly-up by Christmas.

Cedar tried to ignore the corbie and focus on what Alison had said. How do you tell a woman she can't have a baby? What if Uncle Hank had said, Marg, the truth of it is, you've had five miscarriages and each one came closer than the one before it to killing you, so I'm getting myself fixed. What would Auntie Marg have done? Hit the bottle? Walk around talking to herself? Taken a razor blade to her own flesh?

Or just nag, nag, nag, nagged until life wasn't worth living for anyone, all the laughter drying up and scuttling off like dried-up autumn leaves, rattling like Billy Bones when you bumped the table where he stood, clitter clatter and your flesh creeps.

Allie came in smiling, a mug of coffee in each hand, the thermos under one arm, pressed against the swell of her breast.

"If you were to ask Rory, you'd probably have to wait until he gets his Thanksgiving long weekend." Cedar concentrated on her tone of voice, not wanting to sound grudging or unwilling, but also not wanting to sound excited about the whole thing. "Unless, of course, you've decided it should be me who does this."

"I thought about that. And if you want to, that's wonderful. But I also thought, you'd be off work a good four months, and at the wages you make, that's an expensive baby. I can play guitar right up until the door of the delivery room closes behind me. And after all, I'm the one who wants it. It's not fair to ask you to do something this big just because I want it."

Yes, Allie had been pondering this for a while. "And would it be Rory?"

"I thought we'd talk to Rory in October, then he'd have to have time to think about it. He'll be back in December, but supposing he agrees, we'd still have to wait at least until September for the baby. And that's only if it all works right away, which it might not, because I haven't figured out my fertility cycle."

"You know something?" Cedar chuckled. "This is just like the kind of talks Gramps and I have about the sows. Oh yes, let's see now, number seventy-three cycles in a week, eighty-six and twenty-two aren't going to be in until the week after that, so it's going to mean two trips for the AI guy . . ."

"You stop that." Alison slapped Cedar's leg gently. "You just stop it or you're going to get such a bite on the bum as you won't believe."

"Dear me, now I'm terrified."

"So what do you think?" Allie asked, but Cedar had the feeling the decision was made regardless of what she said.

"Would you have to go down to the city for it?"

"No, it can be done here. I thought maybe if it didn't work, or take, or whatever you and Gramps call it, we could still talk to Rory. And if nothing has happened before Christmas holidays, we could try with him then."

"Would you mind awfully," Cedar said, assuming a plummy English accent, "if we bought a new turkey baster especially for the occasion? I mean, Christmas and all, we'd need the one we've got for the goose."

"Oh, you!" Allie snuggled closer. "I kind of like the idea of a reddy-haired kid," she added.

"I'd like a blond," said Cedar, "but hey, who am I to argue? Someone who will grow up tall and with at least a few brains."

"Tall, brains, red-haired and . . . maybe musical?"

"Christ, can you get that specific? We've never tried for musical with the pigs."

"They tell you all kinds of stuff. Was he good in math, everything. And you can hold out for brains—they've got lots of university students who donate because they get paid for it."

"Well, might as well get the most qualified you can find. Be nice to get a brain surgeon. Rory would score high, wouldn't he? Tall, good looking, blond as butter, medical student, sings like a bird."

"There you go. If he had red hair he'd be perfect."

"You're sure about this?"

"I'm sure. I want a tall, brilliant, talented, red-haired girl and I want to call her Molly."

"Oh, we've even got a name for her, have we. Molly who?"

"Molly McCann."

"Molly who McCann? Molly Anne, Molly Jane, Molly . . . Polly?"

"Molly Kathleen McCann."

"Christly Irish-sounding name, that."

"Catherine, then."

"No, Kathleen's good. I like Kathleen. I like Molly, too. So a June or July baby, eh. What's that, Cancer? They're supposed to be home-bodies, that'll be nice. It's always nice when the infant stays home. Such a pain having to chase after it as it crawls off down the road, looking for new worlds to conquer."

Steven Campbell McCann was born at the end of May. He was twenty-two inches long, weighed nine pounds six ounces, and had huge hands and feet.

"Well," Cedar sighed, "at least he's got reddy hair."

"I wanted a little girl."

"What you got was a big boy. I suppose that means you'll have to try again."

"Your turn next. Unless I go insane again."

"He's sure skinny," Cammy said disapprovingly, peering through the glass window of the nursery. "I thought he'd be round and soft. He's a real skinnymalink."

"He'll fatten up fast enough," Gramps promised, grinning widely. "My Ted was scrawny when he was born, and by the time he was a year old he weighed twenty-five pounds."

"That's not much."

"It is if you're carrying it around on your hip all day. You'll see, he'll be worth bringing home. He's a keeper."

"I didn't think I'd be scared to hold him," Cam said. "But now that I see him, he looks like he might break."

"He won't break, boy. He looks small to you, but for a baby, he's a real good size. And we have to be careful with him, but there's nothing to be afraid of. He's bigger than any baby pig you ever held. And he'll be easier to hold, too, not as wiggly and twisty. Come on, boy, let's you and me go celebrate. Do you realize there's more of us now than there are of them? Heh heh heh, it's guy time at our place!"

Cedar watched them heading off toward the elevator, Cam holding Gramps's hand, chattering happily. She looked at Steve and waited to feel for him what she felt for Campbell. Maybe it took a bit of time. Maybe once she knew him better, she'd feel that same surge of emotion. Right now he looked like a loaf of bread wrapped in a pale blue receiving blanket. His face looked like the faces of the other newborns in the nursery. They could all have come off the same assembly line— little round heads, round faces, squinchy eyes.

Cedar went back to Allie's private room but the curtains were still drawn around the bed while the nurses helped her clean up. Cedar wondered what was taking so long. She waited briefly, then went to the elevator, rode it down to the main floor and went outside for a cigarette She wondered, not for the first time, what in hell was wrong with her. Why did she just detach when her emotions ought to be surging? She'd felt more involved in soccer games than she had in the birth of this kid who was, legally at least, her son. Weird.

Weird like being prepared for months of visits to the clinic, months with the thermometer, months of possible disappointment, more money spent for more visits, more attempts, and then, as fast as that, Allie smiling her face off and announcing success. Weird the way a baby due in late June had come in May, and no sign of him being unfinished or anything, in spite of being premature. Weird as in what, magical?

When she got back to the room, the curtains were open and Alison was propped up on pillows.

"Hey." Cedar sat beside the bed and took Alison's hand in hers. "How you doing?"

"Tired. Sore."

"No wonder. That's a big guy."

"They said I can see him if I go in a wheelchair. I'm not to try walking yet. I was up and walking around right away with Cammy."

"Cammy was what, seven pounds? Two pounds isn't much until you're trying to jam it through an opening that usually can accommodate only two fingers."

Alison blushed, and her eyes flicked to the doorway.

"Hush," she whispered, "they'll hear you."

"Stuff 'em. So where do they hide this wheelchair?"

"They'll bring it." Alison pressed the buzzer. "Have you seen him?"

"Oh, you bet I've seen him. Doesn't look the least bit like what you said you wanted, he's not a beautiful little talented and intelligent girl. He's a big raw-boned honker of a ginger-haired boy."

Cedar wheeled Allie to the nursery and stood beside the chair watching as Allie looked at her son.

"Oh, he's gorgeous," Allie breathed. "He's every bit as gorgeous as Cammy was when he was born, and everyone said he was the prettiest baby they'd seen in years."

"They probably tell every mother the same thing."

"Oh, don't you just adore him?"

"Yes," Cedar lied. "I'm madly in love with him. He's much better looking than any of those others in there. He's almost as good-looking as his momma."

"You just keep on thinking that." Allie dared to take Cedar's hand and squeezed it gently. "Oh, he's so nice. He's so nice I don't even mind that he's not a girl."

"Oh, I don't know," Cedar said. "I was kind of counting on using the name Molly Kathleen."

"Maybe the next one," Allie whispered. "In a couple of years. Could we?"

"Jesus, woman, your name is Alison McCann, not Mother Teresa."

She couldn't help it, she just couldn't stop the whirling in her brain. She drove home as carefully as she could, went into the house and was greeted by the almost hysterically joyful Gramps and Cam.

"We brought you some hamburgers," Gramps said. "They'll warm up in a jiffy."

"Not yet." She smiled and kissed his cheek. "My stomach is all fluttery. I think it's called wild excitement."

"A cup of tea?"

"No thanks, Gramps. I'm going out to see the pigs. They always have a calming effect."

"Right. Some would say exhausting, but we don't like that word, right?"

"Such a wise old man. One of the elders of the clan."

She changed her clothes and went to the barn. The old man had been teasing about the exhaustion. There was nothing to exhaust a person out here. The huge bin was three-quarters full, enough food to last most of a week. The smaller bin was filling as the grain auger, connected to a timer, turned slowly, moving sow chow from one bin to another. The small bin had a timer, too, and every four hours the conveyor belt began to move, taking the processed pig food to the feeders. There was never any waste—the pigs ate everything that came to them. Fresh water was always available, too, piped in from the well to automatic waterers, where the pigs could snuffle and slurp at the metal nipples whenever they wanted to.

Cedar and Gramps had refused to consider putting their pigs on metal grillwork, but the old man had adapted one feature—spraying the floor to clean it. The shed had concrete underfoot, sloped slightly to a gutter, and the pressure washer also fed from the drilled well, sending muck and piddle out of the pen and into the gutter. Then, when the pens were clean, Cedar reduced the pressure in the big hose and brass nozzle and sluiced the gutters. They emptied into a series of intercon-nected septic tanks buried deep under the grass in the outdoor pig-pens. Gramps had met with the plumber, explained the how and why of the hose and gutter setup, asked for advice and got it, and also got more help than they could believe. Now the water moved quickly from one tank to another, and in each tank there was an above-ground access pipe. They could put the hose of the honey bucket down, turn on the pump, and pull out a ripe mixture of what they all called liquid gold, a rich fertilizer that they sprayed on the fields and the garden. Every six months the plumber came with his big truck and pumped out the com-posted sludge. Then he processed it, dried it and put it in sacks. They split the profit on the Fine Swine Sludge, straight fifty-fifty. "My grand-kids are gonna go to university riding on pig shite," he joked. "You've really got to get more pigs, the nurseries are going nuts to get this stuff."

"Have to talk to the girls about that, see if you can get them to throw bigger litters or something."

Cedar sprayed the floors clean, sluiced the gutter, got a bucket of cob—corn, oats and barley sprayed with molasses—and moved from pen to pen. The sows knew that the bucket contained a special treat and they pressed against the sides of their pens, grunting wetly, snuf-fling and making a soft *uh uh uh* sound, not a grunt but a greeting. "Oh, yes, my fine ones, oh, you're a good one. Here, something nice for the best sow in creation. You're my favourite, but don't tell the others, no, they'll all get jealous if they know how much more I like you. Oh, such a fine Tammy pig, such a good one."

She had them grouped by breed, the Tamworths here, the Hungarian boars there, the Louisiana razorback hogs off by themselves on the other side of the barn, because if a razorback caught sight of a Hungarian, the fight was on. These sows were as bad as boars. The walls of the pens were made of metal piping and could probably with-stand just about anything, but the pigs weren't made of metal and could be badly bruised as they rammed insanely at the barrier.

Each time a sow farrowed, Cedar checked the piglets. With needle-nose pliers she pulled out the little razors that would develop into tusks. It was nasty enough and difficult enough with the gentle Tams, and downright dangerous with the razorback sows and the Hungarians. Yes, the bacon was lean and they got a specialty price for it, and yes, the market was always ready for it, and yes, the arrangement with the butcher and his smokehouse was a good one. But she and Gramps were considering a change. These were too nasty, even when they were born in the barn and picked up daily to be petted, fed treats, almost pampered. The piglets turned into wild animals, ready to bite, crunch, slash and charge at any opportunity.

"Here, you nasty bastards, see, no matter how wretched and miserable you are, you get treated the same as everyone else. Except for the hand feeding, and we learned our lessons from your sibs, no fingers or hands going anywhere near you when you're this size. Just the babies, and even they can send a person off for stitches. Here, then, yes, we'll pour it on top of the other, there you go, isn't that lovely, oh, we do like our molasses, don't we."

Cedar checked each and every pen, emptying one tobacco can of cob after another, refilling her bucket twice. Then she put it back in the feed room, closed and latched the door, checked the latch just in case, and left the barn. Silk sat waiting, snake tail wagging slowly.

"Hey, my Silk, how's the fine fine dog? Oh yes, she is, a fine fine animal, a noble creature, and a dear loyal friend. You know, I've got something for you. Cedar always has biscuits in her jacket pocket, right? Old covet-love, you. Here, don't tell the others you got one, they'll be *so* jealous."

The others knew anyway, they always did. Either they heard the crunching or they had learned that Cedar was always good for a handout. "Sit" she told them. "No jumping or licking or bad manners, or you won't get squat. That's it. Sit. Oldest dog first." She gave another biscuit to Silk. "Now the sibs. Keeper first, because she's such a bitch, and then Muttly, nice gentle Muttly, oh, he's a good boy, and such a big sook. And Muffin, yes, good for you, yes, and there isn't another pig on the place is as good a friend as you are. Here you are, one for you and another for your brother, got to fatten up that fifth leg, don't we, yes."

Cedar went back inside in time to have a good cuddle with Cam before he fell asleep. She sat on the side of his bed, stroking his head, watching his eyelashes flutter, and wishing she could go back to a time when life was safe and easy.

"Better eat." Gramps handed her a plate with two hamburgers on it. She wanted to walk away and tell him to leave her alone, but instead she sat down in her big chair and started eating. The taste wakened her appetite and she was glad to finish her meal and two cups of tea. Then she felt almost human again.

Almost human, except for the voice in her head that nagged and bitched, pointing out undeniable facts. A baby doubles its weight in the last month of pregnancy. Even if Steve was only a month early, rather than almost two months, he weighed nine and a half pounds. Just figure it, the voice demanded. Nine and a half pounds a month early would have been nineteen pounds full term. Nobody has nineteen-pound babies except those women in the blurry photographs in the supermarket tabloids.

If she asked Rory, he'd soothe her. He wouldn't lie, but he'd turn himself inside out to find an explanation, one that would take the sting out of the questions, one that would remind her that relationships are built on trust.

Or she could go to Doc Forbes. He wasn't in practice any more but if she asked, he'd go up to the hospital, have a good look at Steve and tell her the truth. Except she didn't need Doc Forbes to tell her what she had known as soon as she saw the boy who was supposed to be her legal son. You don't grow a twenty-two inch premature baby.

So who was the father, then? Someone in the band? Hadn't Allie said she hoped the kid would be musical? Could you call someone musical if he hammered out the same two or three chords over and over and over again? Rhythmic, maybe, but musical? Cedar finally let herself know the rest—that when Allie had initiated the cozy late-night discussion about having a baby, she was already pretty sure she was pregnant.

And now that Cedar knew, now that the voice had stopped its damn nagging, now that she knew she'd been well and truly had, what was she going to do about it?

What she did was kiss Gramps goodnight and head upstairs with a thermos of coffee, cigarettes and a book she knew she wasn't going to read. She lay in the tub, drinking coffee, smoking cigarettes until the bathroom was full of blue haze, and laying it all out in front of her, to look at as carefully as if she were planning a new barn. She took everything into consideration, went methodically from step to step to step in a process more precise than linear narrative, delving for every detail she knew for a fact, relentlessly logical. This leads to this, this causes this, for every problem a solution, for every need an answer.

Allie had said that she'd handled everything when Cedar was at work, and Cedar never did meet the doctor who supposedly did the deed. Cedar went with Allie to some of the prenatal visits, for the prenatal classes, for the training to be Allie's birthing coach, Cedar was there for the entire labour and she was there when Steve arrived. Yet Allie had never told Cedar which doctor in which clinic had done the insertion.

She and Gramps had the pig farm, the five-legged pig, the dogs, some equipment and a house. And in that house they had Campbell Ewen McCann, who would go down the road with his deceitful mother if Cedar confronted her with the truth. Campbell would go down the road with Allie, and Steve, the little red-headed stranger, would go with them.

Steve the stranger. Well, weren't they all? If, if and if, and it had all happened, and been true and not a series of evasions and outright lies, and he was an AI baby instead of the product of what, a one-night stand, a two-week fling, what? Would she have known him? He'd still be a stranger, the way we are all strangers when we force our way out of paradise and into the world.

What kind of a place would this be without Cam? What would she do with herself on Wednesday nights and Saturday mornings if she didn't have Cam's soccer practice and games? Would she drive past soccer fields and feel bereft? Would she try to find out where he was living, then haunt the playground hoping for a glimpse of him, would she go to pick him up for the legally agreed-upon access and visitation times and then sob helplessly when she had to take him back again?

What did she have stuck in her throat anyway? What was all of this about? It wasn't like she and Allie were married, or even promised to each other, and you can't commit adultery if you aren't married. No. What you do instead is screw around, fuck around, play fast and loose, bed hop, chippy . . .

Which can hurt just as much, can be as painful a betrayal. Was that it? Really, truly, nobody here but yourself, so no need to protect your Campbell pride. Was she hurt? She was good and pissed off, for sure. What was that joke she and Gramps used to make, about how the assholes who think they know everything are a pain in the face to those of us who really do know everything. That was what had her so mad, so unbearably insulted. That the woman would think for a minute that Cedar Campbell couldn't count to nine!

She soaped her hands and slid the carved silver ring off her third finger right hand. The ring left a wide, untanned band around her finger. She removed her bracelet and that left a pale ring around her wrist.

If she walked into the hospital room and said, hey, Alison McCann, I'm not the one who fell with yesterday's rain, and this is a head on my shoulders, not a cabbage, if she looked her in the eye and laid it all out, there would be a fight. A huge one. Allie would defend herself by attacking, with how dare you, and if that's how little you think of me, and my God have you gone nuts, and no end to it. And because of the fight, and because even while she was fighting Alison would know she was compounding the lies, Cam would wind up going off down the road.

It wasn't as if it was going to cost her an arm and a leg to pull a Kate here, and just go along with the nonsense. But no way was she going to let anyone, let alone Alison McCann, think for one minute that Cedar Campbell was so blind with love and stupidity as not to be able to see the forest for the goddamn trees.

So she waited. Bide your time, my henny, Grandma Campbell said. Every dog has his day, just learn to bide your time. Cedar waited until Alison and Steve were home and the first fuss and furor had calmed.

The living room held masses of flowers—azaleas, gloxinias, and on the porch, a foot-and-a-half-tall flowering snowball bush from Campbell. Steve lay in his bassinet beside Alison's chair, long, lean and already putting on weight. Small wonder, the way he ate—slurp slurp slurp, and the formula level in his bottle went down, down, down.

Cedar sat down beside them and sighed. "Ah, this feels better. Did you see Cam's face when he got to give Steve his lunch? Never saw him look so happy, not even when he saw Keeper for the first time."

"Well, I should hope not!" Allie laughed, and Cedar remembered all over again just how gorgeous she was. "I mean Keeper is a dog, and Stevie is his brother."

"Half." Cedar yawned. "Boy, am I glad you guys are home where you belong. This business of working a full shift, then racing around to get the chores done early so we could head up to ooh and ah and come home without you—it was hard on the sleep patterns. A couple of times Gramps and I as good as gave up trying and just sat in here and planned plans and dreamed dreams. Even Cammy went short of sleep, too excited to drift off the way he usually does."

"Does that mean I was missed?"

"Did you have any reason to doubt you would be?"

Steve squirmed, his face twisted, then he made several soft grunting noises and relaxed again.

"The size of him." Cedar sounded as if she was bragging. "Good job he didn't wait until July, when he was due. They say they double their weight in the last month. He'd have been damn close to twenty pounds." When she looked at Alison, her face was as open and trusting as anybody who was in love and happy. "That's some head of hair! You're going to have to take braiding lessons. Or haul him off to the barber."

"It'll probably fall out," Alison managed, her voice weak, her face pale. "Cam's baby hair fell out by the time he was two weeks old."

"You feeling okay? You don't look all that well. Here, I'll help you up to bed."

Alison lay in bed, her face turned to the wall, her eyes so dry they felt gritty. She wanted to burst into tears and couldn't. She wanted to howl, but her throat was slammed tight, so tight she felt as if she would never again get enough air to breathe.

She hadn't intended it to happen. If she'd been intending anything, she'd have been sure to get her prescription refilled. She hadn't needed the damn pills since she had decided she wanted more with Cedar than just to rent a couple of rooms. It was the eyes, and the shape of the face. It was the hair, and the hands, and it was the laughter. All the good things about Gus were there in Cedar, without the self-indulgent, irresponsible, spoiled brat parts.

She couldn't blame the low-key, something-missing sex life on Cedar. She could have tried to talk to Cedar about it. She could have bought that book—it was right there on the shelf in the bookstore, complete with photographs, and not everybody who bought it was involved with another woman. She could have sat in bed reading it and said, "Listen to this," or, "Look at this." Cedar would have gotten the hint. Cedar could pick up on the slightest change of tone.

She had known that, so why had she been so goddamn ridiculous as to think she could slide this thing past Cedar? And now, beyond doubt, she'd been told that she wasn't half as slick as she had prayed to God she was. It would sit there between them forever, the first lie and then all the other lies she had piled on, one on top of the other, betraying every trust, building her own pillory and shoving her own stupid head into it.

Oh, she'd been told, all right, and told in such a way that she couldn't find any way to clear the air, not ever. If Cedar had come to bed with the small thermos of coffee and two mugs; if she'd said, "Allie, we have to get something cleared up here"; if she'd said, "I think you've been lying to me"; if she'd said, "Allie, that kid didn't come early, what's going on?"; if she'd even yelled, "You lying bitch, it's time to tell the fucking truth!" But all she did was let it be known in an oh-so-Campbell or oh-so-Larson way that the wool had not been pulled over her eyes.

Now what? Oh, God, what if she went off on a Gus episode, yelling and pitching furniture and letting the whole damn world know? What if she gave Alison a deadline: find your own place by the end of the month, get your lying ass out of here, take your bastard children and fuck off? Campbell would never forgive Allie. This was his home, as surely as if he'd been born under one of the trees. Why—Jesus, *why* had she been so stupid?

She couldn't figure it out, even at the time. She knew by the way he looked at her that he was ready, more than ready. He had made it clear he was interested, and she had known just by looking at him that he would be a skilled and effective lover. She could remember the moment she decided. She could remember thinking, why not? And she didn't allow herself to think of the obvious answers to why not, until they had been together several times. And then, driving home from his apartment, she was overcome with all the reasons: the life they all shared, the security, and most of all, her love for Cedar.

She had told him the next night that it was over, and he didn't fight to keep her. And when it was over, it was completely over. Right up until she missed a period.

She had considered having an abortion. If Cedar had said, "Oh, Allie, give your head a shake, we don't need a baby around here, we've got piglets," or, "Not a chance, lady, that's the last thing I want"—but she hadn't said those things. And still she could have salvaged the situation. She could have, should have said, "Cedar, I've been a total idiot, I've done a stupid and awful thing," and told Cedar the truth. But no. And now she had been told that the only thing she had managed to do was to fuck everything to a fine fare-thee-well.

The best thing she could do now was nothing. No use putting it out in the open, no use trying to explain. She'd wrecked any chance of that. From here on in, it was up to Cedar. Completely.

Kate had made a deliberate decision to button her lip. There were enough people gossiping—she didn't have to join them, not even privately. When Cedar had come over to visit last fall, on one of Kate's evenings off, Kate wasn't fooled for a minute. This wasn't just a drop-in for a cuppa. Cedar had never done that. Cedar seldom visited at all.

"Well, how lovely," she had welcomed her daughter. "And just in time, too. The pecan pie is cool enough to cut and I've some of that French vanilla ice cream to go with it."

"Who says I'm not psychic, eh?" Cedar took a chair, the same chair in the same place at the same table of her childhood.

Kate put out cups and saucers and her good cream jug and matching sugar bowl, treating the visit as special, not just a drop-in for a quick mug before zipping off on some chore or other. Cedar pulled out her cigarettes, offered one to Kate and took one for herself.

"It looks great in here with the new paint job," Cedar said. "Brightens up the place. And I like the cupboard doors without those damn ugly handles."

"Don't let your father hear you say that, he'll pitch a fit. He picked those things out himself. Odd, though, he didn't say a word about them being gone."

"Probably can't remember what things look like around here, in camp most of the time and off running the roads the rest of the time."

"Now, now, now, you stop that."

They sipped tea, ate pecan pie with vanilla ice cream, then decided that yes, they really did so need seconds, and had them, too.

"So we've been talking over at our place," Cedar said finally. "Alison has decided she wants another kid. Well, a baby, not a full-grown walking talking kid." Cedar laughed easily and Kate recognized the laugh—different tone, different timbre, same attitude, and it came from Gus when he was being charmingly evasive. "She's researched various and sundry ways," Cedar went on, "and she's making an appointment to see a doctor for artificial insemination."

"Oh, my!" Kate blurted, in spite of her resolve not to rock any boats.

"Yeah, seems a bit cold-blooded, but . . ." Cedar shrugged. "Works good with pigs, so might as well go with what works."

"Oh. Well. My."

Kate didn't say anything that came into her mouth: Are you out of your mind? Have either of you stopped to consider anyone else's feelings? Isn't this entire setup on the verge of sheer insanity? She poured more tea and offered thirds on the pecan pie, and she wasn't the least bit surprised when Cedar said no, she'd just finish up her tea and be off, look what time it's got itself to be.

She had her suspicions when Alison started to show. If the idea had only been in the discussion stage when Cedar came for tea, then Alison was showing very early, even for a second child.

Her suspicions were confirmed when she drove over to see the newborn Steven. She had sent flowers—it's what she would have done for any member of the family, and like it or not, Alison was family. But now she visited in person, bringing along a bag of knitting for the baby and a nice set of bath beads for Alison. And she felt fine, right up until Cedar lifted Steve from his beautiful bassinet and placed him in the arms of the woman who had signed on to be his grandma.

This was no early baby. This was a big baby, even for full term. She looked up, caught the look on Cedar's face and knew all she would ever need to know.

"My," she managed, "he's certainly a big boy. He's got hands as big as most six-month-old babies."

"And feet to go with them," Cedar smiled.

Kate knew what that smile felt like.

"Well, and just look at you." She forced her gaze back to the squirming baby. "If you aren't the nicest little boy. Aren't you lovely? Do you have a big smile for grandma, or will I have to wait a while for one of those?" And on and on, grandma prattle, rhythmic, falling-in-love near-chanting, exactly what anybody would have expected, and all the time she wanted to get up and walk across the room and slap Alison McCann across her beautiful face. You bitch, you whore, you slut! You're as bad as Gus Campbell, no doubt about that.

She thought she would burst with wanting to shout and yell, she felt as if the muscles in her cheeks and throat were going to go into spasms, she was sure her hands were shaking, but when she lifted her coffee mug she was fine, just fine.

Cedar walked out to the car with her. She opened the door and held it while Kate got in. "Don't you worry, Momma. Everything is fine."

"Yes, dear," Kate said. "Just fine."

Every now and again Kate did or said something that exposed to her the ugly streak in her soul. Sometimes she wondered whether everyone had that ugly side. But it wasn't exactly something you could dredge up and dump on the coffee table for discussion, and most of the time she could smother the vindictive mean-minded streak. But there were areas where she let it hang out. Hang out and baldly defy anyone to make any kind of fuss about it at all.

She knew as soon as she saw her photo of Campbell feeding Steve his bottle that it was one of the best pictures anyone in the family had ever taken. She ordered a big print and had it framed and hung on the wall in her living room, right up there with pictures of Cedar and Rory, Tony, Suzie and Chris. Let them all see that she knew who was and wasn't related by blood, if not by marriage. In fact, let them choke on it. And particularly, let Gus Campbell swallow his lying tongue when he came out from camp and saw the boy so obviously the near twin of his own "legitimate" son, saw him with the half-brother who would never look the least bit like him.

Gus didn't say word one. But he looked—often. And because he did, because he so obviously wanted to see Cammy, Kate made sure that there were no other enlargements, although the album she kept for herself was filled with pictures of Cam. She had no pictures of Alison Lyingface McCann unless she was part of a group shot, and of course no pictures of Gus with any of them. She considered enlarging and framing the picture Gramps had taken of Cam and Rory sitting on the sofa with Steve and Cedar on the floor in front of them. Made a person wonder just how much that old man knew. He might be getting old and bent, but he still had his wits. But even Kate had to draw the line some-where. It wouldn't just have been a good solid slap in the face to Gus, it would have insulted Mary and Colin, and they were as old and as bent as Joe Conrad was, as old and precious and tired as Karen and Olaf Larson. Everyone was getting old. Sometimes Kate felt like she was the oldest of all of them.

For Kate's birthday in August, Cedar gave her a family portrait that took the extra step Kate had feared to take. Cedar, Rory and Campbell, three peas in a pod. At least it was only a six by eight and didn't need to hang on the wall. She kept it on the dresser in her bedroom. Sometimes she would try to pretend all three of them were hers. But even if she hadn't lost that third child, it wouldn't have looked like the other two, any more than Steve was going to look like his brother or like his—what was Cedar, anyway, a stepmother?

Alison sat by the river in the shade of an arbutus tree, her shirt wet and clinging to her body, cooling her. She was too huge with her third pregnancy to enjoy any part of the summer. Cedar was in the water with Cam, and Gramps was playing with Steve.

Steve lurched to his feet in that all-of-a-piece, fifteen-month-old gracelessness, took a few steps, then ran for the shallow water. Nobody would have called him gorgeous, but the people in his world said he was as cute as a bug. He didn't have Rory and Cam's beauty. His hair was red, no other word for it, and tight-kinked, in taut little curls that anybody would envy. Steve's skin was as white as Campbell's, but unlike Campbell he barely tanned, and after only a few minutes in the sun they put a T-shirt on him. His arms were faint pink below the sleeve line—today he would wind up in a long-sleeved shirt.

But for now, the day was hot but not yet blistering, and he was starkers. Alison was half asleep, her face pale and beaded with sweat. She didn't look well, and Cedar took her a glass of cold juice, then convinced her that the best thing she could do was lie down on a towel and take a nap. "And you shouldn't lie under an arbutus tree, that's a sure way to get ticks. I'll set you up under the fir tree there, it's nice and shady, there's good thick grass and a breeze, and you can rest."

"I'm fine," Alison insisted.

"I know. But you're supposed to be sleeping for two, remember?"

Nothing about this pregnancy was the same as the others. There were twice as many trips to the doctor, and over a month ago Allie had quit playing with the band and was spending all her time at home, often in bed. Cedar wanted to talk to the doctor about it, but Allie insisted there was no need. The man was busy and had better things to do with his time than calming down nervous partners. "In the time he's reassuring you," she laughed, "he could be saving someone's life."

She had started campaigning for this baby almost as soon as she had got home with Steve. "Just look at him," she said to Cedar. "He's got four people dancing to his tune, five counting your mom, six count-ing mine. He's going to be such a spoiled brat that you won't want to deal with him when you come home from work. If we have another one right away there will be two to share the attention, and someone to play with him and say no to him. He needs to hear someone say no."

"It's too soon. Campbell was an only kid, and he's great."

"Campbell didn't have you, Gramps and Kate adoring him, or Tony, Suzie and Chris fussing him. He didn't have Karen and Olaf going out of their way to come see him and letting me know they accepted him fully, and he didn't have Colin Campbell phoning to invite us all to Saturday supper so he could meet what he called his 'ain great-grandson'."

"That was as much for Cammy as it was for Steve."

"Even so. It's too much oh-you're-wonderful for one kid to han-dle."

"He's only two and a half months old! You can't, not right away. It's too soon."

"No, it is not too soon. It was as easy as falling off a log. I've never been healthier. Only this time, no nameless, faceless sperm donor." She still carried on her half of the game of deceiving each other about the deception. For some reason it made things easier all around—by now it had become a macabre joke. "If you speak to Rory about it, we can—"

"This is the last one. Boy or girl, it's the last one."

"Boy or girl, it's the caboose for sure. I promise, Cedar."

Rory was surprised too, and concerned that the plan might drive a wedge between him and Cedar. "What if—"

"Rory, what if the sky fell?"

"Can I be involved? With the baby?"

"You're involved with Cam, you're involved with Steve, why wouldn't you be involved with Whozit?"

"You promise? I'm not having kids and leaving them all over the countryside like stray kittens."

"You won't be leaving it all over the country, it'll be with us. Hell, Rory, I treat my pigs better than most people treat their kids."

"Yeah, I know. It just feels . . . odd."

"Oh, it doesn't just feel odd, Roarsers, it *is* odd, no doubt about that. But when did odd ever slow any of us down? In fact you might say we thrive on odd. If we didn't, we'd have perished years ago."

Anne Cameron

"This is going to be embarrassing."

"Going to be? It already is!"

Alison's air of desperation faded somewhat when the pregnancy test came up positive, but she wasn't the same. She wept easily and sulked often, and after a week or more of sleepless nights, she decided the problem was getting the better of her and the only way to solve it was to sleep alone.

"It's as if your breathing gets louder and louder until I can hear nothing else, and if you move I jump out of my skin. Next I'll be waking you up, too."

Cedar wanted to argue, but the truth of it was she was short of sleep herself, and had no chance to catch up with a long afternoon nap. She felt as if she was running from the time she opened her eyes—chores in the morning, full days at the gravel pit, more chores in the evening and the endless taking care of Steve and Cam. Most nights Steve slept right through, but sometimes he awoke crying, and then she took him to bed with her. Whatever reservations she had when he was born were far behind her. She loved him for himself, his cheery, jolly, noisy self. But he did like to sleep with her hair gripped in his hand, which was not comfortable, and she couldn't free herself until he went back to sleep and his hand relaxed. She wanted to say to Alison, "Hey, listen, if you're going to be awake anyway, why not take him?" But Alison had him all day, and Cedar didn't have much other time with him. She had no idea where she would find so much as a spare minute for a third child. She'd have to hire someone to help out during the day—there were too many things that Gramps couldn't do any more.

Dianne Marie Campbell McCann was born at the beginning of October, and the entire much-extended family all agreed that she was the most beautiful child ever born on the coast. Cedar could only stare in disbelief. The baby looked exactly like Rory, until she turned her head and looked exactly like Cedar, or scrunched her face before weeping and looked exactly like Mary Campbell. She might as well have had nothing but Campbell blood in her veins. There was no trace of McCann at all.

"Ye've done well, my dear," Mary Campbell said. "I've invited yer dear mother to come tae supper with us tomorrow and then Ewen will drive us all up together."

"Thank you, Mrs. Campbell," Alison whispered.

"I'm Grandma Campbell to you, lass. Now I'll be off. Ye need some rest, ye're as pale as the face of the moon." She leaned over stiffly and kissed Alison on the forehead. "Dinna fash yersel'. Ye've done well wi' yer entire life, girl, and three bonny wains ye've gie us a'."

"I'm sorry." Alison's eyes flooded with tears. "I didn't mean . . . I didn't want . . ."

"Aye, lass, but even a contrary path can tek us hame."

Alison slept most of the time, rousing herself only for meals, or to walk, with help, to the bathroom. On the evening of the third day, the specialist was in the hallway when Cedar and Gramps arrived to visit.

"I need to speak to you, please."

"Is this serious?" Cedar asked.

"Yes, quite."

"Gramps? Please don't go in alone. Could you go back down and get Cam, and take him in with you? And tell Allie I'm moving to the back of the parade for a while to give her time to visit with him."

"Fine." He turned to go back down the hallway, his face showing bewilderment.

"If you go in alone, it'll scare her. If you go in with Cam and that story, she'll be fine. And don't mention this."

The specialist led the way to a small room with "Consultation" printed on the door. "Did Alison tell you she's been seeing me for the past several months?"

"Seeing you? I'm sorry, I don't even know who you are."

"She didn't mention it, then."

"No." She knew from the look on his face that the other shoe was about to drop and that it wasn't a small ballet slipper, but a big black work boot.

Finally she nodded, and he started talking. When he had finished, all she could say was, "When?"

"The day after tomorrow. Alison was supposed to have prepared you. She was supposed to have told you. She said she had."

"Allie has her own way of avoiding reality," Cedar said carefully. "It's not so much a case of ignore it and it'll go away, as it is if you wait long enough you won't need to say anything or have an argument."

"Did you know that her physician recommended against this pregnancy?"

"No."

"Did you know that he wanted to terminate and she refused?"

"No."

"He wanted to terminate and do the operation then. The lump was small at that time. She refused. He told her, very clearly, that the hormonal changes of pregnancy can stimulate this type of tumour, but . . ."

"She still said no, right?"

"I'm very sorry. The prognosis was much better then."

"And Dianne?"

"The baby is fine. We've done extensive blood work already and she's a fine, healthy, normal baby girl." He smiled suddenly. "And beautiful."

When Cedar walked into the private room, Alison knew immediately that her huge secret was out in the open. She held out her arms and Cedar embraced her and kissed her cheek.

"Don't talk about it, okay?" Alison whispered.

"I need to know—why?"

"I wanted to give you something. Something all yours."

"Oh, God, Allie. You and your goddamn secrets."

"Sssh, don't scold. Please, Cedar, don't talk about it."

"Fine." Cedar pulled back so Allie could see her face, see the wink and the attempt at a smile. "Fine, then. Be that way," she whispered.

Rory stared, shaking his head in disbelief. "You're kidding."

"No. The specialist said he'd meet with you and explain it to you. You know me, I could do a great job discussing pig problems, but this other, all I can think is lump, lump, she knew, she went ahead anyway, lump, lump. And now it's lumps."

"Oh God, Cedar." He held her, comforting and being comforted. "If I'd known," he vowed, "I'd never have . . . but she . . . I . . ."

"Yeah. I could slap her cheeky face for it," Cedar sighed. "But what would that change, now?"

Rory was a good half hour with the specialist, and when he came out his face told Cedar everything she needed to know. She turned away abruptly, her sob catching harshly in her throat. "I'll be in there, sis." Rory stood behind her, his arms around her, holding her against him. "I'll be there for the whole thing. Now, let's go tell Allie that. I think it might reassure her to know she won't be all on her ownsome in there."

"It's bad, isn't it?"

"It's bad." His grip tightened. "It's into the lymph system. That's about as bad as news gets."

Allie was in intensive care for six days, then she was taken to a private room on the post-surgery ward. When she wakened, Cedar was there.

"Hey," Alison managed.

"Hey your own self and see how you like it." Cedar leaned forward, kissed Allie's pale lips, then kissed again. "I'm not going to stay long," she whispered. "There's a boy out there nearly ready to come out of his skin with anxiety. And he'll do you a lot more good than I will."

"No." Alison's breathing was shallow and rapid, her top lip beaded with sweat, her lips dry and cracked. "Nobody does me more good than you."

"He needs to see you, Allie, he's terrified."

"So am I. But you're right. And that's one of the things about you I love the most. You don't just think of yourself, you always put my kids—our kids—first. Just give me a couple of minutes with you. I need that time. Hold me, Cedar, please, I'm so scared."

"Sssssh, my darling. Ssssssh, we'll be fine, you'll see. We'll all of us be just fine. The worst is over, you'll see. Ssssh."

Dianne was not quite six months old when her mother died. She and her brother Steve were the only members of the family not completely devastated by the loss.

Cedar mourned for all the times she could have held Allie and hadn't, for all the good times they could have had and missed because of the pressure of work. She mourned the mistakes, she mourned her bitchiness about the circumstances of Steve's conception and birth, she grieved and she wallowed in her grief. She berated herself for many things done and not done, said and not said.

And then Gramps grabbed her in a tight hug. "Pull it together, girl," he said roughly. "I know what it's like. When my wife died, I thought the whole world ought to stop in its tracks. I just about went insane. I couldn't even look after Ted. That's when I lost most of what he and I once had together. Don't you make my mistake all over again. Cam needs you. "

"Gramps, I—"

"Hush. Tough luck. Too bad. Now get it together. Do you know Grandma McCann is trying to talk Cammy into moving in with her full-time? Do you know she's hinting that she ought to be given custody of Steve and Dianne, too? She's saying you're too depressed to look after yourself, let alone them. She's lost her daughter and so she wants whatever of her she can get. You'll wind up with nothing if you don't haul it together."

Cedar sat on the bank of the wide, deep creek that flowed behind Grandma and Grandpa Larson's place and Campbell sat beside her. Their fishing rods lay on the ground, and each of them had one foot on a rod, just in case.

"You need a haircut, darling," Cedar remarked. "You're as shaggy as a sheepdog."

"I want to grow it long, like a hippie," he snapped.

"Okay. You might want to think about getting it shaped, though."

"Shaped?"

"Yeah. It's not really a haircut. Sometimes when they're through, your hair can actually look longer rather than shorter. They've got books you can look through, find the shape you like, the style you want."

"How much does it cost?"

"We won't have to mortgage the farm. I'll pick up the tab."

"Why?"

"Why not?"

"I'm not really your kid. Grandma McCann says—"

"Hey." She put her arm around his tight shoulders. "I'm not insulting your grandma, and I don't want to sound cheeky or nasty, but I really don't give the first part of a fat rat's ass what your Grandma McCann or anybody else says. You are my boy. I'd fight the devil himself for you."

"But I'm not. Not really."

"Cam, listen. I mean this. You didn't move in with us because your momma did and you had to tag along. It was your idea first. Do you remember?"

She felt him relax and pulled him tight against her, his head settling into her shoulder, his body shuddering a bit as the clenched muscles loosened. "It was a weekend, a Sunday, and you'd been out to the farm lots of times. When you first started coming, I think Keeper was about as big as a bread bun and hardly able to walk, and you'd come every weekend. And then she was too big for you to lift, so it was what, two months, three months later? Well, you gave me this talk about how big the house was. Do you remember any of this?"

"I said our landlord was a grouch and we couldn't have even a cat."

"That's right. What else?"

He began to cry. "I said that if you let me live there I'd help you with the pigs. And you said that would be nice, but I didn't have to. You said seeing me smile . . ." He broke down, sobbing bitterly.

"Right. Seeing you smile would be more than enough for me."

"And Mom said . . ."

"Your dear momma said there was no way she was going to stay in a basement if her dear darling love was moving to the farm. She said she supposed if you were moving, she'd move, too. And we shook hands, remember? Well, there's only two of us left, but the deal stands. Unless—" She started to cry herself. "Unless you really *want* to live with Grandma McCann. You are the only one can break the deal."

He shook his head. She pulled him onto her lap and he clutched her neck so tightly she could hardly breathe.

"I miss my mother."

"I know." Cedar held him and let him cry. "Oh, my dear dear Cammy," she crooned. "Oh, my good dear boy. You don't ever have to worry about not belonging. Cedar wants you, Gramps wants you, we'd sob our guts out if you weren't with us. It wouldn't even be fun on the farm any more without you. I love you, Gramps loves you like crazy, Stevie loves you, everybody loves you and wants you. And I promise you, I won't fight with Grandma McCann. We'll invite her for sleepovers, we'll have her for suppers, we'll fuss over her so she won't be sad and lonely any more."

"She cries."

"We all cry, Cam. All of us. We all miss Allie something awful. And because we're all so lonely for her, the thing to do is to group together, be even tighter as a family." She kissed his cheek. "Circle the wagons, pard," she whispered, "circle the damn wagons."

They visited Seamus Kelly and talked to him about what they wanted. Seamus had his entire yard set up as his advertisement, with trellises along the fences and a series of them set up along the walkway to the front steps. Roses of every possible colour and variation flourished, clematis and Chinese wisteria rioted. In the evening the perfume was thick and the neighbours sat on their big front porches and smiled at each other, at Seamus, at the whirligigs he had stuck in his lawn. Seamus had Bottoms-Up Betsy near his front steps, and a four-foot-tall windmill in the side yard between the house and the rose trellises. Bumblebees, hummingbirds and bright yellow daisies spun in the breeze, and an amazingly lifelike great blue heron stood beside a children's wading pool shaped like a turtle. In the pool several rubber duckies floated, along with a sea turtle. "Prefer 'em to the real ones," Seamus chortled. "They never need fed, and all I need to do to change the water is dump the pool. No heaters, no filters, no fuss, no muss, no bother. Now, Cedar Campbell, what can an Irisher do for a heather hopper like yourself?"

Campbell pulled out a crumpled piece of paper. He tried to smooth it, with little success, but Seamus gave it the respect due an architect's rendering.

"A gazebo's what you're needing," he decided. "Here, see, then." He turned over the paper and with a few deft strokes had the design for them. "It could be trelliswork all around at the bottom, waist high. Figure three steps up to the flooring, and if we make it an octagon we'll have eight support posts for the morning glory and such. If it was me, I'd keep the roses trimmed to the height of the railing. We'll make that extra wide, two feet or so, plenty of room for glasses of lemonade and plates of sandwiches. I'd put crushed clam and oyster shell or lime-rock gravel around it at the bottom, just for contrast."

"Concrete," Campbell corrected him. "The grass grows through that other stuff. And it's a pain in the face to try to mow it with the roses and everything growing there."

"Fine. Fine idea." He looked at Cedar, who smiled and nodded.

"Now, the roof. Would you want shingles, shakes, or duroid?"

"Those big wood ones, the really long ones. My mom liked them the best. She said when she built her dream home she was having them on the roof."

"Fine, then, shakes it is."

"And a table with benches around it. Like that one." He pointed to the table on Seamus's huge sundeck.

"Ah, wonderful. See, what we can do with that is put it smack dab in the middle, and that gives us an extra support post. I'd go with a nice peeled cedar log, and if we just alter it here a bit and then change this a tad, it looks as if the thing is growing from the cedar post."

"Not too steep of steps," Cedar cautioned. "We've got a toddler and another who will soon be crawling. I don't want them taking tumbles and putting broken teeth through split lips."

"I'll do them wide and slow-sloped. In fact, maybe you'd be better off with a ramp affair. The old man isn't getting any more spry, is he? Might put the ramp at an easy angle for one of those little electric cart-scooter things, there's lots use them when walking gets to be a problem."

When the place was finished and the propane barbecue was set up, Seamus joined them for the family shed-warming. "Can't exactly call it a housewarming." Cedar smiled more easily with each week that passed. "It's my Grandma Campbell's idea. She's pretty much housebound now. Sort of had the starch knocked out of her when Gramps died. But even if her legs don't work so well, her mind is as fine as ever. People are going to bring rose bushes and climbing vines, or whatever, and they're each making a little tag with the name of the plant and their own name."

"I'll bring an evergreen honeysuckle. I start a few every year from the one I've got at the back of the house. It's from one my mam had outside her kitchen when I was a boy."

"Bring George, too," Cedar smiled. "And don't forget your tag. Seamus and George, Mom's honeysuckle."

George was at least as large as Uncle Hank, and his muscles still rippled when he moved. He was older than Seamus, older than Gus, but even if his hair was snow white, he still looked like what he had been, an Olympic weightlifter. He'd spent his entire career as an amateur, supporting himself and his avocation with a job in the bush.

George and Seamus had been together for more than twenty years. It was one of those things everybody knew and nobody talked about, not out loud, anyway. After all, it wasn't as if either one of them was swishy or faggoty or limp-wristed, and a body could probably get himself crippled if he said the wrong thing.

In the middle of the party, Gus Campbell drove up, a look of defiance on his face.

"Oh my God," Kate breathed.

"Easy on, Mother," Cedar snapped. "There will be no uproar, I promise."

"Don't get into it with him, Cedar, please."

"Me?" Cedar looked amazed. "And here I was worrying about you!" She laughed softly and the smile stayed in place as she walked over to the car. Gus got out, a rose bush under one arm and an azalea under the other.

"Cedar." He stood and waited to see what was going to happen next.

"Gus." She nodded. "You're a bit late, but we've got lots and lots of food. Grab a plate. I think you know pretty well everybody here."

The blond hair was faded and a greying fringe ringed his spreading bald spot. Deep lines creased the corners of his eyes, and others enclosed his mouth like parentheses.

"Hello, hen." He kissed Kate on the cheek.

"When did you get in?"

"Plane landed oh, maybe two and a half hours ago. My mam said you'd probably be here, so . . ." and he kissed her again.

Marg looked away, angry as always at the way Gus publicly assumed ownership of her sister. And Kate went along with it, as if there was some real meaning to the kisses, as if they were something other than post-piddling.

"Hello, son." Gus stood in front of Campbell and smiled, holding out the rose bush. "You might have an idea where this could go. The flowers come out yellow, with orange stripes and patches. Oranges and lemons, they call it."

"Thank you, sir."

"And this," Gus went on, putting the azalea on the ground, "is for Cedar. By way of a peace offering. So, would you help a guy dig a hole or two?"

"Yes, sir." Campbell put his plate aside. "If anyone steals my salmon," he said clearly, "I'll slaughter every living soul in the place. Except for Dianne, I know it won't be her because she doesn't have teeth. The rest of you aren't safe."

"That's my boy." Gus laughed. Cedar stiffened, her pacifist resolutions evaporating. "So, gonna show your grandpa around the place, after we've dug the holes and eaten?"

Campbell dug the hole and laid peat moss, bone meal and loose dirt on the bottom, then Gus ceremoniously planted the rose bush.

"Have to wait," Campbell told him. "I have to flood it, make a slurry. It can sit in there and have a good drink, but we won't be able to put the dirt in yet."

"Oh." Gus nodded as if he'd never planted anything in his life. "Does that mean there's going to be time to dig the hole for the other?"

"Mom's got the hole dug, see?" Cam pointed. "Her and Uncle Rory. They've got it flooded already, too."

"They make a good pair," Gus agreed. "You look like them. You any relation to them?"

Campbell's smile was so much like Cedar's it gave Gus a cold chill. "There's no telling, is there. Cedar says we look alike because we love each other so much, but Uncle Rory, he says there's no use keeping secrets and telling yourself you're doing it to protect me. He told me. Told me I was blood-related to him and Mom."

"Did he, indeed. Did he tell you how?" Gus was uneasy. The blue eyes looked so soft, so gentle, so innocent, but the smile was one he had often seen on Cedar, especially when she was having one of her out-of-touch spells.

"Oh, yes. My grandma Kate was pretty angry about it for a while but Grandmother McCann said it was fine with her that I know."

"Son, I . . ."

"No, sir." Cam shook his head. "I'll go get the hose. We have to finish planting this rose. For my mother."

The card attached to the rose read simply, "From a friend." Cam got a plastic tag and the big marker. "The paper will just shred from the rain and all," he said, as if he was the adult and Gus the child. Carefully he printed on the tag, then attached it to the rose bush. Gus read the tag and felt anger flare, then die as suddenly. The boy had printed "Mr. Gus Campbell" as if Gus was some neighbour who was seldom seen but who upheld the rules of politeness.

"So, then," he said with a warmth he did not feel. "Shall we go join the others?"

"Yes, sir," Campbell agreed.

They returned to the gazebo to eat. Gus filled his plate, then turned to speak to the boy, but Cam had already slipped away and was standing beside Rory. Gus knew he had been snubbed, knew others had seen the snub and recognized it. But he grinned as if he didn't care and tried to tell himself the boy was just a chip off the old block.

"Could I get you something?" he asked Kate. She smiled pleasantly, as if there was nothing between them, no heartache, no anger, no contempt.

"I'm fine, thank you." She moved slightly, making room for him to stand beside her.

"Lovely get-together," he said. He could have been talking to anybody.

"Very nice. Could I get you a coffee?"

"Is there no beer or such?"

"No, Gus," she said gently. "Nothing of the sort."

"Well, a coffee will have to do, then, won't it?" And he smiled that same on-the-tap smile he'd used when she was nineteen and he was in hot pursuit.

Kate got him a cup of coffee, placed it on the railing near his elbow, then drifted off to stand with Cedar and Rory. She stood with one hand on Cam's shoulder as the boy smiled up at her, and Gus could not ignore people's small sighs, the little non-noises of appreciation. He'd been shown. It was worth the drive out just for that. Everything else was icing.

He had a choice—to eat it or to leave. At least that's what everyone thought. But Gus Campbell surprised them. He picked up his cup of coffee and went to join the strangers who were his wife and children.

"Do you like to go fishing, Campbell?"

"Yes, sir."

"I know a few good spots. Want to go fishing tomorrow?"

"Uncle Ewen is taking me out on his prawn boat. Thank you."

"Well, next weekend?"

"I'm going fishing with Uncle Wade."

"I see." He smiled and smiled. "Maybe you could find some time for an old man?"

"I'm very busy, sir. I ride the bus home from school, then Gramps meets me at the bus stop and he and I have all kinds of things to do together. Wednesdays Mom takes me to soccer practice, or if she has to work late, Gramps takes me. Saturdays are games, then there's track and field and cross-country, and I spend weekends with my uncles. I don't want to be rude, but my time is really tight."

"I see." Yet another smile.

Kate had seen that smile too often. She sucked in her breath sharply.

Gus shook his head. "Oh, do calm yourself, Kate," he said coldly. "It's none of your business."

"Gus, please . . ."

"Can you not behave yourself?" He sounded as if he was teasing her, but the smile looked as if it had been carved with a razor blade. "The rest of us have no trouble doing that. Do we, hen?" He looked at Cedar.

"No, sir," she answered politely. "We have no trouble at all. Would you like more salmon? Campbell and I would be glad to get it for you."

"Thank you. I'd appreciate that. And is there any tartar sauce for it?"

Finding kid care for Steve and Dianne was an ongoing pain in the jaw. Gramps hated the idea of driving them to the closest day-care centre, but he knew he couldn't look after them properly by himself.

"I could move in with you." Kate suggested.

"Momma," Cedar sighed, "you and I get along much better when we only see each other for a few hours a week. And you've got your job."

"My job is afternoons and evenings, I'd be here during the day. And I'd be leaving at about the time you came home. We'd hardly have to see each other's faces, let alone deal with each other's odd ways."

"And what about the old man? Do we need the uproar?"

"I doubt there'd be one."

"And who would look after your place?"

"Well, now, it could be rented out, you know."

"And himself? He'd pitch a fit."

"He's as good as moved to his mother's place. I hardly see him."

"I didn't know."

"After the memorial? The shed-warming? We went home, me in my car, he in his, and I got there first. When he came in, I knew he was in a right rare mood. He had that look, you know the one. But I didn't say anything that might tip him over the edge. I just asked if he'd like a pot of tea, and he said he'd make it. So I went back to what I was doing, and the next thing I know the tea's made and he's sitting at the table stir, stir, stirring his tea, clattering his spoon, and I said, 'Well, Gus, I suppose we should talk.'"

"And are you looking for trouble?" he had purred.

"Me? Angus, my dear, I've been alone in this house for six weeks without the slightest sign of trouble. You're here fifteen minutes, and . . ." Kate had pulled her mug toward her, added sugar, stirred. "There won't be any more trouble," she said firmly.

"You saw what they did. And you joined them."

"I did."

"Disloyal bitch."

"No. My loyalty is with my children, Gus. Neither of them has ever hit me, pushed me, shoved me, punched me, terrified me. Neither of them tries to control me, neither of them ignores me or shames me. They have consideration."

"Careful, Kate."

"No. No need to be careful in my own home. Would you like a piece of your mother's butter tart pie?"

"No."

"Well, I'm having some. I don't know why more people don't use a butter tart recipe in a pie. It's much better than pecan, especially when a body can hardly even find pecans any more and has to make do with walnuts."

"Are you going to gab on about nothing all day, then?"

"Oh, it's not nothing, Gus. It's called conversation. People do it all the time."

"What is it you're really trying to tell me? That it's over, is that it?"

"That's about it, Gus. There was a reason for the charade for a long time, but no reason for it now. Cedar's set up on her own, Rory's never here—even when he's got time off from school, he's at Cedar's. I'm in this house alone for weeks on end, then you come back and it's the same old thing, walking on eggshells, waiting for the land mines to explode. It's boring."

"You're my wife!"

"That never made any big difference to you before. You've a string of once-was'es up and down the coast. You'd have one in camp if you could. For all I know, you do."

"Well, and I don't, either!" He looked as if she had just insulted him deeply.

"There's always Bridget Riley, if you can get her sober. Or Alice Carruthers. Or either of the sisters, wotz-their-name."

"Shut up, Kate."

"No, Gus. I'm tired of this, really very tired of it. And something else I'm tired of is this pretending that goes on, even between the two of us. I have my own bedroom, and I'm sleeping there tonight. Alone. I'm not going to pretend that we're close. Not that way. Not any more."

"Cut off your nose to spite your face, then," he laughed. "Go find yourself some on-the-side stud, settle for second or third best. No skin off my nose."

"More tea?"

"Oh, Christ, yes." He casually tossed his mug over his shoulder, and it landed in the sink and shattered. "By all means, a spot of tea. A body would think you were bloody English, you and your goddamn tea!"

Cedar stared at her hands, clasped between her knees. "And he left, just like that?" she whispered.

"Left with most of his clothes. He's been back two or three times, picking up other things. His fishing rods, his creel and tackle, like that."

"Damn, eh."

"I've got money saved in the bank. I could get someone to put up a small place all my own. When I die it's yours, to do with as you want. I'd be here for the babies, I'd be out of your hair, we wouldn't have to grate on each other's nerves at all."

"I have to talk to Gramps about it."

"I've already talked to him. I'd be here for him, too. He's getting very old, very frail."

"I have to think about it."

But there wasn't a lot of room to think. She needed someone full-time, someone who could do more than merely wipe noses and make peanut butter sandwiches. The little ones needed love, needed snuggles and smooches, needed to feel important. And Gramps just couldn't cover all the bases. He could sit with them in his arms, but the up-and-down getting of this and that, the bending, the stooping, the yes dear, coming darling, the constant attentiveness, were too much for him. Sometimes he seemed to lose track of time, sitting in his chair for a few minutes and then half an hour later, or an hour, or two, he would waken confused and disoriented.

Cedar held out for a week and a half, then drove over to Kate's place with Steve in a car seat and Dianne in her car bed.

"Hey, Grandma," she said. "We're here to see if you have any idea at all how to civilize the red-headed heathen."

"No problem." Kate scooped him up and kissed his cheeks. "Warm his bum if he's bad, that's all. Give Grandma big kisses, Stevie? Give Grandma a smooch?"

NINE

Kate sat on the front porch watching Dianne play basketball with the newly raised hoop. Dianne was having some problems adjusting to the change. The hoop was at regulation height now, and Dianne was, after all, only ten years old. You could see the marks where the hoop used to be, a good foot and a half lower. The paint on the wall of the weanling shed was stained by the impact of the ball, and some spots were so worn that the grey concrete showed through.

Kate could hear Steve and Cam practising together inside the house. She enjoyed the sound, liked the strong, steady beat. Maybe it was gypsy music. Kate didn't have much of a background in music—if it wasn't played on the radio, it was beyond her. She would have thought Cedar would be in the same boat, but no, she seemed to know as much about it as the boys did, even Rory, although when he'd have time to sit and listen was a mystery.

Kate wished Rory would settle down, get married, raise a family and have a life beyond the confines of his office and the new hospital. He laughed when she worried about him out loud, reminded her that she had no idea what his life was like. True enough, but how could she? Whenever she called he was at work, or she got the answering service. He was good about phoning back, but still. She'd suggested that he rent out the house he'd inherited when old Doc Forbes died, and move into the big house with Cedar, the kids and Gramps, but Rory just laughed and said he was fine right where he was, close to work, with a beautiful view.

It certainly was a beautiful view. The house sat on the slope that rose up behind the lip of the cliff. At the bottom of the cliff was the sea wall, and beyond that the heaving ocean, visible from two sides of the house. He'd had the whole thing redone two years ago. It must have cost the earth, although he had been able to write off most of it because so much of the expense had gone into modernizing his office, with computers and multi-line phones and who knew what else.

Everything had been fixed, tightened, cleaned, repainted and upgraded. It looked like a mansion now, instead of an old house. When all the work had been underway and the place swarming with trades-men, she had hoped that he was getting ready to surprise her with an announcement, that he was engaged or something. But not so much as word one.

And you'd think, the way he idolized those kids, that he'd want to be closer to them, see them more often. You'd think he'd want to see more of his mother, or at least his sister. He took two days off every week, Sunday and Monday, and he was fierce about it. Nothing short of disaster could get him to see patients on those days. Even babies that arrived suddenly and unexpectedly had to do without Rory. He was as good as gone to the moon from the time his hospital shift ended at ten on Saturday night until his rounds began on Tuesday morning. Every Sunday he showed up for brunch, and Kate got to see him then and to catch up on such news as he cared to share. Then he was gone with the kids, and no sign of any of them until past eight at night. Then he'd have coffee and visit briefly, always taking the time to ask Grandpa Joe how he was feeling. Sometimes he would look him over, although the old man restricted that to the most cur-sory check of his heart, his pulse and his reflexes. "If I need doctor-ing," he said each time, "I'll make an appointment to see you at your office."

"You should come in every six months," Rory lectured him.

"You're just looking to skin my medical insurance. I've had more damn checkovers from you right here in my own living room than I've had in my entire life. I'm not a sick man, Rory, I'm an old man. Everything is wearing out and slowing down. It's supposed to. If it didn't, nobody would ever die and there'd be no place for the newly born. And then what would happen to all those souls waiting to come back for their next life?"

"What do you care about those who aren't even here?"

"Well, shite, son, I might be one of them next year!"   .

Kate wanted to stop them, to tell them it wasn't funny, they were tempting the goolies. But they'd laugh at her, and Rory would tell her she was supposed to be Scandihoovian, she wasn't supposed to believe all those old Scots ideas. Maybe not, but it was no use tempting fate.

Kate's mother and father were gone, their house and land sold, the proceeds divided. Most of the furniture she had in her own small house had belonged to them. And now, without Karen's Sunday dinners to bring them together, she hardly ever saw her brothers any more—they all sort of drifted apart. Sometimes she thought of having a big Sunday get-together here, but the thought always passed. There were so many children, and not all of them used to being around animals. Some of them ran through the flower beds, and others were so intent on clambering onto everything, you worried they'd impale themselves on some piece of machinery.

The music stopped, and then the boys were clattering down the stairs, racing past her, and Dianne was passing the ball to Campbell. He bounced it and passed it back to her, and she passed it to Steve. He almost took a shot, then side-passed it to Campbell, who dunked it. Kate had no idea what the rules of this game might be. In fact, there didn't seem to be any. Dianne was the youngest but she could hold her own and play every bit as well as the boys, with or without rules, even if they ganged up on her and began to play pig-in-the-middle.

Gramps came in from the farrowing shed, walking stiffly, leaning on his cane. Dianne's cockapoo leaped to her feet and trotted over to him, her tail wagging. He stopped to pat her head, then continued toward the porch. The kids called to him, "Hey Gramps, want to play?" and he muttered something that made them laugh.

"Here." Kate fixed the cushions on his chair and reached for his arm.

Joe glared at her. "I can do it," he snapped. "Stop fussing over me."

"Now, now, now," she chided. "No need to be nasty."

"You're the only one of the whole bunch who treats me like a crock."

"I treat you like a priceless Ming vase. Just sit down and I'll get you a cup of tea."

"I don't want tea. Thank you."

"I'll get you one anyway. You might change your mind."

Gramps sighed noisily as she went into the house. Jesus aitch! Maybe she was just trying to show she cared, but the truth was if he drank every cup of tea she made for him, his kidneys would pack it in and he'd wind up on dialysis. Or else they'd declare he had the biggest bladder in the history of the species and put his X-rays in the medical journals. And if it wasn't something to drink, it was something to eat. Even Rory had told her that all those slices of cake, slices of this loaf or that loaf, lemon squares, rum balls and you name it, that she baked up and slid in front of him, weren't good for his blood sugar or his weight. He was all right now, but he wanted to stay that way.

"Here you go." She put the tea on the arm of the chair. Just exactly the right place to get bumped by an elbow and tipped onto his lap. "How's everything in the farrowing shed?"

"Just fine. Cedar's got it all set up, sows are comfortable, piglets are doing well. There's one runty-looking one, but he's up on his feet and scrabbling for a place on the assembly line. She's got the tusk buds pulled on all but the ones born this afternoon. I wish I could help her with them, but between my lousy eyes and my shaky hands I'd wind up pulling off their noses or something."

"Get Campbell to do it. He knows how."

"He's busy, can't you see?"

"Oh, for crying in the night! He's not busy, he's playing! Campbell," she called. The game stopped immediately. "Your Gramps says there's a new litter in there needs the tusk buds pulled. He can't do it, you know how he is."

"Get right on it." Campbell turned to Steve. "Gimme a hand."

"Oh, sure, no sweat," and Steve clapped slowly, mockingly.

Kate was all set to tell him off, order him to get his backside into the farrowing shed this minute and lend a hand, but before she could explode he was moving forward, passing the ball to Dianne. She caught it and dropped it into the string bag hanging from the hook in the wall, then ran to catch up with the boys. Kate followed more slowly. She didn't care much for pigs, not even smooth-skinned newborns, but she wanted to be sure Steve actually helped, instead of pestering everybody else.

When she reached them, Steve was gently gripping a newborn piglet, holding its mouth wide open with a stick. Campbell was standing by with the needle-nose pliers and Dianne with the disinfectant and a roll of cotton batting. Campbell gripped one of the tusk buds and pulled, twisting his wrist at the same time. The piglet squealed and kicked, the tooth bud came out, Campbell dropped it in a tobacco can and Dianne drenched the area with the disinfectant. Another twist, another pull and the tusk buds were gone. The wailing piglet was put back in the pen. He scurried away from them to cower against the huge pink bulk that was his mother.

"He'll be suckling in a few minutes," Campbell assured Kate, "and by the time his belly's full he'll have forgotten all about it. There's no real root there, Grandma, you can check the ones in the can if you want."

"No thank you." She was more than willing to take his word. "You make a good team," she told them.

Steve grinned at her. He had another piglet in his hands, holding it against his chest. He reached for the wooden peg and tapped the baby on the nose with it. The piglet snapped, missed, opened its mouth to bite and Steve popped in the peg prying open the little mouth. Twist-pull-swab, twist-pull-swab and another one was done.

"I'll leave you to it, then," Kate said, glad to leave the farrowing shed and head back toward the house. Clancy the cockapoo greeted her briefly, then turned her attention back to the door. She was waiting for Dianne. That was her job and nothing was going to distract her. She'd have been inside, pressed against the girl's ankles, but no critters were tolerated in any of the sheds.

Kate stopped at the henhouse to collect the eggs. Ten eggs, and that was a good day. Time to go in and cull the unproductive, or maybe she'd wait until the weekend, when Cedar would be taking all three kids down to Victoria—Steve for a soccer tournament, Cam to enrol in university. And wasn't that a caution! Still half a year until the start of the semester, but if he didn't get signed up now, he'd miss out completely.

Cam wasn't playing soccer this year, he was still giving his knee a rest. Rory said that by the time the new season started, Cam would be fit and ready to play, but for now it was rehab. And while he had started running two miles a day, he wore his knee brace when he did. It had been awful, just awful, and Kate had been trying ever since to suggest that maybe Steve and Dianne should drop out before something like that happened to them. They ignored her, of course. What did she know about it? She was the Grandma, older than the pyramids and out of touch with reality. Old fogey. Over the hill. Nearly as old as Gramps.

Cam had the ball when it happened. He was heading up the side, and three of them took him out. They didn't check him, they didn't go for the ball, they went for him. Goon tactics. And when he fell, oh God, everybody knew. Before he even hit the ground the onlookers were groaning with sympathy. A knee is supposed to bend from front to back, not from side to side. Cam said he actually heard the sound when the ligament snapped. He said it sounded exactly the same as when you pull the wishbone of the turkey. The goons got their wish, all right—they got Campbell McCann off the field, not just for that game, but the rest of the season.

No, she'd definitely wait until they were out of town. That way she could go in and cull the chickens without having to listen to all the moaning about how cute this one was or how good a mother that one had been. She'd have it all done and the evidence buried before they got home. Maybe they wouldn't even notice.

But of course they did. They teased her, reminding her that they had a list of every critter on the place, including the grasshoppers and crickets. They even knew when she'd sprayed the house to kill flies and spiders.

"Can't fool us," Campbell told her, his face grave, his blue eyes sparkling. "We knew before we left for Victoria what you had in mind. And don't think you got away with pruning those rose bushes, either. Even the climbers."

"Campbell, they've got to be pruned. Otherwise they'll straggle, they'll look like weeds with thorns on them."

"Gotcha."

"But never mind that. Did you get enrolled for school?"

"No problem. Well, no big problem. I had to show a portfolio of previous work and do an essay to get into the writing course I wanted. And the audition for the music courses was a killer. But I did okay."

"I'm sure you did. Why didn't you try for one of the big universities on the mainland? I know you'd have been accepted, by your soccer playing alone."

"I might be toast as far as soccer is concerned. Besides which, they don't have the instructors I want. And this way," he added, kissing her ear, "if I get hungry, I can just jump on the bus back here, catch a snooze along the way, then walk in, pull my chair to the table and beg for food, food, please, some food."

And before she could tease him back, he was gone, patting her shoulder as he left. That happened more and more often now, so much like Cedar and her way of brushing off any suggestion or idea she didn't wish to explore. Well, fine. Kate would bide her time. She was used to it, and the day would come when they'd realize she wasn't some sagging old gym sock to be tossed into the ragbag and forgotten. She had some ideas of her own, and they were coming together. Other people respected her opinions. Some people even sought them out, listened to what she had to say. If they'd listened to her in the first place, Campbell would have gone directly to the University of Victoria as soon as he graduated grade twelve. But no, he had no intention of going. He had more reasons why he should stay home and go to the local college than a person could write on a piece of paper.

Finally Rory had taken her aside. "He isn't ready to leave home, Momma," he had told her sternly. "Don't pressure him."

"It's time he got himself over—"

"No! Nobody has to get over anything. He lost his mom. You had yours, you have no idea what it's like. He isn't going to go out of his way to lose Cedar and Steve and Di-Di on top of it and why should he? He'll go, don't worry. But not until he's damn good and ready."

"It's a waste of time, Rory. He could be—"

"Momma, stop it. Just . . . stop it."

And so she had, and here they were, and if he'd gone right from grade twelve he'd have been practically ready to graduate. But she wasn't going to remind anybody of that.

Cedar sat in the big chair in the living room with Dianne on her lap, her homework binder open to a map of Canada.

"Steve said you'd know about the fur traders, Momma. He said you helped him a lot."

"Darling, I feel as if I'm fur-tradered out. First I had to learn all about them, then Rory needed help, and after him I think it was one after the other at Auntie Marg's place, then Campbell, then Steve and now you. I am so sick and tired of those guys! By me, they'd have all been street people if there'd been streets, but there weren't so they wound up living in big freight canoes. I bet they stank, and I bet they had body lice and rotten teeth and I bet their hair was greasy and dirty!"

Cedar could hear Steve on the piano in the music room upstairs. Well, his mother had hoped for musical. Those big hands moved with a sureness and dexterity unusual for a thirteen-year-old. His piano teacher had told Cedar to start looking for a new teacher. "He knows as much as I do now," she said, "and he needs challenges or he'll go sour."

"I don't even know where to look."

"I'll help, if you don't mind. But it will be pricey."

Well, who was going to worry about that? Even if all hell busted loose all over the world, they'd manage. Most of what they ate they produced themselves. Cedar had her job, she had tons of seniority, she had money saved in several different accounts.

"Momma?"

"Excuse me, say again?"

"Do they still trap beaver?"

"I guess so. For fur coats and such."

"But you don't know for sure?"

"Not for sure-sure. But I bet if you phone the agriculture department, or the wildlife branch or maybe the one that's supposed to look after the environment, they'd know. Or they could tell you who to phone."

"What do you think about fur coats and such?"

"I haven't really thought about it. What about you?"

"Well, like, maybe up North, you know, where it's really cold for a really long time, it might be all right there. I mean, it would keep you warm, wouldn't it?"

"I suppose so. Be awfully heavy, though."

"But, like, the fashion models, they're wearing a fur coat and it's blazing hot and they've got on, like, shorts and a tit-fall top and—"

"Excuse me? A what kind of top?"

"Tit-fall. You know, they bend over and the whole dairy falls out?"

"Oh. That kind of tit. Okay." Cedar supposed a good, respectable mother would try to correct Dianne. But it was such a good descriptive term, Cedar filed it away for a time when she might use it herself.

"It's not the keeping warm part of it, darling, it's a status symbol. It's like lookie, lookie, see how much money I had to spend on a coat."

"Do we have status symbols?"

"Yeah, we do. We have negative status symbols. We don't go, 'Nyah nyah see how much money we have,' we go 'Nyah nyah, yeah, we've got money, so what? Who cares?'"

"Symbols like what?"

"Like my pickup truck. My pickup truck is older than you are, older than Stevie. It's as old as Campbell! It used to be my work truck, for hauling feed and going to the lumberyard and such. But it started to get rusted out and cranky so I parked it and bought a new one. That old one sat in the shed for a couple of years, but then I thought hell, I really do prefer it. It drives well and it's got better visibility and I like the windows. So I had it towed in to where Uncle Ewen's boy Bob works. And I asked Bob if he could fix her up. He got new panels for the doors, he got new this and new that and replacement something-elses and a reconditioned engine, and now when I drive through town, people know I could have a brand new car if I wanted but I'm too cool, eh, too smooth, too oh-yeah."

"Show-off."

"That's exactly what status is, darling. Showin' off."

"I have math, too."

"You're on your own. I refuse. I absolutely refuse to spend one more minute of my life with the multiplication tables."

"Oh, pooh." Dianne slid off Cedar's lap. "Multiplication tables are easy. I've had them memorized for more than a year. I'm on fractions."

"Okay, I refuse to spend one more minute of my life with fractions."

"It's easy. You just make sure they all wind up with the same number at the bottom."

Campbell brought Cedar a cup of coffee on his way upstairs with a mug of his own. She could see Gramps asleep in his chair on the porch, the motley-coloured cat curled on his lap. Kate was walking out of her house, climbing into her car, heading off to work. She looked like a million dollars—hair just so, dressed to the nines, smooth, sophisticated. She probably outshone most of her hoity-toity customers and she did most of it herself. Made a person wonder what she might have been "if only," and made a person wonder all over again whether Gus Campbell had any brains at all, and if so, where he kept them.

God, Campbell off to university. Well, she'd kept him with her as long as she could, and he'd been more than willing to be kept. In fact he had told her right out that the thought of leaving scared him. Told her he wanted to stay home and go to the local college. Kate had a fit—Kate was always having fits—but Rory calmed her down. Campbell told Cedar he knew he would get over being scared and actually do the work, and do it well, but he wasn't ready to wave goodbye. "I feel like I need all of you," he had told her. That meant a lot. It meant everything, actually. But time to let go.

She would have preferred to be the one who bought Campbell the car he didn't yet know about, but Rory had got there first. She would probably have gone for some sporty thing, but Rory either had better sense or less imagination. He bought the kind of car you'd think an old fuddy-duddy would want. But she knew Cam would be jumping out of his skin when he saw it. Jumping one-legged, perhaps, but jumping.

God, off to university. A place she'd never even thought of going. And didn't Kate make sure to mention that a couple of times a month. "You did so well in school," she'd say, "and it all seemed so easy for you. I guess I thought . . . or maybe hoped and dreamed . . ."

"Yes, Momma." What else can you say, when you'd just as soon say, "Shut the fuck up about it, will you?" You wouldn't say things like that to anybody, especially not your mother.

Damn them all. She'd have to damn them all because she didn't know for sure where to focus, who to blow to hell. She'd been over the accounts six or seven times in the past few days and the news was terrifying. Really terrifying. Where was all that pork coming from, anyway? Who was flooding the market, how were they doing it, and, more to the point, why? On this one you couldn't even point the finger right at the US of A—their pork farmers were dropping like flies, too. And it couldn't be imported pork from Europe. The prices wouldn't pay the cost of shipping the stuff.

She had it all figured out, down to the penny per pound. Even discounting the investment in sheds, repairs, equipment and rah rah, even if she reminded herself that had all been paid for in the past, there was just no getting around the fact that it cost her an absolute rock-bottom minimum of forty cents a pound to raise a pig to market size. so any selling price less than forty cents a pound and she was losing money.

Well, prices had been sliding for more than six months, a steady down, down, down, and now they were sitting right at rock bottom. Forty fuckin' cents a pound for prime pork. She was working hours a day for zip. The electricity, gas, pump repairs, worm medicine, this that and the next thing were like stockholders' loans, not even included in the forty cents. She was just standing in a strong wind taking five-dollar bills out of her pocket and letting them fly off like kites without strings.

When she had made herself sit down at the kitchen table with all the account books and ruthlessly made herself calculate the actual income and outgo, including the vet bills, the utilities and probably a tenth of the incidentals, she was already out ten cents a pound. It was getting to the point where she might as well be raising and selling horses. Now there was a good way to lose money!

Meanwhile, had the price of pork chops dropped? Could you walk into the supermarket and see pork roast for fifty or sixty cents a pound? How did it happen that you would pay at least twenty dollars for enough spare ribs to feed a family of five, and the goddamn farmer who did all the work saw none of it?

Well, there'd be no sitting this one out. She'd sat out the last one, but learned a hard lesson. And the last one hadn't been this bad. She'd heard of a guy who got a backhoe to come in and dig a great jeezly pit, then went to his barns and started in with a deer rifle. It took him two days to bury the corpses, and when it was over, he had what he'd started out with, if you didn't count his confidence, his hopes, his dreams or his years of toil—two pregnant sows and two weanling boars. With the surplus dirt he built a bloody great mound and seeded it with sweet-smelling yellow clover and sweet william. Told them at the feed store he'd considered shooting himself and falling into the pit with his stock, but he didn't know anybody who would take over driving the backhoe to cover them.

And two feed stores down-island were already sporting Closing Out Sale signs, which meant the farmers would have to drive an extra twenty, thirty miles to get feed, which meant their costs were rising again. It was like bowling—if you hit the right one, it'll knock down the others. But damn it, she wasn't getting rid of all the Tammies! The Hungarians, yes, the Carolinas, yes. But not the Tammies, not all of them.

And the bloody government, blithely babbling about whatever

in Christ it was they were always blathering about, and forking over the better part of a million bucks to keep a pack of losers who called themselves a football team for Christ's sake from moving somewhere else, and the damn Tammies were as good as on their way to extinction and who gave a dollar to save them? A good breed, a good solid breed, but slow to mature. Well, of course slow to mature! We're all slow to mature. And if we don't manage to mature, doesn't the voting public just turn around and put us in office?

What in hell was wrong with that goddamn cat, anyway? Screeching and yowling and raising all kinds of bloody hell out there. If she didn't stop with the Hallowe'en grimalkin routine she'd wind up waking up Gramps.

Cedar hauled herself out of her chair and went outside to shut up Motley's yowling. She grabbed her by the scruff of the neck and was just about to throw her off the porch when she glanced at Gramps. She had never moved so fast. She dropped the cat and launched herself into the house for the phone.

Rory got there before the ambulance and police did.

"Oh, Cedar. Oh, baby, I am so sorry."

"Well," she said, as though she were discussing the weather, "at least he was sitting in his chair, on his porch, with his cat on his lap, looking out at his farm, with his family nearby and his grandsons making music. He was so happy when they made music. It was like a miracle to him."

"He had a good life. And you're right, he had a good death, too."

"So why do I feel crazy, Roarsers? I do, I am completely and totally insane here."

"I'll give you something," he promised. "Come on, now, let these people do their jobs. Cam, take your mother's arm, help me get her inside, she'll take root if we leave her here."

The kitchen table was all Cedar could see. The rest of the room faded and disappeared so that she couldn't see what she knew was there—no cupboards, no sink, no counter, no stove, no fridge. There was her, there was the table, there were the kids staring at her with tear-swollen eyes, there was Rory and there was the prick in her arm. The tablecloth was red and white squares, faded to half as bright as it was when Gramps had brought it home from Wal-Mart.

"I don't know what to do." Cedar looked at the kids. "I'm real sorry, kids. I'm real, real sorry."

"Us, too, Momma," Dianne sobbed. "I didn't even know he was sick."

"He wasn't sick," Rory said. "He was just old. Everything wears out. Remember, he told us that himself, lots of times."

"Guess I better go phone Ted." Campbell patted Cedar's shoulder. "I'll do it, Momma, you just sit here and take it easy. Stevie, you might make a pot of coffee."

For some reason Cedar had the idea that a funeral took place three days after death. In Gramps's case it was a full week. Twice in that time she thought she was going to go out back and screech into the wind until her throat wouldn't make any more sound. Once she nearly lost it and punched Ted Conrad in the face.

"You should have—" he started, sad and angry and ready to blame everybody else for what had been inevitable.

"Stop it, Ted." Kate spoke quietly. "Just sit down and watch the video again. Your father made it with exactly this in mind. And don't blow it off as the rambling of a senile old fart, because Joe had his full faculties right up until the very minute his heart quit, in spite of what you always thought. Yes, you'd have had him in an old folks' home years ago, and it would have killed him a lot sooner. Stevie, please, the tape again."

"I don't want to watch it again," Steve said. "It makes me cry."

"Okay, dear. Why don't you find Campbell and ask him if he'll drive you and Dianne into town. Maybe a movie?"

Kate sat on the sofa beside Ted, holding his hand as gently as if he were a tiny child. Ted watched the video, but several times he shook his head in short, hard jerks, and his lips moved as if he wanted to argue.

Ten minutes of tape, ten minutes of Joe Conrad sitting in his chair on the porch, talking to the camera, laying it all out, everything tickety-boo. And the lawyer had everything in writing, too.

"Why," Ted asked bitterly, "is everyone so sure I'm going to raise hell about the goddamn money!"

"Because you did once before. When he and Cedar bought this place and he put it in her name, remember? You had an absolute con-niption."

"It wasn't the *money!*" Ted spoke of the fifteen-year-old argument as though it had happened last week. "He should have retired, and instead he worked himself to death."

Kate let go of his hand. "I'm going to get a coffee, Ted. Do you want one?"

"I'd rather have a good stiff shot of Scotch."

"Be a minute, is all."

She fixed a mug of coffee for herself, then slopped some of Joe's Glenfiddich into a cobalt blue glass. Every now and again Cedar did something unexpected enough to surprise her mother completely. No word to anybody and suddenly there were a dozen cobalt blue glasses in the cupboard. Kate would have bet a dollar Cedar wouldn't even notice things like that.

"Thanks." Ted took the glass, sipped, blinked. "Good stuff."

"Your dad's. He loved good stuff. He'd have a couple of drinks most evenings, before he went to bed. Not always Scotch. There's some fine brandy in there, too. And a golden rum I'm told is very good. I don't know, I don't bother with it, and at work it's the barman's chore, not mine, so—God, listen to me! The dipper stuff we talk about when we're upset."

"I'm not upset," he snapped.

"Of course you are, Ted. And it's not just your dad. I can see your pulse beating in your temple, just above your ear. That's a sure sign. Now what's bugging you?"

"You'll laugh."

"Not *at* you."

"I feel really left out."

"Oh."

"I hardly knew him. Even when we lived together, I didn't know him. He was Dad, he was the boss, he was Joe the pig farmer, he was nobody I had any connection with."

"He felt badly about that, you know. He even mentioned it to me once, about how he closed out the world when he lost your mother."

"Yeah. Things seemed okay before then. He was my dad, you know, and at that time dads were dads, not your buddy or something like they are now. He wasn't affectionate, except with her. And then she was dead and he may as well have died, too."

"He did the best he could, and he did better than most."

"You think so?"

"I'm sure of it. Did you hear what you said? You felt left out of what your dad and mom had. And now you feel left out, again. Maybe you need to do something about feeling left out. Maybe you should look at how you leave yourself out of things."

"What are you, my shrink?" The edge was back in his voice.

She laughed. "Oh, I'm better than any shrink, Ted. I'm a glorified bartender and you know what that means."

"Well anyway, it was never the money. As far as I'm concerned the damn lawyer can divide it up among the others."

"Why the lawyer? Why not you? Or do you want to be left out again?"

Ted didn't answer. He stood up and went into the kitchen to refill his glass.

There was no funeral, no visit to the graveyard, no formal memorial service. The funeral home phoned and Cedar went down and picked up the cardboard box with Joe's name on it, and when she got home, people had begun to arrive.

Nick was wearing an expensive suit and his shoes were shined to perfection, his expression serious. "Not to worry about food," he said solemnly to Cedar. "My staff will deliver. He was my friend. We had cold drink on hot days, or hot drink on cold days, and solve all the problems of the world. Please. Allow me this."

"You're a good man, Nick."

"I am. You should tell that to your mother. She cannot see me the man, she sees only the boss. Such a waste, a woman like that, alone in a house. Such a waste."

"I don't suppose you've ever just walked over to her, taken both her hands in yours and said exactly that?" Cedar hadn't expected to smile on the same day she brought home the last earthly remains of Joe Conrad, Gramps, her friend. But there you are.

"And what if she laughs?"

"Oh, Christ, Nick, what's all that stuff in the history books, the battle of what, Thermopylae, and what about whozit on the bridge or the battle of Marathon and all that other glory of Greece stuff? I thought you were the guys who danced barefoot on broken glass."

"The barefoot part is BS. We wear boots, with very thick soles."

They each took a small handful of the ashes and spread them, and when the bag was empty Cedar turned it inside out and pinned it to the clothesline, so even the finest bit of dust could ride free on the wind. Nobody sang, nobody played music, nobody wept. They gathered together and were awkward, deprived of the formalities and rituals of a regular funeral.

After a while Campbell carried the first tray of deli cold cuts to the table in the gazebo. Steve and Dianne took the hint. Suddenly everyone had something to do, and then the truck arrived with the food from Nick, and Cedar brought out several cases of beer.

By the time evening was closing in, people were relaxed, talking with each other, and when Kate asked Cam and Steve to play some music, they did, but from the upstairs music room, with the windows open, so that Steve could play the piano. Dianne joined them, at least as good on guitar as her mother had ever been, and when she sang, people said that one day she'd have a voice even better than her mother's. Nobody mentioned Gus or his good clear singing voice, and nobody mentioned Mary Campbell, gone now, and the way she could sing the canaries out of their cages.

Seamus Kelly finished one beer and took two others with him when he went inside and began to play as well. Ewen, Rod and Gordon sat on the bench in the gazebo and sang, and even Hugh, Wade and Forrest joined in. Then Marg and Hank, and finally even Kate. Cedar did not sing.

By nine-thirty, Rory had taken charge. He led Cedar inside and made her lie down with a cold cloth on her forehead. She didn't know he was going to give her an injection until the needle was in her arm, and she didn't protest. "Give yourself a break, sister," he said softly. "They can all look after their own damn selves."

When she finally woke up, the first light of day was coming softly through her window. She threw off the quilt someone had put over her and got up, still wearing her clothes from the night before. She had a pee, washed her hands and face, took a swipe at her hair and went downstairs.

They'd cleaned up before they left. The kitchen was spotless, the fridge stuffed with leftovers. Even the gazebo was clean, and when she went out to the barn, she found the scraps in a bucket for the pigs. She checked the pigs, checked the automatic feeders, hosed down the floors of the pens and the drainage funnel down the centre of the barn. She gave the breeding sows the scraps and filled each trough with a bucket of milk.

She had no particular feeling that Gramps was with her, no feeling that his scattered ashes had spread his presence all over the farm. He was gone, and that's all she felt.

When all the chores were done, Cedar went into the house to make the first pot of coffee of the day. She didn't feel like eating breakfast. She sat at the kitchen table with coffee and cigarettes, listening to the radio quietly so as not to disturb anyone. The news took away any appetite she might have had. Pork prices were down to thirty-four cents a pound. What was it Gramps had said only two weeks ago? Something about how more and more things made less and less sense to him.

Ted came into the kitchen and poured himself some coffee. "How you doing today?" he asked.

"Oh, you know, any day above ground is a good one. You?"

"I'm fine. I'm heading back tomorrow."

"Figured you'd be going back soon."

"We don't get along very well, do we?"

"Not so's you'd notice. But we might learn."

"Yeah. Listen, is it okay if I come here this summer? For my vacation?"

"Any time at all. Like the flowers in May." But she really didn't expect to see him.

My God, thirty-five stinking cents a pound. She'd have to go talk to some people. She didn't want to put the butcher in a bind. Didn't want to take any business away from anybody. But she'd bury herself before she'd bury her stock! She could hand off two pigs per unit just in the immediate family, that was two dozen of them taken care of. Where else? Well, the transition house had a big freezer, and there was the food bank, and the guys at work—another ten to a dozen pigs right there.

She'd keep the Tamworths. Every breeding sow of them, plus a young boar. If anybody wanted to raise a pig or two for themselves, they could come and get them, free gratis. People would remember—there would be buckets of berries or fruit from someone's orchard. Something. It was better than destroying them. For crying in the night, she'd have to pay three to five hundred dollars just to get the backhoe to come this far out and dig the pit. Plus all those .303 shells.

Curtis Swenson, old man Swenson's grandson, sipped his beer and listened as Cedar talked and talked. Then they both sipped beer in silence. Finally Curtis talked, and Cedar listened, sipping her beer.

"Helluva thing," she sighed.

"Helluva thing," he agreed.

"Two or three years from now there'll be so few swine left in the country they'll be paying through the nose for the meat. By then, all the independents will be out of business and only the pork factories will . . ."

"A person gets tired of it." Curtis sounded tired. "After the pigs I suppose it'll be beef—again. Or chicken—again. Each time there are fewer and fewer family-farm survivors and the factories . . . Jesus, and the food they turn out is poisoning us."

He drank deeply, then stood and smiled. "So, best I go. You hear a screamin' and screechin', don't worry about it, it'll just be me, pulled over on the side'a the road, yelling like hell."

"I won't hear you for the sound of my own bellyachin' and bitchin'. Thanks, Curtis."

She didn't yell and holler, or bellyache or bitch. Instead she went for a long walk in the bush and wound up sitting on the creek bank where she had sat with Cam after Allison died, feeling as if the whole world was so out of control a person couldn't even find a place to grab, let alone hang on. Good thing she had her job, but how long would that last?

The Hungarians and Carolinas went first, and Curtis Swenson had extra smokehouses set up to handle the overload, extra freezers to store the sides of cured bacon and the pounds and pounds of specialty sausage. Then the giveaway began. Twice Cedar wound up on her knees in front of the porcelain altar, heaving. Both times she waited until Steve and Dianne were in bed, sound asleep.

But there was some satisfaction in parking near the supermarket and handing out roasts, chops and spareribs free of charge. She was only there ten minutes or so before the store manager was in her face, yelling that she was trespassing on private property, so rather than argue with him, she parked just outside the market's property, where he could see her but do nothing except get mad. Cedar didn't care. Another out-of-towner, parachuted in by the American-owned chain that also owned some of the biggest pork factories on the face of the earth, and would own even more once the rest of the independent farmers were bankrupt.

Still, when it was all over and done with and she was down to her
breeding stock, she felt as if she'd lost a vital portion of her anatomy.
And what would she do with all that spare time? The kids, sure, but
each and every day they were closer and closer to being on their own.
She slept in later in the mornings, took no time at all in the barn, went
to work and came home, and the chores were as good as done when she
got there. Much of the time supper was well on its way to being ready,
and then, even with soccer, basketball, baseball and whatever else,
there were hours when she just rattled around like a dried pea in an
even drier pod. She couldn't even get interested in what was develop-
ing between Kate and Nick.

"I'd like to talk to you," Kate said, caught somewhere between
shyness and formality.

"Sure. Anytime." Cedar sat back on her heels and dusted her
hands, knocking the earth from her gloves.

Kate knelt on the other side of the row, pulling on her own gloves.
Much of the difference between mother and daughter was right there
for anyone to see. Kate's gloves were green and white canvas, with little stylized flowers printed on them. Cedar's were leather work gloves,
moulded to her hands like a second skin.

"Nick and I have been seeing each other. On a personal basis, not
as part of the job."

"I know. Auntie Marg told me."

"How did Auntie Marg find out? You're the first person I've—"

"Uncle Hank heard it in the crummy, of course."

"How on earth did *they* find out?"

"Momma, do you remember when I was oh, I don't know, ten,
eleven, and you had a fit about the detective books I was reading?"

"That trash!"

"I was ten years old! What else would I read? Anyway, you could
take *all* those detectives in *all* those pocketbooks and put them
together in one superstar of a sleuth and she wouldn't be able to track
down how the guys in the crummy found out you and Nick the Greek
were starting to think of maybe one day holding hands with each
other."

"Are you laughing at me?"

"No, ma'am. I'm laughing at the guys in the crummy."

"I've been thinking of seeing a lawyer about a divorce." Kate looked as if she expected the sky to part and the finger of God to descend and crush her.

"You know the old fart will go up like a rocket."

"Like one of those Hallowe'en big ones."

"We might wind up really missing old Silk. With any luck nobody has told him she's buried under the golden plum tree."

"I don't think Clancy the cockapoo will be much protection."

"Why did you wait so long?"

"It didn't matter."

"And now it does? Because of Nick? That serious already?"

"He's asked me to go to Greece with him in the fall."

"To *Greece?*"

"You make it sound like it's the far side of the moon! Lots of people go to Greece." Kate was red in the face and laughing nervously to cover her terror.

Cedar gave up any pretence of gardening. "Want a beer?" she asked her mother.

"Love it!" Kate scrambled to her feet like a convict who has been given a last-minute reprieve. "I'll get them. In the gazebo?" She was already walking toward the house.

Cedar pulled off her gloves and put them in the little wooden box Gramps had made for her gardening stuff. She carried a small fork in there, a small trowel, a split-end weeder he had made for her, and there was even a place for a mug of coffee. She took the box to the gazebo, set it under the bench and sat down, leaning back and resting her head against the sill. It was too soon to bring out the pots of fuchsia and trailing geranium. The earth was still cold and damp, the weeds barely growing. Even the eternal raggedy buttercup was no farther out of the ground than a couple of inches.

"Kids not around?" Kate handed Cedar a cold beer.

"Gone up the creek. Dianne wants to collect some fossils and Steve's gone with her, because about the only place he doesn't go with her is the toilet. He's lost with Cam gone."

"He and Dianne always were close."

"Now they're more so. They never complain, but lately I've been sort of wondering. We're awful far from town."

"I wouldn't rush into anything," Kate warned. "I know it seems like a totally different place without the pigs and the business and all, but not everything about living closer to town is a benefit. They're better off up the creek looking for fossils than they are buzzing around in a car full of dope-smoking kids no older or smarter than they are."

"Greece, eh?"

"In the fall. He has brothers and sisters, cousins, like that."

"Hmm. You figure the divorce'll go through that fast? Because I don't. Gus will drag his feet every inch of the way. If he has to, he'll conveniently forget the court date, or he'll go into camp and stay there."

"I know. The only thing that will shift him is court orders, and they don't do that until the last dog has been hung and hide tanned. But I'm getting a lawyer. Actually I've got one already. She says we'll be right flat on top of him every step of the way." She dropped her gaze to her beer can and studied the top of it very carefully. "I got Janet Bridges for a lawyer."

For a moment Cedar couldn't place the name. And then the dime dropped and she was laughing. Kate smiled, then the smile became a grin, and finally she was laughing, too.

"Oh, Mom," Cedar managed. "You can be such a total shit when you set your mind to it."

"She knows. She knows, and I suspect it's her knowing is behind why she agreed to take it. She didn't laugh but she smiled. Not just any old smile, you know . . . I used to dream that you'd do something like that. Become a lawyer or—I don't know, something."

Cedar bit back the bitter words that rose in her throat and pushed against her teeth. Words like Why bother, Momma, nothing I did would ever have been good enough for you . . . Where was I supposed to get that kind of motivation when what I wanted most of all was to be out from under it all and on my own . . . I'm surprised, I didn't think you ever gave the first part of a damn what happened to me. Words like that.

Gus was just in from camp, getting out of a cab in front of his bachelor apartment, with his caulk boots slung over one shoulder, when the sheriff strolled over, grinning from ear to ear.

"Well, hi there, Gus Campbell," he said cheerfully, holding out his right hand. Gus went to shake it, but the Sheriff took his left hand from behind his back and put a sheaf of official-looking papers in the proffered hand.

"What'n hell's this?"

"Court papers," the Sheriff answered. "You take care, Gus, enjoy your time out of camp."

"Yeah, right." Gus stuffed the papers in his back pocket as if they didn't mean anything more than your average grocery list. He waited until he was in the apartment before he sat down with a beer and looked at the crumpled papers. He read each one carefully, then laid them on the coffee table and smoothed out the creases.

After a while he went to the bathroom, turned on the bathtub taps and added a squirt of bubble lotion. Everything in his apartment was clean and tidy. He could have had room and board with any of his brothers, but more and more he liked his privacy, his peace and quiet. There wasn't much of that in camp, machines going from daylight to dark and all the men talking, laughing, trying to be heard over the sound of TVs and radios and God, the stuff the young guys called music! It was nice to get back to his own place and not have the sights, sounds and smells of everybody else assailing you.

He sat in the tub with his second beer, smoking cigarettes and counting the tiles on the wall. Sometimes, if he took things easy and let his mind wander, let his thoughts scud off like fluffy clouds, he found he could suss out other people's thoughts and motivations.

And after a few minutes, he knew that Kate expected a huge hoorah. Why else would she go out of her way to hire the one lawyer almost guaranteed to kick off a go-round? They'd laugh. The entire town would laugh like hell when they found out Gus was going to wind up in court, facing off with his own daughter, named after his own dead sister. And Cedar would laugh loudest of all.

Unless Rory laughed louder. Sometimes Gus felt as if one of his arteries was leaking his lifeblood into the earth, his bonny lassie and his own braw laddie, and neither of them able to remember his birthday or Father's Day. Not a card from either of them for years. No phone call to say Hey, old man, put on some clean jeans, we're taking you out for steak supper. Out of all of them, the whole damn lot of them, nothing.

He'd tried. God knows he'd tried. Tried with Campbell, and what did that get him but laughed at by those dim-witted arseholes who watched and nudged each other? And after Campbell he'd tried with Steve. There were people in town said Rory was Steve's dad. Gus didn't think so—the boy looked nothing like anybody in the Campbell family or the McCanns, either, but you never know for sure. Steve wasn't as polite as Campbell, nor as diplomatic, either. He had just looked through Gus and said, "Not interested, sir." You'd think Gus had been trying to sell the boy a vacuum cleaner instead of offering him the opportunity to walk into the music store and pick out any instrument he wanted. Not interested, sir.

And Dianne! One look at her and his heart ached. She was both of his own children plus his beloved sister, all wrapped into one magical beauty. And the day after he had spoken to Steve, there was Cedar on his doorstep, looking as if she'd been bitten on the ass by a rabid dog, her blue eyes slitted, her voice trembling.

"If you ever go within two blocks of her," she had gritted, "I'll kill you."

"You'd dare talk to your own father that way!"

"I mean it, Gus. If you even walk on the same side of the street as her, I'll shoot you in the back. You don't talk to her. You don't so much as look at her."

"Good God, woman . . ."

"Between the shoulder blades." Cedar spun on her heel and walked off, and he knew that what he had just heard was truer than anything written in the Bible.

And now this. All of them probably checking with each other, did we make sure of this, have we covered the possibility of that, what will we do if he . . . And his own Janet there with her law books. You'd think it was the Battle of the damn Bulge they were planning.

He leaned back, sipped, and imagined the whole shiterooni. They'd have receipts going back to the year zero—who had paid the taxes, who had picked up the tab for the roof repairs and all the rest, and of course it would look as if Kate had been alone in it because she was the one who'd had the time to go into town and take care of business, and she was the one who saved everything, like receipts.

Devious, the lot of them. Backbiting two-faced devious scuts. Well, they didn't need to think they'd get the better of Gus Campbell. The whole lot of them combined weren't as smart wide awake as he was when he was sound asleep.

He pulled the plug, climbed out of the tub, dried and dressed himself and went out to the garage to start his car and drive straight to the Domino Club. Afternoon was fading, and already the thin warmth of the day was being gobbled by the damp chill. He walked into the club, nodded to John Riley, then found Bridget, dealing at the largest of the three poker tables. She didn't see him until he slid into a chair across the table from her.

"Evenin' darlin'."

"Well, as I live and breathe," she drawled, her face flushing with pleasure. "If it isn't Himself."

"You're looking wonderful, as usual." He pulled out his wallet and bought into the game.

Bridget's smile widened, and when she took a sip of coffee, liberally laced with John's own porch-climber, she made sure it was a sip, not a sturdy drink.

Bridget looked as if life had not been a stroll in paradise. Her voice sounded exactly as could be expected of a woman who had spent years searing her pipes with cigarettes, cigarillos and raw hooch. Sometimes her voice reminded Gus of fine sand grating on the bottom of an old porcelain sink. Her hair was a brindling of auburn and white now, and she still wore it in what locals called the Surrey Big Hair. Some said the smaller the town, the bigger the hair, others said the smaller the mind. Gus kind of liked it, though, especially now that she'd stopped trying to hide the march of time with colouring that had never quite fit her complexion.

Her hands were probably her best feature. Bridget went to the manicurist once a week and between visits she did the care and upkeep herself. Gus figured she could easily have modelled rings, watches and bracelets for expensive ads. She handled the cards as if they were part of her own body, an extension of her skin. And she still had great breasts, too. Well, they'd never been stretched by pregnancy and milk, never been tugged and pressed and chewed on by babies. They didn't stand firm and high any more, but if the truth be known, Gus preferred the softer, fuller model, just as he had grown to appreciate her belly now that it wasn't a flat, hard muscle.

"How was camp?" a fisherman asked.

"Same old same old," Gus answered.

"Hear tell your ex is hanging around with Nick the Greek," a young buck dared, a wicked glint in his eye.

"Oh that," Gus shrugged. "Hell, that's been going on for years." He brought out his cigarettes and lit one with the gold-plated propane lighter Bridget had given him as a rare present.

"Kept it a secret for a long time, then." The young buck was really pushing it, and some of the other men slid uneasy glances his way.

"Keeps a lot of secrets, that woman, and keeps them well," Gus agreed, sounding as if he was humouring the guy. "How's your mother?" he asked calmly.

The young man flushed, but managed to smile. "As gorgeous as ever."

"They say," said the fisherman, making his move to divert the conversation, "there's more shutdowns waiting to happen. Closed down one pulp mill already. Closed about a third of the sawmills. They've told us it'll be a short season. Ought to close the bugger completely for the next four to six years, give the fish a chance to come back."

"Close 'er here and the Yanks'll just catch 'em anyway. Got no damn idea at all about conservation, that bunch. Time comes they catch the last coho they'll likely have a public barbecue and invite the TV cameras to film it." The young buck reached for his own cigarettes.

"Have one of these, boy." Gus slid his package toward the young man. "Have one on Uncle Gus."

"Jesus," the boy said mildly, acknowledging what everyone in the club had known for years. "First this guy tries to rot the teeth out of my head with jellybeans and bubble gum, now he wants me to get emphysema. Thanks." He picked up the package, opened it and took one. "Thanks, Uncle Gus," and he laughed.

Bridget was pretty sure the young fellow would leave soon. He'd done his push and shove and Gus had handled it well. There were times less said than that would have had Gus on his feet, ready to swing. Maybe the realization that he was approaching an antique state was having a civilizing effect on him. Or maybe he had really liked the boy. Maybe he still did. Or maybe he had other reasons. You never knew with Gus.

"Thinking of taking the federal package," the fisherman went on, trying to sound as if the mere thought of it didn't twist his entrails. "For a fraction of what they'd pay me to call 'er quits, I could do a changeover on the *Lady Susan*. Get rid of the fish holds, put in living quarters, sort of, get a sign made up, Charter Fishing, and take the tourists out to try their luck."

"Take 'em out to see the whales," a ferry worker added. "Whole freakin' world is going nuts wantin' to see the whales. Crowdin' in at 'em so bad the poor buggers are gettin' claustraphobee. Charge 'em to take 'em over to the damn pulp mill, they got those sea lions over there so thick the noise of 'em honkin' and barkin' is gonna drive people nuts." He laughed. "Just around the point, eh, up where they put in those fancy glass houses for the rich? Well, those damn animals have moved in up there, too. The dentists and such are going crazy—there's sea lion shit all over their little private docks. One guy went out and saw three of 'em lyin' on the deck of his boat, sunnin' theirselves."

"I don't ever remember us bein' up to our arses in those things," Gus agreed. "Seems to me it used to be you hardly ever saw 'em."

"Oh, God, dare to shoot one of the fuckers and they'll be on you faster than if you shot a person."

"Too much pollution down south," the young buck said easily. "Too crowded, too. The damn things are moving. Hey, Martha, she's gettin' congested here, let's us swim North, they say the water's half clean." He shook his head, not quite angry, "And then they run around blaming the bloody weather or something. Try to convince us the reason we've got no fish left is because of naturally occurring cyclic conditions." He looked directly at Gus. "I remember one time you pitched God's own fit about the new ferry terminal because it was going in on what you said had been an oolichan spawning beach. And the outfall from the damn pulp mill, that was another one, once upon a time, in the good old days. So now there's no fuckin' oolichan, they've reintroduced the otters and seals and each of them eating a hundred poundsa fish a day, and now we got them damn sea lions and how much do *they* eat? But we'll blame the dairy farmers because their cows are shittin' in the rivers."

"Right," the fisherman laughed. "What I want to know is who trained 'em to walk down the highway to the riverbank to take a dump? Person who could train a cow to do that ought to be able to teach schoolkids to at least read, God knows."

Bridget listened to the conversation, sipped her doctored coffee and wondered, with no great amount of interest, just what was going on behind the carefully pleasant look on Gus Campbell's face. Something was up. She had no idea what, but something was definitely in the offing.

Big Jake came in at about ten-thirty and pulled up a chair to sit in on the game. She patted Gus on the shoulder as she walked behind him. "Hey there, gorgeous," she grinned. "How's super-studly doing?"

"Oh, you know me, break even if I'm lucky. How's the black cod situation?"

"Desperate. I been thinking of taking the feds up on their buyback. Figure I could turn the *Lovely* into one of them live-aboards, which she as good as is anyway. But fix 'er up, you know? Make 'er real comfortable. Then I could just tootle around pretending to be one of them rich bitches you read about in the magazines."

"I been thinking a charter boat," the other fisher said.

"Nah, not for me. Mosta your customers'd be tourists, and who'n hell wants *them* trompin' around on deck? Put 'em through the brush-muncher, use 'em for crab food."

The club never really closed. As long as there were players to sit in on a game, John Riley kept the coffee fresh and hot and the heat turned on. But nobody was very flush, except Gus, and he didn't lose enough money at cards to make it worth anybody's while staying up late. By two the lights were out, the thermostat was turned down and the burglar alarm was on. By three Gus and Bridget were in bed and she was enjoying every minute of him.

"Ah, Bridey," he sighed. "Ah, and we are good together."

"That's a true thing. Just as long as we keep things casual." She would die a slow death before she would admit to him or anyone else that it was a long, cold time since she'd felt casual where Gus was concerned. Maybe if she'd had to live with him, or see more of him, or maybe any of a hundred things, but for some reason Gus had clung to her like a wood tick, when none of the many others had. Even less understandable, she had not only allowed it, but welcomed it, and done a fair bit of stubborn clinging herself. Maybe it was because whatever could be said about him, the word "boring" wasn't one of them.

Not only did Gus not raise hell about the divorce, he took supreme pleasure in walking into Janet Bridges' office and telling her he wanted to sign over the house and land to Kate.

"She can have it all. They say there's a way she can even get half my pension or something—is that true?"

"Why are you doing this, Gus?"

He looked down at her, at the brand-new top-of-the-line wheelchair, the expensive tailored slacks, the uncreased, highly shined, stylish shoes. "Why, my bonny lassie, no matter what you may have heard from others, I'm not the asshole I've been painted." It was worth every penny, worth every ounce of the effort it took not to rip her traitor head off her shoulders, to see the look on her face. Gus knew he was halfway toward a convert if he wanted one. But did he want one? Her and her fancy goddamn position in life. He'd bet the other half of his pension her goddamn mother and that goddamn Gordon Bridges had never bothered to mention that Gus Campbell was never late with a support payment. In fact, that may have been what paid for her fancy education.

But oh, dear God, she did put him in mind of Jen. Poor dead Jen, who might still be with them if she'd been born twenty-five years later, when she could have had the abortion, legal and safe and quick. And yet, for all she reminded him of Jennet, she in no way resembled Cedar or Rory. The hair was darker and the eyes too. Just the mouth, and that was Jennet and it was Mary, too. She was his, damn it! His!

TEN

The day her parents' divorce became official was the day of the big accident at work. The old mess of a gravel scooper was busy gnawing at the pile, rumbling, grumbling, rattling and backfiring as it filled the bed of Cedar's truck. She wasn't allowed to be in the truck at the time—Compo regulations said so. Fine by Cedar. She got to stretch the kink out of her back, have a smoke and a sip or two of halfway decent coffee.

She stretched once more and turned sideways to put her coffee mug on the top step outside the timekeeper's shack, and suddenly there was the most godawful noise and Cedar was knocked off her feet. Bits and pieces of rusty metal were flying like shrapnel, and she looked up to see Tom, the scooper operator, limping toward her, Cuz running to help him. There was a hollow sound—*whump*—and a ball of flame was belched up into the sky. Cedar scrambled up in time to help Cuz haul Tom away from the explosion. Her truck lurched and bounced, and more crap, crud and corruption flew. She and Cuz gripped Tom and ran, the timekeeper running ahead of them. All Cedar could think of was the line "She might not be a spring chicken, but by God, she's spry," and she nearly laughed out loud.

When they got to the edge of the gravel pit, they looked back. The gravel scoop was a twisted mess of junk, bits and parts of it sticking up out of the bright red inferno and black smoke. Cedar's truck was on fire too, what was left of it, and the trash alder that had taken root just beyond the gravel pit was blazing, the flames heading toward the stand of third-growth fir.

They lowered Tom to the ground. Cedar took off her jacket, surprised to see that it was burned on the back, and covered him. Suddenly Cuz was gone. She worried for a moment, but Tom was more in need of worry than Cuz. He needed a doctor, fast. He was trembling, his eyes wide but seeing nothing, and the timekeeper was trying desperately, with a first-aid certificate but no supplies at all, to stop the blood pouring from his wounds.

And then Cuz came in behind them, driving his near new four-by across the rough rutted ground, pushing aside the alder whips and climbing right up over the half-punky fallen logs and trash. Without a word, Cedar and the timekeeper grasped Tom as gently as possible and dragged him out to meet Cuz. The three of them got Tom into the back seat and pulled a woollen blanket over him.

The fuel barrels started to explode as Cuz drove out of there as fast as he could and prayed on behalf of all of them. Holy fuck this is awful, fuckin' Jesus save my ass. As soon as they were off the rough ground and onto a road, Cuz had his cellphone to his ear. And as soon as he put it away, Cedar lit a cigarette for him and another for herself.

Two miles toward town the first cop car pulled onto the highway ahead of them and turned on lights and siren, escorting them and clearing the highway ahead. Halfway to town the fire engines screamed by in the opposite lane, three of them, lights and sirens and that other awful thing, the *whoop whoop whoop* that always made Cedar's heart leap into her throat.

And then another cop car behind them, adding its siren to the din. The highway ahead stretched open for them, cars, pickups, buses, trailers and transport trucks clinging to the side of the road, the passengers peering out the windows, their faces like little balloons.

The staff in Emergency were ready. Before Cuz had the truck parked they were moving forward, pushing a gurney. Tom was transferred so smoothly Cedar couldn't have described how it was done, and then Cuz was out of the truck and following the stretcher, his face pale and stretched, looking like he was seventy.

Cedar parked the truck in the lot, then went back to Emergency. Cuz and the timekeeper were talking to cops. When one of the cops looked over at her, she realized that she had blood on her clothes, arms and hands, and that some of it was hers. The cop walked toward her, already pulling out a tape recorder. A nurse approached with a wheel-chair. Cedar opened her mouth to say she didn't need a chair, thank you, and then she as good as fell into it, hearing her own voice say, "Thank you so much. I don't feel very well."

She knew who the doctor was in spite of the mask. "Hey, Roar," she managed. She wasn't in Emergency, she was somewhere else. She'd been here before, and it was Doc Forbes standing beside her. "What gives?"

"Well, the short 'n' brief of 'er is, you got a helluva whack on the back of the head, babe, and we're going in to haul out a coupla chunks of stuff that's stuck halfways into your skull bone."

"Oh, Jesus, am I going to come out of this a gibble?"

"Naw, but you don't want to set off the metal detectors, either."

"Feel pukey, Roar."

"No doubt. That's how it is when you've been whacked on the nog-gin."

"Who's doing this?"

"I am, sweetheart."

"I thought you weren't allowed to work on family."

"Everybody else is busy. You'd have to wait your turn. And you're at the bottom of the list, there's hardly anything wrong with you at all."

She wanted to keep talking to him, to take his hand in hers, to . . . and then she was waking up again, in a comfortable bed, and Steve sat in a chair next to her with a three-ring binder on his lap and a ballpoint pen in his hand.

"Stevie." She tried to smile but her face was too sore.

"Mom!" He put the book and pen on the floor and flew out of the chair to take her hand, raise it to his lips, kiss it. "Boy, am I glad to hear the sound of your voice! I was so scared I thought I was going to have to go up to maternity and ask them for a coupla diapers."

She tried to sit up but Steve shook his head and went to the con-trol panel. A low whirring sound and the head of the bed rose slowly, until she was seated comfortably.

"They put Dianne to bed," Steve said, adjusting her covers, stroking her arm—and, she saw, pressing her call button. "She's the lump in the next bed. Gran wanted her to go home but she told her to take a hike."

"Oh dear."

"Told Nick to go back where he came from," he added proudly. "She was all set to tell off Uncle Rory, too, but he asked if she'd at least lie down on that bed and she said sure, as long as she didn't have to leave this room. Then he asked her to take a pill and she did. So there she is."

Steve stepped aside to let the nurse do her professional thing, taking Cedar's pulse, putting something in her ear that made a *neep* sound. She checked the monitors in the wall above the bed, shone a little light in Cedar's eyes, then smiled. "I have offers to make." Her voice reminded Cedar of the way evaporated milk flows out of the hole in the can, smooth and quiet. "Toothbrush, toothpaste, mouthwash, basin of warm water, soap, facecloth and, finally, very cold orange juice."

"Do I have to do anything particularly obscene to qualify?"

"Just wink and it's all yours."

Cedar winked. The drop-dead beautiful nurse with the cap of burnished bronze hair and a name tag that read "Sorrel McLean" winked back, then left the room.

Steve watched her go, then shook his head. "Momma, when I grow up, can I have one of those?"

"Little boy, when you grow up and you're a big man with a good education and a good job and your own car and everything, you can probably have one of them, or a short one if you want, or a blonde one if you want, or one of each if you want." And he was Steven again, no kin to her, not a drop of blood. Hers totally and completely, her son, her darling, her precious. She felt tears slipping down her face.

"It's okay, Mom." He took her hand. "They've got pills for the pain."

"It's not the pain. It's just nerves."

"Yeah, right. We've been meaning to talk to you about that, we all think you should go on Prozac or something, your nerves are driving us to a nervous breakdown." His own nerves must have been acting up, because his eyes were brimming and his voice had a thin tremor that didn't sound like him.

He reminded Cedar so much of Alison. "Did I ever tell you," she said conversationally, "that the very first time I held you, I fell madly in love, for life and beyond?"

"No, you never did tell me." Steve pulled his chair closer and sat down, holding her hand in both of his.

"You didn't have an ounce of fat on you. In fact, you were the skinniest baby I ever saw. And big! We made jokes about how with hands like yours, we could train you up to be a pugilist." She closed her eyes. "And your momma! Oh, Stevie, I wish you could have had more time with your mom."

"Yeah, everyone says that. And I always want to holler that I do so know my momma. You're my mom."

Tears slipped down Cedar's face. She had a sensation of floating in that state between sleeping and waking. When she shifted her weight, she could feel each individual bruise, laceration and abrasion. And the feeling in her head defied all description. She raised her hand carefully and felt a bandage. Around it she felt her shorn scalp. "Oh shit," she breathed.

Sorrel McLean returned and the sponge bath began. Steve helped, his touch gentle, his face concerned. The water in the basin changed colour as the dark flecks dissolved and reddened. Cedar made a sound and Sorrel patted her shoulder. "Not to worry," she soothed, "not to worry."

After the bath, Cedar knew she still had dried blood in what was left of her hair, probably more of it between the bandages on her back and definitely even more of it under her fingernails, but she could wait a while before tackling it. She brushed her teeth and rinsed with the hospital mouthwash.

"I'd probably kill for a good smoke," she hinted.

"Oh, no, not in here," Sorrel said. "There's a smoking lounge at the end of the hallway. We'll get you down there just as soon as we can. In the meantime, here's that orange juice."

It was so good Cedar could have jumped into a tub of it and drunk her way back out again. Then she felt the prick in her arm, knew what it was and was glad when the pain began to fade a few minutes later. She'd just finish this juice and get Steve to help her get down to the smoking lounge, and then she'd be fine, just fine. She could taste the cigarette already.

Dianne was pacing, arms folded across her chest, stubbornly ignoring Kate and Nick.

Cedar watched briefly, then lifted her hand. "Di-Di."

In a flash her daughter was there, holding Cedar's upraised hand, peering at her. "Momma?"

"Hey, how's the most gorgeous creature in the world?"

"I don't know, how are you?" Dianne kissed Cedar's face repeatedly and began to sob. "Oh, Momma, you looked so little, and your face was so white. And then cousin Brendan came in and he said what happened and I got so scared."

"What did Cuz say? Because I don't know."

"He said when you were helping him get that guy out of there, he said the gas tank blew up and stuff pelted you. He said you got hit but he didn't know how bad because you didn't say anything about it and he was kinda busy."

"How's Scoop?"

"The hurt guy? They took him to the city in a helicopter. It landed on the roof of the hospital, Steve and I went outside and watched. They wouldn't let us up on the roof, eh? It was right over our heads when it took off and someone in it waved at us."

"And you thought angels had feathered wings. Now you know— they ride around in helicopters."

"I am *not* going home with Grandma," Dianne announced.

"Of course not. You're going to stay with me today, and then tonight you can go home, sleep in your own bed, go to school tomorrow, and come up here after school. If I'm still in here, which I doubt."

Finally she got to the smoking lounge. She didn't need the wheelchair and she certainly didn't need to be lifted into it, but the duty nurse insisted. "Not on my shift. Besides, it isn't every day I get the chance to wheel a hero down the hall."

"Hero my arse." Cedar shook her head. "Scared rabbit is more like it."

"Tom McLendon, that scoop operator, is my brother-in-law," the nurse said softly, "and between you and Brendan McKenzie, you saved his life. I don't care much for Tom, but my sister Lily is crazy about him. So, I owe you."

Cedar settled her sore backside in the chair. "You know full well if the shoe had been on the other foot he'd'a been lugging me out of that mess. You don't owe me. And if you did, this trip to the nic-fit farm would more than pay me back."

"Yeah? How's about a nice fresh coffee to go with it? Real coffee."

Cedar wanted to hold Dianne, wanted to cuddle her daughter on her lap, but when they tried, her arse protested and her left leg raised hell. Dianne knew it before Cedar said anything, and slid off her mother's lap to sit as close to her as she could.

"I love you, baby."

"I know you do. But I love you more because I've loved you my whole entire life."

"Ah, g'wan, I loved you before you were born. Hell, I loved you before you were even conceived."

"Want to know what's really funny? It's really funny that Uncle Rory is my dad. Why can't I just call him Dad? Why do I have to call him Uncle Rory?"

"You don't have to call him Uncle Rory. You can call him anything you want. Spot. Rover. Late for dinner. Anything."

"Everybody else just called him Uncle, so I guess I . . ."

"But you know he's really your daddy."

"Yeah. With my other mother, right?"

"That's it."

"But he's not Steve's dad, right?"

"Nope, your mom was too shy to ask Rory when we decided we wanted someone to keep Cam from being an only kid," Cedar lied. "She got over being shy, but that was later. And so she went to this clinic, and they had, like, a catalogue, and so she picked what she wanted. Red hair and musical, she said."

Cedar thought fast, digging up answers for the questions she knew would come, but she was saved by the arrival of the nurse, wheeling in a small cart. "Coffee wagon!" Cedar knew the tray on the cart wasn't hospital equipment, and that wasn't a hospital coffee pot, either. Nick came in behind the nurse with a wide grin and a platter of food.

"Look what we have here!" he grinned. "Health food."

Before she even sampled the delicacies, Cedar finally had her cigarette and a cup of absolutely excellent coffee. Dianne made a big enough dent in the food to satisfy even Nick, who seemed to feel that almost everyone in this country was anorexic. Nobody suggested that Dianne might want to leave when Nick did, nobody hinted that she might find it boring in the hospital now that her mother was fine. Nobody suggested anything of the kind. That's probably why Dianne decided to do what everyone had been hoping she would do, and went home with Nick.

Before they left, Nick bent down and touched Cedar's arm. "You scared me," he said. "When Stevie phoned I thought I was going to . . . We're a very emotional people, us Greeks."

"Yeah," Cedar grinned. "Us oatmeal savages, too."

She managed the trip back to her bed, she got from the chair to the bed under her own steam, she even held up her end of a short conversation, but then the room started to blur at the edges, her eyelids felt as if they weighed a ton each, and the nurses' voices seemed to be coming from the far end of a very long tunnel. She knew she was falling asleep, and without one word of apology, she went with it.

When she woke up she knew she had missed lunch, but that didn't matter because someone in a pink uniform was sliding a supper tray onto the over-bed table. Cedar would have told her to please take it away, but it was too much trouble to speak. She ached from ankle to neck and throbbed from the neck up, the pain so bad she would gladly yell and holler but for the noise, which would hurt even more.

And then Sorrel was there, sliding the business end of a hypodermic into her upper arm. "Only a minute or two," Sorrel whispered. "Just take a few deep breaths, Cedar. Steady on, we're prepared for this. You're about one shot short, so of course you hurt. I didn't want to waken you."

Cedar spent four days in hospital. Rory would have preferred her to stay longer, but once her headache faded, the dizziness was gone and so was the nausea, which had come in waves and left her feeling weak and sweaty. The patches on her back where she had been whapped with bits of flying debris were healing quickly. She had a constant low-back ache that had Rory concerned, but he had to admit it wasn't bad enough to forbid her to go home.

"You should stay at my place for a few days."

"I'm not staying at your place. Between the phone and the No Smoking signs I'd go nuts. Besides, the kids have enjoyed about as much of Gran's full-time ministrations as they can endure."

"She tries hard to be extra good to them," Rory said, pushing her toward the elevator in her wheelchair. "But she's so old-fashioned, she's like a visitor from another planet. And your kids aren't exactly . . ."

"Is there such a word as manipulate-able? Manipual? If not, they should invent one."

"I think it would be manipulable."

"For that you went to school all those years."

The hospital had areas set up like patios, which had benches and a few ornamental shrubs and some flowers, and big ashtrays. Rory sat on a white plastic lawn chair, peeling an orange, while Cedar lit up and sighed with enjoyment.

"Kind of surprising that you never started to smoke," she said. "Kate and Gus both smoke, and I smoke."

"Never even tried it out, not even when I was a kid. *He* smoked. I wasn't going to be like him. He ate, too. If I could have figured out how to not do that, I'd have given up food." Rory ate his orange one segment at a time, looking like someone who had something to say and wasn't sure how to get to it.

"Dianne said an odd little thing," Cedar said. She wanted to move her chair so she and Rory could look at each other while they talked, but she knew it would make him uncomfortable. He talked the way other guys she knew talked—they'd sit side by each and not look at each other, directing their words straight ahead instead of at each other directly. She told him what Dianne had said about how funny it felt to call her dad "Uncle."

"Yeah." He nodded. "But I can see how it came about. She picked it up from Cam and Steve."

"Do you mind?"

"Of course I mind. I mind like go-to-hell. I *mind* the entire situation, Cedar. I want time with her—alone. I mean, I like Stevie. Hell, I love him. But Di-Di is—Jesus, it's so cliché, but I look at her and it's like drowning or something. She looks like you, she looks like Cam, she looks like me, and she's there because of *me*. Dumb, eh?"

"No." Cedar patted his leg. "Not the least bit dumb. So—who do I have to fuck to get a cup of coffee around here?"

He came back with two lattes from the hospital cafeteria. Because he was who he was and because he treated everyone the way he did, the drinks were in real mugs. The one he handed to Cedar had "Tawny" written on the side in nail polish.

"Who's Tawny?"

"One of the nurses. Used to work here. Moved away to get married or something, I think."

"Hmm, really good stuff." She licked foam from her top lip. "So what do you want to do about it?" she said, as if there had been no interruption.

"Have her stay over on my days off."

"Fine."

"I want to be able to take her to the city, stay in a hotel, eat in a fancy restaurant, go to Science World, stuff like that."

"Fine."

"I just don't want to hurt Steve's feelings."

"Stevie knows you aren't his dad. Besides, I can always bop off with him while she's with you."

"Do you ever miss Grandma Campbell?" He held up his hand, his thumb and forefinger half an inch apart. "Ever feel like she's this close, even though she's not really here?"

"Yes."

"I wish things had been different and we'd known her better."

"Yeah, well, things weren't and we didn't. And that's it. That's what our life was."

"You ever go to one of those groups?"

"You mean adult children of dysfunctional assholes?"

"Yeah."

"No, I never did. You?"

"No." He checked his watch and sighed. "Hell, my break is just about history."

She was back in bed reading a magazine article about guns in America when Gus walked into the room with a potted azalea in one hand, a small brown bag with Windflower Books printed on it in the other and a hesitant smile on his face.

"Hello, bonny lassie."

Cedar just stared. She wondered what she would do if she had one of the guns in her hand, the ones the article said were so easy to get below the forty-ninth.

"Gus," she said carefully, determined to be at least as polite to him as she would be to a total stranger.

"Only found out about it an hour or so ago, when I saw the paper." He put the azalea on the over-bed table and handed her the bookstore bag. "I just saw Rory in the hallway. He says you're going home tomorrow?"

"Yeah, he told me I couldn't leave until after lunch. Maybe he figures I'll eat the hospital food and get so sick I have to stay longer."

"Bump on the noggin, it said."

"Yeah. Couple of little hunks of something, kind of ripped the scalp a bit, stayed in there until Roarsers cut them out."

"Rory said it wasn't dangerous, though."

"No. I was well away from the real uproar. Tommy McLendon got the worst of it, he's still at the big hospital in the city. I guess if we hadn't had the timekeeper there, he'd'a never made it. "

"Did you know the mayor is gonna give her a certificate? And the crown and robe to her, instead of having a Miss Town contest this year. She's gonna ride in the big convertible in the Sea Fair parade."

"Hey, that's nice," Cedar grinned. "And, of course, it won't hurt the mayor's re-election campaign one little bit. Betcha he's got a thing in his speech about the nobility of the working class."

Gus grinned back, and then his face turned serious. "I guess you know your mother and I . . ." He hesitated.

"About time, I'd say."

"It's not the way I wanted it." He studied the pattern in the floor tiles.

"Well, even you can't have everything exactly the way you want it."

"Guess she's hooked up with that Greek now."

"Guess so."

"Do you remember that time your mother was ill and you came out of your bedroom and as good as ran into me in the hallway? And I was carrying something?"

"I remember."

"Well, your mother had a miscarriage. I've always wondered whether the Greek was the father of that baby. And if not him, who was it? Because it wasn't me."

"I've no idea at all." Cedar showed no sign of the deep shock she was feeling. She had assumed there had only ever been Gus in Kate's life. Not Kate. Not her *mother!* But her voice sounded past calm to totally uninterested. Gus looked at her, his piercing blue eyes slightly narrowed.

"You're sure, my bonny lassie?" he purred.

"Come on, Gus. How old was I? How would I have known? Do you know that most of the time I have no memory at all of those days? I'll be chatting away with someone and they'll start in on the old "remember when" routine, and about all I can do is smile and nod and pretend I do. But I don't. Entire weeks and months of every year of my life are gone. I don't have a clue what she was doing with her life, and no understanding of what you were doing with yours."

"Christ." He stared at her.

"And now, when there's nothing can be done one way or the other to change, alter or improve any of it, the fact is, I don't *want* to know. Okay?"

But Gus wouldn't let go. "I just wonder if it was him. Or that other one, the old farmer's son, the big warrior pilot."

"Ted? Oh Gus, for crying out loud!" Cedar began to laugh, and she was still laughing when Sorrel walked into the room with her dressing tray.

"Dr. Campbell says every second stitch can come out," Sorrel announced with a pretended fiendish grin. "Oh, I'm going to make you suffer."

"Hello, bonny babe," Gus smiled widely.

Sorrel looked at him, and in that glance was everything Cedar needed to know.

"Hello, Uncle Gus." Sorrel sounded as if all her memories of him were warm ones, affectionate ones. "You're looking good."

"Me? I'm an old relic, darlin'."

"Small wonder. I've heard of burning the candle at both ends, but you may have taken it to extremes. In your youth, of course."

"My youth? What would you know of that? I was losing my hair when you first met me."

"More like lost, my dear, but none of us said anything because we didn't want to upset you."

"And your dear mother?"

"Fine. Just fine." Sorrel put her tray on the over-bed table beside the azalea. "Gonna have to boot you out early, Uncle Gus."

"No, no, bonny lassie, I was as good as on my way anyway." He walked over to the bed and for one awful moment Cedar was afraid he was going to bend down and kiss her. She didn't know what she would do. But he just reached out and touched her hair. "Jesus, my darling. You'll have to get it all taken off and evened out. And maybe nobody else will tell you, but I'm your dad, so I will—you have to change your hairdresser." He patted her arm. "You take care."

He turned and headed toward the door, smiling over his shoulder at her and Sorrel. It wasn't until after he was gone that Cedar realized she hadn't thanked him for the plant or the book, whatever it was.

"You ready for this?" Sorrel lowered the bed. "I need you on your belly."

"My belly. Sure." But Cedar didn't move. "Did you see that old English movie . . ."

"The one with the daffodil?"

"You've got it. Can you be trusted?"

"No. On the other hand, daffodil season is over and we're well into the pansy and lilac and rosebud stage."

Cedar rolled onto her belly, grunting with discomfort. She shifted uneasily, to the left, then to the right, trying to find a comfortable position. And then she felt Sorrel's hand on her back, patting gently. "Lift up a bit, darlin'," she said softly. Cedar lifted and Sorrel very carefully slid a small, flat pillow under her. "You might want it a bit lower, but I'll leave it to you to position it. Wouldn't want the super or anyone else to get any wrong ideas."

"Of course not. I hate it when you get the name without a chance to play the game."

"You aren't going to be playing any games for a couple of weeks."

"Hell, it's been so long since I played that game I probably don't even remember how anyway. *Jesus!*"

"Oh, did that smart?" Sorrel sounded too innocent to be believed.

"What are you doing?"

"Just taking off the bandages. I guess the adhesive stuck to the little hairs on your back. It's like a goldy fuzz. I bet you glow in the sunlight."

"I'll glow, all right—bright red, where you yarded off my skin."

"I'd never yard off your skin, Cedar Campbell. I have great respect and admiration for your skin. Though just at the moment it's a wee rashy."

"Itches like hell."

When the stitches were out, Sorrel sprayed something on Cedar's back instead of putting the dressings on again, then helped her into a clean pyjama top. "If we put it on backwards, you can sit on the edge of your bed and get some sun on your back. Maybe that'll help."

"Or I could just lie on my belly here, on that pillow you gave me, and really let the air at it. My Grandma Campbell used to say fresh air was a cure for anything."

"Yeah, in the days before acid rain. Okay, we'll try belly-down. But first you take your pill."

"You're turning me into an addict."

"No way. You're too stubborn to be an addict. Here you go—pill, then water. And now, that's it, on your side first and then . . . here, I'll just move the flaps, and I think maybe we should haul the sheet up over your butt. Otherwise we'll have a traffic jam in the hallway, people lined up for a chance to have a look."

"Nobody gets a look at my butt," Cedar agreed, suddenly feeling very sleepy. "Not unless they buy a ticket."

"How much do you charge?"

"For you, a discount. Professional courtesy and all that."

"Go to sleep, fool."

Cedar went home and told everyone she intended to spend as much time as she possibly could cashing Workers' Compensation cheques. She chuckled when she said it, but more than once she sat out on the porch at two or three in the morning, in the comfortable chair she had bought herself for Mothers' Day, smoking cigarettes and drinking tea and worrying. Not about money, but about her working future.

What do you do when what you're good at is on the block? Cuz had come to visit her and said he was worried, too. "Not as much construction happening, what with the downturn and all. Government claims it's too broke to do much more than upkeep, no new roads or anything. Company's making noises about how it can't afford new equipment, says the gravel pit's exhausted according to the geological survey guys. More it changes, more it's the same old, same old, eh?"

"Makes my heart pump piss," Cedar grumbled. "How come it's the ones with the most money are the quickest to plead poverty? Rant and rave in front of the TV cameras about level playing fields, blah blah blah about private enterprise and free market economy, then apply for every goddamn government grant they can scrape up. Well, I'll maybe do that myself. Get a grant to study the effect of undeserved wealth on someone who has previously worn herself down to a nub for every cent she ever got."

"Hey, I could help." He sipped his beer and yawned. Brendan

always yawned when he was talking about something that made him uneasy. "Dixie thinks we should move to Alberta."

"What in hell for?"

"Supposed to be jobs there, again. Oil patch is looking healthy. Again. Plus they're going in for pulp in a huge way. Guess they've got a whole helluva whack of deciduous, up north a ways, and they're putting in pulp mills, running roads here there and everywhere. Her brother Blake is up there already, logging, although how you can call it logging when the damn trees aren't any bigger'n a foot across is something to make a guy wonder. Anyway, he phoned. Says there's a big gravel deposit up there and they need someone who knows pit run from pea to set 'er up and get 'er going." He yawned again. "Dix, she made up this resumé thing for me, sent it up to Blake. He took 'er into the company and, well, I guess if I want it the job is mine."

"Go for it," Cedar said quietly. "If this bunch of peckerheads won't give you any sort of security, then you don't owe them sweet tweet. Go for it, Cuz."

"You really think so?"

"If Dix did that, she's worried sick, too. You've got kids ready to hike 'er off to college or trade school and they can't do that without a lot of help from the folks at home. And you need to set 'em an example, show 'em that just because somethin's new, it isn't necessarily bad. You don't want *them* doing what we did and staying here because this is what we knew and everything else scared us."

"Yeah." He nodded, then rubbed his face with his hands. "But Jesus, Cedar. Alberta?"

"Hey, it could be worse. It could be Ontario."

"I'd never go if it was."

Cedar went into the kitchen and came back with two beer, then lowered herself gingerly into her chair.

"Back still acting up?"

"Aaagghhh," she growled. "But it's getting better. Rory did a whack of tests and stuff, says there's some bulging going on with a coupla disks, they're pressing on some nerves. Gonna start physio for it. Keep me on compy a while longer. He figures the bang on the back started it, and then dragging Tommy out finished the job. Or at least that's what he's telling compy."

"Good job you don't have a thousand pigs to feed right now."

"Funny how that worked out, eh?"

On the first of July long weekend, Rory took Dianne and Steve to Vancouver with him, and from there they went up the Duffy Lake Road to Lillooet. Cedar stayed home—sitting in a car for a few hours or days wasn't high on her list of things to do with a smile on her face. And the prospect of some time alone was one of the best ideas she'd heard in a long time.

On Friday evening she finally got back to her flower beds, not really working but nipping a wilted leaf here and killing a slug there. And there, and there, and there—the sun had hardly begun to slant toward twilight and the slimy little buggers were already heading out for their nightly ravages. She looked up to see a car coming down the long driveway from the back road, and Muffin ambled toward it, doing her guard-pig thing. Clancy raced after her, yipping and yapping, all noise and bluster. "Clancy!" Cedar yelled. The dog didn't seem to hear her and Cedar didn't feel like hollering until her throat bled.

The grey import stopped between the barn and the house, the driver's door opened and Sorrel stood there smiling, waving, looking even more gorgeous in jeans and a T-shirt than she had in the nurse's uniform. The shirt had something printed on the front of it that Cedar couldn't read from a distance.

"Hey," Sorrel called. "That's a very bizarre-looking watchdog you've got."

"Wait until you hear her bark."

Up close, she could see the T-shirt read: "How dare you presume . . . ?" "What a nice surprise," Cedar smiled.

"I figured I had to catch you off-guard or I wouldn't catch you at all." Sorrel looked around. "So this is your place. Really nice. I mean *really* nice."

"Yeah. I like it." And Cedar Campbell, usually self-possessed and in control, suddenly felt very shy, as if the place revealed more of her than she wanted known.

"And that's the gazebo. God, those rose bushes look like the ones in the seed catalogues."

"They get a lot of attention. I think everyone in the family fusses over them. Kids spend a lot of time on them, Kate's always mothering them up. They probably get far more fertilizer than they need and I bet each and every one of us sprays them for bugs, mildew, black spot, leaf curl, you name it."

"I didn't know Alison. But people say she could sing like a bird."

"She was more of a musician than a singer, but yeah, she could sing."

"Brought some ice cream." Sorrel held out a brown paper bag. "Didn't know what your favourite was but I thought butterscotch ripple wouldn't get wasted."

"No, ma'am, it sure won't."

They went into the house, and while Cedar dished up the ice cream, Sorrel walked around the living room looking at pictures. "A regular rogues' gallery. You've got pictures of the kids from the time they were infants right on through."

"Yeah. Let's eat this out on the porch."

"Great. You need any help?"

"No, I'm actually in great shape considering the shape I'm in. I'm just goofin' off, scamming the compy people."

"Yeah, I know. I saw the X-rays."

They sat on the porch and watched the mosquito hawks chase bugs, swooping and diving against the glory of the sunset. "Not as many hawks as I remember," Sorrel said wistfully. "Remember how many of them there used to be, especially up at the lakes? I guess all the sprays they're using wiped out most of their food supply. Or something."

They finished their ice cream and put the bowls on the porch for Clancy to lick clean, then sat sharing the quiet. Cedar lit a cigarette. Sorrel held out her hand and Cedar put the cigarette package in it. Sorrel laughed, shook her head, laid the cigarettes on the arm of Cedar's chair, then extended her hand again. Cedar held out her own hand and Sorrel took it in hers.

"So I've been asking around, very diplomatically, of course, and the way I hear it, you haven't hung out with anybody since Alison died."

"Too busy. Three kids, Gramps, a thousand pigs, full-time job, you know how it is."

"No, I don't. I guess that's part of why I came out here tonight. Is that a gazebo, or is it a shrine?"

"Just a gazebo. The roses and other flowers are kind of special, but that's because they were given to us by people who are still pretty important to us."

"So how busy are you now, what with the kids just about grown up?"

"I'm not busy at all." Cedar smiled at Sorrel. "Hours and hours and hours every day to call my own. And every night."

"That's good."

Cedar felt something in her lower belly shift, but not tighten. "I even have spare toothbrushes."

"Oh, no need. I brought my own. Just in case."

They lay in bed, the sweat drying on their bodies, moonlight filling the room with a silver glow.

"Look at you. Christ, you've got scars up your back, and another one here. What are you, a refugee from a war zone or something?"

"Accident prone, is all." Cedar showed the scar on her shin and calf. "Swimming accident."

"And this one?" Sorrel traced it with the tip of her finger, and Cedar felt the cool touch of fire.

"Pig bite."

"That funny-looking Muffin thing bites?"

"No, but her daddy did. Or maybe he was her uncle. He was bacon and sausages in no time flat after that one."

"No scars on your belly."

"Nope."

"Hey, lady." Sorrel squirmed around and lay her cheek on Cedar's shoulder, her breath warm on her neck. "I guess everybody tells you you've got absolutely incredible breasts, eh?"

"Oh, yeah, the whole world calls me a big tit."

They laughed, but not at the stupid joke. They laughed because they were together, and because passion was growing again, and because there was moonlight in the room and because they were both very happy.

"Anything more than a mouthful is a waste," Sorrel whispered.

"God, but you are the most gorgeous creature I've ever seen," Cedar answered.

Cedar and Sorrel stood together on the sidewalk with Rory and Kate and Campbell, cheering and clapping as the kilties swung by, Steve in the Campbell tartan marching with the rest of the pipers. As he went by, he winked at his family and swayed his hips to make his kilt swish from side to side.

Sorrel grinned in acknowledgement. "How did you ever live through it when he was first learning?" she asked Cedar.

"Oh, it's easy," Cedar answered. "You just go blank inside your head, get yourself a temporary case of amnesia."

"There's Dianne with her drum! Oh, she is *so* gorgeous!" Sorrel breathed. "Just look at her."

"She plays the dying cat too, but they needed a drummer when Brendan moved. His boy Jody used to drum, but . . . so Dianne said she'd just as rather, anyway."

Dianne winked at them, grinned widely and twirled her drumsticks, rolling them over the knuckles of her hands, showing off. The crowd roared approval.

"What a ham," Cedar breathed. "Way to *be!*" she shouted. "Yay, Di-Di!"

"She won't even hear you over the caterwauling." Kate didn't approve of such noisy public displays, but she didn't want to say much more because someone in the crowd might hear. And anyway, heaven only knew what Cedar might say in reply.

Rory stood on top of a fire hydrant, his hand on Cedar's head for balance. "That's my kid!" he shouted. "Hey, world, look!"

"Oh, Rory, for heaven's sake settle down," Kate hissed. "Whatever will people think?"

"Who gives a shit, Momma?" he grinned, then waved again.

Campbell reached up and grabbed Rory by the belt. "Easy on, old man. You'll wind up on your arse on the sidewalk and everyone will point at you and say look, another Campbell passed out in public."

"Yeah? Get sassy with me, boy, and they'll be saying, oh look, another McCann just got himself punched out for talkin' out of turn."

"As if!" Cam laughed.

"Oh, look," Sorrel called. "Across the street. Uncle Gus is over there with—" She stopped suddenly, blushing, afraid to look sideways in case Kate was giving her the Larson glare.

"Oh, this is ripe." Rory got down off the fire hydrant. "So is that Marjory Peel's mom or her aunt?"

"I don't know," Cedar answered. "I could never tell the one from the other anyway."

"That is Marjory's mother," Kate said stiffly. "Marjory's aunt moved away years ago."

"You'll come for supper at our place?" Nick asked hopefully. "It is big Sea Fair special buffet tonight."

Kate tucked her arm under his. "You know very well it's a smorgasbord, not a buffet."

"Everybody come. You tell all of them. Marg, Hank, everyone. I'll set up a big family table." He looked hopefully at Campbell. "You might come? I have a new idea for the place. I bought a very fine guitar, pretty good violin, got a nice old piano. Maybe we try to get some people to do something. Maybe you? Maybe you and Steven and Dianne start it off?"

"If you want the clients doing something like that, you're going to have to make it worth their while . . . like oh, I don't know, five bucks off the bill, or a drink on the house?"

"Sure. I give you free drink," Nick beamed. "I give you big jug of water."

"Right, and pour it over my head, too. Hey look, here come the cadets!"

Kate was her most elegant when they arrived at Zorba's, and she took time off from hostessing to join them for supper. Nick sat proudly at the table with them, basking in his moment, a chance to show his pride and joy establishment to the people he considered his family, a chance to show his family to his best customers. The staff bent over backwards to make sure everything was perfect.

They ate until they couldn't eat any more, and then they had coffee and listened to the music. When Cam got up and walked over to the small roped-off stage area, Marg slid into his chair and leaned toward Cedar.

"Listen to me," she whispered. "You have got to talk to your mother."

"About what?"

"You have to clear the air with her before she and Nick leave for Greece. She came to see me last week and she cried buckets. She feels bad, wants to apologize or something. She isn't sure why, or what she's done wrong, and she doesn't know if apologizing would do any good."

"Apologize for what?"

"She said there were times she had to run home from work just to make sure he wasn't beating on you. Said there were times she pulled him off of you. She said she had to sacrifice part of her life to save the rest of it, and she's dying of guilt because now she thinks you were the part she sacrificed."

Suddenly, as if she was watching a movie, Cedar could see the kitchen in the old place. She saw herself, backed up against the old porcelain sink with a knife in her hand, holding it out in front of her, and she saw Gus, his feet bare, facing her, his eyes snapping sparks of fury, his fists clenched. Now she saw Kate, standing in the doorway, her face pale, her mouth open with shock, and something else—distaste? horror? something—and then Kate spoke. *What in hell is going on now?*

Gus didn't even bother to look at her. "None of your goddamn business," he gritted.

"Go to your room, now, Cedar," Kate said quietly. "Just go to your room."

And Cedar, wearing her school clothes—a tartan pleated wool skirt, her school skirt, a pale yellow V-neck over a white blouse—put down the knife and obediently, without a word of explanation, walked past Gus and Kate and down the hall to the stairs to the second floor, and to her bedroom at the end of the hall, the entire length of the house away from Gus and Kate's room.

"What's wrong?" Marg asked, touching Cedar's forearm.

"Nothing, Auntie. Nothing's wrong."

"Are you going to talk to her?"

Cedar shook her head. "No. She might have talked to you about it, but she hasn't said word one to me. Not then, not since. And anyway, what would I say to her? You know I can't remember diddly-doo about most of what went on."

"Is this a private conversation or can any old body participate?" Sorrel asked.

"Family only." Marg tried to smile and couldn't quite bring it off. "Pull up a chair, dear. You qualify."

Cam was singing "Bridge Over Troubled Water," accompanied by Steve on piano and Dianne on guitar, when Gus and Colleen walked in and stood by the Please Wait To Be Seated sign.

"Oh, the cheek of the man!" Kate hissed.

"Oh, Momma, not everything in the world is about you," Cedar said tiredly, as fed up with Kate's reaction as she was with the cheek of Gus going out of his way to stir the pot. Could neither of them just let the ghosts of the past rest, and maybe one day fade away? Did every event have to be another episode in a wretched soap opera? "This is a public place. Everybody knows this is the best eatery in town. He's got as much right to be here as any of us."

"But he knows—"

"Stop it, Momma. I'll say it again. Not everything Gus Campbell does is about you, or us. Now let me hear my kids sing, okay?"

Gus and Colleen followed the waiter to a table for two, and Gus stood politely until the waiter had seated Colleen. He watched the stage area intently, and if it had been anybody else, in any other circumstance, Cedar might have been moved by the look of yearning hunger on his face. But it was Gus, and he had always most wanted what he couldn't have.

The song ended and Nick moved to the stage, fumbled with the mike and had to get help with it from Steve. Cedar suspected that the fumbling was intentional, a pretence to put the patrons at ease, show them they weren't in the presence only of smooth experts and professionals. Nick spoke briefly, explaining that the stage was open and that anybody who played, sang, did a standup routine or danced would get a free drink for everyone at their table. "If nobody gets up here," he warned, grinning happily, "we go from table to table with the microphone, so everybody see you anyway. This place is Greek! In Greece everybody sings, everybody dances, everybody makes music. That means you!"

And wouldn't you know it, there was Gus Campbell, walking forward as if Zorba's belonged to him! Kate's face turned pale, then beet red. She glared at Cedar as if everything was her fault, then got to her feet and stalked away from the table, her heels tip tip tipping on the polished slate floor. Gus watched her leave and smiled as if this was Christmas and Santa had finally, finally left a cocker spaniel puppy under the tree.

He leaned forward and said something to Steve, who turned to look at Cam, who nodded. Dianne put down the guitar and picked up a violin, plucked the strings, adjusted the tuning and plucked again without looking at Gus.

Cedar felt like the person in the threadbare saying, the one who didn't know whether to shit or go blind, steal third or go back to first. Part of her was so used to being pissed off at Gus Campbell that being angry was easy, and another part was all set to admire the sheer nerve of the old fart.

"He's an asshole," Uncle Hank said softly, "but he's got more guts than you'd find on the floor of a slaughterhouse."

"Right," Marg snapped, "all mixed in with the shit and sawdust."

"Wouldn't you know it would be Uncle Gus," Sorrel sighed, smiling and shaking her head.

"Yeah," Cedar answered, her tone neutral. "Wouldn't you just know it."

Kate had returned to hostess duty, almost out the door and onto the sidewalk, trying not to think about her ex-husband, her children or her grandchildren. Of the entire bunch of them up on stage she shared blood only with Dianne, and Dianne was the one who was behaving as if it was no big deal. Everybody came up to the stage at Zorba's, it was same old, same old, and she didn't have to do anything about it but fiddle.

Gus didn't take the mike because he didn't need it. Gus had never needed a mike, or any kind of encouragement, either. He looked at Cam and nodded, and he began to play. Two bars later, Steve picked it up on the piano, and then Dianne joined, the violin perfectly tuned, each note pure and clear. "Maxwelton's braes are bonny, where early fa's the dew," Gus sang, "And 'twas there that Annie Laurie gave me her promise true."

In spite of years of cigarettes and booze, in spite of late nights and protracted bouts of hollering and shouting, in spite of the lies that had slid up through his throat, Gus Campbell's voice was still what it had been when he was fifteen, and it had steadied into a strong tenor with a wide range. He locked eyes with people at each table, deliberately including them in the song. He smiled and sang as if directly to and only for Marjory-stuck-like-a-tick-Peel's mom, Colleen, who looked exactly like someone had just handed her a rainbow on a string.

And Colleen couldn't help it, she looked for Kate, to give her a look of sheer, raw triumph, but Kate seemed to be totally occupied with an arriving party of six, who had dropped in without reservations. Ordinarily she would regretfully have sent them and their money on their way, referring them to one of Nick's other places. Right now, however, she had no intention of sending anyone anywhere else. She welcomed the chance for a distracting flurry of activity.

And all the while, Gus sang. With "Annie Laurie" finished, he consulted with his son, granddaughter and Steve, and then they were singing together, "Galway Bay." Between the first and second verses, Gus wiggled his hand, the instruments faded, the other three voices stilled and he spoke. "Oh, for crying in the night, the lot of you! You're sitting there like posts in a field. Bertie Fiddick, you know that I know that you could sing the birds out of the trees. Get up here, man. And you, Lois Carson, what's your excuse for pretending you don't know the words? Listen, Nick has said free drinks, and we're Scots, right? When did we ever let anything free slip past us? Come along now, young Bruce Gailus, don't tell me you can't sing every bit as well as the rest of us up here. I happen to know, boy, that your grandparents on both sides could sing better than anybody in the world. Except the Campbells, of course. Come up here, lad, or sing from where you are. But let's drink the Greek dry here tonight!"

Brucie Gailus stood, grinning challenge. "Any Gailus, awake or asleep, can outsing any Campbell at any hour of any day or night. And what's more, Gus, so can the Frasers."

Nick grinned. He knew Kate was upset, he knew she probably felt she had every reason in the world to be upset, he even knew there was every chance in the world he'd wind up paying for more than free drinks, but right then and there he didn't care. If he'd had any idea of how Gus could work a crowd, he'd have hired him for the night.

"Galway Bay" knit the crowd together. Even Marg and Hank sang along, and Sorrel was so happy that she held Cedar's hand, knowing full well that the entire town would know about it before noon the next day.

"He's got a way about him, no doubt," she said.

"If you only knew the half of it," Cedar answered.

"I know the half of it." Sorrel looked serious, but not sad. "My mom and dad got divorced because of Uncle Gus. And my mom intended to wind up with Gus, full-time and exclusive. And didn't. I know Gus! Jesus, darlin', everyone for miles around knows Gus. He's still the best sideshow you'll see on or off TV."

Cedar Campbell laughed. She squeezed Sorrel's hand gently. "You have a way with words, my dear," she managed.

Nick got up on stage again and stood facing Gus. The patrons in Zorba's knew as much as the family did about how things stood with Gus and Nick and Kate. The quiet in the room was as thick as hummus. This could wind up a very public punch-up.

Except that Nick was grinning from ear to ear. "Campbell, my boy." He looked out at the crowd and winked. "Campbell is almost my grandson—in here," he said, thumping himself on the chest. "In here, all three of these young people are my grandchildren. These wonderful ones I love very much. And you, Gus Campbell . . ."

Cedar thought she might fall into a faint, or go to that other place where she had spent so much of her childhood, the place where nothing ever touched you, not really.

"Do you know this song? I know those kids know it because Grandpa Nick taught them."

Nick burst into song—the Greek version of "Never on Sunday." His voice was not as smooth as Gus Campbell's voice, and he didn't have as much technique or practice, but he was just as good at making music and pleasing a crowd. Everyone in the room relaxed and cheered Nick on as he sang. Gus stood, smiling widely, clapping rhythm, and when Nick finished a verse and waved at him, Gus sang in English. Then Nick began to dance. Not to be outdone, Gus danced, too, but only when he had finished singing and the music was swelling.

"They'll gossip about this forever," Cedar sighed. "The night Kate Larson Campbell's men decided they were best friends and made displays of themselves in public."

"As if anybody really gave the first part of a good damn!" Sorrel laughed. "People are having fun, Cedar, that's all."

"Gus is—"

"Oh, I know what Gus thinks he's doing. Gus is right into the middle of his own fantasy. He thinks he's pumping testosterone and everyone else thinks it's hot air. So what?" She was laughing, and so was Cedar.

Kate would dearly love to go over and give Cedar a slap in the face. But not in front of all the customers and staff! She had a thing or two to say to Nick, too. But not here, not now. More people were arriving, and this time she just didn't have room. She'd have to send them to one of Nick's other places.

When they had gone on their way she turned back, steeling herself against whatever she might see. Cam, Steve and Dianne were still on stage, with Bruce Gailus and another man. Gus sat with Colleen Davis Peel, drinking a beer and smiling at her as if she was the only reason the moon was going to shine that night. Kate knew what it was like to be on the receiving end of that smile. She also knew what it was like to wear the look on Colleen's face.

Kate felt very conspicuous, and then suddenly she realized nobody was looking at her. In fact, hardly anybody was paying attention to Gus. They were watching the stage, where Dianne was putting aside the violin and picking up the guitar again and Bruce Gailus was standing next to Steve, demonstrating something on the keyboard. Steve nodded and looked over at Cam, who nodded back. The music started again, the waitress walked up to Gus and Colleen's table, and Marg and Hank got to their feet, obviously saying their goodbyes.

When Dianne was sure Cedar was watching her, she turned her head and looked at the big clock above the bar. Cedar held up ten fingers.

"You guys don't even need words." Sorrel sipped her wine, holding the glass in one hand and stroking Cedar's leg with her other hand, under the table so that no one else could see.

"Ah, well." Cedar lifted her glass of beer and reached over to touch her glass to Sorrel's in an unspoken toast. "You know how it is. Sign language. A gift to the world from the Native people of North America."

"I'm very fond of sign language. And Braille. Braille may be more important than rocket science."

"Sometimes it seems as if Braille *is* rocket science. I've gone to the moon a few times because of it."

"Listen to you. Anybody'd think you were related to that bald old fart who was up there singing a while ago."

"Who? Him? Heh heh, I taught him everything he knows."

The Fiction of Anne Cameron

"Anne Cameron's fictional voice is unique in Canada. She can cuss like a logger or set down words as tender as lullabies. Her West Coast, small-town characters, like her prose, are rough and tough, sweet 'n' tender."

—Ottawa Citizen

"The anger and passion with which Cameron writes lift the ordinary into something stronger."

—Quill and Quire

"Cameron understands the way a woman's work affects every other sphere of her life."

—Feminist Bookstore News

Daughters of Copper Woman
Legends • 5¼ x 7½ • 200 pages, paperback • 1-55017-245-X • $19.95 Can, $14.95 US
Since its first publication in 1981, *Daughters of Copper Woman* has become an underground classic, selling over 200,000 copies. This new edition includes fresh material added by the author.

Hardscratch Row
Novel • 6 x 9 • 378 pages, paperback • 1-55017-290-5 • $24.95
In this funny and heart-wrenching novel the characters grapple with the very meaning of the word "family," just by living their lives.

Sarah's Children
Novel • 5½ x 8½ • 288 pages, paperback • 1-55017-274-3 • $21.95
This is a story about one woman's slow and painful recovery from a serious illness; a story about a family taking an honest look at itself; a story about the power of love.

Those Lancasters
Novel • 6 x 9 • 398 pages, paperback • 1-55017-227-1 • $21.95
A novel that puts the fun back in dysfunctional—a light-hearted look at the trials and tribulations of a family that defines disadvantage.

Aftermath
Novel • 6 x 9 • 400 pages, paperback • 1-55017-193-3 • $18.95
An examination of the child-welfare system through the lives of hauntingly memorable characters.

Selkie
Novel • 6 x 9 • 192 pages, paperback • 1-55017-152-6 • $17.95
One morning it starts raining in Cassidy's house, and nobody can get it to stop. Like everyone else, Cassidy figures it's just a problem with the pipes. She doesn't know that she's about to embark on the ride of her life.

The Whole Fam Damily
Novel • 6 x 9 • 264 pages, paperback • 1-55017-134-8 • *$17.95*
This story is told in Cameron's signature style—direct, smart and very funny—with the undertone of anger that marks the most provocative fiction.

DeeJay and Betty
Novel • 6 x 9 • 264 pages, paperback • 1-55017-112-7 • *$16.95*
A story about two women who overcome their pasts to forge strong futures for themselves and each other.

Kick the Can
Novel • 6 x 9 • 160 pages, paperback • 1-55017-039-2 • *$15.95*
Rowan Hanson refuses to get involved with "the ex, the kids, the house, the car, the boat or the lawyer who's apt to wind up with it all, anyway." But in the end she has to take the advice her grandmother gave her twenty years earlier: "When it's your turn to take your kick at the can, kiddo, you do 'er."

Escape to Beulah
Novel • 6 x 9 • 236 pages, paperback • 1-55017-029-5 • *$16.95*
Guided by streams and mountains, helped in their arduous journey by Native Americans, sustained by their own vision of a better life, an unlikely band of women and children pushes northwest to make a new home. Their story is a tribute to the strength of women everywhere and a passionate statement about human freedom and dignity.

South of an Unnamed Creek
Novel • 6 x 9 • 200 pages, hardcover • 1-55017-013-9 • *$26.95*
This novel focuses on five women from diverse backgrounds who find common ground in the dance halls of the Klondike Goldrush.

Women, Kids & Huckleberry Wine
Short stories • 6 x 9 • 258 pages, paperback • 0-920080-68-5 • *$16.95*
With clear-sighted realism and wry humour, these stories enchant, move, disturb and provoke.

Available at Better Bookstores or

HARBOUR PUBLISHING
P.O. Box 219
Madeira Park, BC, Canada V0N 2H0
Phone (604) 883-2730 • Fax (604) 883-9451
Toll-free order line 1 800 667-2988
Toll-free fax order line 1 877 604-9449
E-mail orders@harbourpublishing.com
Website www.harbourpublishing.com